OF SECRETS AND CROWNS

DAWN J BRAITHWAITE

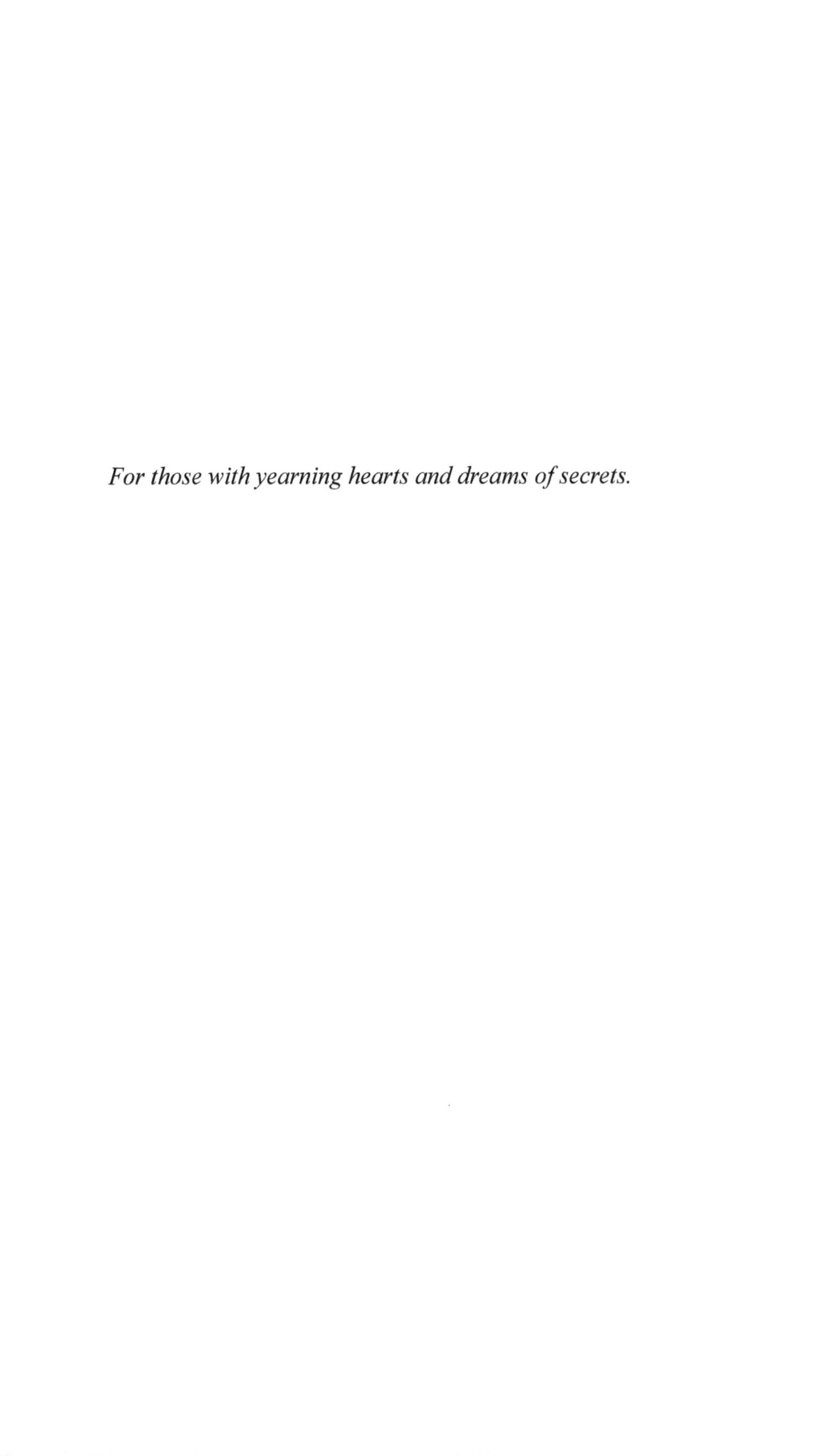

For those with yearning hearts and dreams of secrets.

CHAPTER ONE

he cool, gray early morning mists of Apoidea seeped through my broken window, the damp chill waking me from my sleep. The temptation to curl deeper into my make-shift bed, comprised of a small heap of blankets and straw, wrapped its fingers around my heart and beckoned me to travel back to my dreams.

In them, my mother crept into my tiny room to wake me with a quiet birthday tradition. She carried a plate stacked high with her amazing honey cakes. I took one with reverence, Mother's honey cakes were truly special. Locals described her as a bee charmer. She harvested the already fermenting golden honey directly from hives carved deep into the forest trees herself. No smoke or other diversion needed. The bees just accepted her in their midst.

Crumbs from the sticky, sweet squares clung to my fingers and lips while she combed my hair and told me of how brashly I had entered the world. Soon, I buzzed from the intoxicating sugars.

My father came in, wearing a sly smile and handed me a small package. Even though the paper was plain and clearly reused, I opened it with care. I didn't want to rip it, it too was precious just because my father gave it to me. Inside the paper, I found a pretty dagger in a box. Its silver handle was inlaid with delicate filigree and small pink gems.

A dagger like that had to have taken some true dealing at market to acquire. Father promised we would practice throwing before we went into the village that night.

My parents smiled at me, their eyes full of promise and love. Full of their hopes for me. Mother leaned in, her soft lips kissing my cheek, with tears in her eyes. Her expression darkened, "I'm so sorry, Merinley. Your life is about to change. Do not lose your way."

I woke with my own tears clinging to the corners of my eyes. It had been a wonderful, though somewhat confusing, dream. Mother's strange words changed the whole tone of the dream. I brushed it off, letting my mind linger on the rest, even though it made me sad. My heart ached for my long-dead parents and what could have been.

Once I left my little room, I knew my birthday wouldn't be anything like my dream. Aunt Rowena and Uncle Peter rarely acknowledged anything about me, unless I had made them unhappy. I had been under their guardianship since the flash flood that claimed the lives of my parents. My time with them had been unpleasant, to say the least. They did everything in their power to keep me beneath them. In all these years, not once had they acknowledged my birthday. Today would not be any different.

On Apoidea, your sixteenth birthday was considered to be one of the most important days, the day that you would learn if the magic of our Fae ancestors would manifest in you some way. The Ceremony of Gifts. Families would visit the elders who would determine whether you would be gifted and how powerful you would be. Those the elders found to have the most promising gifts were granted a place on the council when a seat became available.

When evening fell, the birthday celebrations would heighten and a great feast would be held in the village. The whole island gathered to celebrate and toast to the future. Thinking of the celebrations to come, my saddened heart constricted in my chest. This honored tradition was not in my cards, thanks to my aunt and uncle.

The reality of the day hit me hard as I pulled myself from the mild warmth of the straw beneath me. I had no intention to let it keep me down. I intended to be happy. Nothing made me happier than practicing with my knives, as I did most mornings, as long as I possibly could, even if it meant getting too little sleep. Throwing on a ratty dress without looking, I rushed to ready myself. I knew this would be the only time I would get to myself today, the rest of the day would be spent on doing my chores. When I was ready, I kissed the old brassy locket that hung around my neck on a delicate chain and sent a silent loving message to my parents. The locket was my most prized possession, it was the only thing I had left of either of my parents. I never took it off.

I peeked out of the door of the tiny shed I lived in, to search for signs of life from the family cabin. The chimney spouted no smoke, no sounds escaped the walls. All was quiet, given the early morning bird calls and wind caressing the treetops. I breathed a sigh of relief and hustled into the thick woods beyond.

The woods hummed with early morning activity from the local fauna. A pair of ix scampered across the leafy floor, their rust-colored fur almost camouflaging them in with the reddish dirt beneath them. When they noticed me, they vanished into their invisible state faster than I could blink.

The thumb-sized, bumblebees which made the extra sweet honey that we all valued and took pride in, were beginning to drone out of their over-sized hives that sat at invaded many of the trees. They buzzed in a lazy fashion as if they too longed for a delay in their day. A tenacious bee flew right into my leg and dropped into the wooded ground. The fuzzy creature shook its silvery wings. With a little hop, it flew back into the air to join its hive-mates, paying no attention to me. A relieved sigh escaped my lips. A male. Had the bee been a female I would likely have been stung and injected with venom, ending up in a twitching puddle for at least half an hour before being able to move again. That would have ended the precious little free time I had, and possibly make me late for chores, the last thing I wanted.

Despite the mild danger some presented, I adored the variety of unique forest life that Apoidea offered. On a typical day I would linger and watch these creatures go about their peaceful way, but today my thoughts were obsessed with the large oak where I hid the knives that I had collected for throwing. I knew that practicing my knife skills would bring me a sampling of joy and make me feel closer to my parents. Something told me I needed that.

My feet hurried along the fern covered path, anxious to get to my destination. Every step made my fingers itch more for the cool metal handles waiting for me.

As I approached the clearing my feet faltered, something was wrong. The air became heavy with negativity; with anger and irritation. I strained my ear to listen for anything that should not be there. It didn't take long for me to catch a distinct cadence of speech, multiple voices. At least two male and one female. My heart sank low as my hopes for the morning were dashed to pieces. The female voice had the unmistakable pitch belonging to my Aunt Rowena. Her shrill voice pierced through anything like a hot knife through butter.

I wanted to turn around and head home, begin my chores and avoid this confrontation, but she spotted me through the trees. The pleased look on her rawboned face told me that something very unpleasant lay ahead for me. Everything in my body told me to turn and run, but I knew I had to face her, and the men. My parents had raised me to do the right thing. To face your expectations no matter how unpleasant. I straightened myself and marched towards her with heavy, slow steps.

"So this is where you disappear to when you're shirking your responsibilities?" No doubt she already knew, I wasn't sure how. Perhaps one of the little ones had figured it out and told when promised extra goodies. Maybe she had followed me at some point, saving busting me for when it would truly hurt. It didn't matter how, in truth, what mattered was that she had.

As I approached, I noticed Rowena also found my small stash of knives and daggers. She held one in bony hand and the rest had been discarded at her feet. "You know you shouldn't play with knives dear, it's not becoming of a girl."

"So this is the girl?" A gruff, unfamiliar voice pulled my attention. My uncle stood unsteadily with two large men to my left. The men wore the ragged and weary look of having been on the road for a long time, for longer than they would have liked according to the air around them.

"Come here and let the man see you," Uncle Peter barked. The scent of cheap ale wafted off of him, it was very likely he was still drunk from spending yet another night at the tavern in the village. I knew he would rather be there than in this small clearing. He loved his drink far more than he did his family. The only thing he loved more was coin.

I stepped up to my uncle and the two strangers like a beaten dog. My eyes darted back and forth searching for clues to the reason they were there and why they wanted to see me. A set of irons hung from the belt of one of the men, and the one that spoke held a small leather purse that bulged with coins. The set of irons and full purse a dead giveaway. These men were a special sort of trader. The kind that dealt in people.

My heart thumped frantically against my ribs and my palms went cold. My aunt and uncle had sold me to traders. The desire to flee surged through me again, but I stayed my feet. Running would be fruitless. These men, though weary from travels, would overpower me as soon as I started to run. More importantly, I had no place to go that I wouldn't be easily found. I would be hunted like a beast.

Aunt Rowena valued money and power over everything else, in that she and Peter were a perfect match. These traders were known for paying out a great deal for their wares. Causing them to second guess their agreement to buy me would cost me dearly. A cost I would pay with a pound of flesh beneath Rowena's switch. I couldn't count the times she had taken a thin branch to my backside for spilling food or ripping dresses when I was younger. My back ached from the memories.

The man with the coin smiled when I stopped before him, instantly making me think of a predatory animal. I flinched when he reached for me. "Now now, girlie. Og won't be hurting you." His rough, sun-darkened hands quickly moved to check me over, squeezing my cheeks and feeling the quality of my hair. I suppressed the urge to bite his fingers when they prodded into my mouth to check my teeth. His eyes glimmered with the prospect of fortune as he finished his evaluation, "She will fetch a handsome price; she is young, healthy and pretty. Yes, any good named family would pay well for a maidservant like her." He rubbed the black stubble growing on his chin. "It'll be tough though with her being Apoidean. Now you are sure she got none those powers you people get?"

Rowena laughed insincerely, "No sir, she does not. She had her ceremony months ago, not a drop of magic in her." Her lie caused me to shoot her a look of shock, she knew my Ceremony of Gifts was supposed to be today. She also knew I'd been a strong empath since I was very little, my gift having appeared early. I was thankful for that, it helped me avoid unpleasant situations many times. Unfortunately, today had been one of the rare times where it failed me. If I had not been so focused on reaching my hidden stash, I would've noticed their presence earlier.

Rowena returned my glare, a venomous warning in her aging blue eyes.

"Good, good. She'd never sell if she did; the last thing any proper folk want is Fae magic sullying their good homes. I guess I can pass her off as something else. No one needs to know her origins. Looks like we have a deal then." Og smiled and motioned for his partner. "Bachman, collect the girl," he quipped, handing his purse to Uncle Peter. My uncle's eyes shone with greed as he hefted the purse between his hands. I could see him fantasizing about how to use it. I knew a good portion of the gold would be squandered at the tavern on drink and gambling, much to Rowena's dismay.

Disbelief knocked my legs out from under me, and I crumbled to the ground. My body shook with each heaving sob and my mind spiraled.

I always knew my aunt and uncle did not love me, not as any normal family would. They thought me to be a burden to them, and a reminder of the power they would never have. They tolerated my presence only because they needed me to make their lives more comfortable. I had never imagined that their distaste for me ran deep enough for this betrayal. Sold into a life of servitude; sent away from my childhood home. It was unthinkable.

Since the day that they became my guardians, they had been careful to ensure that the village only saw that they treated me well, keeping the emotional abuse and mistreatment confined to our walls. They had only allowed their goodness to be seen, that they had opened their home and taken me in when my parents had tragically died.

Confusion, anger, and sadness competed for control in my head. All these years, under my relatives' guardianship, I'd been thankful and obedient. I kept my true thoughts and opinions hidden, my unhappiness tucked away and made sure my free time did not interfere with what needed to be done. I kept quiet, doing as I had been told to do, often doing more than my share to make sure that I stayed in their, somewhat, good graces. My younger cousins were always appreciative of my help, but my cousin Kizzy seemed to want nothing but to add to my misery.

Rowena gripped my arm with her claw-like fingers and pulled me up off the ground in a huff. I looked at her through my tears, "Why?"

"Because it suits us," a wicked grin smeared across her face.

"What does that even mean Rowena? I've never wronged you, always done what I've been told? What did I do to be treated like an animal?"

"It would seem, dear niece, that you have garnered some attention that does not suit you; despite being told to keep to yourself. Attention better suited to someone else." I stared at her wide-eyed, completely baffled what she refered to. "You thick girl! Must I spell everything out for you? For some reason, Tristan, Elder Tam's grandson, has asked for your hand. I would assume the only reason he would do so is if you threw yourself at him. Been doing things young girls should not be doing. God knows you are not pretty enough, or interesting enough for that kind of match."

Her stinging revelation shocked me, "Rowena, I swear on my mother's grave that I had no idea of Tristan's intention; or why he would choose to ask for my hand. I'm cordial with him when he greets me in the village, but that's the extent of any interaction between us. I treat him no different than anyone I come across."

Rowena sneered, "Lies, I am sure. No matter." She shrugged "Now that you will not be here, I will not have to deal with your deceit any longer, and Tristan will to come to his senses and ask for Kizzy's hand. She is far more worthy of holding such status than you are. You'll never be more than a filthy servant." With that, she threw me towards Bachman. He gripped me roughly as he clamped the irons around my wrists and began to lead me away.

Rowena's words cut deep. My tears flowed free and wild as I allowed the traders to lead me away.

A cold hand suddenly grabbed my arm from behind. I turned to see Kizzy's stone gaze and twisted smile. How had I missed her presence?

"Goodbye cousin, I'll be sure to comfort Tristan for you. Oh, and Happy Birthday." She laughed and let go of my arm. I turned and marched in sadness towards an uncertain and bleak future.

As the men led me through the woods, the sound of our feet on the beaten path lulled me into a sullen, trance-like state. I wondered what the village would think when I no longer came around. What would my relatives would tell them if someone came looking for me? No doubt they would tell lies that I ran away, make up some story that I'd been unhappy with them no matter how well they treated me. Rowena and Peter would tell them anything to keep themselves in good standing with the rest of the island. Their lies about me would bring shame to my father's memory. The daughter of an Elder abandoning her people would be scandalous and cursed.

I wept in silence as the traders pulled me along, leaving behind all I had ever known.

CHAPTER TWO

After a long journey, my first glimpse of Realta came through the slats of a crowded carriage stuffed with human cargo. The capital city, which shared its name with the country, loomed before me. The massive city left me both frightened and amazed. Feeling small. I had never seen anything like it before in my life. Everyone back home had heard of the crescent-shaped city that filled the outer bailey of the palace, Bua Tur, which itself was surrounded by fortified star-shaped walls and a thin moat, but never had I dreamed any place could be so large or hold so many people. There were easily twice the number of people walking the city streets than there were on Apoidea all together. Behind the city and castle loomed an eerie forest, dense with tall, dark trees draped with wisps of fog. Behind the forest, the small but majestic Eira Mountain range, perpetually capped with the only snow ever seen in the kingdom, jutted into the pale blue sky.

"Well, kiddies, this is it," Og said. I barely saw him make a sweeping gesture beyond the slats as if he were showing off our new home to us. An empty gesture to be sure. This place could never be my home, no place would be ever again thanks to Rowena and Peter.

The carriage rattled through the gates and into the bustling city. People and animals roamed everywhere I looked. My eyes clenched shut against the immediate onslaught of the emotions that came with the high population of the city. It was overwhelming, to say the least, and I knew this was the first taste of how I would have to adapt in order to survive. There was a lot of work ahead of me to keep this number of emotions in check.

We stopped before a plain, brown brick building with matching brown shutters, innocuous enough to the passing crowd. For us in the carriage, it was not. This place was a depressing stop on the way to the auction block. Og ordered us out of the carriage. My cramped muscles welcomed the chance to stretch, but also protested stiffly after such a long stretch of being unused. He and Bachman led us into the building, telling us to find a space and make ourselves comfortable for the night.

The inside of the building was even sadder than the outside, practically barren. The high windows were caked in dirt and cobwebs, matching the dirt strewn floor. Old, discolored chamberpots adorned each corner, along with piles of dusty looking piles of fabric. The only furniture was the beds, and those could barely be passed off as anything more than flooring; a thin layer of straw that smelled of mold, and blankets that were falling apart. My old palette on Apoidea seemed a luxury in comparison.

Og caught me by the elbow and led me to one of the sad straw beds. "Settle in, make no trouble," he instructed before wandering off into the room, stopping every now and then to talk to other traders dropping off their haul for the night. I wasn't sure what made him think I'd do anything troublesome. All I wanted was to get away and be by myself, try to rest.

The straw itched against my skin the moment I sat on it. There was no sense trying to get comfortable. My best bet would be to distract myself from thinking about what kind of bugs could be lurking in the musty bed under me. Switching focus, I watched the room in silence, observing the crowd that I'd be sharing this room with for the night. Most girls huddled together, seeking comfort from each other. Some of the young men joked loudly, masking their fear by playing rough. Traders lolled about, checking on their people or leaning against the bare walls to share their tales from the road.

It was obvious that many of these people had formed bonds on their journeys from wherever they came from. I wasn't sure if I thought them to be lucky to have one another or not. They would likely be ripped from one another the next day. I decided I was glad I hadn't gotten to know the few others Og and Bachman had collected on their journey. I didn't have to fear losing anything more than I already had.

"Hello there," a man squatting next to me pulled my attention away from the rest of the room. A trader, he was older, blond and wore a set of shackles on his belt. There was no trace of worry or fear in him, only desire and greed. "You know, a girl like you should not have to sleep in such deplorable conditions. You could have a nice comfy bed. Would that be nice, after such a long journey?"

Lust oozed from him. He wasn't just being kind, he was looking for something more. For someone to share his bed with. "I am fine here," my voice trembled.

"Come now, girlie, you cannot really be fine with sleeping surrounded by strangers in this smelly place. Share a bed with me, I know you'll enjoy it." He reached out and stroked a piece of my hair.

"No, thank you." I shied away.

"Come on."

"The girl said no, Wallace." Og's heavy hand landed on Wallace's shoulder. "I think you should move on before I make you."

"Whatever, there are plenty of others that would rather have a bed." Wallace stood, wiping his nose with his thumb. He didn't move along very far, only a few straw piles away. He'd turned his sights on another young girl with tears staining her cheeks. She couldn't have been much older than me, petite with crimson gold hair. I prayed she would not be susceptible to his lecherous offer, but her fear of this place overtook her good sense. She slipped her small hand into Wallace's and let him lead her away.

Og clicked his tongue and shook his head, "It sickens me the way some of these traders think they can treat girls however they like. As if the deal they made was for their personal satisfaction rather than business," he grumbled to himself as he set a crusty scrap of bread next to me. He moved on without another word.

. . .

Sleep was not my friend that night. The whole of the past week kept playing over and over in my head; my family's betrayal and the arduous journey to Realta. It all swirled in my mind like a bad dream I couldn't wake from. My physical and mental exhaustion, paired with the added anxiety of each person crammed in the little building with me, made true rest near impossible.

The moment the sun rose, the traders filtered into the room clanging their shackles against anything metal. My aching body was not refreshed or relieved when I attempted to stretch away the exhaustion that had taken up residence in me. I'd been through too much to be comfortable. Not to mention there was no time to wake up slowly. The traders were in a rush to get us to market.

The men and women were herded to opposite sides of the open room. A large, dingy swath of white fabric draped across the room, separating us for modesty. With a loud whistle, maids descended upon us, armed with buckets of cold water and lye soap. We were stripped bare and scrubbed until our skin was pink and shiny. Sobs echoed across the women's side of the curtain and mingled with the splashing of water on the floor rinsing away the grime of our pasts. After the aggressive sponge baths, we were each given simple brown dresses with aprons to wear. The fabric itched from collar to hem. They then pulled our hair into tight buns that stretched the skin on our faces back ever so slightly. In the end, we were all only distinguishable by our faces and heights. We were blank slates capable of being molded into what our future masters wanted us to be. When we were all prepared and the fabric wall was taken away, it was time for final instructions.

A trader I wasn't familiar with barked out what would be expected of us at market. He emphasized the importance of being on our best behavior in order to garner the attention of a good employer. If we were really lucky we could land positions in the palace. Anyone stepping out of line would lose the opportunity to be auctioned off. Anyone not sold at auction would be sent to mills, labor camps, or pleasure houses to work off their debt to their trader. The mention of possibly being forced to work off my debt in any of those places sent chills through me. I may have been isolated away on a small island, but I knew the reputation that came with those jobs. Most who worked them did not have long lives.

I would rather be a servant my whole life than dead before my time.

"Listen you lot." Og took over the instructions. "In a few minutes, we will make our way to the market. You will line up, single file, and wait to be processed out. What that means is, you will each be marked with a string tied to your left wrist as you exit this building." Og held a bundle of strings above his head. There were lengths of several colors dangling from his fist like some twisted version of a maypole. "This string will let buyers know the minimum price you can be purchased for." He paused studying the crowd, a harsh look in his eyes. "Now, get in line."

Every bought person in the room scrambled and shoved their way to get into line. The chaos froze me, and I felt as though I would explode from it. I couldn't get a grip on my own feelings to overcome everyone else's frantic energy. It was only when someone grabbed my arm that I was able to snap out of the daze.

I looked over to see Og, full of something close to sympathy. "Let's get you in line," he said tugging me towards the forming queue and leaving me to oversee the placement of the strings. He walked next to me as the line moved and spoke in hushed tones, "Listen, you need to keep your mouth shut about where you come from for the rest of your life here. Any word from you that you are Apoidean and you are done. You will not be bought, you will not be able to work anywhere, and you will not be able to work off your debt. It is likely that you will be killed for your heritage. Am I understood?"

I kept my eyes on the dirty floor and answered in a meek voice, "Yes, sir."

"Good girl. Without doubt, you will fetch a hefty sum at auction; you are healthy and easy on the eyes, a good combination for maid-servants. Had you been anything less, I would've left you on Apoidea with your miserable relatives. If anyone asks where you are from during the viewing you tell them you are an orphan and unsure of your heritage."

I nodded again and he patted my head before ushering me forward to receive the string that put a price on my head. My anxiety regarding being sold off like livestock doubled after the brief conversation with the gruff yet caring trader. The reminder that being Apoidean meant I was undesirable to most, thanks to rumors spread by past rulers, sat heavy in my heart. Thankfully, Aunt Rowena had lied about my gift. Being an Apoidean with magic was even worse. My magical gift made me something less than undesirable. It made me evil in the eyes of the rest of the kingdom.

THE MARKET SQUARE bustled with activity. Farmers and merchants set up their stalls to sell their wares and customers haggled over prices. People wandered back and forth between stalls, exchanging pleasantries. Children whined about their boredom to unhearing parents. Animals called and cried from their pens for a savior that would never come. Inside I felt the same pain as those poor creatures. I was no better off than them, being sold to a fate I had no control over.

Everyone's eyes seemed to follow us when we passed them, gawking at the poor souls that they were glad not to be. Their pity seeped off of them. It was worse when we neared the platform where the auctions took place. The square around was packed already with those seeking to buy. The rich and the servants of the rich. Their haughty, hungry eyes at the first glimpse of what could be theirs. The rich itching for their pocketbooks to be lightened so that they could have leisurely lives. Their gazes burned into me long after we disappeared from sight into the holding barn next to the auction block.

We waited there, penned like animals, as prospective employers examined and evaluated us before deciding if they would bid on us. This hour-long viewing was torture for me. The close scrutiny left me feeling naked, and I was terrified I'd slip up, reveal something I shouldn't when they questioned me about my skills. Most never questioned me on anything else.

One, a short woman with frizzy, graying red hair, did ask of my origins, along with many other questions about what I could do. My heart fluttered nervously as I gave the answer that Og had asked me to. As she considered my answers my nerves grew, and I became certain my lie was about to land me in hot water. My mind reeled with the possible consequences. What would happen to me? Would Og deny his inside knowledge of me? Certainly, I'd end up rotting in a cell until they decided to execute me for merely being Apoidean.

The woman moved along. My fears diminished into the small knots they began as, leaving me to wonder more about where I'd end up after the auction.

MY TURN on the auction block came last, my time to take center stage came far too soon. The crowd of potential employers and spectators eyed me with greed. I trembled under their judging and hungry stares. The auctioneer raised his voice high to reach over the din of the busy marketplace, "This servant is sixteen, has many household skills, and experience caring for youngsters. She would be a fine addition to any household with young children."

The bids for my servitude came fast and furious. As my price went higher and higher, bidders dropped out until there were only two left to war over who would own me. One, a well-dressed man with light hair and cruel brown eyes. He had a frail-looking woman, with the same color hair, clinging to him. I assumed she was his wife, a soft aristocrat unable to lift a finger of her own. She eyed me warily with jealousy in her heart. Her adverse reaction to me made me pray the man would not win this one. He had obvious other intentions for me.

The other was the short, red-haired woman that had asked me the bevy of questions during the viewing. With every bid the man threw against hers, her eyes flashed with irritation. As the bidding war dragged on, it was her that took action to end it once and for all. She clenched her skirt in her fists and marched to the man, determined. I thought for sure she might physically attack the man if he continued to bid against her. Her small hand waggled in front of her wildly as she berated the man and his frail companion. His face fell in defeat instantly. I had no idea what she had said, but it worked. The small woman had won the auction. Just like that, I became someone's property.

A man grabbed my arm and led me off of the platform and down the small set of creaky steps to meet with my new owner. She waited at the bottom with a warm smile that I couldn't help but want to return, mostly because she had answered my prayer not to be bought by the fair-haired man. "Hello there," her nasal voice squeaked as she spoke. While her voice and stature were small, I could tell she was a force to be reckoned with. "I am Mrs. James. What's your name?"

I curtsied as I greeted her, my voice weakened and wavering from nerves."I am Merinley, Ma'am."

"No need to be so timid, or formal with me girl. While I am in charge of you, I'm not your master. You are going to work in Bua Tur."

My heart stopped. No wonder she had won. Bua Tur, the grand palace of Realta. All my life I had been told to fear the palace, the home of those who had made monsters of my people. The idea of being walled in with them was frightening. What if they saw through me. Knew I lied about where I came from. I swallowed hard at the thought. I would have to tread more carefully than Og had warned in this life I'd been forced into.

CHAPTER THREE

"Now, don't think things will be easy in the palace just because there are a lot of us. Far from it." Mrs. James called over her shoulder to me as we bustled through the market. Though she was small, I had a difficult time keeping up with her rapid pace. "Everyone helps out, all the time. If you finish one job, you move on to another; help where you can and where you are told."

"Yes, Ma'am."

She spun on her heel, quick enough to startle me. "What was that? You will need to speak up to be heard, especially in my kitchen. If I can't hear you over a few chickens, I certainly will not hear you over an active kitchen."

I nodded, suddenly too nervous to respond any other way.

"Good. Now, try to keep up. It's easy to get lost in the market if you don't know your way around." She turned and continued on her way, weaving around the bustling people. I quickened my pace to keep up and opened up my senses to help me be more alert and avoid bumping into anyone.

Mrs. James continued talking to me as she walked, giving me brief details about what would be expected of me in the kitchens of Bua Tur. She stopped at stalls selling various foods to purchase supplies to be delivered to her at the palace. Her command at each stall impressed me; she never let any of them intimidate her. In fact, she did most of the intimidating.

At each stall we stopped at, Mrs. James made sure whoever ran it took note of me. "You see this girl," she would say, "she is not to be taken advantage of if she ever comes to your stall. She's my new kitchen girl. Treat her as you would me when selling to her. Harass her and you can be sure King Bern will hear of it."

At the mention of King Bern, every stall owner turned ashen. Their reactions had me curious, I had to ask, "Would King Bern really care if a kitchen maid was harassed?"

Laughter erupted from Mrs. James. "No. He only cares for himself, his grandson, and his fortune. I'm just clever enough to use his power to make sure we get fair prices. A lot of these vendors take advantage of women at the market, charging them more than men. Throw around his name and we get the best prices."

"So, I will be doing this? Ordering what the kitchen needs here at the market?"

"Eventually," she shrugged. "Like I said before, you will start out doing odd jobs in the kitchen. Helping make bread, washing dishes, prepping meals and whatnot. When you have earned it, you will be running kitchen errands in the palace. It is my hope that in time you will be appointed to taking over on my errands so that I can keep my focus on what is happening in the kitchen. Then you will be doing this."

"Your errands?"

"Yes, my errands. Making orders at the market and serving private meals to King Bern and his family." She let out a reluctant sigh, bringing her hands to her hips, "If you want the honest truth, I could have selected any of those poor souls up for auction to come work for me in the kitchen and run menial errands, if I were not looking to unburden myself of errands outside of the kitchen. I am no spring chicken anymore, and as terrible as it sounds, King Bern and his family prefer to be served by servants who are pleasing to look at. You fit that bill more than anyone else back there. I no longer do. Understand?"

"Yes, Ma'am." It was my turn to swallow hard. The revelation that I would eventually be the primary server for King Bern and his family intimidated me; frightened me enough that the rest of the trek to the palace was made with shaky steps and my heart pounding in my ears. My racing mind struggled to focus and the emotions of the people surrounding me seeped in, amplifying my lack of focus. This always happened when I was upset.

"Here we are," Mrs. James declaration pulled me from my nervous thoughts.

I looked up; an overwhelming feeling of being small filled me at the sight of the palace looming over me. Seeing it up close was far different from seeing it towering over the city, like comparing beetles to butterflies. A strange sensation of relief and fear bubbled in me. I was afraid of this place, for reasons other than my hidden identity that I couldn't pinpoint. Yet, I was relieved I would not be thrown into errand running right away. Getting a sense of direction within the walls of this formidable place would take some time to do, of that I was certain.

Instead of heading straight into the palace, Mrs. James led me around to the eastern end of the inner bailey and through a crumbling stone passage into an open area that seemed not quite as picturesque as one would imagine any part of a castle grounds to be. The ground was barren of almost any plant life, a sad blanket of dirt and very little grass. Two weathered, medium sized cottages leaned up against the bailey wall. A stone wall separated them, blocking the windows that faced one another; offering privacy yet taking away a source of natural light. A lone guard stood at the end of the wall, boredom written all over his face.

About twenty or so feet away from the cottages sat stables and paddocks filled with horses, cows, and pigs. There was also a string of cages which were occupied by a variety of fowl; chicken, ducks, pheasant, and peacock. The animals were lucky enough to have a few large shade trees, the cottages were exposed to the elements with no protection from them.

Mrs. James stopped in front of the cottage on the left. "This is the female servant house, the other is the male. This is where servants who do not have families to live with outside of the palace grounds stay when they are not working. There is always a guard on duty out here as well, as you can see." I looked to the guard who seemed to appraise me with his eyes. I suspected he was not really there to guard the servants from danger but to make sure they behaved.

Inside, the lodging almost felt homey with its centralized crackling fireplace. But everything else screamed that it was merely a place for us to sleep, just like my little hut back home. The wood floors were creaky and graying with age. A dozen cots occupied most of the floor-space, each one made neatly with simple blankets and flat pillows. In the far left corner of the cabin was a closed off area for bathing.

Mrs. James instructed me to choose one of the unoccupied beds, distinguishable by the lack of a ribbon on the bedpost. She handed me a bit of yellowish ribbon from her apron pocket so that I could mark my bed as taken. I picked one that lay under a high dingy window and tied the ribbon to it. It surprised me that none of the other girls wanted the tiny bit of natural light it provided. I could deal with the smell and sounds of the stables if it meant a little bit of natural light to look forward to.

After I picked my bed, we left the servant house and followed a dirt path past the stables. I could not help but peek in the stalls at the magnificent horses housed inside. The strong and sleek creatures seemed to acknowledge my admiration, responding with excited nickering. At the end of the stables, we passed through a doorway in a high vine-covered wall. The doorway led into a stone passage illuminated by thin slits in the walls. The passageway echoed our footsteps back to us, adding to my building anticipation at what would be on the other end. I didn't have to wait long to find out that the passageway let out right into the kitchen.

Mrs. James wasted no time putting me to work the moment we stepped foot into her domain. There was no time to get to know my surroundings. I had to learn as I went, taking moments to study what was around me between listening to instructions. She immediately led me to an area in the kitchen where two older women were busy making bread at a large wooden table. "Ingrid, Suzette, this is Merinley. She's going to be helping you out for a little while." The women both looked up to give a brief and courteous hello. "Show her the basics of what we are doing with the bread today. I will be back in a little while to check your progress."

Ingrid, a dark skinned and plump woman with dark silvery hair, wiped her hands on her apron and stepped over to me with a heap of dough in her hands. I was familiar with making bread, but I paid close attention just in case there was something special they did with their loaves. The older woman worked fast, breaking off a handful of dough and shaping it into a small round loaf, the kind used to hold thick stews. When she was done forming the loaf, she slashed a small cross into the top of the loaf for ventilation. When Ingrid finished showing me what needed to be done, I jumped right in and began kneading mounds of dough and forming them into small round loaves. My arms grew sore after only a few minutes from the repeated action of working the heavy dough. But I was proud of my work. The loaves I made were identical to Ingrid and Suzette's. By the time that Mrs. James came back, I had managed to cover myself with a fine layer of flour.

"Well, look at you girl. I think there is more flour on you than on the table. Such waste is unacceptable."

"Sorry, Ma'am. I just wanted to do a good job. I guess I got carried away. I didn't mean to waste, it won't happen again."

"Be sure of it. I will let it slide this one time since it is your first day, but in the future, you can expect some punishment. Every ounce of what is used in the kitchen is precious. King Bern may be rich, but he is selfish. He gives us limits. As bought and paid for servants we earn nothing, so waste comes out of our provisions. You will have to learn to work clean. Now, clean yourself up. I am going to show you the rest of the kitchen and then we are going to polish serving ware."

"Yes, Ma'am." I wiped my hands on my apron as I responded. I was a little sad to be leaving the bread station. I enjoyed the silent company of Ingrid and Suzette, as well as the task we were doing, despite how hard it had been to work so much heavy dough. It had almost been cathartic.

CHAPTER FOUR

"Merinley!" Mrs. James called for me, her voice sharp. Her abrasive demeanor served a purpose; it let others know who was in charge. She was a sweet and caring woman, completely fitting to her diminutive stature, so she had to make up for it for adopting an abrasive demeanor in the kitchen. Had she not, she would not have been successful in her position. I knew many in the kitchen didn't see this, they only experienced her while working. My gift gave me a look into her true self. In the short time I had been in Bua Tur, I had grown fond of her.

I wiped my hands on my apron and rushed to answer her call. I found her standing near the central serving station, her frizzy red and gray hair stuck out in erratic coils from her cap and her hands on hips stance made clear to anyone her impatient mood. I saw the bad day she was having. "Yes, Mrs. James?"

"Take this tea to the Quaintrelle quarters, and hurry." She nodded her head in the direction of a tray sitting on the table near her. "Mistress Anwen should not be kept waiting for her afternoon tea. Her time is precious."

I curtsied and grabbed the tea tray from the table. The steam wafted over my face as I hastened carefully through the halls going to the

Quaintrelles' quarters, the sweet rosy scent wrapping around me as I went. The luxurious smell added to the giddy feeling forming in my heart. I was about to enter the most secluded area of Bua Tur. In the month and a half I had been in the kitchens, I'd never been sent to that particular wing of the palace, but had always been curious about it. Very few saw behind the doors at the end of the corridor, their world was considered mysterious.

The corridor bridging the Quaintrelles' quarters to the palace was under the watch of more guards than necessary, three stood at the corridor entrance itself. One would think that whomever lived beyond the corridor was as important as the King himself. The theory was practically true, from what I understood. King Bern considered the Quaintrelle to be one of the most valuable assets of Realta.

The moment I stepped into the corridor, the air became charged with something I couldn't quite identify. My head buzzed with something close to excitement laced with nerves. Much like the anticipation of something special about to happen. I was about to step into Bua Tur's greatest secret. By the time I reached the end of the corridor, my heart felt like it could fly.

Four more guards stood watch at the doors to the Quaintrelles' quarters. Yes, these girls, these women, were the safest residents of the palace. "I'm here with tea for Mistress Anwen," I announced, approaching the doors. Without words, the guards parted and one opened the doors so I could enter.

The breath was stolen from my lungs when I entered the opulent wing of the palace where the most coveted creatures in all of Realta lived. White marble floors shone bright, reflecting the golden filigree accents on the equally white walls. Lush, jewel tone fabrics draped from the windows; the same fabric used in upholstering the furniture and for the pillows scattered on it. The air was fragrant, feminine, and soft. This was a place where beauty resided.

I passed an open room and peered in to see a small group of girls around my age being read to by a plain brunette woman, their blond heads leaning intently towards her. I stopped and listened to her for a moment. Her voice dripped with sweetness as she read a sultry poem of forbidden love. When she noticed my eavesdropping she gave me a small nod to indicate that I should move on. I wished for a moment that I could stay and join the girls in their lessons. Stay and hear the end of the poem.

Venturing further into the quarters, a soft flowing melody caught in my ears. I turned a corner and discovered the source of the music. A pretty woman with pale red-blond hair sat at a large harp, plucking out a heavenly melody. I hated to interrupt her song, but I didn't wish to upset anyone by serving cold tea. I approached timidly. It only took a moment for her to notice me and stop playing. "I beg your pardon, Mistress, do you know where I might find Mistress Anwen so that I may deliver her tea?" She pointed off towards her right and told me that I'd find her languishing about in the Quaintrelle gardens, returning to her harp immediately after.

After a minute or two, I was rendered awestruck as I came upon my destination. The gardens were the most beautiful sight I had seen since coming to the palace. Sunlight dappled through the towering trees, offering ample shading for the coveted ladies when they studied poetry or picked flowers from the wide variety in the garden. Cherry blossoms bloomed throughout the area. Some blossoms fell from the trees like a fragrant snow flurry.

A gentle cooing came from the golden dovecote in the center of the garden. I thought the doves were lucky to live among such beauty; even though they lived in a cage. This place reminded me of the stories about the Fae that my mother told me as a young child. I could almost see the magical creatures frolicking under the cherry blossoms and singing the enchanting songs to the birds, their silvery wings twinkling in the soft sunlight as they flitted about. Perhaps a few would have been sitting under the trees making flower crowns or braiding their hair. I sighed and forced myself from the fantasy, then returned to the task at hand.

The magical garden appeared empty at first, but as I ventured further along the path I saw a woman sitting at a small stone table. She was an exceptional beauty wearing a soft blue dress. Her honey hair sat in loose curls that reflected golden in the minimal sunlight. She hummed as she read something to herself. A wave of bashfulness swept over me. My disheveled, labor dirtied appearance painfully obvious in her presence, I felt as though I'd somehow disturb the serenity she may have sought from this place with my ragged appearance. If it weren't my duty to interrupt, if only to deliver tea, I would've run from there as fast as my feet could carry me.

"Excuse me, Mistress Anwen, I have your tea," I announced with trepidation.

"Why thank you, dear." She took the tray from me and smiled as she set it on the table before her. I couldn't help but smile back. "You must be Mrs. James' new girl. She told me she found someone to help her out. She was not kidding when she said you were something special." The way he eyes appraised every inch of me scattered my nerves.

"Thank you, Mistress."

"Tell me, where do you hail from? Your features are so striking, but I see no resemblance to any that I have yet encountered in the kingdom. Though, I admit I have not traveled to every corner. Yet," she added.

I fidgeted with the side hem of my stained apron. So far, I'd listened to Og's instruction to hide my true identity. Then again, no one showed any interest in getting to know anything about me other than my name and how well I did my chores. Yet, something in me screamed to tell her. Perhaps it had been her earnest face and gentle demeanor that made me want to trust her the instant I met her. Or maybe it was that she was a Quaintrelle, a position full of secrets to be kept.

I wanted to tell her, I felt like I had to. To be sure, I closed my eyes and opened up the gift that I'd barely used since my work at the palace begun. I sensed Mistress Anwen's kindness; that her nature was generous and understanding. I knew for sure that I could trust her with my secret."I am from Apoidea, Mistress," I said. After a moment, I panicked and added, "I shouldn't have told you that. Please do not tell anyone. I was ordered not to tell anyone because Apoideans are so undesirable that I'd be imprisoned, or even killed, if I did."

"Your secret is safe with me." She gave me a wink and sipped her tea. "I must say, I've never met an Apoidean before, I'd be very interested in learning more about you. What's your name and age dear?" She spoke with an educated air about her. Her warm attitude about my revelation made me like her even more.

"Merinley. I am sixteen, Mistress."

"Thank you, Merinley. Perhaps I will see you again?" I nodded in response; curtsied and dashed back to the kitchen. I hoped with all my heart that I would be sent on an errand for her again. I knew that I could learn much from the kind and world-wise woman.

CHAPTER FIVE

Over the next few weeks, Mistress Anwen called on me to deliver her tea almost daily. Some days, I'd even see her in the kitchen speaking with Mrs. James. She'd ask me something about my life, both before and now, or tell me something she thought I'd find interesting. I took care when answering her questions so I didn't accidentally reveal too much to anyone that could overhear. When I showed an interest in a book she read, she came to the kitchens the next day with it and read to me while I did my chores. Her visits were the highlight of my days and led me to believe that life here could be good. Having her as a friend made me feel important; special for the first time since my parents died.

I looked forward to seeing Mistress Anwen each day, but then she suddenly stopped sending for me. My spirit fell at the apparent abandonment, it hurt as much as Rowena's betrayal. I assumed I'd done something wrong, that somehow I did something to offend her. I even questioned my gift. Had I read Mistress Anwen wrong? Had she decided that who I was made me too undesirable to befriend? Would she out me?

The loss of seeing Mistress Anwen led to a bout of lethargic moping. My chores took longer to do and I accomplished less and less each day. I was constantly on guard and expected to be arrested at any moment.

Mrs. James took away my errand privileges. With how much I'd flourished after those began, she was certain the mild punishment would be enough to set me back on path. Her plan backfired. My paranoid skulking continued to interfere with doing quality work. My polishing was spotty and I wasted more resources than I had when I was new. With that, Mrs. James decided a harsher punishment was needed to snap me back into the girl I'd been when I first arrived. She denied me food for a day and a switch was taken to my backside. Not hard enough to lash the skin, only enough to leave me sore a day or two. It had been enough.

Though I still mourned Mistress Anwen's absence, I set aside my wishing for her company, pushed down my fears, and threw myself back into my work. I didn't want any sort of punishment ever again. I left my pain as tear stains on my cot.

My threadbare bed itched beneath me as I lay with my eyes closed. I lost myself in thoughts of my childhood, brought on by the sound of the rain tapping on the window above me. The tolling of bells told me I had to rise. Stretching my back, I sat up. The lingering fog of sleep took minutes to dissipate before I realized the day seemed much brighter than it should be, despite the overcast sky, and no one else lingered in their cots. The bells continued to toll longer than they should have.

A ball of panic knotted in my stomach. I had overslept. On top of that, I was hurt that none of my roommates had cared enough to wake me with them. A harsh punishment would certainly be waiting for me when I arrived at the kitchen. I berated myself for giving Mrs. James a reason to punish me yet again, just as I was beginning to get back in her good graces. I scrambled out of bed and into my over-sized work smock, I had to make a mad dash to the kitchen.

As if the heavens had seen it fit to punish me for my tardiness as well, the skies opened up and the pattering rain turned into a torrential downpour. The cold rain pelted against me harshly with every step across the yard to the tunnel to the kitchen. My feet and ankles were splattered with mud by the time I arrived at the kitchen looking like a drowned kitten.

My mud caked shoes slipped on the stone floor as I hurried in search of the kitchen master to receive my duties for the day, as well as my punishment. Fellow kitchen staff gave me strange looks, a few tittering in amusement, as I passed through. I squelched to a halt when I found Mrs. James leaning against the central table, her back towards me. Her tiny frame relaxed as she laughed with the tall blonde next to her. There was no mistaking who that was, for there was no one as elegant as her anywhere near the kitchen. Mistress Anwen. I watched, stunned at her sudden appearance, as she gracefully lifted a teacup towards her face.

I cleared my throat to gain their attention without completely interrupting their conversation. Their gazes fell on me simultaneously, each of them allowing their eyes to take in my sopping form from head to toe. Mrs. James' eyes widened in irritation, the knowledge of the mess I must've dragged into her kitchen with me playing in her mind. She bit her lip, taking control of the lashing her tongue was dying to give me. Mistress Anwen, on the other hand, snickered in delight. Not at my appearance, but at her amusement of the shade of pink Mrs. James had turned. Her eyes continued to hold a note of pity for the sad mess I was in.

"There you are, girl," Mrs. James chided. "I was beginning to think I'd have to fetch you from bed myself."

I kept my gaze low and shuffled my feet, "Sorry Mrs. James. I don't know what came over me this morning. I'm prepared to accept my punishment."

"No, dear. There will be no punishments today." Her words astounded me. As much as I saw past her tough exterior, I knew Mrs. James would always be liberal with the switch when someone deserved it. With how late I'd been, I deserved it.

She moved from the table and stood before me, hands on her hips as she usually did. "You no longer work in the kitchen dear. You will now be training under Mistress Anwen."

"What do you mean?" I asked in disbelief.

"I mean just that, you will be training to be a Quaintrelle under Mistress Anwen now."

Mistress Anwen confirmed Mrs. James' words with a nod, her bright curls bouncing, "It is true, Merinley. I've seen great potential in you, from the first time you were sent with my tea. I've arranged to take you on as my trainee, pending approval when you meet our Matron, of course. Your life is going to change in ways you could never imagine."

My eyes widened. For a moment I was thrown back to that fateful morning I'd been sold, to the words my mother had spoken in my dream. It seemed like fate that Mistress Anwen repeated them now, as my life began to change again.

At the same time, I was frozen with trepidation. I admired Mistress Anwen a great deal. She was beautiful, kind, and full of knowledge that astounded me. I'd often wished to be more like her, but never thought it would happen. In truth, I envied the seemingly easy life Quaintrelle had, and their pretty clothes; but I never wanted to be one. I knew what the job of Quaintrelle truly entailed. I also knew nothing could be done to change what had already been agreed upon. Whatever exchange there had been to make this happen would have been binding. It would be best to remain agreeable; I didn't want to cause trouble.

"Well do not just stand there a gape-seed, Merinley," Mrs. James said. "Go fetch anything you may wish to keep from the cottage and come back as quickly as possible. Then you will follow Mistress Anwen to your new home."

"There's no need for me to do that, Ma'am," I managed after a minute of stunned silence. "I don't have much of anything else there. I have all I need on me." I had acquired very little when I came here, just a few articles of clothing. I doubted I would need those. The only thing I valued, my mother's necklace, never left my neck. In truth, I wanted to change into something dry. That would be a pointless task with the current weather. Whatever I changed into would just become wet as well. Best to move on without hesitation.

"Very well then, off you go." Mrs. James motioned to Mistress Anwen. "Good luck, Merinley."

Butterflies filled my stomach taking my first steps towards the Quaintrelle quarters as Mistress Anwen's trainee. I'd so little luxury in my life, the idea of being one of the palace beauties daunted me. Yet, curiosity and excitement filled my belly as well. Despite my apprehension, I hoped I'd do well in this new life. The last thing I wanted to do was disappoint Mistress Anwen.

CHAPTER SIX

The Quaintrelles' quarters seemed different as I walked in them side by side with Mistress Anwen. Everything in them seemed lighter, brighter. The air even smelled sweeter. I knew deep down that nothing had changed, that my perception had only been altered by my new circumstances. This would be my new home, not just a place I got precious moments in while fulfilling my duties.

"I wish I could let you have a day of rest before we begin your training," Mistress Anwen explained as we passed through the beautiful living space, "but you are behind the others as it is. There will be no time to adjust, and for that I'm sorry."

"What will I be doing first?" I expected that I would be sitting in a lesson like I'd seen many times when delivering her tea.

"First, we get you cleaned up." She led me through rooms I'd never seen, which I attempted to see as much of as I could as we went. Glimpses of real beds and tables littered with flowers and sparkling bottles of exotic oils flashed before me. I couldn't wait to explore these areas further; to try the contents of the bottles and snuggle into the large beds.

We ended up in a large communal bathing area. A row of large, white basins stretched across the room, a soft-looking rug sat at the foot of each one. The blue-gray marbled floor glittered under a large skylight. Through it, I could see that the gray skies were giving way to beams of sunshine and bright patches of blue. A light rain still sprinkled down.

"Strip down, Merinley," Mistress Anwen ordered, stopping beside the basin at the end of the room, steam rising steadily from the water inside. A chill of excitement jolted through me at the sight. I couldn't remember the last time I had a hot bath.

"Here?" I looked around for a privacy screen of some sort. We may have lived communally in the cabin behind the stables, but there were at least privacy screens for dressing and sponge baths. "There's no privacy screen."

"Of course not, why should there be? Our bodies are nothing to be ashamed of. You're going to have to learn to be comfortable with yours as well as other people's."

Nerves overwhelmed my eagerness to luxuriate in hot water. I gulped back my inhibitions and slipped out of the dirt caked slippers and peeled off my rain-soaked dress. I tried, in vain, to keep myself covered with my arms as slowly lowered myself into the steaming water.

My body instantly relaxed once submerged in the bath. The luxurious bubbles and oils made the water feel like silk. I slipped into a state of pure bliss as one of the maids scrubbed my hair with something that smelled flowery. Another maid gave me a hand sized sponge and poured the same flowery substance on it, which I used to wash the rest of my body.

The whole experience had relaxed me more than I had been in a long time, that is until a maid came at me with a straight razor and cream. I splashed out of the bath in a panic. "What are you doing?"

"We need to remove the hair from your legs, Miss," the maid explained.

"Why?"

"It is what needs to be done."

I looked over to Mistress Anwen for a better answer. The idea of shaving, to me, was complete insanity. I knew that shaving had been a luxury only meant for men, a means to having well groomed facial hair. A status symbol for many.

"We shave because we are soft and delicate creatures," Mistress Anwen explained. "Works of art if you will. Every bit of us must be pleasing, from our minds to our bodies. This practice sets us apart from other women, namely prostitutes. We are not ordinary women, Merinley. Nor are we whores. We are Quaintrelle, special and refined."

Her explanation did little to comfort me; more reminding me of what I was to become, on top of fearing strange women dragging blades up and down my legs. Despite the hesitation, I got back in the bath. If I was going to be a Quaintrelle, I would have to abide by their rules and rituals. Including rituals I thought to be alarming.

After all was said and done, I felt amazing, cleaner than I had in ages. I was even sold on the idea of shaved legs, they were wonderful in all their smoothness. One of the maids had given me a silky powder blue robe to cover myself with and taken to the trainee dorm. The flimsy material clung to my body, feeling more like spiderwebs than decadent fabric. The material was not for me, I couldn't wait to change into something else.

We made our way back to the trainee dorm at a whirlwind pace, maids in tow. Mistress Anwen wanted to incorporate me into lessons as soon as possible, as if every moment wasted would be detrimental to my progress. Once again, the beds called to me as we passed by them to a dressing area separated by a large room divider. The partial wall was a work of silver and gold metalwork flowers hinged in three places. Before my mind could wonder on the curiosity of a dressing screen when none was offered near the baths, I saw the answer of its existence. The other side of the gilded work revealed mirrors running the full length of the structure, as well as lining the alcove it created. A way for trainees to ensure their appearance was suitable across every inch, every angle.

Despite being truly clean for the first time since Apoidea, my appearance was raggedy to say the least. I was worn down from years of mistreatment and hard hours working in the kitchen with Mrs. James. Certainly a far cry from a promising Quaintrelle trainee. My mouth turned down at what I saw, I wondered what it was Mistress Anwen had seen in me to sweep me into this life. Whatever it was, I couldn't see it.

A maid interrupted my self-critique, shuffling in with a neatly folded dress in her arms. In a flourish, Mistress Anwen unfurled the dress as she took it from the maid and revealed the butter yellow garment in its entirety. Even though it was slightly wrinkled from storage, it was a finer garment than I would have ever seen in my life, had it not taken the path it had. The soft yellow fabric had barely noticeable white flowers on the bodice, and the cap sleeves were entirely white with yellow ribbons around the cuffs. I could hardly wait to try it on, even though it, on some level, represented that my life was no longer my own to do with what I willed.

I quickly disrobed and the maids helped me into the pretty dress faster than I imagined possible. I was transformed when dressed, even looked a little newer. But the tired girl still lingered in my eyes and posture. Perhaps she would always be there.

As I studied my new self in the many reflections before me, Mistress Anwen's reflections beamed at me over my shoulder. The pride I saw and felt in her emboldened me. "Mistress, I don't wish to offend, but may I ask why you chose me?"

"When I first met you, I sensed something truly special in you, Merinley," she replied. "Someone as special as you needs to shine, not decompose in manual labor. Something told me that this is where you belong."

Her answer satisfied some of my curiosity, but I felt something had been left unsaid. Not wanting to stir the pot, I left it alone. "Thank you."

"No need to thank me, Merinley. I'm more than happy that you're here." She tried to smooth a lock of my curls into obeying, but it did as it wanted. She gave up on it and smiled, "Now, it's time to begin. You are already late for your first lesson."

Mistress Anwen escorted me into my first lesson, a poetry discussion. I peered with hesitation into the parlor being used as a learning space. The scene held a serenity that I longed to be part of. My stomach fluttered as if to remind me that I now was. The tutor sat in a large cushioned chair next to a small bookshelf. Scattered about the parlor were five girls seated upon big, overstuffed, cushions. "Are these girls just starting their training as well?" I asked.

"Normally we begin training at thirteen years of age, and only recruit every five years. You are starting later than these girls, but I have no doubt you can keep up and advance with them. You see, only a select few girls are ever chosen to train as a Quaintrelle; they train for four years and have one year of advancement. Fewer still progress to full Quaintrelle status, in this group I'd say only that one or two would progress. Some groups yield no Quaintrelle at all. As for you, I don't worry about your future here, Merinley. Like I said, you are something special."

I looked again at the small group of girls in the room. The second glance did confirm that the five other girls were about the same age, maybe a year older than I, and were all fairly similar in appearance. They all had blond hair, in varying tones, and sun-kissed skin. Looking down at my pale arms and the ends of my dark auburn hair, I realized how much I'd stick out in this group. This fact made me nervous. I knew coming in that I'd be different from the others, but looking completely different somehow made it worse.

I wondered how many, if any, of these girls would progress to Quaintrelle status. "So this group is nearing the end of their training?"

"Yes, that's correct. I sense you are bright enough to keep up. It would be unorthodox to have you reach Quaintrelle status a few years early, but not unheard of. I became a Quaintrelle at sixteen because I started training very early. My mentor had seen something in me at a prepubescent age and knew by the time the next training group was chosen I'd be over the age of recruitment. Now I'm nearing my time to retire. I may even retire and become a handler by the time you advance."

A whole new set of nerves took over. I was ages behind these girls, starting training years late and expected to advance with them in a little over a year. My lips sucked in at the daunting thought. No matter how much confidence Mistress Anwen had in me, I had my doubts. I spent my earliest years chasing the exotic creatures of Apoidea and throwing knives at trees. My adolescent years working my fingers to the bone. While these girls likely came from affluent families and had proper training for years.

My new mentor's intuition was keen, picking up on my nerves as easily as breathing. "You'll be fine. Come along," she guided me towards the room with her hand on my back. With a dainty clearing of her throat, Mistress Anwen interrupted the class to introduce me to the tutor, Miss Harper, and my peers. "Girls, this is Merinley. She'll be joining your class from here on out. Please make her feel welcome and help her adjust to our routines." She smiled reassuringly at me as she gave me a final nudged into the room.

The girls all greeted me in turn as I timidly entered the class. "You can sit here," a bubbly girl with platinum blonde ringlets patted the over-sized cushion next to her, her face bright and welcoming. The fluffy green cushion was like a cloud when I sat on it, returning the girl's smile. "My name is Lorna," she said, her voice smooth. I learned later that her whole life had been preparing her for this life. She'd been the third in her family's history to enter the Quaintrelle trainee program, making her a legacy. Her aunt and great grandmother had both been Quaintrelle. A lot of pressure rode on her shoulders to do well. Something that made me indemnify with her more than the others.

The class settled and Miss Harper continued on with her lesson, breaking down the importance of how one recites poems for an audi-ence. When she finished, she instructed us girls to all read to ourselves, imaging regaling a crowded party with the words before us. We all rose from our seats and picked a book from the selection available near Miss Harper's chair.

The books were like everything else, gorgeous. Supple leather binding decorated with filigree in silvers, gold, and bronzes encase each one. Their beauty made me hesitate in choosing one to read, spending far too long admiring them. "Having some trouble, dear?" the tutor inquired when she noticed how long it was taking. "Do you need some help," she lowered her voice, "with reading?"

"No, Miss. I can read, and write, fairly well. My mother taught me before she passed. They are all just so stunning. I can't choose." I reached to pick a book for myself, pulling my hand back with uncertainty once more.

Her face crumpled piteously at my response, "I can recommend one, if you like." She placed a hand on my arm while she perused the selection of books. A minute passed, then she pulled a light brown book with bronze filigree and handed it to me. "I think you might enjoy this one. It has some particularly touching poems."

I thanked her and went back to my seat, hugging the book close to my chest.

THE BUSY DAY left me exhausted. There had been so many lessons my head swam; poetry, tea etiquette, dance, vocal, and politics. Even our meals were learning opportunities. It seemed everything we did was one. I wanted nothing more than to remove my day dress and snuggle under the covers of my new downy bed. I looked forward to it more than a bride did her wedding day.

I felt mildly crestfallen when I was informed it was not yet time to retire for the day. Mistress Anwen and the other mentoring Quaintrelle led us all past the dorm and into the bathing area once again, where I was bathed and rubbed with oils and lotions to keep my skin soft and supple. Mistress Anwen gave me a pair of gloves to wear at night after I applied lotion; she explained they were to help undo the dry damage caused from years of manual labor. This time I made sure to ask for a cotton robe.

After brushing my hair and teeth, I was finally led to the dorm. The bed called to me, but Mistress Anwen would not let me rest yet. She had more to discuss with me.

"How was your first day, Merinley?"

"I enjoyed it, but I'm still not sure I belong here. I'm not used to any of this. "

"You're going to be just fine, don't worry. It will take some time to adjust, but you will."

"Mistress Anwen?"

"Yes?"

"What are we allowed to do in our free time? I noticed the girls napping, practicing needlework, or just sitting about talking in our free time, but what if I wanted to do something else?"

"As in?"

"Well," I paused. "What if I wanted to train in weaponry?" I fidgeted with uncertainty. I itched to be able to throw some daggers once again. I'd not been able to practice since before my family had sold me.

"That's certainly the strangest request I've heard from a trainee. What makes you ask?"

I had already confided in her of my true origins, I knew I could trust her not to judge or overreact. "I love it. My father taught me when I was young. After he died, I continued to practice in secret. It's the one thing I have left to connect with him. I'd hate to lose all he taught me by not being able to continue the practice."

Mistress Anwen's eyes filled with compassion, "I can't make any promises, Merinley, but I will see what I can do for you. There must be some reason I can think of to get the approval for it." She paused, "Now get some rest, tomorrow you must meet Matron Hattie."

"Who is Matron Hattie?"

"She is in charge of the Quaintrelle program, she makes all of the major decisions that affect us."

"Was she once a Quaintrelle herself?"

"No. She wasn't a Quaintrelle, I believe that she was affiliated with a convent before coming here," Mistress Anwen explained.

It found it odd that someone who'd never been a Quaintrelle would choose to run the program, let alone someone that had previously been religiously affiliated. To me, it seemed as if the Quaintrelle were everything a religious woman stood against.

"I'll let you get your rest now. You've had a busy day, and tomorrow will be even busier."

Mistress Anwen blew out the oil lamp on the bedside table and left, her silk skirts whispering along the polished floors. With a deep sigh, I looked about the Quaintrelle dorm, at my new sisters in trade. Each one lay their golden heads on downy pillows dreaming. A contented warmth filled my heart, they felt like family already. Their kindness to me today evidenced the bond that I was about to share. My eyes grew heavy and a yawn stretched my muscles into total relaxation, signaling sleep was not far off. I snuggled down into the extravagant bed and fell asleep in mere moments.

CHAPTER SEVEN

The next morning, the contented feelings from the previous night were gone; replaced with overstimulated nerves. Going to meet Matron Hattie made me like I was back on the auction block, with her deciding if I was good enough or not to be bothered with. Even though Mistress Anwen assured me all would be fine, her words did little to calm me. This meeting would determine my new fate. She led me to a door deep in the Quaintrelle quarters. I wondered if I'd seen Matron Hattie at all in the limited time I'd been here, or if there was some exclusive passage out from there.

As we reached the door Mistress Anwen gave me a quick once-over, then rapped on the door lightly. Moments later the door opened with a slow creak, revealing a small and frail woman. She had wide green eyes and mousy brown hair in a low bun. A few strands of her hair wisped around her face, adding to her timid look.

"Good morning Tabitha. Please inform Matron Hattie that I'm here to introduce her to my trainee, Merinley," Mistress Anwen said.

"Of course, Mistress, come in. Matron Hattie is expecting you." Tabitha welcomed us into the room and led us to a small tea table that she instructed us to wait at. I tried to take a seat across from my mentor as we waited, but Tabitha stopped me just as my bottom touched the chair. I understood; I would be standing for this meeting. "I'll inform Matron Hattie that you are waiting."

Tabitha left the area only to return minutes later, followed by an austere woman, Matron Hattie. She looked neither old or young and had her gray hair pulled into a severe bun that stretched the skin of her face back slightly. Her high-collared black dress only enhanced her severe look. Everything about her screamed modesty and propriety. She looked like the pious woman I'd expected her to be. I couldn't help but feel intimidated by her.

She sat across from Mistress Anwen and eyed me where I stood. A small smile graced her thin lips but I couldn't decipher her exact feelings about me. I used my gift, hoping I'd be able to sense her opinion. Her emotions seemed walled behind a fierce control, steady and solid. Yet, there were cracks in her rigidity; a soft and caring light twinged with a deep and sad regret. Her harsh presence was definitely brought on by something in her past. Perhaps a self-punishment of sorts, or maybe she felt her soft-hearted nature had been the cause of misfortune. Whatever it was, she was intimidating now.

"Matron Hattie, I'd like to introduce you to my protégé. This is Merinley."

"Pleased to meet you, Matron Hattie." I gave a half curtsy, fighting to hide my trembling under her scrutiny.

'No need to be afraid child," Matron Hattie soothed. "My bark is worse than my bite."

"This is true. I recall being quite intimidated when I first met you," Mistress Anwen laughed. "What do you think of Merinley?"

Matron Hattie instructed me to step out from the table so that she could inspect me. She stood and approached me, putting on a pair of thin, wire spectacles as she did."Well, you certainly are different from the rest of the trainees, definitely not fair of hair, and there is something else about you that I can't quite place, a certain unnameable charm. Mistress Anwen was not wrong there. Lots of potential, I can definitely see you being very successful." she nodded in approval. "You picked very well Mistress. Though, are you certain that there will be no issue with her beginning so late?"

"I have been observing her for some time. Merinley is a quick learner and a hard worker. She's very disciplined, and smart too. I'm certain she will do just fine."

"I'll try my best to keep up, I promise," I added, just in case Matron Hattie needed more convincing.

"Very well then. Let me tell you all you will need to know in order to succeed."

My mentor grinned and gave my hand a squeeze. Her happiness at Matron Hattie's approval washed over me, I couldn't help but feel a buzz of excitement about the possibilities my future was beginning to have.

Matron Hattie sat back down and she asked Tabitha to retrieve a chair for me. She then wasted no time continuing the meeting. She began to cover the rules that I'd be expected to abide by in order to succeed as a Quaintrelle trainee. My head spun with all the information I learned. I hoped I'd remember it all.

There were a lot of rules. As complicated as I knew a Quaintrelle's life to be, a trainee's life was even more so. We were learning to be much more than pretty playthings. We had to be knowledgeable in many subjects and capable of multiple forms of art. Trainees were required to spend much of their days studying; learning history, politics, music, dancing, and conversation. Trainee's also spent hours dedicated to perfecting etiquette. We were living art, fantasies, comforters, and, to a select few, lovers. Above everything else, we were ladies.

On top of the rules of what we would spend our days doing, there were rules regarding almost every aspect of our lives. For example, Quaintrelle weren't allowed to have any relationship with a man other than clients. Nor were they allowed to have children until they retired from the trade.

There was one rule that shocked me more than others; trainees weren't allowed to leave Quaintrelle quarters until our debuts at the Butterfly Gala, even then we could only leave with a proper escort. When the time came that we became full Quaintrelle, we would have free reign over where we went. The goal was to keep us secreted away so that when we made our debut, it would be the first time we were seen by future clients. Until that day we only interacted with our fellow trainees, the Quaintrelle, female servants, and our maids.

When Matron Hattie finished going over the rules, she asked if there were any concerns I had that I'd like to address. I still felt hesitant about the request I made to Mistress Anwen the night prior. I wondered if asking would even be worth it.

"Merinley did request something last night that I think would be beneficial to all of the girls. Something even the other Quaintrelle and myself could benefit from." Mistress Anwen replied when she noticed my hesitation. "You see, she lost her parents at a young age. Before that her father had been teaching her the art of knife-wielding; throwing to be precise. This is something she enjoys doing still. This got me thinking that it wouldn't hurt if the Quaintrelle and trainees learned some sort of self-defense."

"I'm not sure such lessons would be well received," Matron Hattie said. "We wouldn't want any accidents that could damage any of you."

Not being able to continue doing something I loved would crush me. I had to fight for this. "Please, Matron Hattie," I begged, "I know no other way to continue feeling close to my father."

"Aside from Merinley's wishes, don't you see how important defending ourselves is these days?" Mistress Anwen continued. "Tensions are high in Relata. With the constant threat of pirates and the growing tensions with the Savage Lands, knowing some self-defense is crucial. Not to mention, I've heard whispers of discontent in the kingdom. I'd hate to think that any of the girls could get hurt if some rebel zealot somehow made his way into the palace."

"I have heard these whispers as well." Matron Hattie mulled over the argument laid before her. "Very well, I'll see to it that defense lessons are added to your routines. But, if there are any detrimental accidents, the lessons will be pulled."

"Thank you, Matron Hattie." My heart thrilled. To be able to do this one small thing elated me, gave me a piece of me to hold onto as I transformed into what the program would make of me.

With my one little request being granted, my evaluation was complete. Matron Hattie truly seemed pleased with Mistress Anwen's decision in me. My future was now set; I'd officially begin training to be a Quaintrelle.

My nerves about being accepted abated, and a whole new set took hold. Mostly about being a Quaintrelle. There would certainly be many things in my new life that would threaten to break me. I vowed to myself that I'd try to maintain my true self so that would not happen.

CHAPTER EIGHT

Many months passed, my graduation to Quaintrelle drew near. So much had changed in the last year, including me. My transformation was astounding. Without doubt, I still remained lily white with an unruly mess of dark auburn curls, but otherwise, there was little evidence left that would suggest I'd once been a neglected workhorse.

I no longer looked worn or gaunt. My new lifestyle had allowed for me to fill out to a more desirable shape, though I often fretted that my body did not have the same softness that the other girls' did, thanks to the extra time I took in our defense training. Mistress Anwen said it was nothing to worry about; though my figure was not ideal for a Quaintrelle, my natural appeal would outweigh any physical flaws. My innocent features, not to mention my ability to read others, helped to catapult me into the possible position of being a well sought after Quaintrelle. But first, I had to get through the Butterfly Gala. The elegant celebration of introducing upcoming Quaintrelle to court, was approaching faster than I would have liked. The prospect of being a full Quaintrelle made all of the trainees nervous, as did appearing before the royal family for the first time.

The Butterfly Gala often signified a turning point for trainees; a night where there would no doubt be losses to our ranks. We had already lost two of our sisters when they did not show a mature nature when we learned certain topics of intimacy. The idea of losing more of our friends put a damper on the upcoming celebration.

Despite our nerves and worries, we were also looking forward to it. The gala marked the beginning of the end of our training, something we'd all been looking forward to. I, for one, was most looking forward to being allowed out of the Quaintrelle quarters. The limited freedom that came with advancing was my favorite part of the event. The amount of time I'd spent daydreaming in the garden about wandering free of these walls was immeasurable.

Our mentors hand selected our debut gowns for the gala, selecting gowns that would reflect what our signature looks would be. Cerisse, Lorna, and Oona were given beautiful jewel-toned gowns that complimented them perfectly. Their gowns were the epitome what I expected Quaintrelle to wear, attention grabbing and sophisticated. Dresses that marked them as the jewels they were.

When Mistress Anwen took me to see my Butterfly Gala gown I'd been blown away at the vast difference between my dress and what my peers had. The dress was far simpler, and not the traditional jewel tone that Quaintrelle usually wore. Mistress Anwen picked a dusty rose colored sleeveless gown for me, with a wide black sash separating the bodice from the full skirt. The skirt itself had a lacy black floral-patterned overlay, which gave the dress a more sophisticated look than it would have had otherwise.

While I loved the dress and how it complimented my pale skin and dark hair I couldn't help but think of how I would compare to the other girls in their jewel-toned gowns. Instead of looking like my sophisti-cated sisters, I feared I'd like I look like an overgrown doll. Worse yet, that I'd look like the girl of poor origins that I was; merely playing at being a jewel of the court rather than truly being a promising Quain-trelle trainee.

I wanted to ask Mistress Anwen why she had decided to stray from tradition with my gown, but I held my tongue. I didn't want to offend her, or make her think that I didn't like it. As a matter of fact, I loved it.

It was a dream dress, my mother's favorite color. The color of the wild roses she encouraged to grow outside our little home when I was young. The ones I would pick and make crowns out of and dance wildly through the woods as I followed father to our spot. It was as if my mentor had pulled those memories straight from my mind when she had this dress commissioned.

WE GATHERED JUST outside the ballroom preparing to be introduced at the half-way mark of The Butterfly Gala. As tradition, we were to be introduced one at a time rather than as a group. Each of us given a moment to shine on our own, not stealing the spotlight from any of the others. Despite the excitement in the air, my stomach was in knots. I worried that I would not be as well received as the others. I didn't look like any of the others, and my dress only enhanced that difference. I'd been taught that being different in Realta was never a good thing. I hoped that would not be true tonight.

I also worried about being in close proximity to the royal family. I'd seen them in passing glimpses during my time in the kitchen but had never had to interact with them. Other kitchen staff accounted that the royal family had harsh opinions that they were unafraid to voice. Why should they be? This was their kingdom.

Besides my own feelings, I was having trouble controlling my gift. The buzz from the awaiting party washed over me as we waited. Between my own nerves and the excitement from the crowd, I felt more than scattered. My emotional state didn't go unnoticed by Mistress Anwen.

"Merinley, be calm my dear. Everything is going to be fine. Everything will be more than fine." She guided a stray hair that had escaped from my barely managed curls back in with the rest. "You'll be introduced last. I'm hoping doing so will garner you the attention you deserve. You have excelled in training and have grown to be an exceptional beauty."

"I thought we were introduced individually as not to distract from the other girls."

"This is true, dear girl, but you are worthy of exception. Besides, my sister Quaintrelle and I all secretly hope it is our girl that wins the night."

"Mistress Anwen?"

"Yes?"

"Can I ask as to why my dress is not the traditional formal dress of a Quaintrelle? I fear I will look foolish compared to the others dressed as a doll." I could no longer hold in my curiosity about the gown I'd been given. I was sure knowing why she styled me so different from my peers might boost my waning confidence.

"You're right that your dress is far from what a Quaintrelle usually wears to a ball or celebration. And yes, I did fashion your look to be very different and that of something delicate and pure on purpose. Merinley, like I said before, you are special. Not like any other girl ever to be a Quaintrelle. You have more fire in you, an air of being stronger than you seem. Not to mention you're much more capable of handling yourself than the others. Making you seem more innocent through dress, softens that, and makes you stand out so much more than a traditional Quaintrelle's dress would. Besides, I want all eyes on you, even though you're supposed to be equal to your peers."

Though I felt flattered by Mistress Anwen's kind words, my nerves were still frayed. Even if I were calm there would be no way I could overcome the emotions coming from within the ballroom. But, I couldn't tell her that. My abilities weren't something I was comfortable sharing with her just yet, if ever. I wasn't sure she would handle that I had Fae abilities as well as she had my true heritage. "I'll be fine, Mistress Anwen. Thank you."

A trumpet sounded, announcing that the introductions were beginning. I watched with bated breath as Lorna made her entrance into the ballroom, her emerald silk gown and golden up-do were impeccable. She oozed confidence as she made her debut, making her all that more beautiful.

The herald called for Cerisse next, she entered in a cloud of blue shimmering taffeta with her honey-colored hair flowing gracefully down her back. Of all the girls I'd always suspected Cerisse would be the most successful of us. She knew everything and did everything with absolute poise and confidence. The hushed gasps that accompanied her entrance told me that I just might have been right.

A commotion just to my left drew my attention away from watching Cerisse's introduction. I turned to see Oona struggling against her mentor before running off. I wished, momentarily, that I was brave enough to follow her. Yet, I knew I owed too much to Mistress Anwen to throw away everything she had invested in me.

Mistress Anwen didn't miss a beat when Oona made her hasty exit. She made a few tiny adjustments to my gown and ensured that the lacy black sash was securely tied. She gave my hair a quick inspection and tightened the flowered combs, which held my unruly curls back. My cheeks were pinched to make them extra rosy just as the herald sounded again. My turn had come.

With a nod of confidence from Mistress Anwen, I stepped through the doors trying to emulate the confidence that Lorna had shown and Cerisse's grace. The chattering of conversations about the previous two girls abruptly ended as I came into view. All eyes were on me. Waves of approving emotion emanated from all in attendance. I dared not look about, afraid I would lose my nerve, and kept my focus on the front of the room and on the royal family, who were gazing at me with intense looks upon their faces. King Bern was leaning over the side of his throne whispering something in the ear of Prince Talbot. They both wore grins of approval as they nodded in unison. I became more ill at ease the more that I looked upon them. I had to look away to keep my composure.

I turned my attention to Duchess Emile, Prince Talbot's mother. She sat just behind the two men and was indifferent to the whole event. I understood that she felt that way about most events. Gossip among the Quaintrelle quarters was that she was unhappy and desired to return to the life she had before she married Prince Declan, the only member of the royal family that had a good reputation. Too bad he had died many years ago, long before I'd come to Realta.

My legs wobbled as I ascended the few steps onto the small dais at the head of the ballroom. Presenting myself before the royals quickened my heart more than anything else about this night, and their strong egos threatened to overwhelm me. Stopping before them, I lowered myself into a graceful curtsy. My eyes locked with Prince Talbot's ever so briefly, and I was hit with another overwhelming emotion from him. Greed. A chill ran through me under his intimidating gaze. The breath trapped in my lungs released slowly as I turned around to present to the crowd, but I felt no relief. I could still feel eyes staring from behind me. Want enveloping me. After a quick curtsy, my introduction was over. My legs could not take me from the dais to wait in the wings with my sister trainees fast enough.

"You were amazing. They all love you." I gave her a half smile; still unnerved by the moment I had with the Prince. I hoped my mind would be taken from it as the night stretched on.

THE REST of the night we were paraded around the ballroom and introduced to potential suitors. We advertised our talents, even gave small performances of song or spoken word when asked. We were praised and evaluated by those we met. I was taken back my first day in Realta; when I was set to be sold at auction. It seemed to be a running theme in my life since then.

As the ball wound down, the Quaintrelle gathered their trainees to announce that there had been a contest going for the second half of the gala. Potential clients had been bidding for the chance to be the first to escort us on the dance floor. The coin collected would be placed into accounts that we would have access to once we became Quaintrelle. I was grateful that this bit of information had been kept from us until then. Knowing this was happening would've crippled me.

After the announcement, the Quaintrelle each pulled their respective trainee aside to give them the details on who they'd be dancing with. "You have done wonderfully, Merinley, and have won the attention of many future clients," Mistress Anwen said to me. "Many of them quite prominent."

"Truly? I was terribly nervous, afraid it would show and that I'd be a failure."

"Not in the least, dear. Your nerves did not even show once."

I was relieved, even more so that I'd been as successful as the other girls in their debuts.

Mistress Anwen continued, "The final waltz is soon, and I must tell you that you have managed something that has not been managed before. Prince Talbot won your first dance. You've indeed garnered the attention I thought you would, and more."

I felt my face go pale at the revelation of whom I'd share my first dance in court with. I relived the moment between Prince Talbot and myself earlier in the evening. Imagining being held closely to him and his cold gaze locked with mine, filled me with fear. "Mistress Anwen," I couldn't manage to say more, my ability to form words had been stolen by her news.

"You'll be fine dear." Mistress Anwen observed me for a moment or two, "I'm entirely unsure of what has come over you this evening. You're generally much more confident than this."

"Just nerves Mistress. Tonight is a big deal, and now it feels even bigger."

"This is a great honor. I know that Prince Talbot can be quite intimidating, but you have nothing to fret from him. Under his grandfather's watchful gaze I am certain he will behave himself. Now come, let us mingle until it is time for your dance." A flame of disgust rose in her as she spoke about the prince, pointing out her lie to me. Rather than argue with her, call her out on her lie, I let it go and nodded obediently. "Shall we continue mingling until the waltz? Are you good?"

"Yes, Mistress. I am good."

We continued to walk about the ballroom, meeting and greeting all we passed. When the herald sounded the announcement for the final waltz, Mistress Anwen escorted me back to the dais. As we approached, I saw that Duchess Emile had gone, leaving King Bern and his like-minded grandson to themselves. Prince Talbot was already standing at the base of the dais and appeared eager to begin the dance. But his mood said something else too, his eagerness was tinged with something dark and boastful.

Phantom spiders crawled over my skin as he watched me approach.

He looked handsome as he stood tall and straight in his stark white jacket adorned with crown jewels. He stretched his hand out when I was steps away, waiting for me to take it. His green eyes were glowing with pride the moment my hand slipped into his, but his face remained stony. I hoped he had not noticed it trembling.

Audible gasps chimed throughout the ballroom when the crowd noticed who had won the bid of my first waltz in court. Their disbelief swept through the crowd, intensifying the awkward fluttering in my stomach. From what I understood, the royal family had never participated as more than observers at any celebration. The response of the gathered nobles pleased Prince Talbot; a prideful sneer spread over his face. He liked the power it gave him, the shock of the crowd. The way he craved it made me ill.

We glided onto the dance floor as the crowd settled; joined by my fellow trainees, mentors, and their dance partners. As we moved into dance position, I was overcome with a heavy feeling of being trapped, like I had been put into a cage and placed on display. Possession and greed rolled off of Prince Talbot's body. Even without my ability, it would have been easy to tell he enjoyed having me in his arms. Hiding my true feeling was more important in this moment than it had ever been before. With a deep breath, I put on the first of many shows to come. I smiled at my dance partner with all the sweetness I could muster, hoping that smile would cover any unease I was feeling.

No words were uttered between us as we danced. The silence was uncomfortable, strangled even. I counted the seconds, anxious for the waltz to end. By the time the music stopped, I was fighting to keep my composure; but I had to remain calm. I curtsied, thanking the prince for his gracious beginning to my career. He showed no emotion in return, no interest at all. His eyes had lost their prideful glow and were now as cold the rest of his face had been. He left me in haste without any gesture of gratitude. He had gotten what he wanted, there was no reason for him to do anything else.

CHAPTER NINE

I became a full Quaintrelle shortly after my eighteenth birthday.

As she said she would, Mistress Anwen announced her retirement. Instead of moving on and finding a life outside the palace, she opted to stay within the Quaintrelle program and become a handler, my handler to be specific. Her decision to stay, elated me. I would've been lost without her, and my career as Quaintrelle would've fizzled rather than bloomed. Though, I sensed there was more to her decision than she let on outwardly. She had a secret, something that made her nervous much of the time. The only reason I didn't press was to keep my own secrets. A time would come for her to reveal hers, as much as the time would come for me to share mine. At least these secrets we knitted tightly to our chests did nothing to come between us. Our closeness was that of family. She became my closest friend and confidant.

Quaintrelle life was comfortable and happy, for the most part. Not only did I have Anwen, I had my sister Quaintrelle. We were a small, tight-knit family of women held together by our calling. It was a semblance of the life I'd longed for since I lost my parents. A family that cared for me. Everything else about being a Quaintrelle was filler, nice but not necessary. Sometimes it was too much. The constant late nights, parties, being at the beck and call of whomever bought my time, was exhausting.

Deep down, I longed for a simpler life. One where I wasn't a glittering jewel of the court, sought for by dozens. A life where I'd be free to do anything and everything I wanted to do. Able to have love, able to have a family. A life I knew I'd possess if Anwen hadn't plucked me from the kitchens, if my aunt and uncle hadn't sold me. My disgust for them seethed whenever I thought of that morning, a black tendril hidden deep a corner of my heart. They'd always be the ones that stole my chance at a normal life.

Where would I be, if that morning hadn't transpired? Married to Tristan with a gaggle of sweet rosy cheeked babies to call my own? Would my days be spent in the family cabin, tending to little ones and being a doting wife? Or would I be sitting next to Elder Tam, a leader of Apoidea, just like my father? I could see myself there more than anywhere else, if I'd not been sold.

As for Anwen, I held no animosity toward her. She saved me in some way. Since my debut, I'd seen the kind of unwelcome attention the female servants endured. Becoming a Quaintrelle had protected me from the aggressive and often forced affections they suffered at the hands of those they served and worked along side with.

Despite the longing in my heart, I flourished as a Quaintrelle, just as Anwen said I would. My schedule was full, with few evenings where I wasn't called away from Bua Tur. Most nights, I could be found attending some party entertaining guests with songs, poetry, or my so-called parlor trick.

My skill with knives became somewhat of a novelty at parties, thanks to Anwen fooling some drunk merchants one night. She made a wager with them that a woman could throw as well as a man, and thrust me into the bet. My skill was a hit, and became the talk of parties for a crone's age. I'd earned quite the reputation that night. That was when the invitations for parties came flooding in. With each party, I charmed my way deeper into the hearts of Realta's wealthy class. Which in turn filled my account with lavish gifts from men seeking more intimate engagements with me.

I was glad I had the control of choosing which of these invitations I accepted, an advantage of the acclaim I'd earned. It was my secret weapon which gave me an advantage that my fellow Quaintrelle didn't. My gift, which I used to guide me in choosing whom I accepted invitations from. My gift felt less of a burden because of it, though the secret of it still weighed on me.

Despite my popularity, there was one aspect of being a Quaintrelle that I wasn't successful in. I hadn't received any requests to choose a Premier, a man that would be the only man that could ask for private engagements. I wondered at this for a long time, never having the courage to ask Anwen for her opinion on it. Until one day when she pulled me from my studies, concerned for my career.

"What is this I hear about you swaying your suitors away from intimacy during your private engagements?"

Certain aspects of being a Quaintrelle had never sat entirely right with me, though I knew it was better to grin and bear it than refuse and end up someplace unsavory. This didn't mean I rolled over and followed all of the rules. I found ways to do things my way. Yes, I'd bedded a few who sought intimacy, it was part of the job after all. It was my gift of empathy that was key to being able to surrender myself that way. I was able to shut out my feelings and use the feelings of my suitors in those cases.

At the same time, it was also my empathy that made me able to sway those whom I knew could be. I used my gift to loosely bond with the men that sought my company, rooting out a need, one much deeper than physical pleasure, which needed to be fulfilled. In this, I became more than what a Quaintrelle was supposed to be, more than a pretty and witty doll for their entertainment. I was the embodiment of catharsis. Was it wrong to manipulate men in that way? Perhaps. Did I feel bad about it? No. I had to maintain myself above others in order to survive this world.

"Anwen, I don't feel that it's always necessary to always appease a man in such ways. True they think it's what they want, but it is not what they always need. Mostly they just need to feel appreciated and understood; to have someone to listen to them. A companion that will not judge."

"It's the job." Anwen's unhappiness worried me. She took my hands in hers, "I thought what was expected of you was clear."

"It is clear Anwen, and I do appreciate all you have made possible for me. Might I ask why it is so bad that I make my suitors happy without sex? Have there been complaints?"

"Well, no, there hasn't. Still, think how this could hurt you." I could see her genuine concern for me, but this was something I would not relent.

"How can this hurt me if no one is unsatisfied with my services?"

"You could end up being passed over so much that you are no longer viable as a Quaintrelle. There would be no choice but to dismiss you and who knows what would happen to you."

Anwen had a valid point, there was no knowing what would happen if I were turned away from the palace. "I do understand that Anwen, I really do." Perhaps I had hurt my career. I was, after all the only one who still had not received a Premier request. Maybe this was the reason why. "Anwen, do you think this is why I haven't received any requests to select a Premier?"

"No, my dear. There is another reason why that has not happened yet. They fear King Talbot."

"What do you mean?"

"His interest in you at the Butterfly Gala has yet to be acted upon. They don't wish to be the man that gets in the way of his pursuit of you, if he chooses to."

I thought back to that night. A cold feeling passed through me as I remembered the possessive feelings he emanated when we danced. I was unsure if there was any interest beyond that, though. He showed no interest at all once the dance ended. "I don't believe there was any real interest there. He certainly departed my company quick enough. Besides, wouldn't he have said something already?"

"I know the lack of word from him has nothing to do with disinterest. King Talbot must surely be waiting until he has settled into his new position. King Bern's death came so suddenly. The burden of King is a lot to adjust to, even for men like them." Anwen's certainty didn't comfort me, mostly because of my discomfort with King Talbot. "Trust me, Merinley. Once he is settled, he will ask for you. Until then, can you promise me to not sabotage yourself?"

"I promise that I'm not sabotaging myself. I will be as good a Quaintrelle as I can be. However, if I can find a way to be a Quaintrelle and avoid feeling like I'm little more than a toy, I'll continue doing my job as I see fit. If formal complaints are ever made, then I'll rethink my methods. Until then, or until I have a Premier, I will be the one who decides what I do with my body."

She sighed in defeat, "Since there's obviously no deterring you, I will accept that, as long as you hold to your word." She embraced me. "How could I have ever thought you would do anything any way but your own. You may have the training of a Quaintrelle but your heart is as determined to be free as it ever was."

The conversation left me uncertain of my choices, of my future. All I could do is hope that I was able to continue on doing things my way. And that I had lost King Talbot's interest.

CHAPTER TEN

The masquerade ball celebrating King Talbot's thirtieth birthday had been in full swing for an hour, and there was still no sign of him. Each minute that passed without his appearance was a sigh of relief. There was something about this night that had me on edge nearly as much as my introduction to court over four years ago. At least this time I had an idea of what to expect. Whispers around the palace indicated King Talbot had some big announcement planned.

I tried to lose myself in the party and did my best to take part in meaningless conversations and distracting heated political talk. I enjoyed the performances of my fellow Quaintrelle, ate the decadent food and drink. The rich swirling colors of the dresses on the dance floor were as marveling as ever. I danced with countless noblemen, each wishing to have one of the palace beauties on their arm; and each wanting to ensnare me into their beds. My reputation as the most selective Quaintrelle had not hurt me, it had made me a desired conquest. Every man out to do what few had been able. But, the upcoming announcement nagged at the back of my mind. I couldn't shake the feeling that it was going to be something horrible.

The constant long waltzes had my feet aching for a break, and my head buzzing from anxious anticipation of what King Talbot had in store. I was dying for a break by the time I reached the last in the long line of promised dances. My partner had been a young Earl with large teeth and oily skin. He was pleasant enough, made light conversation and attempted, poorly, at flirting with me. Poor thing was sorely inexperienced with women, that was easy to tell. It was easy to feel sorry for him, but not enough to linger when the song ended. My pity wasn't stronger than my need to rest. My obligation to the young Earl complete, I thanked him and wandered toward the outskirts of the crowded ballroom. I was eager to retire, if only momentarily, to the veranda to catch some air. The chill night air teased my skin as I neared the quiet seclusion outside. Freedom was inches away when a strong hand caught mine. I cursed inwardly.

"I've been waiting a long time to dance with such an exquisite flower," the strange and haunting voice purred as I turned to see who was seeking a dance with me. He was tall, lean, and masked; as were most of the people here. His eyes were the most astounding blue I had ever seen. I knew I had never crossed paths with this nobleman before. I would've remembered those eyes. His presence was intense and confident, traits enhanced by his eyes and height. Despite his intensity, I couldn't feel anything but a calm excitement as I studied him.

"How could I pass up a dance with such sweet words," I flirted, as I was trained to do, despite my aching feet and deflated hope. Quaintrelle rules made it impossible for me to refuse a dance with someone, if I hadn't yet danced with them. I replaced my disappointment with a bright and alluring smile as the dashing man led me back to the ball.

We stepped onto the dance floor and he pulled me tight against his tall frame as the music began. The music built as our bodies swirled around the room. His grasp on my waist remained firm and warm, but his hand on my shoulder wandered to caress my neck and my face. I truly blushed under his persistent touch and gaze, something I was not often guilty of doing, making me wish I'd been allowed a mask to hide behind. "Tell me, sir, are you new to the court? I don't believe I know you."

His eyes glinted with mischief, "No, I have been before. My appearances are often more," he paused and smirked, "discreet when

I'm in Realta. But, I admit, this is my first ball. Had I known the palace held such beauty, I would have frequented more of these affairs."

"Surely you knew Bua Tur's Quaintrelle attend every ball?"

"Yes, that I was aware of, but if I'd known there could be a Quaintrelle such as you I would've come much sooner. You are quite different from your sisters, not to mention quite young to be a Quaintrelle."

"At nearly 21, I am the youngest of my coterie, but not the youngest Quaintrelle ever appointed at Bua Tur."

"But by far the most desirable."

"You flatter, Sir. May I inquire of your name?"

"You may call me Sir. I prefer a little anonymity," the man teased.

"Well then, Sir, I must tell you that it's most fortuitous that you have chosen this ball to attend. The celebrations surrounding a king's birthday are always much grander than others."

"Fortuitous depends on your perspective of this night," he said.

"What do you mean Sir?"

My dance partner smiled, "You see, Sweet, it's a great fortune for me to escort a beauty such as you around the floor. Yet, at the same time, this small fortune is but a fleeting moment that may leave me crushed, for I may never have this pleasure again." He leaned closer and whispered, "I could care less about honoring King Talbot's birthday. He's an insufferable git. I care about this moment, for this moment there's just you and I. That's what this night is about."

Though I was shocked at his candid confession, his words caused me to blush and avert my eyes, as an innocent maid would when amorous words are secreted to her for the first time. "I think King Talbot would disagree with you."

He lowered his voice into a gentle purr, "Well this night should be about you. You are the most exquisite creature in this room, and that deserves celebrating. The women envy you. The men all watch your every move as if you are a prize stag in an illustrious hunt. I think even a man as foolish as the King would agree with me."

His words hung heavy, waiting for my witty comeback. Yet, I found none. He had reminded me of my true place, Quaintrelle of Bua

Tur. A woman not swept away by flattering speeches. That reminder somehow brought back memories of the night Anwen thought my career was doomed, and how the entirety of the noble class waited with bated breath to see of King Talbot would stake his claim. There was no way I could let this stranger in on the momentary unease. My lips drew up a coy half smile and I batted my lashes, hoping he would see only them and not my reeling mind.

We finished the dance in silence, the whole time his piercing gaze never leaving my face. Despite the selcouth fluttering he caused, and the unease from minutes before, it was the calmest I felt all evening. All my fears and aches melted away as we danced together, and the ballroom seemed to blur.

When the song ended he bowed, "Thank you, Sweet, for the dance. I shall remember it always." He pulled my hand to his lips and winked at me, sending flurries through my body. When he stood, he gazed into my eyes; yet again, causing me to blush. Before I could thank him in return, he had gone.

I stood on the dance floor, bewildered by the mysterious man; mostly for the unfamiliar flurry of feelings that he had caused and the careless, brave way he spoke his mind. Had any other noble heard his traitorous words, our dance would have ended less pleasantly. Without though, my hand fluttered to my chest, to fiddle with my mother's locket as I always did when lost in thought. Panic seized my heart. The locket was gone. My recent dance partner's honeyed words were revealed to be nothing but a distraction in order to thieve away jewels. He likely seduced many treasures off of the necks of every woman he had danced with this evening. Surely a man so gifted with charm enough to seduce a Quaintrelle could make a bounty stealing gems from women with less harness on their feelings.

My bewilderment ebbed to anger as I hastened after the silver-tongued scally-wag who had just charmed my most cherished necklace away. Part of me was impressed that he had out charmed a Quaintrelle and that I had not picked up on his intentions. I blamed myself for being too distracted by the strange feelings he caused to pay attention to his feelings.

I removed my shoes in preparation to take after the thief. I needed to move swift and silent, a feat my pinching shoes would not allow. It was a long-shot that I'd even catch him, but I had to try; even though leaving the ball early broke the rules. I broke even more Quaintrelle protocol as I dashed out of the party, ignoring the calls of men seeking my attention. I had something more important to do, try to catch the thief. My mother's locket was more important than any man.

Luck was on my side. I spied the man I sought in the hallway, his long, dark braid and height easy identifying features. His back was turned as he paused to admire his ill-gained treasure. His emotions were high, like he'd just stolen some crown jewel. I couldn't fathom what his attraction to the tinny old locket had been. It was not worth near as much as other jewels I had on.

Alerting him to my presence could backfire. As quiet as I could, I pulled at my skirt to grab the small knife that I almost always hid against my thigh, despite that it was not allowed. I knew for certain my status would make me an unassuming opponent. No one expected much from a Quaintrelle, other than anything beautiful. When I was prepared, I called out, "Stop right there!"

He turned, surprised anyone had been able to sneak up on him. After a moment, a crooked smile adorned his face, "What are you going to do? Flirt with me?" He pulled his hands to his chest to emphasize the condescending, yet playful, remark.

I drew a quick breath and assessed the distance between us. "No, Sir, I am not. I'm getting my necklace back, scoundrel."

"This necklace?" he asked, dangling the locket up in the air. "Do you really think you can?"

"Yes." I let the knife fly from my hand. My aim held true. The locket was knocked from the thief's hand and transported to the wall tapestry, trembling from the abrupt stop.

The thief's mouth gaped and he removed his mask in shock. When I saw his whole face for the first time my heart nearly stopped. He was as intense and beautiful as his presence suggested. The mask had hidden the high angular cheekbones and long straight nose, which was a little on the large side but complimented his other features well. The one flaw would be his ears, which were large and stuck out quite a bit near the bottom. Despite their oddness, I found them endearing.

There was something familiar about him that I couldn't place. I shook off my daze and refocused on the task at hand. I smiled at my accurate aim and finished the distance between us to confront the suave robber.

I reached past the man and yanked the precious necklace and knife from the tapestry. "This, Sir, is mine." I glared at him in contempt of what he had done. No wonder I'd never seen him before, he was a thief crashing the ball for treasures. I was curious as to whom else he may have lifted jewels from this night. His face was still plastered in a look of surprise as I continued my lecture. "I care nothing for jewels, if you had stolen any other thing from my neck I might have let you get away with it, but not this. This is import…"

The strange man pulled me to him and kissed me, cutting me off. The kiss was filled with more passion and purpose than I ever allowed anyone before. Our lips parted and he exclaimed, "Woman, you are amazing." He released me and looked back at me with awe.

His kiss stirred feelings that I was trained not to have. "You need to leave, Sir, before I alert the guards." I wasn't sure why I was giving him a chance to get away, possibly with pockets full of stolen trinkets from other ball patrons.

He smiled and bowed, "The name is Felix, Captain Felix Wade." As soon as he came up from the bow, he turned and ran.

His name rang in my ears, and I knew it well. Captain Wade, a wanted pirate. His wanted posters exaggerated his features and did him no justice. No wonder I didn't recognize him.

I couldn't believe what had just happened. I encountered a famed pirate, besting him in a way. I'd been kissed by the most hunted man of the sea in the kingdom. His kiss haunted me into a daze as I stood there. I didn't hear the footsteps coming from behind.

"Merinley," Anwen's voice shook me from my thoughts. "What are you doing girl? King Talbot has arrived in the ballroom. He prepares to give an address."

I looked back to where Captain Wade had been. I was perplexed at the whole encounter, and made a silent wish that I'd see him again. He was intense and exciting; a fresh breath of air compared to the monotony of the life I led.

Anwen cleared her throat, I turned to find her impatiently tapping a foot. I gathered up my skirt, stealthily placing my blade in the hidden hilt, and resigned myself to go back to the ball. I really did not want to.

The murmuring crowd in the ballroom had already gathered around the dais when I returned to the ball. Anwen escorted me through the maze of bodies to the front of the crowd, to join my fellow Quaintrelle. My eyes instantly fell on King Talbot, sitting in his throne with a smug expression on his face. He glared over his subjects, cooly, proud of the glittering crown on his head. His crisp white suit, decorated in lavish ribbons and gems, seemed to accentuate his arrogance. I knew many found him handsome, and he truly was. But, for me, his looks did nothing to eradicate the ill at ease feelings I got any time I was near him. For me, he was repulsive.

The herald trumpeted twice and the crowd trickled to dead silence, each and every person eager to hear the big news. King Talbot stood and moved towards the front of the dais, the purely decorative medals on his lapel clinking softly with each step. His steward, a short man with bulging eyes and thinning strawberry hair, shadowed him closely. The steward stopped half a foot behind him, and two feet to the right, unfurling a sheet of parchment between his hands. As usual, King Talbot merely stood by, seemingly uninterested in his own announcement, as his steward made the announcement for him.

"His Majesty, King Talbot, thanks you all for your attendance to this celebratory ball. On this night we are not only here to celebrate the beginning of his thirtieth year, we are here to celebrate the announcement of his engagement. From this night forth, Mistress Merinley will no longer be known as a Quaintrelle, but as Milady Merinley future Queen of Realta."

That announcement was the last thing I expected to hear. It was near unheard of for royalty to pursue Quaintrelle, to seek to marry one seemed impossible. Yet it was happening, to me.

The roaring applause that followed dulled to silence in my ears. I felt every eye in the ballroom searching for me, wanting to witness this uniquely remarkable event. Their faces blurred into each other. My body tingled and felt leaden at the same time, I couldn't think clear enough to make any sort of movement. It was only after I felt a nudge on my shoulder from Mistress Cerise, that I snapped to enough to begin my shaky walk to the dais.

My eyes locked onto King Talbot, once again. He waited with a gloved hand outstretched, silently calling me to join him. I did my best to hide away my surprise and put on a charming smile. I knew I must be more gracious and elegant than ever before. Taking a deep breath, I found my center and allowed my gift to take over. It was the only way I'd get through this moment.

Emotions from the surrounding crowd washed over me. The pride from fellow Quaintrelle and other palace staff for one of their own. The sadness of opportunities lost from former clients. Approving joy radiated from the majority of the nobles for choosing an enchanting bride. The jealousy and anger from the rest who felt I had no right to marry into the crown. None of them realized I'd change places with any of them in a heartbeat. I'd give up this path chosen for me if I could.

I slid my hand into the King's, taking my place beside him. Though my stomach churned, I bravely gazed out over the crowd, over my subjects. As I surveyed the crowd my thoughts drifted back to my dance with Captain Wade. He was right. Fortuitous depended on the view of whom you asked.

CHAPTER ELEVEN

The next morning, I was woke by a maid much earlier than I was accustomed to with a message. King Talbot summoned me for breakfast. I dressed in a light blue petal sleeved day dress and pulled my hair into a chignon; keeping my appearance simple and clean, which had been the usual way I dressed when I did not have an event to attend to. I took a deep breath to calm myself as I left my chambers and followed the maid to my fiancé's rooms. The word sloshed around in my brain, fiancé. It was unwelcome there, brought none of the joy it should. Instead, it brought a sense of being trapped.

I found him seated on his veranda, already eating his meal. He didn't even bother to look away from his plate or stand to greet me properly when I approached the table.

"Good morning, Your Majesty." I greeted with a small, polite curtsy before I sat across from him.

"You are late." His replied in a curt manner; he did not look up, he just continued to shove his breakfast into his mouth, bits of it falling from his lips back to the plate below.

His indifferent attitude towards my requested presence unsettled me, diminishing my appetite. The idea of eating made me nauseated. Yet, I knew that it would be rude to refuse any of the offerings before me. Starting my engagement off by offending my fiancé wouldn't be a wise thing to do. Offending King Talbot at all was a bad idea.

I perused the offerings of breakfast foods on the small table before me. There was so much to choose from; pastries, fruit of every variety, sausages, guinea fowl, fresh butter, porridge, and potatoes. There was enough food to feed at least a dozen people. There was no way that Talbot and I could finish all of it ourselves, and that turned my stomach even more.

My short time in the kitchen with Mrs. James taught me anything leftover from this meal would be thrown out rather than shared with the staff; many of whom went hungry. I simmered in silence knowing most of this extravagant meal would go to waste.

After a moment of reflection, I decided that I'd work on changing that rule. I held a position to do so now. Perhaps I could be a good influence on the King.

I selected a bunch of bright green grapes, a handful of berries, and a flaky pastry to appease the social expectation that hung over my head. Just as I popped one of the grapes into my mouth Anwen entered carrying a tray with my Quaintrelle's tea, a contraceptive drink made of a special blend of tea leaves, honey, Queen Anne's Lace, Pennyroyal, Rue blossoms, and Silphium. Quaintrelle were required to begin drinking the concoction daily after the Butterfly Gala. Of course, some Quaintrelle would choose not to drink this, which usually ended their careers. That is how we lost Lorna mere weeks before graduating to full Quaintrelle.

Anwen threw a bright smile my way, though the caution she felt emanated freely from her. She, like I, had never spent more than a few passing moments with the man in the room with us. Anwen placed the small tray onto the table so that she could offer us a formal greeting. The formality of her demeanor seemed strange to me. Considering my new position, I'd have to become accustomed to those I knew treating me in a different manner.

"Thank you, Anwen," I said as she turned her attention to pouring the tea for me.

"No," Talbot looked up at Anwen with a stern look on his face.

"My fiance is to no longer have your un-sanctimonious concoction." He switched his gaze to me "You will give me an heir. I expect you to transition into my chambers as quickly as possible."

His demand caused me some dismay. "Surely you do not mean for us to share a bed before we are joined in matrimony?"

Talbot's eyes flared for a brief moment at my query. "I'd think that you wouldn't hesitate to enter a man's bed. Has that not been your profession up until now?" His implication at my previous station stung, I maffled an incoherent response.

Anwen seeing my flustered state, spoke for me. "I think, Your Majesty, that Merinley simply means that she wants to put her past behind her and go through a purification period before your vows, as many Quaintrelle do, if and when they wed. She confided in me just last night that she wishes to be pure again when she enters this marriage." She looked at me with understanding in her eyes. I thanked her with a small nod for her rescue.

"Does your maid speak the truth?" Talbot inquired.

"Yes. I do wish to reclaim my purity for our marriage, out of respect for you." I played up Anwen's lie.

King Talbot's scowl never left his face. "Very well. I can agree with your reasoning, give you time to dry out before I claim you. Though, do not expect me to return the gesture in kind. I have needs." He wiped his mouth with his napkin, "Since we have an arrangement which differs from my previous plans, you will move into your own separate quarters, away from your Quaintrelle friends. I do not wish for their bad influence to affect you in any way. I'll have a valet escort you to the south wing when you are ready." Talbot's tone remained snide, despite his cool demeanor. Anyone could've seen my rejection stirred his anger.

Talbot finished the rest of his meal in haste and with no other words. As he departed he had one last demand, "From now on dress appropriately for your station. You are on the cusp of becoming a queen and are held to a higher standard now than a palace whore."

Talbot's parting words brought to the surface feelings of worthlessness I once felt daily. I kept my composure, despite wanting to cry. I never had been just a palace whore; Quaintrelle were much more than that.

The moment I felt certain that we were alone, and would remain so for some time, I broke the heavy silence King Talbot left in his wake. "Thank you Anwen," I gave her a grateful hug. "I panicked at his demands and couldn't think. He gives me extreme feelings of unease, he frightens me. I don't know what I'd do without you."

"I care for you a great deal, my dear girl. I will always be here for you, as a friend or guiding hand, no matter what."

"Would you stay and join me? There's far too much food here, I don't want it to go to waste." I knew offering this to her went against the rules, but I didn't care.

"Merinley, Talbot does not allow food to be shared with the palace staff. You know that. And as I'm now your maid, rather than a Quaintrelle or handler, I'm considered staff. My years of dedication to the court means nothing."

"Nonsense. You are much more than just a maid to me." An idea played in my head and I smiled mischievously at Anwen, "As future queen, I command you eat something, and take the leftovers to share them with whomever you wish. Discreetly, of course." We both giggled at my absurd command and she sat to join me. She picked out a simple meal, much like the one I chose. We finished our meal together, chatting away about things that didn't matter. There had been enough serious talk for the day already.

TALBOT GIFTED me the wing that Prince Declan had shared with Emile, as it were no longer in use. The Duchess had returned to her home country, Mattine, surprising no one. She cared little for her life in Realta. During my brief encounters with her I'd been able to glean she never truly loved Prince Declan or their son. Only her fear of King Bern kept her in Bua Tur. When King Bern passed; she no longer felt bound to Realta and left for her home with very little notice. She left even before her son had his coronation.

My new rooms seemed like a place I could turn into a true, albeit temporary, sanctuary for myself. The wing had a spacious garden that rivaled the one in the Quaintrelle quarters, a private bath, and a library that I couldn't conquer no matter how much time I spent in it.

After the abrasive breakfast that morning, I needed to distract my mind with something unimportant. I decided I would spend my first day in my quarters doing the simplest of things; reading under a tree in my new garden. The weather was pleasant enough for it. I smiled at the thought of even climbing up one of the larger trees to hide away. Doing so would not be proper for my station, which made it appealing.

I perused the vast collection of books in search of something light to lose myself in. My mood did not call for a serious read; I needed something that would lift my spirits. A book simply marked with a band of flowers along the spine stood out from all the others and piqued my interest. I pulled it from the shelf, noting that it seemed a little lighter than it should have been.

When I opened the tome, I hoped to discover poetry. Instead, I found it hid a smaller plain leather book. Someone had gone to great lengths in gutting the bigger book, destroying what appeared to be some beautiful illuminations, to hide this.

My curiosity heightened. What did the small book hide inside that needed to be squirreled away? I removed it from the fake outer book, which I discarded on a nearby table, and opened the pages to reveal what secrets it held. The first page merely had "Declan" written neatly upon it. I flipped through a few more pages, each covered in slightly sloppy writings. This had to be the late prince's journal.

I buzzed with excitement over my find and longed to read the thoughts of the man I never had the pleasure of meeting. All I knew of him had been what I had heard from others. King Talbot and his grandfather had regarded him as a weak man; the palace staff that knew him regarded him as being kind, caring, and a little rebellious. The book I held would tell me so much more than anyone ever could.

I swaddled the journal close to my bosom and headed out to the garden to discover what secrets it hid inside.

. . .

IT DIDN'T TAKE me long to read through the first three-quarters of the journal. Like I had predicted, it taught me so much more about the man that would have been my father-in-law. He seemed to have been everything the palace staff had said he was, and more. If only he hadn't passed so young.

The pages I read were filled with his rants against his father's harsh rule and his plans for what he would make of the kingdom when he inherited the crown. Most of it alluded to opening up the palace's resources to the people; being more giving to those who needed help. My heart leapt when he had written about his plan to re-establish a relationship with Apoidea, an idea he had frequently brought to King Bern only to be rejected each time. Just the fact that he was willing to see past all the lies and give my people a chance was inspiring.

I wanted to read more, but felt a desperate need to stretch after sitting so long. The sun above signified that it was nearing mid-afternoon. A sure sign Anwen would be coming to check on me soon.

As if on cue, I heard Anwen's familiar voice calling me from within my rooms. I called back, letting her know that she could find me in the garden. I had just started standing and brushing the skirt of my dress clean when she found me.

"Enjoying your new space, Merinley?" she asked. I noticed her eyes lingering over the book that I held, "I can see you are making good use of the library and garden. Duchess Emile never used either, they were more Prince Declan's than hers."

"I am, I think I'll be very comfortable here for the time being. Is there something you need Anwen?"

"I've brought some afternoon refreshments for you if you would like."

"Is it that time already? I had been so rapt in what I was reading, I lost track of the time."

"That must be a very good book then."

I nodded in reply and wondered to myself if I should share with her what I'd been reading all morning, if she would have any interest. Part of me worried of secret ears hiding in Bua Tur. If the wrong person overheard, I'd likely get into trouble for reading Prince Declan's journal. Yet, something nagged at me to share, "If you would be willing to join me I will tell you all about it."

"You found Prince Declan's journal!"Anwen's enthusiasm over my find surprised me.

"He would have been a wonderful King."

"Yes, he would've. I only knew him briefly but he was a good man, sad but good."

"Sad?"

"I'm not one to spread rumors, so I'll just say that he didn't lead his life the way he wished to. King Bern controlled everything, even took over how Talbot was raised."

"That's fairly obvious, Talbot's far from the man in those pages, he had no good role-models to learn from. I must admit I'm a little terrified of him. Were there a way out of this marriage, aside from death, I'd take it."

Anwen looked at me with an apology in her eyes. She took my hand in hers but said nothing, she had no need to. She felt for me. She knew how deplorable Talbot could be. He'd been a spoiled and arrogant brat before his grandfather died. His new found power had only made him more cruel.

Like many times before, it seemed Anwen knew more than she let on. My gift gleaned an internal struggle. I didn't push it. Silently, I vowed that if I didn't discover whatever secrets she may have held in Declan's journal, I'd inquire further about them.

CHAPTER TWELVE

nother boring afternoon was promised. King Talbot demanded I join him in his meetings with the citizens of the land. Yet again, he expected me to be seen and not heard; which came as no surprise but was still disappointing. I discovered, a few weeks into my engagement, that my new duties appeared to be little more than sitting and looking pretty while listening to the men discuss important business. I prayed this would change when I officially became Queen, but wouldn't hold my breath. Part of me knew this would be how it would always be.

I took great reprieve in my time spent away from being a silent observer of meetings. Respite that annoyed my husband to be, or would if he cared enough to notice what I did when I wasn't in his company. If I wasn't reading in my new garden, I was reinforcing the bonds of the friendships I forged before becoming engaged. I often found myself in the kitchen having tea with Anwen and Mrs. James, playing tables out in the run down cabin with the female servants, or practicing arts with the Quaintrelle. I had no plans to give up on those bonds, I thought I'd go mad if I had to.

That afternoon, the meeting was particularly tedious. My focus drifted as I looked around the room and fiddled with my mother's necklace. As I dragged the old locket back and forth over the chain, I only half listened to the current issue being discussed. King Talbot and his men had been discussing the same matter for well over an hour. My mind naturally wandered.

The sound of people entering the throne room broke me from my thoughts. I re-focused to see a small priest and a stately looking nun approaching. They stopped and bowed a few feet from the dais.

The priest addressed us. "Your Majesty. Milady. We come to ask for assistance with our convent. A tree fell during the last storm, damaging the building, the dormitories where the orphans are housed. We humbly ask for your assistance in restoring what has been lost. Our convent, Saint Ludo, is nestled up in the Eira Mountains behind Realta, with the weather threatening to turn again we must repair quickly."

King Talbot mulled over the request, his annoyance was choking. "Priest, I don't have the manpower at this time to send someone to even assess the damages. My men are stretched thin in deflecting threats to my great kingdom. Surely you can gather help from another religious facility in Realta?" he replied in a cold and heartless manner.

His uncaring response pierced me. The Eira Mountains were cold even on the warmest days. With a possible storm coming, I feared for the children enough that I forgot to hold my tongue.

"My King," I interrupted, "perchance I could go survey the damage and take some warm supplies for the children in the meantime. I could bring back my findings and send volunteer laborers on my return. We can't let the orphans suffer, please."

Talbot's eyes narrowed at my interjection, but I felt something playing within him which suggested he might've been considering it. After a minute he smiled, but his annoyance never left his eyes. "My dear, how fortunate the people are that they should have someone like you looking out for them, willing to sacrifice for them." He turned his gaze towards the priest and nun, "Will this suffice?"

"Yes, thank you, Your Majesty. Thank you, Milady."

"Very well. Expect the arrival of Milady and her maid soon."

The pair bowed once again and took their leave. A deep, happy warmth washed through me, pleased that I'd been able to find a solution toward aiding them. I contributed to the well being of some of my people.

Once the priest and nun had left the room, King Talbot dismissed his council and motioned to the guard to not let in any more citizens. My good mood dissipated when I turned my attention to King Talbot. His anger rolled off of him in waves. I knew in an instant my interference had gotten me in trouble. He grabbed my arm with a rough grasp, "You're lucky your idea suits me, but you're not to speak up again in my meetings. I am the ruler; you are something pretty to look at. Do I make myself clear?"

I agreed with a silent nod, fighting the tears threatening to spill. It was all I could do to keep myself from panicking under his now wicked stare. I never considered myself one to cower from anything or anybody, until I found myself betrothed to the king.

"Good. Now go alert your maid and ready for your trip. I'll arrange for one guard and a carriage for you. We cannot have you traveling alone, anything could happen."

His words and actions unnerved me, like he knew something that I didn't. A dark glee swam around him, which only made my suspicion worse. Something about his entire demeanor unlocked a new knowledge about him, why I always felt so uneasy around him. I realized King Talbot's rueful and harsh nature weren't just side effects of his spoiled and cruel upbringing. He was a natural monster.

I HAD a hard time sleeping that night. The excitement I felt for my upcoming journey coursed through me, even though I was disappointed that Anwen wouldn't be joining me. She said she would find a maid to journey with me in her place. I trusted that she would pick well.

After tossing and turning for what seemed hours, it became obvious my mind wouldn't relax. I sat up and lit the lantern on the little table by my bed. Picking up the lantern, I padded across the cold floor and made my way to the library to get Prince Declan's journal. I needed to finish reading it.

Butterflies formed in my stomach as I sat back in my bed and opened up to where I left off. What secrets would I discover as I continued to read?

I didn't expect the tumultuous array of emotions that assaulted me as I finished the book. The final pages were a love story so beautiful and sad that I understood what Anwen meant when she said Declan had been unhappy. He'd fallen in love with a peasant girl named Rosalie, and had been forbidden to see her by King Bern. Not being one to be told what to do, he married her in secret. But, King Bern had kidnapped her shortly after learning she was pregnant. There were a few entries regarding his desperate search for her, but after that the pages were blank. He never said if he found her, reunited with his love and his child. The answer was plain as day, but I still wished there had been more to their tale.

My mind reeled with the information as I flipped through the blank pages hoping for some resolution. As I neared the end of the journal, a folded and worn piece of parchment fluttered onto my lap. My heart pounded as I picked up the well read note. I unfolded it with reverence and read.

The message there answered my questions. It was a letter from a nun at a convent, Sister Maria Benedict. Prince Declan never reunited with his secret family, his wife and child both died during the birth. Heavy tears sprung into my eyes at the tragedy. He had love, real love, and a growing family. Then his controlling and vile father ripped it away from him. Who knows what might have been had that not happened. Would they still live? Would his first-born have been a good man like him? I found myself wishing into the darkness that things had been different; maybe I wouldn't be preparing to marry a monster. Maybe I wouldn't be here at all.

I needed to share what I discovered with Anwen. I hated the idea of disturbing her sleep, but I couldn't shake the feeling that talkingto her couldn't wait. News this big wouldn't keep well.

I threw on my robe and started off to Anwen's room, which was adjacent to mine due to her huge role in my life. I had moved a few paces before I turned back. I'd forgotten the journal and secret letter.

Anwen would want to see them. I hastily retrieved them and continued on my way.

As I approached her room, I noticed a soft glow coming from beneath her door. Happy relief eased my tension. I wouldn't be disturbing her sleep after all. But as I got closer, I heard hushed voices and an angry and hateful aura was seeping from the other side. Concern welled in me for Anwen's safety.

I pounded my fist on the door. "Anwen! Are you all right? Open the door, Anwen!" Panic replaced the anger beyond the door. Whoever was in there with Anwen had been started by my knocking. I heard scuffling and the distinct sound of the other door opening and closing in haste.

Moments later, Anwen opened the door looking flustered. "Milady, what brings you here at this hour? Is there something wrong?"

"Is there, Anwen?" I looked at her with a skeptical eye. She was hiding something from me, something big. "Who was in your room with you? You can't tell me no one was in there; I heard someone. I can sense that you are hiding something. You know I can."

She sighed in defeat, "Alright, Merinley. I can tell that you won't be content until you know, and I don't want there to be secrets between us. You have trusted me with all of yours over the years. I want you to know you can trust me. Come in and I will explain."

Anwen allowed me in her room and motioned for me to sit at a small table in the center of the room. I placed my lantern down in the center of the table and waited for her to join me.

"I'm sure you're wondering why I would have guests in my room at such an hour, and why I tried to hide the fact that I did. I'm hoping I can sway you away from needing to know, even though I said I want no secrets. Know that I am only trying to protect you by keeping you in the dark."

I said nothing in return. I had no intention of letting this go, not when I felt the hate and anger so clearly. Something of ill intent seemed to have been happening beyond the door and I needed to know what.

Anwen knew me well by now, she knew my determination could

be fierce. "Fine. If you must know, I met with some friends who are working on something for the good of Realta's people. We have to meet in secret, during late hours so that we are undetected by those who don't want to see change."

"What does that mean Anwen? Please don't be vague with me. I can handle whatever it is, and you can trust me not to betray you."

Anwen bit her lip in hesitation, "We want to overthrow Talbot." The words rushed from her like they tasted bad and she couldn't wait to expel them. "The people are tired of his family's rule, they have brought nothing but hate and ruin to Realta and the far-reaching regions of our kingdom."

Anwen's revelation shocked me. I never pegged her for being part of the rumored rebels that we'd been warned against all these years. I understood why she wished to keep me out of it, seeing how I was set to marry our king. The wheels in my head spun, all I could think of was that there may be a way out for me.

She continued on, "Merinley, please believe me when I say that this in no way reflects on you at all. The rebels know what position you're in; the danger that this poses to you, an innocent who has been thrown in the way."

"Anwen," I interrupted. "You mistook my silence. I felt no concern over my safety. I just want to know one more thing about this matter."

"What?"

"The plan, and when it will be exercised."

"No. You cannot be part of this Merinley. It is too dangerous," Anwen insisted.

A wave of anger blew over me. How could she expect me to stand aside when she knew how I feared King Talbot, of what would become of me once I became his wife? "And so is being married to Talbot! Do you not have any idea of how horrifying my life will be if I marry him?"

"I do know. That is why I am trying to urge them to act swiftly, despite their hesitation to act without a fully formed plan. They don't want to worsen things by trying and failing. Such an outcome would be worse than death for the whole of Realta." Anwen paused with a wistful memory lingering in her gaze. "If only there were a way to just dethrone him without replacing him with someone just as bad. Or worse even."

"That would be much easier had Prince Declan's first born had lived." The words came from me without thought. I slapped my hand over my mouth once I realized what I'd said.

"What did you say?"

"Nothing, Anwen. It is not helpful in the least, just wishful thinking."

"No, that was something. First born?" Anwen pushed for more information.

"Yes, the reason I came to see you in the first place tonight. I finished Prince Declan's journal because I couldn't sleep. As soon as I did, I had to share what I discovered with you. Did you know that Duchess Emile was not his only wife?"

"Yes, I did know that. Not many do. The rebels all know, as much of their work is inspired by Declan's rebellion against his father. After his death, his compassion is what sparked the rebellion into being. One of the leaders of the group had an accidental witness to the wedding. When it was discovered that he knew about Declan's defiance, King Bern had him imprisoned and tortured. They released him only because it had been ensured he wouldn't tell a soul. King Bern had his tongue cut from his mouth. Then kept him on as palace staff so that he could keep a close watch on him. He obviously found ways around keeping silent."

"The gardener?"

Anwen confirmed my hunch with a nod. "We believe Prince Declan was killed by Bern so that Talbot could inherit the throne instead. King Bern wanted an heir with a like mind. He knew Declan would change things."

"Is that what spurred your secret alliance with the rebels?" I asked.

"No, I was fulfilling my philanthropic work that all fledgling Quaintrelle are required to do." I nodded at Anwen's reference. Matron Hattie desired to balance the sin of our line of work with doing good works for those in need. "I worked with the sick at the convent up in the Eira Mountains. One day an aging nun approached me. She rambled about a lot of things, including about how she had cared for Prince Declan's wife during her pregnancy.

"I was a little taken aback because I hadn't realized that the palace had ever employed nuns. When I asked if she liked the Duchess she looked at me as if I had offended her. 'I have never met Duchess Emile,' she told me, 'I was speaking of sweet Rosalie. I only regret that I shall never get to apologize to the prince for lying to him about his son.' With those words, she left. Another nun then approached me and told me not to worry about the old woman, her mind wandered and she very seldom could tell reality from delusions anymore.

"A few days later I discussed what happened with Mrs. James in the kitchens. It had been so bizarre, that I needed to share. Well, she wasn't shocked in the least and told me that it was true, Declan had been married before and Bern disapproved. He made the girl disappear. Mrs. James never heard of them having a child, though, and we dismissed it as part of the old nun's going mind.

"It was at that time that Mrs. James let something slip about being a rebel. I decided I wanted in." Anwen released a deep sigh when she finished her tale.

"The old nun, she mentioned she lied about the child though?" I asked, my mind tumbling. Stories were lining up. I pulled the letter from the pages of the journal. "Do you recall the nun's name?"

"Sister Maria something."

I opened the letter and skimmed it once more before handing it to Anwen. "Maria Benedict?"

"I think so," she responded off hand as she read over the letter. Her face went slack as she neared the end of the page and she sank deeper into her chair in disbelief. After a few minutes of stunned silence she looked back at me with a wide smile across her delicate features, "Merinley, I think you may have just given the rebels exactly what they need. If the nun I encountered was this Maria Benedict and she sent this letter to Prince Declan, which says his son died at birth with his mother..."

I interject with new found excitement, "And she told you that she lied to him about his son. That means…"

"Talbot is not the true heir to the throne! Declan's first born son, wherever he is, didn't die and should be king. All we have to do is track him down."

"That won't be easy," I said.

"I wonder if she kept any personal records of this. If she did they would still be at the convent." Anwen tapped her chin with her manicured finger.

"You said she lived at the convent in the Eira Mountains? Saint Ludo?"

"Yes, why?"

"That's the convent I'm headed to, to assess the damage from the storm. I could ask."

My friend beamed at me with more hope swirling around her than our conversation started with, "That would be an excellent idea, my dear girl. I will tell my friends in the rebellion what we have pieced together here tonight. With any luck, we can do two wonderful things with this information. Dethrone King Talbot, and prevent you from having to marry him."

We hugged in excitement. I couldn't wait to head to the convent tomorrow. I left Prince Declan's journal and Sister Maria Benedict's letter with Anwen for her to share with her friends. I raced back to my bed to try to get some rest for the next day's big journey. Though, I knew sleeping would be near impossible after everything we'd learned.

CHAPTER THIRTEEN

The carriage bumped along the muddy road as we headed towards the convent with our meager supplies, a bundle of blankets and loaves the kitchen whipped up at my request. My lack of sleep weighed on me, but the excitement of the discoveries I made had me fully alert. I just wished I could have brought Anwen with me; it would have given us an opportunity to discuss them further. She had other responsibilities, that I understood completely. Not to mention, she had to get our discoveries to her friends.

As promised, Anwen chose a maid to go in her place, Lily, a sweet and cheerful girl with chestnut hair and wide hazel eyes. She would be of no help where it came to what I wanted to accomplish most, but I did appreciate her company. Our ages were close enough that we could chat idly without too much awkwardness. Though, I mostly listened to her. Her fresh and innocent view of the world was refreshing.

"Thank you, Lily, for coming with me today. I'm certain this trip would be terribly dull without your company," I said, a yawn escaping from me.

"Milady, you can rest if you need to. I don't mind if you do. I'm more than happy to gaze at the scenery to entertain myself. I don't often get to travel outside city limits."

"Thank you for your concern, Lily, but I'm fine. I'm tired, indeed, but also anxious to make it to the convent and offer aid."

"You are a blessing to the kingdom, Milady. I can tell you are going to be a good queen."

"Thank you, Lily. I do hope I can be."

The carriage stopped without warning, jostling Lily and myself against the seats. Our guard ordered us to stay inside, assuring us not to worry, that it was routine to stop other travelers as a royal carriage passed.

"Halt," the guard called out to the travelers. "Make way for this carriage." A long silent minute passed before the guard spoke again. This time his order took on a more aggressive note.

Our guard's orders were not being heeded.

I reached out with my ability, getting a sense of what was happening on the road. When their intentions met my mind, I gasped. These were no mere travelers. They had greed on their minds, greed and trouble. A knot formed in my chest and my nerves spiked, amplifying the high tensions coming from the rest of my traveling party. Lily trembled in fear to the point of being on the verge of crying. I opened my mouth to give the guard an order to barrel through the men on the road when we heard the first gun shot. We were officially under attack.

"Lower your weapons!" our guard yelled. His face appeared in the carriage window, slick with panic, "Run Milady." Another gunshot rang out. The guard's face turned ashen as he grunted in pain. His face contorted before going slack. Moments later he toppled from the carriage, sliding down over the window. His impact with the ground made a sickening thud.

I moved with haste to get out of the carriage. There was no time to gather anything to salvage from these men. Our lives were more valuable than possessions, I had zero intention of being captured or killed. The carriage door stuck in its mechanisms, sending a shiver of horror through me. I tried again, empowered by my desire to remain safe. The door gave with the second push. Regret bubbled up my throat the moment it did. The guards lifeless body, slick with mud and blood, lay there just under the door. One hand flew to my mouth, the other pressed against my stomach.

Centering myself, I leapt from the carriage and over his body, nearly landing on my bottom on the slick ground. With a quick glance around I saw our attackers advancing closer. Time grew short, but I needed to make sure Lily made it out safely too. I wouldn't abandon her to these men. I turned back to see her frozen in terror, curled up on the seat inside, crying.

"Come on, we need to get to the trees over there," I urged Lily to come out. I pointed westward towards a thicket. "These men are robbers, they'll raid the carriage and leave. We get up in those trees and we'll be just fine." My words were uncertain, but they were the only plan I had. "When they leave, we can take the carriage back to Bua Tur and explain what happened. This trip will have to be delayed."

Lily hesitated. I urged her with more authority before she moved, hesitantly taking my hand and emerging from the carriage. She dropped my hand and stumbled back when she caught sight of the guard, her head shaking furiously in protest. "I can't," she sobbed.

"Lily, I know this is scary. I'm terrified too, but we'll be safer away from the carriage. Come now, please." I stretched my hand out for hers once more, hoping to embolden her. She nodded timidly, screwed her eyes closed and grabbed my hand. With a mighty yank, I pulled her from the carriage and begin to dash towards the tree-line. We had only moved a few steps towards our goal when I felt Lily tug backwards and her hand slipped from mine. Looking over my shoulder for her, I saw a tall, lean man with black hair and almond shaped eyes had her wrapped in his arms. She screamed and flailed in fear. Though I knew my chances of beating him were slim, I had to do something. I wouldn't let this thug harm the sweet girl.

I lunged for him, "No! Do not hurt her!" My body connected with his and I pounded my fists against him in a desperate attempt to save her. My focus on rescuing Lily distracted me enough to forget about the second man. That is until a set of rough hands grabbed me from behind and threw me to the ground.

My back slammed against the wet ground, knocking the air from my lungs. I shook off the momentary shock knowing I had to defend myself. I needed to defend Lily from these men. Her innocence needed protecting more than mine. I fumbled with my skirt in search of my dagger. My habit of keeping a blade on me had never changed. It was a habit my fiancé would disapprove of if he knew of it. In that moment, I was thankful I maintained it.

My attacker was shorter, with thinning, stringy, greasy, gray hair and a rounder belly. His pock-marked face contorted into a sneering mess as he gazed down at me with a happy glint in his cruel eyes. I realized neither man made a move to ransack the carriage. They weren't after the wealth of supplies, or the hidden stash of coins that could always be found in a royal buggy, after all.

Fight or flight instincts kicked in and my chest tightened in response to the realization of how serious the situation was. These men were most likely after me, the future Queen of Realta.

I grasped the hilt of my dagger and freed it from its sheath. "What, what do you want?" I stammered, brandishing my weapon. I pointed it with a shaky hand towards the round man.

He moved swift, faster than I imagined he would. In a quick move, he grasped just below the hand I held my dagger with and twisted; I dropped it. "Ain't it obvious pet? We want you." The short man's eyes flashed with greed. "Alec, get rid of the girl. She isn't what we were hired for."

I watched in horror as Alec chuckled, lifting his weapon, and aimed at Lily's head. The innocent maid cried ragged and desperate tears at her impending fate. She struggled against the mud to scoot away from Alec and his weapon's deadly stare. The wet earth seemed to be against her, sucking at her hands at feet.

"Stop! Please, stop. You do not need to hurt her," I begged through my own tears. "She is no threat to you, please."

Alec was given an order to halt. "Fine. It would be good to have a witness to deliver a message anyways. Knock the maid out, then bind this one's hands. I'll have a look-see around the carriage for any treasures to sweeten our bounty."

"Righty, Jim." Alec returned his firearm to his hip and hit Lily hard enough to render her unconscious before moving on to bind my hands.

I listened to Jim rummaging through the carriage as Alec tied my wrists together. I tried to keep my sight on anything but the skinny man. A wave of guilt washed over me. This was my fault. Had I not insisted on being the one to help the convent, I'd be safe at Bua Tur. Lily would be safe, rather than lying unconscious on the side of the road.

Jim reappeared with an armload of spoils from within the carriage; gold, the food we had packed, blankets, and clothes. Sitting on top was a small scrap of paper and a quill. He ordered Alec to take the pile of jewels and finery from him and take it to their battered wagon down the road. He then used the scrap and quill to scrawl out a message.

"There. Now your fiancé will know your fate, but it's missing something." Jim turned about as if he were searching for something; something to complete the message. His eyes fell on me and he grinned broadly.

I cringed as Jim's lanky hands reached towards my face. His hand shot past my face as he grabbed the white ribbon from my hair. He then grabbed my hands and took my engagement ring from me as well. He strung the ribbon through the ring and tied it around the message. The message was tossed next to Lily's unconscious form.

Alec returned as Jim finished up, "Pick her up Alec, let's move before anyone comes along."

CHAPTER FOURTEEN

The wagon came to an abrupt stop. I could hear my kidnappers muffled voices as they prepared to dismount. I assumed they were preparing to make camp somewhere in the dense woods yet again. This would be the fifth night that I spent in their company, and I still had no clue of their intentions or why they kidnapped me. All they talked about were their past conquests and adventures; and their forthcoming fortune. Not once had they mentioned who hired them or why I'd been taken.

I'd given up on attempting to appeal to their better natures, offering them riches beyond imagination if they would just return me home. They only laughed and said they'd been paid handsomely enough.

Sunlight assaulted my vision when the canvases covering the wagon were pulled back. When my vision cleared, I saw that the surrounding landscape had changed. We were no longer in the dense forest, but in an open area with scattered trees. The salty air hinted we were nearing the coast again. We hadn't been near one since the first day when we ventured near the Fenian Cliffs.

Jim pulled me roughly from the wagon and tied a rope around my already bound wrists, fashioning a lead of sorts.

"Jim, all clear!" Alec called from behind me. "Not a soul here, anymore." He chuckled at his last statement. My stomach turned when I understood the meaning of his words. He slaughtered somebody to keep my presence secret.

"March," Jim instructed as he jerked the rope, signaling me to turn and move. As we rounded the wagon I saw an old building looming before me. The unimpressive, graying inn looked sad. The dirty, salt crusted windows made it all the more depressing. I noticed the road seemed rarely traveled, but worn enough to determine people did, indeed, still pass through. I assumed this place saw little business, but enough that it did not fall into total disrepair. I could hear sea birds in the distance and even spotted a faint shoreline far beyond the inn.

Alec waited at the door to the inn. He grabbed my arm as I passed him and leered at me with lust. "Our accommodations for the next few days. The beds look very cozy," he laughed with oeillade dripping in his voice. I gagged on his rancid breath. I didn't need special abilities to understand what intentions played through his lecherous mind.

The rope Jim led me with tugged, pulling me further into the inn. My eyes adjusted again to the change of light inside. The inside of the inn showed little of the sadness of the outside. A fire blazed in the hearth that warmed the building. The simple tables and chairs were well taken care of. A stage sat on the far end of the room, next to a well used piano. Were I there under other circumstances, I would've found it charming.

Under current circumstances, all I saw made me feel imprisoned.

"Go tie the girl up over by the stage," Jim ordered, handing the rope lead to his partner. "I'll find us some drinks before we clean up this body. And feed the girl, instructions were to keep her healthy or else she will be worthless."

Alec led me across the main room. I spied the dead innkeeper lying behind the bar, his beard a deep, garish red from the blood spilled when Alec slit his throat. A sob escaped my throat at the sight. Another victim of my abduction. The poor man had been innocent, his fear still lingered in the air.

Alec tied me to a pillar near the small stage at the far end of the inn's main room and disappeared to fulfill the rest of Jim's order. The rich fabric of the curtains pooled on the floor, offering some cushioning on my weary body, a welcome feeling after near a week on the hard earth and in the back of a bumpy wagon. I had to fight to keep myself from dozing in the meager luxury.

Alec returned minutes later with some ale and a molding apple he found. I pushed the small meal away from me, despite the ache in my stomach for real food rather than something foraged from the forest ground. I'd rather have starved than do what these men expected me to. The stein scraped the floor with more sound than it should have.

"Oi, eat up there cunny. You don't want us to force that down that pretty throat of yours do ya?" Alec leered over his shoulder as he crossed the inn.

I drew a long drink of the ale to appease them. The bitter flavor made me sputter and the sticky drink spilled down the front of my already dirty dress.

"Well little whore, that won't do," Jim crooned from the stool he had perched on. "Alec, take her backstage and see if we can find her something clean to wear. Our contact will be sore if she isn't presentable when delivered tomorrow. He might assume we ignored the order to keep her well. Just think, by this time tomorrow we'll be rich men."

As Alec untied my binds, voices drifted from outside of the inn.

"Hurry you dolt," Jim ordered. "Gag her and keep her quiet back there. I got to clear this body from sight. We don't need any trouble." Jim tossed a filthy handkerchief at him. Moments after we were backstage, the old brass bell on the door rang out. A loud clamor of men's voices filled the room.

"Welcome, gentlemen," Jim greeted the men with a jolly imitation of an innkeeper.

Backstage, Alec tied me to an abandoned chaise and wrapped the dirty handkerchief around my mouth. He began a hurried and silent rummage through the backstage inventory, searching for something to replace my dirty dress. After minutes of searching, he returned with a brown tunic and a cat-like grin.

Alec drew the dagger from the sheath at his side. I recognized it as mine, a fact that made me feel violated. He straddled me; his excitement of dressing me evident thanks to the growing bulge in his trousers. I tried to struggle against him, but my bucking movements only excited him more. He became more aggressive in his task.

I could still hear the men who entered the inn before. I wished Alec had not been so quick in listening to Jim, that those men had seen me. Maybe they'd have seen my distress and stopped Alec from dragging me backstage. Maybe they would've helped me if they knew my predicament. Before that could happen, I had to figure a way out of the situation; I had to help myself before I could hope to seek help from others.

An idea struck me.

I decided to lay limp and bide my time. Alec had to untie my hands at some point to pull the tunic over my head and arms. I thought if I were able to lull Alec into believing I'd given up that I'd have a chance at escaping his grasp. I only hoped that the men beyond the curtain were more honorable than my captors.

"That's a good little whore," he whispered hoarsely when I stopped struggling against him. "Would hate to have to hurt ya, accidentally that is."

He dropped the moth-eaten tunic next to my head and ran the flat side of my dagger against my cheek. Alec's cold dark eyes glimmered with greed as he cut my dirty dress from my body to reveal my naked breasts to the dusty air. He leaned in and pressed his torso against mine and breathed my scent in as he untied my binds. I turned my face into my arm to escape his rancid breath. I just needed to let him dress me in the tunic; I didn't want to to be naked if I escaped into the room full of strangers. The tunic at least offered me some covering.

Alec grabbed hold of one of my wrists and pulled the tunic over my head and other arm. He changed grip to the dressed arm and finished pulling the tunic over my head. A lecherous smile spread over his gaunt face.

"No wonder King Talbot chose you," he whispered. His free hand lingered on one of my breasts. Alec took his time; enjoying whatever fantasy he had created in his mind. I winced as he ran his tongue over my neck. A grim intention shadowed his emotions, but I sensed he had become distracted enough for me to make my move.

He released my wrist to search for the rope to re-tie. This was the moment I'd been waiting for. I drew my arms to my chest then pushed into Alec with all my might, knocking his balance off just enough to free a leg. Before he had the chance to react, I brought my knee hard into his groin. Alec toppled over onto the floor.

"You bitch!" Alec screamed in pain.

I threw the handkerchief from my mouth as I jumped off of the chaise to make a break for the fusty curtains. "Please, help me!" I cried as I broke through to the other side.

The men scattered about the room all jumped to their feet at my appearance, staring towards me in surprise. Some drew weapons, while others looked bewildered at the appearance of a half-dressed woman. I scanned their faces, looking for one who looked like he might be inclined to help me escape my captors. My eyes stopped on a familiar and haunting face. Captain Wade.

His eyes flashed with recognition and he started towards the stage.

I made to run off the stage to meet him halfway, but a savage grasp circled my waist. Alec roared in my ear and dragged me back towards the curtains. I saw the situation registering on Captain Wade's face, his expression changed into fury just as we passed through the curtains.

Alec threw me, head first, back onto the lounge. My head made contact with the ornate backrest with an audible crack. The impact had been hard enough to open a wound; I felt a warm trickle of blood and a tintinnabular sound filled my ears. He came at me, angry; I barely had time to shrink away from him. He slammed his open palm across my face and straddled me once again.

This time there would be no pretending, I fought against him. Every time he reached for me I would scratch and push at his hands and arms. But he managed to capture my hands and hold them together with one of his. He drew back his free hand, making ready to strike me again. I bucked to throw him off balance. The move failed. I closed my eyes and prepared for his hit.

The hit never came.

Alec lifted off of me. I opened my eyes and witnessed him being hurled back through the curtains into the sound of brawling men. I knew instantly the fight beyond the curtain would be unfair, and would not be ending well for my kidnappers.

The Captain's formidable form loomed into my vision. His face was stony and intense, as though he were ready to kill someone. His face softened as he offered me a hand, I grasped it with shaky fingers. He squatted in front of me, inspecting the visible damage Alec inflicted. With a ginger touch, he caressed my face and wiped the blood away from where my head and met the lounge.

"Did those men harm you?" His question obviously asked if the abuse I suffered was more than what he could see.

I hadn't cried since Alec and Jim had first kidnapped me on the road to the Eira Mountains; I refused to. The relief I felt then, along with the true compassion emanating from Captain Wade, opened up something inside of me. I no longer needed to be strong. A hard sob plowed from me, stealing my words. I could only shake my head in response. I'd been lucky Alec had not had the chance to finish what he'd started.

"Stay here, Sweet," he said. "I have some dogs to put down." He stood and removed his long coat, placing the heavy gray garment over my naked legs before he disappeared through the curtains. I felt the anger he bottled when he checked on me swell once more. An anger like a swift tide on a storm ridden sea, dark and fierce. I understood the fearsome reputation he had, how his wrath could come out of nowhere on swift wings.

I listened through my dying sobs to the scuffling sounds beyond the wall of fabric near me. The distinct sound of flesh being beaten. An untuned cacophony mingled with the sound of a crash; no doubt someone had just been thrown into the dusty old piano lying dormant near the stage. Captain Wade roared. Alec and Jim whimpered like the dogs they were.

After long minutes had passed, the beatings stopped. Jim and Alec could no longer be heard. They had either been knocked out or beaten to death. I heard the Captain's voice, ragged from the fight, order his men finish the job.

Felix returned backstage; his anger slaked. He paced a few moments to cool his head. I wanted to say something, but the abrupt ringing of gunshots interrupted me, startling me enough to gasp. My alarmed outburst drew the pirate's attention back to me. He resumed his squatted position and took my hands in his. The touch sent the warmth of security through my body.

"Thank you, Captain, for saving me." I managed a whispered gratitude.

He shushed me in a manner which meant to soothe. "Felix, call me Felix. Come on then, Sweet, let's get you fixed up." He helped me to my feet and led me towards the main room. "You should cover up. We may have just released you from those rakeshames, but we are pirates. A beautiful, half naked woman may cause trouble." His eyes glimmered with mild mischief, emphasizing his remark. He helped me into his long coat and buttoned it so that I would be a little more covered. Satisfied with the result, he continued to lead me away from where he'd found me.

The crew was scattered about in a manner that suggests nothing violent had ever happened here. The only signs that Jim and Alec had even been there were two red stains smeared across the floor and the remains of the broken piano.

"Men!" Captain Wade shouted as he continued to escort me through the inn. "Change of plans. Return to The Fura. I'll not waste any more time in this place." They complained at the order but did as they were told. We stopped at the door and he grabbed an exceptionally large man with wild red hair and matching beard with one more order. "Burn it."

CHAPTER FIFTEEN

woke to the sound of a door closing and heavy footsteps. My heart raced, nervous about whomever approached. In my sleepy haze, my brain struggled to recall where I was. All that registered were memories of being terrified.

When the heavy sleep began to clear from my head, I remembered Alec and Jim no longer held me captive. I'd been rescued from whatever their plans were for me. I'd been rescued by Captain Wade. Though I didn't recall much after that, just bits and pieces. The burning inn. The passing forest. Being lifted into Felix's arms. The safe feeling I had nestled against him. I didn't, however, remember arriving at the ship. I must've fallen asleep after Felix insisted he carry me.

I drank in the remarkable room around me. I lay on an ornately carved bed made up with rich blackberry colored blankets and over-sized pillows. A desk sat across from the bed. It, and the chair it paired with, had carvings that matched the bed. Tapestries and maps adorned the walls. A large cushioned chair sat in an inglenook, a surprising thing to see on a ship, heavily decorated with various exotic treasures. I never imagined a pirate ship could hold such decadence; could rival any room in the palace.

Felix sat in a chair in the inglenook, a glass of amber liquid in his hand. Weariness etched his angular face. He seemed deep in thought. Gratitude swelled in my heart. This man, this pirate, saved me in more ways than one the night before.

I tried to sit up, eager to express my thanks again. The swift movement caused my head to spin, and I fell back into the pillows again with a dizzy groan. I closed my eyes and I brought my hands up to cup my face; waiting for the dizzy spell to pass. With my fingertips, I could feel the small cut I suffered on the lounge had been stitched. I wondered how they were able to do that without waking me. The kidnapping and subsequent travel must have exhausted me more than I realized.

A warm hand on my cheek caused my eyes to fly open in a panic. After what I just went through, the unexpected touch alarmed me more than it usually would have. Jumping back against the headboard of the bed, my arms flailed out to protect me. After a moment, my head took over my body's natural reaction and I realized that Captain Wade had touched me. The realization calmed me.

"I should have waited to approach after you got your bearings. I couln't help myself, though. You've been sleeping a quite long time. I was beginning to wonder if you would ever wake. Smith said it was a possibility with a head injury." He sat on the edge of the bed and touched my cheek again. I blushed under his touch. This had been the second time this man had made me feel more than I was used to allowing myself to. Part of me felt confused; the other part was exhilarated by it.

"How long have I been asleep?" I asked.

"About a day. Don't worry, no one bothered you, and your necklace is still yours." Captain Wade joked about our first meeting, causing me to smile a little. He let out a breath and I felt the anxious tension he carried drift into relief.

My stomach grumbled and my cheeks flushed. Back in Realta, the station I held made me a fantasy, it had been frowned upon to show humanity.

Captain Wade laughed, "Sounds to me like you could use some food. Might not be the fare you are used to, but I can assure you what we have is better than nothing. Plus, Cook is quite picky about what is served upon The Fura." He took my hands in his and began to lift them to his lips as if to kiss them. He didn't follow through, though, as if he thought the gesture would upset me. Instead, he patted my hands. "I'll be right back."

I took the opportunity of being alone to have a closer look around the cabin. I walked around the room touching the tapestries and trinkets with a gentle hand. Upon exploring, I became delighted and surprised to find Captain Wade had many books in his possession. They were scattered in small piles and broached many different subjects. Hidden in some of the books were jeweled trinkets. I wondered if any of them had been lifted at King Talbot's birthday ball. Thinking of that night led me to recall my first meeting with Captain Wade. The memory glowed in my mind fondly, and yet again my emotions stirred in unexpected ways.

My stomach rumbled again, reminding me of my hunger. I spied a bowl of fruit sitting ups the desk. The fruit tempted me. I saw no harm in taking one of the luscious treats to sate my appetite for the time being. I plucked a pear from the offerings of fruit and bit into the soft, nearly too ripe, fruit. The delicious flavor exploded in my mouth. I ate with greed as I continued my exploration of Captain Wade's domain.

I had just finished the pear when he returned with some bread, an apple, and a flagon of water. "I apologize I don't have more to offer you. I'm afraid we haven't supplied the galley recently. What supply we do have at the moment is not ours to take from."

"The meal is fine, I'm grateful for anything. I helped myself to some of your fruit as well," I explained, sitting at the desk. My mouth watered at the humble offerings. No need for propriety, I dug in to the bread with the gusto of a starving dog. It was dry with a delicious sour tang that danced on the back of my tongue, and was far better than any of the fancy breads I'd eaten at the palace.

"By all means, have all you like," he replied, sitting on the edge of the desk. He watched me patiently as I ate.

"Captain Wade," I began.

"Felix," he interrupted to correct me.

Something about his informal attitude warmed me, I liked that he wanted me to call him by name rather than his title. King Talbot had grown very angry the one time I slipped and called him only by name. "Felix, I want to thank you again for saving me from those horrible men," I said between mouthfuls of bread. "I shudder to think of what could have been."

He beamed. "My pleasure, Sweet. But now, what to do with you? It's my understanding that our cockalorum King Talbot should be aggressively searching for you, or did I hear false that he announced your engagement at his party? If that's true, I certainly find myself pleased I missed that part of the evening."

"That certainly was as much a surprise to me as the rest of the kingdom. I had no idea of his intentions at all. We hardly ever interacted before."

"That's a shame, nothing so beautiful should be wasted on a fool." Felix's eyes danced as he paused in search of his words. "So, now begs the question, do I return you to your fiancé, or do I keep you? Both prospects have their benefits, but the latter seems to be calling me. I assume you would prefer the first?"

I missed some aspects of Bua Tur, but the king wasn't one of them. My stomach and face twisted at the mere thought of returning to him. I felt no fear about being truthful with Felix; after all, he held no fondness for the king either. "I would almost rather have remained in the company of my kidnappers."

Felix chuckled, "I see you hold your fiancé in as high a regard as I do. How did you end up with those vermin anyways? If I were Talbot, I wouldn't have let you out of my sight for any amount of time."

"They abducted me. My maid and I were journeying to a convent to assess damage from a storm in lieu of soldiers being sent out. The carriage was ambushed, my driver and guard killed; my maid injured and left on the side of the road. They wanted to kill her too, but I begged them not to."

"Talbot allowed you to travel so lightly?" He voiced his shock that I'd been sent with only one guard. "The fool."

"He said he could only spare the one. In truth, he didn't want me to go in the first place. He didn't like that I offered to go; he was very cross with me for it. He only allowed it to save face."

Felix thought over my tale for a moment. "Well, Sweet, if you do not desire to be reunited with your fiancé, I guess you'll have to remain with me. Unless there is another place you would rather go?"

"No, there is nowhere else I want to be."

I SPENT the rest of the day in the cabin. Exhaustion from the kidnapping still raked my body, and I didn't feel ready to explore the ship. Felix spent a fair amount of time ensuring my comfort and that I had what I needed, but otherwise his attention was where it should have been; on his ship and crew.

At first, it seemed strange for me to be in a man's room who didn't expect anything of me, except for me to make myself comfortable and relax. Whenever he would pop in to check on me, I felt the urge to greet him formally or offer him some comfort; the way I would've when I was a Quaintrelle. He'd shake is head a laugh when I did; reminding me I acted out of habit rather than as I wanted to. By the end of the day, I grew comfortable in my new surroundings. Felix had been very kind and assuring, never once making me feel as though I'd gotten in his way. It almost felt like I'd always been there.

I had just lit some candles, stoked a small fire in the fireplace, and was making myself comfortable in the cushioned chair in the inglenook when Felix came back to the cabin to end his day. He looked worn from the long day. He shirked off his long jacket and hung it on the back of the chair at the desk before sitting there to remove his boots. He looked about."This is nice," he said, "coming back to a warm cabin to a friendly face."

"You seem tired. Would you like me to put some of the candles out so you can sleep? I don't mind." I offered.

"No, I have more work that must be done. Logs to keep and all. You are no bother." He pulled out a piece of parchment and began to write. He looked so serious hunched over his writing. The scowl he wore as he worked seemed familiar, but I couldn't place why. I watched him a few minutes more before continuing to look through the book in my lap.

What seemed like mere minutes later, Felix startled me awake by shaking my shoulder."What are you doing sleeping in the chair, Sweet? Take the bed."

I yawned, "I don't mind sleeping here. The bed is yours, after all, I would hate to steal it from you yet again. I feel bad enough for having kept you from it while I slept before."

"Nonsense. I insist. A chair is no place for a lady to sleep."

"I haven't always been a lady."

A puzzled expression crossed Felix's face. I couldn't determine if was my statement which confused him, or that I argued with him about it. After a moment he said,"Besides the point, Sweet. You must understand, I'm a pirate and have not always been Captain. I can sleep anywhere."

I could tell there would be no convincing him otherwise and had to concede.

I stood and stretched, noticing Felix's eyes light on my legs when the tunic pulled up from the action. I corrected the tunic. I wished I had something longer to wear. Perhaps I'd inquire about better clothes for myself in the morning.

CHAPTER SIXTEEN

The morning came like a springtime breeze, welcoming and refreshing. The heaviness in my soul dissipated, and I felt reborn. Free. Free until Realta came looking. For the time being, I'd savor the deliciousness of it. Thrill at the lack of expectations held for me. For the first time in years, I could truly be me. Best of all, the company of an intriguing man filled the salty air with a promise of adventure. Company I very much wanted to keep.

The realization had me giddy. I lingered in Felix's ornate bed, relishing the fact that I could. There was absolutely nothing expected of me for the first time in over a decade.

I still lay marveling in my new found peace when Felix came back to his cabin.

"My, oh my, Sweet, you seem mighty at home in my bed," he quipped. His long legs carried him to the edge of the bed where he stopped, a glint in his eye and hands secured behind his back. "Were I a weaker man, you would find yourself with a bed-fellow most eager."

My cheeks heated. Felix was a man of confidence and integrity for sure. Much different than the men I dealt with before. Men that took what they wanted, or needed persuading to choose a different action. I couldn't place any reason why he had so much affect on me. I sat up, throwing the covers off and swinging my legs over the side of the bed. His eyes flicked over me, his Adam's apple bobbed with a heavy swallow. But the captain remained settled otherwise.

"I suppose I should be thankful then, to be rescued by a man of strength," I responded as I stood.

Felix chuckled, a half smile remaining behind as evidence of his amusement. "If you are up for it, I'd like to show you around today. Since you are going to be with us for the foreseeable future. No reason for you to be holed up in here all the time. You are not captive, after all."

While I wanted to see more of Felix's ship, I didn't think it would be a good idea to flit about in just a man's shirt. Felix may have been iron-willed, but not all men were. "I'd like that very much, but…" I fiddled with the hem of the tunic.

"You feel a bit under-dressed?" He summed.

"Yes,"I replied with a ghost of a laugh.

Felix revealed his hands, bringing out a a graying dressing gown he had been holding behind his back."I noticed last night you are in need of something more suitable to wear."

"Thank you." I had no intention of questioning where it came from, I was just grateful to have something other than the tunic Alec had placed on me days before.

"I'll be waiting just outside."

I held the dressing gown up, inspecting it closer. The garment had to have been fairly old, grayed with age and having been either white or pink when it was newer. I could make out faint needlework along the bodice, small flowers. Nor was the gown thin, being entirely opaque. I pulled the tunic over my head, noting my body was no longer sore from the week of hard travel and lack of sleep. It seemed everything was getting better, not just my circumstances.

The dressing gown was a little tight, but at least it covered me. It would do until I could get something else.

I caught a glimpse of myself in the simple standing mirror in the corner. I was a fright. My already unruly hair seemed to stand out in every direction and there was an obvious layer of dirt on me. Pride told me I needed to fix that before seeing the rest of the ship.

Looking about, I spied a was basin and pitcher. It was empty, of course. Nothing could be done about the grime covering me. Accepting defeat on looking presentable, I merely ran my fingers through my hair to make it a little smoother and was ready to face the day. I'd have to ask about a brush and getting some water to wash with later.

I found Felix right outside, just as he promised. The large man he grabbed in the inn stood with him. My distress had prevented me from getting a good look at him before. The man towered over Felix by several inches and had a large strong build. He had a leathery face that was scarred from his left eye down to his chin.

"Allow me to introduce you to my First Mate, Mister Bimble."

"Miss," he greeted me with a nod of his head and an outstretched hand.

"Pleasure to meet you, Mister Bimble." I offered my hand in return with confidence, which seemed to surprise the pair. I supposed they had expected hesitation; I assumed most who met Mister Bimble would've been intimidated by his appearance. Thanks to my secret, I knew him to be a gentle man at heart. I felt absolutely no fear of the man.

"I was just giving my man here the order to take over for the morning," Felix explained. "Your tour is my priority for now. Shall we begin?" He turned and offered me his elbow. I looped my arm through his and we were off.

As we toured The Fura, I marveled at how well maintained it appeared. Felix obviously took pride in his ship. I didn't blame him one bit in that, the ship was beautiful. Much more so than I thought a pirate vessel would've been. Main doors and railings about the deck were carved in intricate patterns that matched those found in Felix's cabin. When I commented to Felix on the beauty of the ship, he beamed back at me with prideful mischief. He explained the ship had once been part of the Realta fleet. Keeping it well maintained was just another jab towards the monarchy.

"How did you manage to get a fleet ship?" I asked.

"That is not my tale to tell," Felix replied with a wink.

Along the tour, I met many other members of Felix's crew.

I first met Smith, a former doctor who joined the crew a few years back. His dirty blonde hair was short, with a little curl to it. His eyes were deep brown. He was jovial at heart, with a free spirit. A genuinely nice guy. He checked the sutures he had done while I slept. I thanked him for what he had done and complimented his skill.

Felix briefly introduced me to Hawthorne and Domhnall. Hawthorne, Mister Bimble's second, had skin as black as midnight and the kindest eyes. He was loyal to the core and a hard worker. Domhnall, a thin and wiry fellow with one arm, had dark hair and a face that defied his age. He recently joined the crew; having only been on The Fura for a few months.

Lastly, Felix took me down to the galley for some breakfast. There I met Cook, the older man who ran the galley. I felt instantly drawn to the skeletal man with mounds of gray curls on his head and large bushy eyebrows over an intense blue eye and an eye patch. I imagined he looked much like an angry owl before he lost his right eye. For a moment, I thought I'd seen a flash of a familiar bushy red tail scurrying over his shoulder, but was sure I had imagined it and brushed it off. Though, it would have been wonderful to see the creature it made me think of.

After we had something to eat, we returned to the deck. Felix had called his crew to gather for instruction. Felix stood large at the helm; the minute change in his demeanor, as he went from tour guide to Captain Wade, impressed me. His men loved him. Devotion poured from each one as he addressed them.

"Men, as you are aware we have recently acquired the future Queen of Realta." I prideful murmur swept through the crew. Felix waited for them to settle. "I've discovered something surprising in speaking with her the past few days; she is not set on returning to her fiancé. It would seem she loathes him as much as we do." The crew laughed at this. "So it would seem she is going to remain in our company, for now at least."

Felix's speech created a perceptible change to the mood of the crowd. A few strands of fear and distrust weaved through the air, mixing with the good mood their captain had created in them. There were even a few shouts of protest. They feared retribution from King Talbot.

Felix set to assuage their fears, "Men, there is no reason to fear King Talbot coming after us. We had no hand in her abduction, in fact we saved her from a cruel fate. The fool has no clue Milady is in our possession. If he happens to learn she is with us, so be it. King Talbot's no match for us." They cheered at their captain's bold statement.

"So where to now Cap?" Mister Bimble inquired once the crew has settled.

"Where else, Mister Bimble? We have business and no reason to change that because of our current company."

"To Apoidea?"

"To Apoidea." A chorus of agreement surrounded me as the men began to hustle back to their duties.

My heart lurched in my chest when I heard their destination. I never expected to return to my birthplace. For me, it had been a place of bittersweet heartache, the only happy memories were fleeting images of my early childhood and the stolen moments of peace with the few friends I had. Apoidea held nothing for me. I felt certain that no one would be pleased to see me. Not even friends that I held dearly once, my relatives would've made certain that their love for me turned to hatred once I involuntarily left.

CHAPTER SEVENTEEN

e reached our destination in the next few days. Apoidea, a place I deliberately forgot, or at least tried to. There had been too much heartache in thinking of my home while I lived in Realta. I could feel my stomach tying itself in knots as I watched the shoreline approach from the port window. I wanted to malinger, stay in bed with a made up illness, in order to avoid stepping foot on the island; my childhood home. But I knew Felix would leave Smith to care for me and the ruse would be blown. Instead, I tried to convince him there may be someone from the palace that would recognize me; after all King Talbot must have deployed men all across Realta to find me. I didn't tell them that I knew I would be recognized; that I feared being seen by the family that sold me years before. That I was afraid of the disappointment my people likely hold for me. I thought hard, trying to come up with how I could avoid accompanying them.

I failed.

Wanting to be as invisible as possible while on shore, I asked for clothes that would disguise me. The crew pitched in and offered me items they had so I could blend in with them better while we were ashore. They gave me a cream tunic, which hung askew over my shoulder due to it being two sizes too big. I was given a pair of brown buckskin pants, which must have been from someone's younger years since they were skin tight on me. The haul also bestowed me a brown leather belt and a musket, which Hawthorne insisted that I needed in order to be a convincing pirate. The outfit came to completion with some old knee-high boots, a vivid blue scarf, and a rather large, floppy feathered hat. I appreciated the hat most of all; it would help hide my face. I debated braiding my hair but decided on leaving the black cherry tangle of curls down. Though my hair might have been be a dead giveaway to my identity, it also aided in hiding me.

I stood admiring my new pirate look in the Captain's mirror when I heard a chuckle to my left. "You look good in my pants."

I turned, amused at his statement. "Your pants?"

"Aye. I have been on The Fura for a while. Like I said, I haven't always been Captain Wade. You know, I could have sworn you wished to remain invisible while we are ashore. You make a mighty alluring pirate." Felix drank me in, appreciation gleaming in his eyes, then stepped next to me with a grin plastered across his face. "Might as well go out naked, Sweet. You'd be far less noticed in your birthday suit than you are in this."

In his words, I saw the opportunity for me to stay behind. "This is what Mister Bimble and Hawthorne gave me to wear. If you think it's not appropriate I shall remain here." I began pulling the hat from my head, but Felix stopped me.

"Oh no, you don't get out of coming ashore with us that easy. Death from boredom awaits those who stay behind," Felix laughed at his own joke."You are going ashore. But I fear I'll have to guard you closely. Young Apoidean men will be falling all over themselves as we pass through the market." He brushed a stray curl away from my face. "You'll blend just fine. If I think rightly, your fame has not yet reached Apoidean shores, the monarchy shares nothing with these people. No one will suspect you are not one of us, that you do not belong among them."

I felt the color drain from my cheeks. Felix must have noticed. His brow furrowed, "What did I say, Sweet, to make you look so afraid?"

I bit my lip in hesitation; I had to tell him the truth about why I was so worried. Everyone on that island would recognize me. Peter's 'runaway' niece, Nicolai and Tish's orphan. I took a deep breath and unbound my secret, "I'm still nervous of being recognized and causing a scene for it." Felix started to respond, but I interrupted before he had been able to utter a word. "But not by anyone from Bua Tur. I spent my childhood years on Apoidea. I'm Apoidean."

He was shocked by my revelation but took it in stride. "The future Queen of Realta, a wicked Apoidean? Oh, old King Bernie must be turning in his grave. How did you ever become a Quaintrelle? Lord knows they usually don't look this far for recruits. And you definitely don't seem the type to seek the position out."

My past caused me to bow my head. "I was sold, when I was sixteen, to traders. My relatives were jealous the Head Elder's son had asked for my hand rather than my cousin's. In truth, they hated me long before that. They sold me because they wanted to be rid of me. I've hidden my lineage from most everyone since that day. I was sold at auction to the kitchen master of the palace. The decision to train me as a Quaintrelle came later when my mentor saw me. She changed the course of my life."

Felix pursed his lips and gave a nod as he digested the information. After a moment, he kissed my forehead in a comforting gesture. "Don't fret, Sweet, being recognized won't be as painful as you think. I'm certain there are many here that will be glad to see you return. As for your family, do not give them another thought. Are any of them worth a king's ransom?" He beamed a crooked smile at me.

I shook my head and smiled meekly in return.

The late afternoon sun beat down on the market place, which buzzed with the same activity I remembered from my youth. The restrictions placed on Apoidea seemed to have been little hindrance to the people. I knew differently though. I knew King Talbot, like those before him, took much from them. He gave nothing in return. It left them with less than what they needed, less than they deserved.

I caught glimpses of people I knew from between the spaces the crew created as they carried their bountiful cargo around me. None seemed to notice me, for that I was grateful.

Children whooped and hollered as they ran alongside the pirates, playfully daring the gruff men for their attention. The men were almost as excited as the children, roaring in fun and breaking off to chase them for a few steps before returning to ranks. Nearly everyone in the market stopped to shout hellos as we passed them. These pirates, these wanted and feared men, were anything but. They were important and welcomed friends.

My heart swelled seeing the interactions. Nobody treated anyone with fear or hatred. The pirates accepted my people, and my people accepted them. It was a window into how my people should've been treated by outsiders. It made me want to weep.

"They're all so happy to see you," I remarked to Mister Bimble, who walked to my right, carrying a large crate. He only winked and smiled in response before roaring after a little boy who had just tried to scare him. This only caused more little boys to join in and jump on the big man.

We stopped at the tavern I recognized as the one my loathsome Aunt Rowena often sent me to in order to fetch drunken Uncle Peter. I remembered the warm atmosphere inside feeling strange to enter as I sought out the inebriated man. He bore his wrath on me more than once. I knew, even then, his drunken anger was the reason Aunt Rowena sent me to fetch him instead of going herself. Better I receive his abuse than to have her husband angry with her.

I took a deep breath and prayed that Uncle Peter wouldn't be inside.

Each man carrying cargo made a beeline for the bar when they entered the tavern, dropping what they carried with the barkeep before dispersing into the crowd. As Smith passed me, I grabbed him. "You help the Apoideans."

"We do. You see, miss, the restrictions King Talbot's predecessors placed on trade have made it hard for some things to be available for the people here. We do a lot of trading on their behalf and share the spoils of our raids as well. Been that way for years. The people would be bad off otherwise, and Captain has a soft spot for helping the underdog. We follow Cap because he is as good to us as he is to these people."

"You giving away our secrets, mate?"

I smiled at the voice that came from behind us. In the short time I'd been with Felix and his crew, I'd grown fond of them. I'd grown particularly fond of Felix. My feelings grew more now that I knew what he did for my people.

Smith took Felix's appearance as his cue to take his haul to the bar and join in the merriment.

"Well, Sweet, guess the cat's out," Felix said, stepping into my view. "We are not the big bad pirates we're made out to be. Don't misunderstand me, we are quite bad when we need to be; and we also revel in sticking it to the monarchy. Helping those the royal family despises does just that. If it restores our reputation, we take the tavern for all the bochet we can," he remarked, in jest.

Apoideans may be looked down upon, but it did not take away their pride. They accepted very little for free. The bochet was in trade for whatever the crew provided.

"Oh I don't misunderstand at all, I've seen how ferocious you can be," I flirted, playing into his game while referring to the passionate man I'd seen rescue me from Alec and Jim. "You want to know a secret, Captain?" He leaned in closer with a beguiled look. "I already knew that you were one of the good guys, ever since you tried to lift my necklace."

He arched his eyebrow in question.

"I have my ways."

"You are brimming with secrets, Sweet." He laughed in wonderment. "I suggest that if you wish to be less noticed, go sit in that corner over there." He pointed to a darkened area of the tavern where no one else sat.

I nodded, agreeing that it seemed a good place to sit. I lowered my hat enough to keep my face hidden as I walked through the tavern. I wasn't taking any chances of being recognized by the wrong person.

"No kiss for being helpful?" Felix teased across the room. My face flushed at the thought of what it would be like to kiss Felix once again. A real kiss, not one done in haste.

Walking across the tavern, I heard a female voice cut through the crowd, "New crew, Captain Wade? I thought it bad luck to have females on board." The pair chuckled with one another, and a twinge of jealousy settled in my belly. She knew him well, but how well? I reminded myself that he didn't belong to me, there was no point in my jealousy. Our brief encounter at the ball had been just that. His rescue of me hadn't meant anything else, despite his flirting.

In truth, I felt attraction, a common occurrence for me since I became a Quaintrelle. But, attraction and true feelings have always been strange bedfellows. So similar in the way they emote, yet not the same at all. I couldn't count on what I felt from Captain Wade to tell me an absolute.

I sat in my darkened corner taking time to study the tavern. Felix still talked to the young woman, relieved to see their body language portrayed nothing but keen friendship. The woman had dirty blond hair swept in a messy bun on top of her head and a very visible pregnant belly protruding from her midsection. She seemed familiar, but I could only see a sliver of her profile. Not enough to make a positive guess at her identity.

I moved my sight on to the rest of the tavern. Every detail looked exactly as I remembered, right down to the few local patrons. I breathed a sigh of relief when I noticed that one in particular was missing, Uncle Peter. I sat back and removed the floppy hat.

Another glance around now placed Felix at the bar, laughing with the man who owned the place. His name escaped me, but I recognized him as a grown version of the son of the owner. His father had always been kind to me when I would collect my drunken uncle. Felix caught me staring at them and gave me a wink. I averted my gaze, not wanting him to see the flush on my cheeks, only to see the young woman waddling towards me, carrying a large mug, I assumed it was filled with Apoidea's famous bochet, and a dish of food.

I scrambled for my hat, which I'd somehow sat on. Before I

managed to get it back on, she arrived at the table. I kept my gaze down and squeaked out a thank you as she placed the mug and bowl of slumgullion on the table next to me. She didn't move on. She continued to stand there as if she was waiting for something. It was possible she needed a rest. I recalled how tired Aunt Rowena became after the smallest tasks when she was pregnant with her youngest. Then again, Aunt Rowena had been a woman prone to exaggeration.

I waited anxiously for her to move away. She never did. The woman continued to linger longer than just resting would take. Her curiosity pierced me.

I looked up from under my lashes to see the girl studying me intently. This time, I recognized her in an instant. Esme, one of my childhood friends. My heart pattered, thrilled to see my old friend. Yet, I was apprehensive about revealing myself to her. I couldn't imagine the hurt my disappearance caused her. That was enough to keep my excitement at bay. I hated that my relatives lies probably hurt her deeply.

She, too, didn't need more evidence to know my identity.

"Oh my God! Merinley!" Esme almost jumped up and down; her belly being the only thing that prevented her from doing so. She moved swift for a woman so far along in her pregnancy. Before I realized it, she slid onto the bench next to me, giving me the tightest hug imaginable. She broke the hug and slapped my arm, then hugged me again. "My world ended when you ran off. Not that I blame you. Those relatives of yours are unbearable! Well not the younger ones, but Kizzy and her parents, they are downright nasty! Let me tell you, I was surprised the tavern didn't lose money when Peter died. Do Kizzy and Rowena know you are here?"

I shook my head no while a wave of relief washed over me. I wouldn't be seeing my lush of an uncle. Esme chattered away rapidly, I barely kept up with what she said. She had always been a very loquacious person.

"Now look, here you are back in town, and a pirate!" She squealed once more. "And you are so pretty, like those Quaintrelle girls we always heard so much about. No wonder Captain Wade keeps staring at you like you are the only one here. So romantic. Gosh. Is it exciting to be a pirate? Those relatives of yours would have a fit if they could see you now. They were so odd when you ran off, not even a tear shed." She stopped to take a breath.

"It's good to see you too, Esme," I replied, amused. If only she knew how true some of her words were.

I wanted to say more, but Smith interrupted our little reunion. His cheeks and nose were flushed with alcohol and he seemed nervous. "Would the Queen care to dance?"

I blanched and looked quickly to Esme, readying my brain with an explanation. Her grinning face was lit with a mischievous idea. "Oh I see what's going on here," she declared as she nudged me. "Pirate Queen, of course! I knew there was something going on between you and the Captain the second I saw you come in with the crew. Well, I mean I had no idea it was you, I just knew you were not a male crew member. You lucky little wench. So many women have tried to gain his attention here, but he never paid more than a few moments of polite attention to any of them. Captain Wade is a picky man with good taste."

I liked her revelation, that Felix had shown little interest in other women. At the same time it occurred to me that I could receive the same. I'd have to squash my budding feelings for him and be as unaffected as I would've been as a Quaintrelle. That seemed an impossible task. Felix had some power over me that kept me from recalling my training.

I gave her a sheepish smile; I let her believe the fantasy she created. Better that than tell her the truth of how I'd come to be with Felix and his crew. I turned my attention to Smith, who waited with patience for a reply. Diving into my dormant Quaintrelle skills, I brought a coy playfulness into my voice, "Of course, Sir. I would be delighted."

Esme excused herself and gave me another hug before she waddled back to work. Smith led me out onto the open floor.

The fiddler played a jocund tune. Smith spun me to the music, making my hair flare out like black flames. I allowed his happiness to wash through me and the last of my trepidation melted away. Laughter, real laughter, bubbled out of me for the first time in ages. I didn't want the music to end.

"Sure is grand to see you smile, miss. Warms my cockles, it does." Smith said as the music ended.

"I do believe that I needed just that. I'm sure you knew that though, being such a talented medic. And thank you, again, for taking care of me when I was injured." I placed a gracious small kiss on his cheek, causing Smith to blush and grin.

"May I cut in?" Felix's voice came from behind.

"Of course, Cap, I was just tryn' to cheer the lass up. Thanks again, miss, for dancin' with me." Smith scuttled away like a kid caught doing something he shouldn't have been.

I turned about to accept the dance with the handsome captain. He pulled me into dancing frame. The fiddler's instrument sang out a slow and sweet ballad. The tune cued Felix to adjust our frame into a much more intimate one. His emotions surged with warmth as he did so. Inside, a flame had been lit from the new closeness; I had to remind myself to keep my new feelings at bay.

"You spend a bit of time with Smith, Sweet. Need Talbot be worried?" Felix broke the silence with a playful query.

I smiled and looked back over to where he'd returned after Felix cut in. The small doctor already found himself another pint of drink. "No, King Talbot has nothing to worry from Smith." I caught myself staring into Felix's deep blue eyes and felt myself flush. A small wave of relief emanated from Felix. "You and your crew are lucky to have someone trained in medicine with you."

Felix nodded in response and silence filled the air between us yet again. After a moment or two he spoke again. "I noticed that someone recognized you. Was it as painful as you imagined?"

"No. I mean yes, an old friend. No, it wasn't painful. It was nice." I warmed fondly recalling Esme's giddy reaction to Smith's dance request. "You know she is under the impression that I'm a Pirate Queen, thanks to Smith. Is there such a thing as one?"

Felix pondered my query for a brief moment. He leaned his face in, millimeters from mine, and brought my gaze to meet his. "If there were, you would certainly be worthy of the title, Sweet. Could I grant you with the title, I would, and I would make you mine." His voice developed a lusty purr that stoked the growing flame in me. His eyes, full of longing, kept their focus on mine as we danced to the slow melody; we were in our own little reality. The scorching desire became tangible. I knew then I'd already been lost to the selcouth emotions he gave me. Could it be possible that what I felt from him was real? That what I felt from him was not the same passing fancy he would afford others?

We stopped dancing, but the music continued to swirl around us. My head spun in anticipation, realizing what was about to happen. Felix closed the minimal space between us and kissed me. The kiss was unlike any other I'd ever experienced; not hurried or desperate for something else to follow. This had not been an erratic kiss from some molly-nogging fool out to dip his wick in any well that would have him. No. The gesture felt sweet and pure; free of any wanton thought. It spoke volumes in seconds. The air froze around me and everything seemed still, yet everything buzzed with the glowing vibration of excitement. It felt as though Felix delved into the core of my soul and deemed to share his with me.

When the music stopped, our lips parted. A cacophony lifted the spell we had woven around ourselves. I looked about, blushing, and saw the men whooping and cheering at our display. I spied Esme near the bar, smacking the owner's son. Her husband. She berated him loud enough for the whole tavern to learn she wished he would make the same kind of romantic gesture.

Felix still held me in an intimate embrace. "Sweet, would you accompany me back to the ship. I desire to know you more," he suggested in a whispered voice. I looked at him and nodded. The implication of his question left me breathless. "I must attend to my men's bill. I'll be but a minute."

Returning to my darkened corner seat, a new sense of nerves overtook me. I'd never been alone with a man I actually desired. I reached for the bochet Esme had brought me, hoping its fire-like sweetness would steel my nerves. As I raised the glass to my lips, I noticed a harried blonde rushing into the tavern. Her pace implied she came on an emergent issue, but I heard no cry for help from her. Only sensed urgency.

Something about the sight of her made me want to hide, but my body still buzzed from my dance with Felix. I didn't want to lose that feeling. I brushed off thoughts of the blonde and finished my drink. As I put down my glass, I saw the blonde stalking towards me., a look of disgust written all over her face. My heart jumped into my throat as recognition finally soared into being.

Kizzy.

The shock of seeing her face, full of an anger that matched her father's, caused me to knock over my almost empty cup. My hope of not seeing one of my vile relatives dashed into a million pieces.

Kizzy stormed up to my table with a malevolent sneer. My stomach flipped in queasy circles, my heart pounded. I was on the verge of being sick. Perhaps finishing the bochet hadn't been wise.

On closer inspection, the hard years were written plain on her. Kizzy's rail thin body pained me to look at it. Her stringy hair and gaunt face were aged beyond her years. She obviously hadn't had an easy life. Rowena's prediction, with me out of the way Kizzy would gain the attentions of Tristan, didn't come to fruition.

Her closeness also allowed me to gain a solid read on her. Despite her haggard appearance, she held a high opinion of herself. She still felt better than others, that she deserved what she wanted no matter the cost. Kizzy hadn't changed at all. Why would she have?

She was also deeply annoyed by my presence. After all these years, I was still seen as a threat.

"Well, well, well; look who came crawling back home, pretending to be a pirate." Kizzy's voice dripped with smugness. "I guess you're not good even enough to scrub the floors of Realta's wealthy citizens after all. End up in a mill, did you? Or more likely a whore house."

Her words stung, even though they weren't true. I should've corrected her, bragged of the extravagant life I led as a Quaintrelle. Boasted of how desired I became, and all of the lavish gifts admirers gave me. I could've revealed my engagement to King Talbot. But I didn't dare tell her the truth; she wouldn't believe me. In her eyes, I was unworthy of anything good.

Worse yet, if she believed me there'd be a whole lot of questions to be answered. Questions I'd have been obligated to answer no matter how much I did not want to.

I couldn't reveal the truth to her.

I shot back with a lie I thought she'd believe, "I ran away, from the palace actually." I leaned in close and whispered in her ear, "I do that sort of thing, right?"

Kizzy's eyes widened at my hardihood. I'd never stood up to her when we were younger. She hadn't expected I would now. "Just proves you are too lazy to earn your keep, and a disrespectful little bitch too."

"For your information, dear cousin, I ran away to escape the abuse I was tormented with daily as a servant. You can't imagine the vileness I endured for years because of you and your parents. You sold me, you were the reason I was there."

She fumbled for a come-back, glaring maliciously when she found her words, "How did you convince these pirates to take you on anyways?" She tapped her dry, pointy chin for a moment and then offered an evil smirk. "Let me guess it has something to do with what lies between your legs and a darkened room?"

Her insinuation unleashed something in me, made me want to hurt her back. "You would know, for that is all you seem to be here for." I suggested with an arched brow. My words stung her. Kizzy, with no other verbal maneuvers left, moved to strike. I grabbed her hand before her palm made contact. A new look of surprise crossed her weary face. She wasn't used to anyone having the upper hand, she didn't like it. "I have died a little every day since your parents sold me, and I have never gotten over it. I would suggest not pushing me further, Kizzy."

Over Kizzy's shoulder, I spied Felix approaching us. I dropped her hand and moved my gaze from her to him, and then back again; giving her the clue that someone else approached us.

In response, she peeked over her shoulder, then leered back at me with a wicked, sweet grin. Her face changed; she shifted into being sweet as she turned to greet him. "Hello, Captain," she cooed, oozing lust and pride. She sought to make me jealous. To knock me down now that I had the upper hand. She wanted Felix. "I heard you had returned to Apoidea and got here as soon as I could. I had to see you. I truly missed your company. I was just getting acquainted with your new crew member here." She swished her shoulders, playing the sweet and welcoming girl she had never been. Surely, this was the Kizzy he knew. The fake Kizzy.

Felix gave her a charming half-smile. I sensed he had clued in on the tense air between Kizzy and me; that he knew her sweetness to be an act. The Captain was not addle-brained. His response to her confirmed my suspicion. "Hello, Kizzy. I was hoping to bump into you too."

Her face lit with preemptive victory and she tried to snuggle into him. "Of course you were."

Felix pulled away, "I deeply wished for you to meet Merinley, my, well for lack of better definition, she is mine," he emphasized his last words and winked at me. My heart fluttered.

Kizzy's jaw sagged open in shock and she stepped further from Felix. Her jealousy grew as her emotional distress welled.

"But, Felix," I played along, seeking to deliver a blow that would knock her from her high horse for good. "We already knew one another. This is my older cousin, whom I haven't seen in years."

He understood my hidden words. Felix's cool demeanor erupted. His face darkened like a fast moving storm as he glared over at the girl he once tolerated. "Leave, you pettifogging wench. Do not seek out my crew or myself for company ever again. You will regret it if you do."

Kizzy's last bit of pride demolished into tears. She fled from the tavern. Her pained rejection ran deep and pierced me as if it as deep as if it were my own. A small part of me felt guilty for being so cruel.

"Fret none, Sweet, over revealing her to me," he said, seeing my inner turmoil. "She deserved a little bit of hurt in return for all the hurt she and her family caused you years ago." He kissed the top of my head, "Come, The Fura is ours tonight."

I stopped by the bar to say goodbye to Esme on our way out of the tavern. "Thank you, Esme, for not being mad at me. For understanding the truth when you hear it."

Esme hugged me goodbye, "Oh Mer! I can't imagine what you must have gone through all these years. Promise me you'll come back."

"If not for sharing stories, then to meet your little one," I smiled and gave her one last hug before I left. I vowed to myself I'd try to come back someday when I'd be able to make a difference the way Felix and his crew did.

I met Felix just outside the tavern door. He leaned against the building, waiting for me. Silhouetted in shadow he looked every bit a dashing pirate with trouble on his mind. Despite the amazing kiss in the tavern, I felt a little odd about approaching him., though I was confident of his interest in me. Whether his interest went further than a passing fancy would be seen later. My hesitation rooted in my life as a palace jewel. I'd untied my emotions from intimacy for all of my years as a Quaintrelle. I had no idea what to expect doing this on my own terms.

My worries were brushed away when Felix beamed at my appearance. His smile had a way of lightening me. He grabbed my hand, pulling me up against his masculine figure. He lifted me so my face leveled with his and whispered in a husky tone next to my ear, "Ready, Sweet?" His words ended in a quick, rough kiss that stilled my breath. My knees were jellied when he set me back on solid ground.

CHAPTER EIGHTEEN

To say the Captain and I were inebriated was an understatement. The bochet continued flowing from the moment we stepped into his cabin. He sat atop his desk, swirling a glass of the drink from the tavern. His eyes studied me from across the cabin. A sudden devilish smile spread across his face, sending flutters through my abdomen.

"You find me amusing, Captain?"

"Oh, I find you much more than amusing." He downed the remainder of the drink in his glass and poured himself another, "But, I was thinking of our first encounter. The masterful way you retrieved your precious necklace from me."

"What of it?" I pushed, eager to see where his thoughts were headed.

"Was it a fluke, or are you as skilled as I remember?" Felix slid off the desk and came around behind my chair, purring his challenge in my ear. "Shall we test your skill?"

"My dear Captain, you have seen nothing of my skill." I grinned back at him over my shoulder. I had this, even in my drunken state. My throwing skills were never something I questioned, they were the one thing I knew I was good at.

I stood and walked over to the desk. A large red apple in the fruit bowl on the desk called to me. I plucked it from the bowl, admiring it. The fruit made a perfect target. Felix came up right behind me. He snatched the sweet, crisp fruit from my hand and took a large bite out of it. The satisfaction he wore emphasized his playful, and contagious, mood.

I turned, reached into his belt, and pulled out the short dagger he kept there. Felix choked out a playful grunting remark. With my free hand, I stole back the apple and pierced the ruby skin with the dagger, cutting out a wedge of the fruit.

I held the apple slice out. "Here, you can hold my target," I challenged. "Or are you scared?"

In response, he snatched the apple wedge from between my fingers and marched across the cabin. When he turned back to face me, I saw he had stuck the apple wedge so it protruded from his mouth. Felix arched his brow and turned to the side. Challenge accepted.

I hadn't meant for him to stick the wedge in his teeth. I assumed he would just hold it a safe distance from his body. Felix felt bold. No matter. Either way, I knew I could impress him.

I finished the bochet in my own glass. Breathing deep, I steadied myself, aimed, and let the small dagger fly from my hand. Time slowed as the dagger turned end over end through the air, hurtling towards the tiny target. For a brief moment nerves that my drunken state may have made this a terrible idea, took over. I could've missed, or I could've hit Felix. Why did this man constantly make me question myself?

A gasp of relief escaped my lungs when the dagger made contact, making a neat slice through the top half inch of the apple wedge and nestling itself between two panels on the back wall.

Felix removed the apple wedge from his mouth. Despite being impressed, he wanted more. "Ah, Sweet, you can do better than that," he smiled slyly as he removed the dagger from the wall. He handed it back to me before repositioning himself and the apple slice.

He wanted better, I planned to give him better. I took a small step to the right, preparing to throw the dagger again. The dagger flew from my hand for the second time. This time the dagger whispered across Felix's face, missing his lips and nose with little room to spare. The apple slice had been whittled down to next to nothing.

The captain chomped down on the apple bit in his mouth, a huge smile spreading across his face. Rushing me, he scooped me up into his arms and spun us about until we were both dizzy. We toppled into the cushioned chair near the fireplace, laughing.

Felix repositioned me so that I sat on his lap. "Amazing, Sweet. That was absolutely fantastic; surely they don't teach that in Quaintrelle training."

I smirked, "No, knife work is not Quaintrelle taught. Although, I did convince the Matron to provide the girls in some defense training just so I could practice with my daggers." I paused for a moment, "Many men did marvel at my skill, as a parlor trick, but I'm sure they would have shrunk impotently if they saw what I could really do. None were as brave as you."

"Not I. I find your skill rather impressive. The joy and light brings you only adds to your allure. It's quite sexy."

I poked at his chest playfully, "Indeed you must, to remember that I had such skill at all. It has been a long while since you last seen it."

"Oh, Sweet, your skill is not the only thing that left me impressed, you are indelible. An intoxicating creature." Felix ran his heated gaze over my body. The look sent mass shivers through my entire being. "I did so obsess over our brief encounter. I was absolutely gorgonized when I first saw you at the ball. I imagine most men are. My crew was driven insane by the distracted state you had caused me to be in. I must admit, I'm quite disappointed I didn't think to kidnap you in that very moment." He offered a toothsome grin.

"Oh?"

"Oh, yes. Imagine the scandal. Captain Wade absconds with King Talbot's bride to be. That, Sweet, would have been the bounty of a lifetime."

"I have to disagree. The scandal would have been much less. I hadn't become betrothed to King Talbot until after we met."

"No. There would definitely have been scandal worth noting. You were a prized Quaintrelle." Felix paused, "Speaking of scandal, I learned of your scandalous reputations."

"Scandalous reputations? Oh, my dear Captain, you must have learned of the wrong Quaintrelle. My reputation is entirely pure." I fluttered my eyelashes and offense at the insinuation.

"That there is the scandal! The virginal Quaintrelle! Please tell me it isn't true, for such news would be so shocking I may cease to breathe. My soul would be crushed, my hopes dashed." He grasped at his chest dramatically.

"That is an inane rumor. One cannot be a Quaintrelle without bedding men. In truth, though, I bed far fewer than a Quaintrelle usually does. Let's say I was choosy and satisfied my clients in other ways."

"And yet you were the most sought after Quaintrelle." Felix touched the tip of my nose in a playful gesture. "Or so I hear."

"That, Captain, is partially true. My sisters were just as popular as I," I retorted, refusing to believe any of my coterie were better than the rest.

"From what I hear, I doubt that. So tell me, how did you do it then?" he asked.

"That is my one true secret, one I haven't ever fully revealed to anyone before."

"Which is?"

Perhaps the bochet had emboldened me, or maybe I felt I could trust him more than I did Anwen. He knew I was Apoidean. He was good to my people. Yes, I could trust him with this one thing. "I'm one of the Fae blessed Apoideans. I can feel what others feel. An empath."

My words peaked his curiosity, "How exactly does that play into your previous station?"

I leaned in towards him and caressed his face. I lowered my voice into a seductive purr befitting of secret-spilling, keeping my lips inches from his, "I feel out a man's deepest desires, his truest needs, and fulfill them. Those needs, aren't always as physical or short termed as sex. Even if they don't know it." I pulled back, examining his face; he was rapt with anticipation. I dropped my hands from his face and placed one over his heart. "I offered those who sought me out much more than that; I offered an ear or a shoulder more often than not. Satisfying their emotional needs leaves them just as, if not more, fulfilled than intimacy does. Most are just as surprised as you look right now."

Felix shook his head, breaking some unspoken spell. "Oh but you are wicked, Sweet. Which leaves me to believe your other reputation is quite true. Enchantress. You are, oh, so enchanting. Illecebrous even. You get under the skin of those around you, becoming all they can think of. People want to be near you."

His words filled my head with images of my father, and how much the people loved him. "My father was like that, it is a part of our gift. He and I shared the same gift." The thought had me wistful."I miss him so."

"How did you lose him?" Felix asked.

"He died when I was very little, saving some kids in a flash flood. Him and my mother." Felix rubbed my arm soothingly and I wiped away the stray tear on my cheek. "What of you, Captain? Do you come from a long line of fearsome pirates?"

"Far from it, I imagine. I don't know who my parents are, or were. I am an orphan, born and raised in a convent. A convent very near to Realta in fact, in the Eira Mountains. Set for a life devoted to God, as many orphans in convents are. When I was ten, I encountered the moment that changed my life, led it to be one of adventure. It was as if God himself was telling me something."

"What? A convent? Did a band of pirates pillage the convent?"

He chuckled. "No, Sweet, something far more intoxicating than that, I accidentally stumbled upon a novitiate bathing. She was vision-ary, like a saint depicted complete with aureole. The sight of her naked bosom sang to me, I felt awash with apricity, as though I had been warmed from a lifetime of coldness. My loins stirred for the first time, and it became clear to me that I wasn't to be a man of God; not after that. I tried my best to set it from my young mind. After weeks of being tormented by the memory, I was finished with torturing myself. With my apostasy complete, I ran away, living as a beggar and sheep-bite for a bit until I came across a band of pirates. I joined up as a cabin boy and made my way up through the ranks as the years passed. And now, here I am." He smiled. "I thought I'd never get over that woman's beauty." Felix's voice grew low and husky, "until that fateful night I made the mistake of lifting a tinny old locket off of a palace Quaintrelle." His lips grazed along my neck in a tortuous fashion.

The breathy teasing caused my body to respond without thought.

"Tell me, Sweet, do you know what it's like to long for someone so unattainable? Someone that belongs to another, someone what has made you feel something you haven't in over 20 years time, but you can't help yourself. You find yourself with this perfect creature, somehow, and all you can do is have a small taste, have stolen moments?" Felix's eyes grew heavy with desire as he stroked my skin with the lightest of touches.

My heart screamed at my head, telling me to let go. Could I chance to tell Felix what selcouth feelings he caused? "Felix, I," I hesitated and lowered my gaze. I looked back at him through heavy lashes as I finished what I longed to say. "Being a Quaintrelle, true feelings of desire were always been lost on me. No man ever made me feel more than obligation to duty. But you, you've damaged me. Every interaction, every touch and every kiss we've shared since we first met at the ball, has me swimming in an unknown sea. I've tried to push them away, but can't. Though I'm set to be wed, I find myself thinking only of you; thinking of you in ways I've never thought of any man before." My cheeks flushed with my indecent thoughts.

"Merinley," Felix said my name in a feral growl of a whisper. His hungry lips smashed against mine and his hands tangled in my hair. My admission to what I felt gave him the permission he sought to make me his, if only for a short time. In one swift motion he lifted us from the chair onto the waiting bed.

I WOKE to the gentle rolling of the ship on the water. The night's activities lingered fresh in my mind. I felt like I was glowing and as though I could vibrate through my skin. I hadn't been this happy in a long time. I stretched my arms out towards where Felix had been sleeping next to me, finding him gone. He must have had risen earlier; a captain has many responsibilities.

I rolled over and snuggled deeper into the bedding. I didn't want to leave my dreams behind. I played the night over and over in my head and could still feel Captain Wade's kisses. The phantom memory of his gentle, fiery touch still scorched my skin. The way our bodies intertwined like they belonged together. The memories ignited my desire to see him, to touch him, once again. My desires were all the motivation I needed to force myself to open my eyes.

As I rubbed the last remnants of sleep from my eyes, I spied Felix sitting at his large desk across the room, his profile to me. He sat hunched over, intent on whatever he worked on. He paused and grabbed an apple from the bowl on his desk. His whole face lit with a smile as he examined the apple before taking a bite. Without doubt, he was reliving the night before in his mind too.

I studied him in silence. I loved the seriousness of his features; his long straight nose, his high cheekbones, and deep, focused eyes. I loved how the simple addition of a smile upon his strong mouth would change everything about his face, taking it from serious and strong to light and playful. His feelings were not well hidden, they were like an open book.

A glow spread through me, reminding me of feelings long forgotten. Warm and caring feelings that made me think of home. In that moment, I realized that I'd already lost my heart to this man. There was no turning back.

An adoring laugh escaped me as I continued to watch his admiration of the apple. Felix's attention zipped from the apple to me. His smile grew ten-fold as our eyes met. "Morning, Sweet. I trust you had a restful sleep?"

I nodded as I sat up, clutching the bedding to my chest in an attempt to remain covered.

Felix lounged back in his chair, "Why so shy? I would think it clear that I'm intimately familiar with each and every inch of your exquisite body. If you think otherwise, I would gladly look again."

I rose from the bed, still hugging the blankets around me, and made my way over to Felix. I sat on his lap in a coy manner, I felt his struggle to remain collected. I loosened my hold on the blanket around me. A sliver more of my bare skin revealed itself and Felix sighed. Wrapping an arm around me, he pulled me a hairs breadth away from him. His other hand wound into the folds of the blanket and caressed the small of my back. My body shivered in delight at the gentle caress of his calloused fingers.

Our kiss began tenderly, intensifying into a burning passionate kiss. My grip on the blanket around me loosened more. We couldn't get enough of one another.

A brusque knock sounded at the cabin door seconds before it swung open. The interruption broke the spell we had woven ourselves into. I drew the blankets tightly around myself in haste. Our heads whipped around.

Hawthorne.

"This had better be extremely important, Hawthorne," Felix groaned, "else you find yourself adorning the ship's bow."

Hawthorne, flustered, maffled before finding his words. "Mister Bimble has requested your presence on deck, Captain."

A heavy sigh escaped Felix's lips just before he planted another quick kiss on mine. "Later, Sweet. I have things that need attending to." He gently guided me off of his lap as we both stood. He gave me one last longing look before joining Hawthorne at the door.

Felix turned back, "Before I forget, Esme sent a package back to the ship with Smith early this morning." He pointed over to where the package could be found and gave me a wink. As the pair left, I saw Felix smack the back of Hawthorne's head. The poor fool wasn't going to have a good day. Mister Bimble likely shared his fate.

I decided to dress, somewhat, before opening the package Esme sent for me. I threw on my rumpled tunic from the day before and made myself comfortable in the inglenook. The soft and bulky package had a good weight to it. Esme must've thought I needed quite a few things. I pulled open the packthread and opened the muslin wrapping. The contents delighted me.

Esme had gifted me three simple day dresses, a long woolen cloak, and a few small containers of lotions and soaps. I cracked open a container of soap, the clean lavender smell washed over me. It reminded me of my mother; of helping her make the same soap when I was small.

A gentle rapping at the cabin door interrupted my reverie. "I hope yer decent, Cap' says I got to feed ya," Cook quipped as he opened the door to the cabin before I could open it myself. He carried a wooden pitcher of water and a plate piled with bread and fish. He placed the meal on the desk, looked about the room, and grinned. "I see why ya and Cap' disappeared last night." My eyes swept about and saw all the evidence from last night. No wonder he smiled so broadly. Nothing advertised sex like empty bottles, a crumpled bed, and clothes strewn about.

Cook scowled. "Hey now, that's not for you."

I was taken aback by his words and stared at him bewildered. "I…"

"Oh, not you Miss. Clara." He pointed a long bony finger towards the plate he sat on the desk. I turned to see what he pointed at. An ix sat on the corner of the desk, holding a chunk of bread in its paws. It laid its large round ears flat and took another defiant bite from the starchy treat she stole. Sassy little thing.

"You have an ix! I thought I had spied a red tail over your shoulder the other day, but convinced myself I had only imagined it."

"Clara's more like a demon. Little bugger always causin' trouble," he remarked.

"She is an ix. Notoriously mischievous, and prone to moodiness," I stated. I was more than familiar with the native Apoidean creature known for its masked face, russet fur, and tendency to vanish in thin air.

"Jus' like a woman. Bah. I know. Had her for near forty years now."

The little food thief jumped onto my shoulder and made a short chuffing sound while nuzzling up to my cheek.

"She's a traitor too," Cook grumbled and stuck his tongue out at his pet, who mimicked his action. "Come on ya little beast, I got food for ya in the galley."

On cue, Clara leapt from my shoulder into Cook's arms and snuggled into them like she hadn't been angry with him m moments before. He cooed at her and scolded her all at the same time. I laughed. I would never have guessed that rough and gruff Cook had a soft spot.

After my meal, I took it upon myself to tidy up the cabin while I continued to wait for Felix to return. I gathered our clothes that had been tossed around the room in haste and placed them in a neat pile in a corner of the room. The dagger from my display of talent still stuck out of the wall. I removed it and placed it on the desk next to my empty dishes. I also picked up and arranged the empty bochet bottles on the desk.

Having finished the light cleaning of the cabin, I found myself getting restless. I wasn't confined to the cabin, but I still felt uncertain of moving about the ship without purpose. Being underfoot was the last thing I wanted. Despite my hesitation, I decided to return the bottles and dishes to Cook. The task would give me reason to roam.

I changed into one of the dresses that Esme had sent to me; a pale gray, cap-sleeved dress that was a little snug but would be much better to venture out of the cabin in than just a tunic or the clothes I had worn the day before. I fashioned a bundle out of the muslin from the package Esme sent me, wrapping the dishes and bottles in it to make carrying them easier.

Satisfied I had everything secure in the bundle, I set off to the galley.

Cook worked alone in the galley, cleaning up and prepping some of the goods acquired at the tavern last night. He looked up from his task when I cleared my throat. "I brought back the dishes you dropped off earlier." As if my voice summoned her, Clara popped into her visible form and scampered over to me.

"Nice ta see ya are not a pampered plaything, like some Quaintrelles can be." His remark, which held a note of truth, left me wondering how he knew that, and what other little-known facts he knew.

"It's no problem, Cook. I've always been one to tend to my own needs rather than rely heavily on others. Being a Quaintrelle wasn't always in my cards. I worked in the kitchens at Bua Tur for a short time."

"Did ya now?" He arched his left eyebrow, intrigued by my confession.

I nodded and handed the muslin bundle over to him. "You seem to be quite busy here. Could you use some help?"

"If yer willing, I'd be more than happy ta have an extra hand." Cook straightened his back, which creaked with age, and looked around. "Ya think ya can carry some of those bottles of bochet below to the store room?"

"I certainly can." I headed over to the bottles he mentioned with Clara on my heels. I gathered them up and made my way towards the store room opening. The little ix followed me about, and I almost stumbled because of her circling me.

"Clara!" Cook snapped without looking up from the task he had set himself on. "Ya leave the lady alone. Last thing I need is her tripping and hurting herself. Felix would have ya skin."

Clara scampered off and turned invisible.

I continued my way down into the store room to put away the bottles. The store turned out to be spacious, which I expected since The Fura had once been part of the Realta fleet. Cook kept it well organized. I could easily to tell where the bottles were meant to be placed.

I heard someone enter the galley as I worked.

"What ya got left this morning Cook?"

"Nigel. Yer late, and out o' luck. Maybe ya should get yer lazy ass up when the rest o' us do," Cook scolded.

"Could not be helped. Found me an excellent little tart to warm up with last night. Only got back moments before anchor was lifted. Are you sure there is nothing for me to eat?"

Cook grumbled something unintelligible under his breath and began to scrape around.

I finished my task and started up the ladder for more bottles.

"Speaking of excellent little tarts," Nigel quipped with what sounded like a mouth full of food. "Cap's got himself a fit bit of cunny."

I froze half way up the ladder when I heard the way Nigel referred to me.

"Shut yer hole, ya buffoon," Cook warned.

"What? That's all she is really, a glorified whore that we happened to stumble upon. Maybe now that Cap's had her we can ditch her somewhere, women have no place on The Fura." Nigel's statement turned my stomach and chilled my blood.

A loud thud and a clattering of dishes sounded above me. "I said, shut yer hole. I will not abide ya speaking about a nice lady that way. Cap's guest is no whore. If he wants her on this ship, that is where she belongs. If he were ta hear ya speak that way he would do more than throw ya over a table and point forks at ya. Now get out before I put yer eye out with one."

Nigel huffed out loud and stomped out of the galley. His words hurt. A few tears spilled down my cheeks as I finished going up the ladder.

Cook took one look at me and his face fell. "I am sorry ya had ta hear that. Forget Nigel. He is nothin' more than a flea bitten mongrel."

I nodded and wiped the remaining tears away. My thick Quaintrelle skin had thinned considerably since joining Felix and his men. Since giving in to the feelings I didn't understand and fought so hard against.

"Good. Now back ta work."

CHAPTER NINETEEN

The Fura made port in Icharo five days later. On first sight, the tiny island kingdom seemed fascinating. Small vessels teeming with laboring men dotted the outskirts; the men on them either casting their nets or unloading their hauls.

I had some knowledge of Icharo, thanks to my political lessons as a Quaintrelle. Those lessons, though, seemed to not do the actual place justice in my mind's eye. Icharo was a unique island, having no shallow water surrounding it; its shorelines were sheer drop-offs into the depths of the sea. Due to the size of the island, small enough to cross on foot in less than an hour, a majority of the villages were on floating docks connected to the main island by a maze of planked walkways. The single port, for larger visiting vessels, was tucked away in a cove created by the vast network of floating sections of the independent kingdom. To see it in person was incredible.

Icharo's precarious and unique geography was the reason it was such a prosperous nation, despite its size. The deep seas surrounding it provided an abundance of sea life, making it a major trading hub for the region. Realta had tried and failed at acquiring Icharo. Valuing their independence, they rejected the deal. But, their significant contribution to many kingdoms in the region had protected them from the fate

Apoidea suffered when they stood up to Realta's bullying. This made them blessed, in my opinion.

I could hardly wait to explore Icharo for myself.

"You excited?" Hawthorne asked in jest when he saw me bouncing in anticipation while I waited for Felix.

"Yes. I have never been to a land outside of Realta's rule," I replied.

"Yeah, I get you. I was the same when I first started out." It was easy to feel Hawthorne's own love for the place.

Nigel came up to us and scoffed, rolling his eyes.

"What?" Hawthorne challenged.

"Nothing," he scoffed once more walking away. I knew Nigel did not care for me, he avoided me at all costs. Cook's threats surely had something to do with it.

"Ignore Nigel, Merinley. We all do, he is an ass," Hawthorne excused.

"I already figured that out."

"Well, Cap wanted me to escort you off the ship today, take you to meet him on Icharo. He had to head out early," Hawthorne explained.

Cook joined our little circle, carrying a crate of bochet.

"I see you do not keep all the bochet from Apoidea. Smart," I commented.

"Bah, smart has nothin' ta do with it. Bochet is our most valuable supply. But, being a former Quaintrelle ya knew that."

"Being an Apoidean, I knew that," I retorted, having become more comfortable with sharing my heritage. Felix's crew were is family, that meant I could rust them as much as him. Hawthorne and Cook exchange surprised glances. "Yes, I know. Shocking. Bochet is the only reason my people are still bound to Realta." The extra sweet and extremely potent honey wine was highly valued across the kingdoms because Realta's monarchy hoarded it for themselves. Trading it was considered illegal almost everywhere. It seemed Felix was mad enough to defy that law. With the bochet, they could get mountains of fresh supplies for their stores.

"Well, then," Hawthorne beamed, "Merinley, secret Apoidean, shall we get a move on?" He offered me an elbow.

"I am more than ready." We headed down the gangplank with Cook on our heels.

FELIX WAITED at the edge of the market. He smiled when he saw me approaching but it was faded, not as bright as his usual smile. He was irate, disappointed. Something was wrong.

"What is it, Felix?" I asked.

"You need to get back to The Fura," Felix explained through a clenched jaw.

"What? Why?" I looked past Felix, trying to determine what would make him give me that order. It only took moments for me to see why. I was stunned to see the market was crawling with Realta soldiers. There was no ship in the port flying Realta's colors. The soldiers had been left there for a reason.

My heart sunk. I'd been looking forward to exploring a new place.

"It's not safe for you," Felix's voice dripped with concern.

I understood what he really meant. It wasn't safe for me at the market with him. It wasn't safe for the crew at the market with me. Separately we weren't in any danger from the soldiers. With Icharo being a haven port, they couldn't touch him without probable cause. If I was seen with him, he would lose me and his freedom.

"Hawthorne, take her back to the ship then meet me back here," Felix ordered. "We'll finish up our business and move on as quickly as possible. Spread the word to others on their way here that we must use extreme discretion while trading today."

"Yes, Captain."

RELAXING WAS IMPOSSIBLE, my mind went to a thousand places the longer Felix and the crew were on shore. Nothing helped to calm me. I practically wore the floor of the cabin out with my pacing. As the day wore on, I ventured out of the cabin, desperate for any sort of company; any sort of news.

I wandered in an aimless manner, eventually finding myself at the galley once more. My subconscious must have led me to the one other place I'd grown comfortable in onboard.

Pushing the door in, I stuck my head in to see if Cook had returned. The bushels of fresh produce and seafood sitting on the central table only meant that someone had placed them there. Maybe Cook, maybe not. Either way, making myself useful seemed like a good way to pass the time. I popped down to the store room to gather supplies.

"Ah, thought that was ya down there," Cook greeted when I emerged from storage.

"Sorry, I saw the supplies piling up and thought I'd help."

"Yer no bother, yer good here. 'Bout the only one I trust ta work with no instruction." Cook's vote of confidence in me felt good. I hadn't been with these men that long at all, so it meant a lot.

We worked in silence, Cooked preferred it that way. Even without words, we worked instinctively; moving around one another in what could almost be described as a graceful dance. But, I couldn't work silently for too long. My mind was dying to know how things were on Icharo.

"How was it? The market." I dared to break the silence.

"That damned brat Talbot's got his fingers in the market. Not sure how that ninny managed it, but he somehow has a strong presence on Icharo now. Market gossip says he's been up to all sorts o' nasty in Realta. The people are suffering for it. Most likely has somethin' ta do with ya going missing, but if ya ask me I think he's using it as an excuse to get his way, a learned thing from his grandpa no doubt. It certainly made trade a lot harder than it had ta be."

Cook's words hit me hard. People were suffering because of me. I couldn't sail free with Felix and his crew knowing I could fix it. I knew what I had to do. I had to return to Realta, make this better, even though I desperately didn't want to.

Nausea swelled within me. I excused myself, not feeling like I could work anymore.

"Now I know ya be thinkin' of goin' back," Cook's words stopped me in my tracks. "Ya think that it'll fix the king's tirade. That decision is on ya and is not my place ta stop ya. I understand how ya feel that way. But know this, Miss, I been around a long time and know somethin' about monarchs. A lot 'o time, there's no fixin' them.

"I have ta look out for mine. With ya, well, Felix is better with ya. You've given that boy more happiness than he's had in a long time. I know he'll fight to keep ya safe. And losin' ya might just end him."

"You really care for Captain Wade," I assessed aloud.

"Aye, I care for the boy. I've known him longer than he has been Captain of this ship; since he was a lad. He is brash and bold headed, just like… Well, let's just say he's like a son to me."

Cook fell silent after that; my cue to take my leave. He'd given much to think about. I had decisions to make. Decisions that needed be made before Felix returned from shore.

CHAPTER TWENTY

I sat at Felix's desk weighing my options: return to King Talbot and hope he'll calm down, or live a life on the run with Felix, letting others suffer for my freedom. The choice I wanted to make was clear, I wanted to stay with Felix. He made me happy. I didn't have to worry about propriety. There was no duty to be bound to. I didn't have to worry about angering him. I could just be me.

But ,was it the right choice to stay? Something within me begged that I gave more attention to returning to King Talbot. I couldn't shake the feeling that I was overlooking something important.

The stress gave me a headache so severe that I couldn't focus. I needed to step away from the matter and rest. I hoped a nap would clear my head and help me find the answers I needed.

I DREAMT OF MY MOTHER, which I hadn't done in years. She walked with me along a dark wooded path, much like the ones we walked together on Apoidea before her death. She carried with her two objects: a bottle of bochet and a set of shackles. I thought it odd for her to be carrying them.

We came to a hedge wall with a narrow passage in the middle. Mother entered, I hesitated.

"Do not fear, my love. I'll be with you every step of the way, as I've always been," she said.

I followed her into the passageway. Each step taking us further from the light, until the passage was in complete darkness. Long minutes ticked away in the dark until the passage abruptly ended against a cold door.

The door opened, revealing a dimly lit room. My mother stepped through, turning to smoke the second the light touched her.

"No! Come back, please." Despair bubbled through me, it felt like I had lost her all over again.

"I've not gone anywhere. I promise I'm with you, every step of the way." Her disembodied voice filled the room.

I stepped through the door, trepidation in my heart. I almost expected to disappear as well. For a moment, I thought I had.

The dim light brightened and faded again, revealing Felix's desk in the center of the room. On the desk were the shackles and the bottle of bochet.

Mother's voice filled the room once more, "Look at the objects, Merinley. What are they?"

"Shackles and a bottle of bochet."

"No, dear. Things are often more than they seem. Look closer."

Curious, I stepped up to the desk and looked at the objects closely. There seemed to be nothing special about them.

I picked the shackles up. Their cold weight filled me with despair. I heard voices, they were muffled but grew clearer the longer I tried to listen.

"*You will give me an heir,*" King Talbot's voice rang clear through the room. "*I would think you would not hesitate to enter a man's bed.*" My stomach churned, I knew this conversation.

On cue, Anwen's sweet voice entered the room. "*Merinley simply means she wants to put her past behind her...*"

The more I listened, the heavier the shackles became. It didn't take long for them to become heavier than I could bear and I dropped them on the desk. They landed with a deafening thud that seemed to shake the room.

I picked up the bottle next. The bottle felt light and warm in my hands, the polar opposite of the shackles. I waited for the voices to begin, as they had with the shackles, but there was nothing. I shook the bottle, expecting it to trigger something. Shaking the bottle didn't give me the voices, nor did I hear the sloshing of liquid. Instead, a faint tinkling sound filled the air. There was something other than liquid in the bottle.

I pulled on the cork, but it wouldn't move. I had to work for this one. I pulled with all my might for minutes before the cork even budged. Finally, the cork was freed.

"Do you come from a long line of fearsome pirates?" My voice burst from the bottle.

"Far from it, I imagine." Felix's voice swept through me, filling me with warmth. I listened, rapt, once again to his tale of being born and raised in the convent in the Eira Mountains. I became so invested that I forgot about the tinny sound I was investigating by opening the bottle, until Felix ended his tale and a light streamed out of the bottle.

I peered inside and saw a glowing ring sitting at the bottom. Suddenly, the ring began to grow. I could hear it scratch the sides of the bottle. Soon after, the bottle began to vibrate.

I dropped the bottle just before it shattered, letting loose a blinding light.

The light slowly faded, seeped into the spot here I dropped the bottle. When the light fully subsided, a silver crown sat in the middle of a broken pile of glass.

"Do you understand, Merinley?" My mother's voice returned, seeking to give me guidance.

I looked back at the desk, my gaze switching back and forth between the shackles and the crown. After a minute of this, I knew what it meant. The air seemed to be sucked from the little room, the lights dimmed. I couldn't breathe. My vision blurred. Everything went dark as I passed out.

. . .

AIR FILLED my lungs as strong hands shook my shoulders. I opened my eyes.

Felix hovered over me, his face etched with concern. He pulled me up into a tight embrace. "You had me worried. I couldn't wake you and then you stopped breathing," He pulled back and stared into my eyes, "I thought I was losing you."

"No. No, I just had a very bad dream. I could never leave you," I knew the words were a lie as soon as I said them. I had to leave, if just for a short time. Yet, I also knew I wouldn't be leaving him forever. I couldn't do that. True happiness had found me, and I wasn't about to lose that forever.

The revelation in my dream was clear. With King Talbot, I would never be free.

Had that been the only revelation, my next move would've been easy. I'd stay with Felix. But there had been one more revelation that could not be ignored.

Felix was Prince Declan's first-born son.

That part should have been clear to me, even without Mother's help. He revealed he'd been born and raised in the convent in the Eira Mountains. He spoke of Saint Ludo, the convent where Prince Declan's bride was hidden from him. I wasn't sure why I didn't piece that together sooner. I could only blame myself for being too distracted by my growing feelings.

It was clear to me that I had to return to Realta. There was no question about it. While Anwen knew about the lost heir, no one, besides myself, knew Felix to be that rightful heir to the crown of Realta.

What made it harder, I couldn't tell Felix any of this, my plan had to remain secret. That killed me. I couldn't tell him he should be king until the right time came. I had to leave him in the dark, for now, to protect him.

I doubted he would even believe me.

TWO DAYS PASSED. I hadn't been able to bring myself to tell Felix my intention to leave. I delayed, for two reasons: I didn't want to leave, and the news would not be welcome. I feared what would come of it. Felix would be hurt. The crew would hate me for it. Cook might kill me.

Yet, with every passing day the need to return to Realta grew. So did the guilt. With the guilt eating away at me, I felt worse and worse as the hours passed. I needed to tell him. With a heavy heart, I set out to locate him.

I found Felix at the helm of the ship. He stood, cross-armed, calling out orders to his men. His brilliant blue eyes squinted against the morning sun. The way he commanded was cool and calm. It was beautiful to behold.

When he noticed me his face lit with a signature, goofy smile. He handed the control of the ship over to Mister Bimble and rushed across the deck. He swept me into his embrace the moment we reached each other.

"Could I speak to you in private?"

"Of course." Felix motioned to Mister Bimble, signaling his departure. Taking my hand in his, Felix rushed us off to his cabin.

"Felix, I have something I need from you." I started the second the cabin door closed behind us.

Desire glinted in his eyes and he nuzzled into my neck, "I will give you anything, Sweet, all you need is to ask."

"Not that. I need you to do something important for me." I kept my voice somber and low. The decision to leave had me wary; I expected Felix to become ill-tempered when I told him. If it were him asking this of me, I would be furious.

My resolve quaked with our closeness; I had to put some distance between us for me to get through this. I removed myself from his strong arms and sat on the bed. The playfulness in his smile disappeared. He realized I was being serious.

"I..." my voice faltered; tears began sliding down my cheeks.

"Whatever it is, Sweet, you can ask." Felix sat next to me and took my hands in his.

"I need you to take me back to King Talbot." The words pierced me as I said them. They pierced him as well.

His face fell. Anger began to grow beyond the concern. "No. I will not do it, Sweet. Taking you back to that man is not a good idea. I thought you wanted to be here, with me."

"I do, Felix. There is nothing I want more than to stay with you."

"But…" Felix prodded.

"But, I cannot rest easy knowing that there are people suffering because of my absence, or that my presence on this ship risks your safety. With me here, you and your men are in more danger than you would be without me. What if the wrong person sees me with you?"

"We can handle ourselves against anything that fool can throw at us."

I shook my head, "I need to go back to Bua Tur, just for a short time. I have the means to end this misfortune. The means to free myself from the threat of his grasp."

Felix stood and crossed the cabin, coming to a stop by the fireplace. "No. I refuse. In time, King Talbot will calm, he will think you are dead. He will move on. We will have our freedom."

"That could take years, Felix. All I need is a month, maybe two. Please trust me. In my heart I know it's a bad decision to return, but I have to. I'm needed there. Nothing you can say to convince me otherwise."

"You are needed here," he argued.

"I need to think of more than our feelings, Felix. We are not the only one's affected by this."

"If you…" he ran his fingers through his hair in frustration, losing his words. "Fine. We set course for Realta." Felix turned and walked away. He stopped a few feet away and looked back. My heart shattered at the dejection coming from him. His mouth opened as if to say something else, but he decided against it and stormed out of the cabin. The door slammed behind him.

What had I done?

CHAPTER TWENTY-ONE

elix avoided me for days after I asked to return to Realta. He took his meals in the galley and slept with the crew. My time was spent holed away in his cabin, alone with my misery. My heart ached from the pain I caused him, and it broke in the resulting silence.

This stalemate threatened my mission. I needed Felix to have faith in me, to trust me. He was an integral part of why I had to return. If our bond remained broken when we reached Realta, the mission would fail. Time was running out. In less than a day The Fura would reach the far shores of Realta. I needed to do everything in my power to get in Felix's good graces again.

The ship sailed on, eerily quiet as I hastened on silent feet towards the galley. Cook's territory had been Felix's sanctuary since our fight. He would be there. The skeleton night crew remained above deck before sun-up, leaving no chance of an awkward encounter of any of them. I only had to worry about Felix and Cook. I didn't know which one I worried about encountering more. I tiptoed in, praying I kept the element of surprise on my side.

Felix sat slumped over the table with his back towards me. His dark long hair disheveled rather than in his usual elaborate braid, a bottle of bochet in his outstretched hand. A stormy sadness swirled in him. He was broken.

Tears sprung into my eyes. Feeling his anguish with such acuity added to the guilt and pain I felt myself. I hurt him more than I realized possible. I wiped the tears away and dug into the resolve of my mission. Tears could wait until I knew whether or not I could change his mind. Whether or not I'd lost him completely.

Clattering and exasperated curses rose from the storage beneath the galley. The unmistakable noises of Cook gathering supplies. Relief filled me that he busied himself below. I feared his underlying anger being directed at my head. He loved Felix like a son, and protected him fiercely.

I hesitated. The thought of making myself known sent waves of nausea rolling in my belly. I worried Felix wouldn't stay and listen to what I needed to say. He held the cards. I had to employ every Quaintrelle trick and ounce of stubbornness in me to force him to listen.

My hesitation lasted too long. Before I even had the chance to approach Felix, Cook emerged from storage, Clara by his side, as she always was. He startled at my unexpected presence, but not enough that it alerted Felix. He glared at me with his face twisted sourly, and pointed a long bony finger at the door. He wanted me to leave. His disappointment was clear.

A lump formed in my throat, threatening to choke my determined spirit away. I shook my head. "Please," I mouthed. I needed him to let me talk to Felix.

Cook tipped his head back, rubbing his face with his hands. I was sure this was the end, that he would send me away. But when he righted his head, his face had softened. He came around the table and placed a hand on my shoulder. In a barely audible voice, he questioned, "Ya set to fix it?" Clara cocked her head at me as if she were asking the same thing.

I lifted my shoulders in an unsure gesture, "I want to try." My whisper came out laced with pauses in order to fight off breaking into tears.

Cook pursed his lips and nodded, patting my shoulder as he did. He gave one last sorrowful look at Felix and left me to my mission. Hopefully, Felix had it in him to give me a chance too.

I took a minute to compose myself before speaking. "Captain?"

He turned his head slightly and groaned, his weary face enhanced by scruffy, new facial hair. "Go away, Woman," his head slumped back towards the table.

"No, Felix. We need to discuss this." I fought to keep my voice from wavering.

"Like hell we do. You made your choice, now just leave me be. You'll be dropped back at your castle tomorrow and we will never see one another again. It's better that way." He took a large swig and stood somewhat straight. Felix stumbled a step forward, then back in an attempt to leave.

I closed the distance between us and held his shoulder, defying his attempt to shrug me off. "You know that isn't what I want, Felix! I want to be with you. What I'm doing scares me to no end, but it has to be done. No one else can, no one else knows what I know."

"And what is that, exactly?" He swayed then steadied himself.

"I can't tell you. Not now."

He turned around with a defiant air, scoffing as he did.

"Please, Felix. Do not shut me out," I begged.

"Then tell me why you are leaving me," he roared, slamming his fist on the table.

"No," my voice held steady despite my trembling body. He'd never hurt me, I knew that. His hurt drove his outbursts. It killed me to keep this secret from him, but it kept him safer than if he knew.

"Why not?" he growled.

"I need to stop Talbot first."

"Right." He moved to push past me. I pushed back.

"Felix, stop this. How many times do I have to say that I do not want to do this."

"Then change your mind, don't go," he half commanded, half plead.

"I have to." Somehow, my apology turned into a fight. I had to redirect. This was only making it worse. "Look, I hate that I've hurt you, I hate that I can't share why I'm going back. I want to, I really do. It's just not possible right now, but I will. I promise. When I come back to you. I will come back."

"How can you be so sure?"

I placed a hand on his cheek, which he reluctantly pressed into. "Because Bua Tur is not my home. You are."

Felix's stubborn aura cracked, hope glimmering beneath his surface. His anger warred with the tender feelings breaking through. He wanted us to return to how we were before my request as much as I did. But, he wasn't ready to give in.

"Could you just listen to me?" I asked in a firm tone.

"Go on then, Sweet. Make your case, though it's doubtful it will make any more sense than it did days ago." He stubbornly held on to his dwindling anger.

I took a deep breath, measuring my words carefully for the best chance at swaying Felix. I was confident that appealing to his pirate side would help my cause. "I know you're against my being reunited with King Talbot, I am quite against it myself. I can ensure that it will be worth your while to do so."

Felix raised a quizzical eyebrow. "Enlighten me." He crossed his arms over his chest and cocked his head to the side. He sat back on the stool and waited for me to explain.

"For one; there will be, without doubt, a sizable reward for whomever returns Talbot's intended untouched." Felix chuckled, his wry smile giving away his lewd thoughts on my choice of words. "Unharmed," I corrected with an exasperated, amused, sigh. "Second, I'd petition him for your pardon for all past crimes that he feels you've committed. You'd have the freedom of remaining in and near Realta for as long as you wish."

My proposal garnered some real interest from the headstrong Captain just then. "I'm not sure if that's a sweet enough deal to sway me into being more agreeable." His playful smile returned; he hinted he understood what I meant.

I was breaking his resolve.

I returned his smile, "I don't plan a lengthy return to Talbot's side.

As I said before, I'll need only a month or two tops. In this time, I believe that some good changes will happen for Realta. During that time, should you be pardoned, I don't see why we can't continue on as we are. Meeting discreetly. Right. Under. His. Nose." To add emphasis to my words, I sat on his lap. "Can you imagine it? It would be dangerous. It would be thrilling. King Talbot's betrothed and his enemy having a secret, torrid affair." I planted a delicate kiss on his neck, just behind his ear. His skin pimpled with a shiver of delight. "Do we have an accord, Captain Wade?"

His lips crushed against mine in desperation. All of the passion of the last few days cumulated into this moment and burst through us. The hurt, the anger, the wanting all meshed together; I couldn't tell where his feelings ended and mine began.

Felix stood, lifting me. I wrapped my legs tight around his waist as he moved us across the room, colliding with the galley door. Felix's heated lips moved along my jaw, down my neck, and across my collar. Each spot his lips touched blazed. His hands found their way into my skirts, squeezing and stroking my thighs.

Passion erupted in my veins. My hands responded to our growing desire as they traced down his front to the waist of his pants. I fumbled with the laces that contained him. My body needed his like bees needed flowers.

"Wait, Sweet." Felix pulled away and placed my feet back on the floor. "Not here. Cook wouldn't appreciate our sullying his workspace. One does not want to anger that man."

I wrapped my arms back around Felix's neck and kissed him again. "Cook is a pussy cat, I'm not afraid."

"I mean it. You don't know him the way I do. Besides, Cook's been known to put surprising ingredients in the food of those that anger him. You care to eat rat, Sweet?" I made a face at the thought of Cook's revenge. "I thought not." Felix scooped me up and threw me over his shoulder.

Using his free hand he pulled open the galley door, ready to make a break for his cabin. He faltered.

"What were you doing in my galley, Boy?" Cook quipped with

mild amusement, though his irritation was greater. The crew members gathered nearby, seeking their breakfasts, all wore sheepish grins. No doubt they heard the commotion we caused with our fervent reconciliation.

"Galley is all yours, Cook." Felix sidestepped the men before him. A fit of laughter erupted from me as I watched the men disappear from sight, all laughing save for Cook, who wore an irritated scowl while shaking his head.

WE LAY TANGLED in Felix's bed, reluctant to return to reality. In bed we had no worries, just the warmth of each other's bodies and the sound of our hearts combined. Beyond the borders of the mattress, lay a slew of problems that needed facing. Those problems were far too important to ignore, no matter how tempting it was. Our main concern focused on getting Felix into Realta without getting arrested, or blamed for my abduction.

"Brainstorming is difficult, Sweet, with you like this; doing that." Felix chided me, in jest, for running my fingers along his bare arm.

"Doing what?" Playing coy, I kissed along his jawline, intent on avoiding reality for a little longer.

He responded with a playful growl and flipped himself over me. "You know exactly what you do." Felix closed the space between us, planting kisses in a path from my ear to my lip. I delighted in my apparent victory, until he planted a final kiss on my forehead, got out of bed, and began dressing. I groaned in protest. "We have work to do, unless you've changed your mind?"

The loaded question tempted me; the last thing I wanted to do was to return to Realta or King Talbot. My heart ached a little at the thought of leaving the warmth of Felix's bed and trading it for my cold and lonely suite in the palace, but I knew that I had no choice if I wanted true freedom. Not only for myself; my return would be for the good of the kingdom.

"No," I replied with a reluctant pout. "Returning is for the best, for the time being." I followed Felix out of bed and dressed, too. Then, I joined Felix at the desk where he studied a map.

"We can't make port in Realta itself, we'll be arrested the moment we are seen. We need to pass it and port somewhere else, not in an actual port either. Not to mention we need to be covert entering the city."

"Out of curiosity, how had you planned to get me to Bua Tur, without being arrested, before we came to our agreement?" I asked.

"I had no plan. I wanted them to," Felix admitted.

The sting of guilt welled in my chest. I had no idea that he planned on being arrested. "They would have killed you. I wouldn't have been able to live with myself."

"Good thing you changed my mind then," he quipped.

"Felix..."

He pulled me into his arms to comfort me. "Sweet, you know as well as I do that you would've intervened. Found a way to spare my life. Probably the same way you plan to allow me to stay close to you while you take care of what you need to."

"But you were so mad at me."

"Yes, I was cross. Despite that, I had absolute faith in you."

I warmed at his words. I should have realized he had a plan all along. "You sly pirate."

"Did you expect anything less?" He beamed. "Now back to planning."

I peered over the map trying to think of anyplace that I knew of that allowed us to port and make the trek into Realta within a day. When my eyes passed over the Fenian Cliffs a chill came over me. I recalled the day Alec and Jim kidnapped me. They had backtracked to pass Realta and went through the farms near the cliffs and down to the cove at the bottom to travel along the shore in a dinghy for a day.

An idea formed in my head.

I pointed to Fenian Cliffs, "We can port here. There's a trail that goes from the beach below to the top. We could make for one of the farms there and borrow a wagon and maybe some sort of disguise. These outlying farms are no more than an hour or so from the city."

Felix nodded. "Yes, Fenian Cliffs! Why didn't I think of it? My predecessor told me of a hidden alcove, a large cave that a ship will fit in and not be seen from above or the coast. We could moor there without worry of being seen at all." He rubbed his chin in thought. "Looks like I need to have a talk with Cook."

"Cook?" I asked.

"Cook is my Captain, Sweet."

"Captain Cook? I don't recall hearing of him."

Felix laughed. "No you would not have heard of Captain Cook, that's not his name. We may call him Cook, for that is what he does now. Before he retired he was known as Redmayne."

My eyes grew wide. Captain Redmayne had been the fiercest and most notorious pirate for years and then he just disappeared. He spent his career making life hell for King Bern. Most figured he died. I'd never have pegged the wise old cook with a twinkle in his eye as the dangerous pirate. I wondered how the old man had gotten away with speaking to Felix so brashly, never referring to him as Captain, but as his name or "Boy".

After a moment or two of stunned silence, I finally responded, "Now I understand why you said it wouldn't be wise to upset him."

CHAPTER TWENTY-TWO

Cook easily led us to the hidden cavern at Fenian Cliffs. Had he not been there to point it out, no one would have found it. It truly had the definition of being hidden. The cavern lay nestled beyond an illusion making outcropping covered in thick cascading brush-like vines. Every member of the crew nervously watched the old man navigate The Fura directly toward what seemed like a cliff wall, eyes glinting with a keen cunning and little assurance coming from his lips. We all sighed in relief when the bow cut cleanly through the vines into the passage leading to the cavern.

Near complete darkness enveloped us. The crew quickly lit torches to guide the way in the low visibility. Only minutes passed before the ship entered the main cavern, surprisingly lit naturally by vents at the top of the cliff.

Cook called for anchor, bringing The Fura to a stop in the middle of a small lake underground. The ripples caused by our mooring lapped quietly on the thin beach lined with large rocks that lined the far side of the cavern. The roaring of a waterfall echoed in the distance, beyond sight.

Once anchored, an excited calm swept over The Fura. All were shocked at the ease Cook demonstrated navigating to this hidden place.

Much of the crew witnessed his captaining for the first time, seeing with their own eyes the tales they had been told of Captain Redmayne; a man so of the sea he could navigate any waters. Salt water ran in his veins instead of blood. Cook made no big deal of it, handing the reins directly back to Felix the moment the ship ceased rolling with the settling waves. He wasted no time jumping right back into the role and hammering out details of the mission, namely who would be embarking on it.

The selection of the men who would carry out our plan proved to be the hardest part of the journey. Every man on board clamored to volunteer, eager for a change. A change of scenery. A change of pace. Not to mention the chance to be welcomed into Realta and witness King Talbot essentially bow to a pirate.

Then there was the chance of action, on the chance things wouldn't turn in our favor. Every man onboard looked forward to a fight.

Felix picked Domhnall first, an easy choice. His relative newness to the crew made him least likely to be recognized as one of Felix's men. He got the role to act as head of our group when encountering others. Smith became the second obvious choice, being the medic. On the off chance there was a fight, he had the know how to patch up the injured. Hawthorne and Mister Bimble both volunteered, though only Hawthorne was selected. It was better for Mister Bimble to stay behind and run the ship. His size and reputation made him easily recognizable, too.

After that, the process of getting ready to depart the ship flew by. In the blink of an eye, the away party made its way through the passage in the waterfall, onto the beach at the bottom of the cliff, and began the ascent up to the top. I dreaded this climb almost as much as I did returning to Talbot. As I recalled, the trail teemed with treacherous terrain complete with spectral hands that had scratched at me the whole way down.

As we ascended, I realized my distress had warped my limited vision of the descent down to the beach where Jim and Alec had parked their small boat. They had thrown me unceremoniously into it and steered it to a coastal settling. There they'd stolen the wagon that took us to the inn. The memory sent chills down my spine.

We reached the top in good time, and stopped for a moment to change into the disguises Domhnall carried in his pack. I wore the heavy hooded cloak Esme gave me. The garment proved perfect for hiding my face so I wouldn't be recognized by anyone we might encounter. I aimed to remain hidden until it became necessary to reveal myself.

Felix and his men donned monk tunics he had stashed on board for less than honest purposes. He became an image of what his life might have been had he never left Saint Ludo's. Even in a holy man's robe he had a mysterious and cunning air. His devilish charm would have been torture to the poor nuns at the convent. The imagery stamped itself clearly in my mind, drawing an amused chuckle from me.

"Yes, Sweet?"

"I still can't believe that you had monk tunics stowed away," I covered.

He laughed. "We are pirates, Sweet. I think you forget we are less the honorable sometimes."

His words were true. While I'd been with them, I had witnessed many accounts of evidence to the side of them that helped the people Realta oppressed. That said, I also saw their fierceness in a fight; but I hadn't witnessed many acts that would paint them as anything less than good.

With our disguises complete, we set out on the next leg of our journey; finding a farm and acquiring a wagon. We walked for near an hour in open fields before spotting a small farm that fit our needs. A simple home with only two other buildings that were obviously a stable and wagon house. Flocks of sheep dotted the fenced in field next to the home. Bits of a garden peeked out between the wagon house and stable. This was a farm with multiple means of living. We were certain to find a wagon large enough for our needs.

Picking up his role as man in charge, Domhnall scouted the farm ahead of us; to see if we would encounter trouble. The men and I watched, lying low in the tall grass with bated breath, as he made his way down the sloping landscape towards the farm. Long minutes passed before we heard the call. A series of whistles, close to natural bird calls, drifted back to our ears, signaling that we were in the clear.

By the time we reached the farm, Domhnall had already been to the wagon house and began hitching a horse up to the rickety old wagon inside. He'd done an impressive job considering his physical limitation. We moved quiet as leaves, infiltrating the old building to join our friend. We worked together in silence to finish prepping the wagon, amazed at how easy this had been.

The air shifted as Hawthorne started to help me into the worn wagon. The silent victory prickled with something else. Anger began to crawl towards us. I turned to determine its cause but found no evidence of where it came from. The farmhouse, framed by the wide open wagon house doors, remained still. I turned my attention back to getting in the wagon.

Then a door slammed. We froze, save for our heads whipping in unison at the unwelcome sound. A pair of angry looking men had stalked toward us. Nerves spiked across our party, along with a slight buzz of anticipation of a fight.

"You failed to check the house?" Felix berated Domhnall, his long finger jabbing the man in the chest. "How could you be so dull?"

"I checked. No one appeared to be about."

"Not well enough then." Felix rubbed his face in frustration. He hoped to reach Realta without incident. We all had. "Men, prepare to take the wagon by force if we have to."

At their Captain's command, the three pirates pulled their hoods and drew their swords. Felix kept his hood in place, his identity had to be as secret as mine.

"What do you think you are doing?" the older man yelled out. He brandished a familiar looking sword in his left hand. It looked similar to the ones the ones issued to the guards at Bua Tur. Perhaps he was once a guard and retired here, having inherited the farm from a family member. His courage astounded me, even more so than the unexpected sword. It raged like a fire, though his heart trembled at being outnumbered. A fact that did not hinder him from the confrontation. He was just as ready to fight as Felix's men.

The younger man, likely the farmer's son, glared with malice as he stalked across the space between the wagon house and his home. His presence was a strong silence, all brute with no words needed to be intimidating. There was something about him though. Something familiar. A deeper sense of being like someone than looking like someone

These were not bad men. They were honest, hardworking men just defending their property. I couldn't let this fight happen.

Hawthorne made to make first contact; I stepped in front of him. He grabbed my arm, meaning to move me out of his way so he could strike first. Felix, however, stopped him with a glance.

"Let me speak with them," I implored my companions. "There shouldn't be need for a fight, it can be avoided. It must be." Felix nodded, his men stood down, and I faced the pair of farmers again. "Good sirs. We need to borrow your wagon. I'm sorry that we tried to do so without your knowledge, but we are in dire need to reach Bua Tur."

The old man gaffed, "Whatever it is you seek there , you won't find it. My advice is you seek what you need elsewhere. King Talbot cares not for the plight of any person, even if they are disguised as holy men." He tightened his grip on his weapon, "Now leave my property, without my wagon."

I felt the men behind me tense with the old man's order. I raised my hands up in a double signal: telling my friends to hold and telling the old man I meant no harm, and stepped cautiously closer. Felix's nerves spiked as I did, and he stepped up to my side to keep me guarded. He sheathed his weapon and raised his hands to keep the peace as well.

I addressed the farmer again."Please, good sir, I need your wagon. You have my word that it'll be returned tomorrow."

"Why should we trust the word of thieves?" The old farmer questioned my promise. He needed to be shown the truth in order to trust.

"Because I am not a thief." I raised my hands to remove my hood. Revealing myself would be the only way we'd acquire this wagon.

Felix reached to stop me, but I shook him off. "This has to happen," I assured him as my hands slid the hood from my head. The conviction in my voice had Felix do the same. "I'm Milady Merinley. Captain Wade and his men are escorting me back to the palace."

The men wore equal expressions of shock at our revelation. The younger of the two gaped. The older man looked as if he'd seen a ghost, but his gaze wasn't on me. He dropped his sword on the ground and his aged blue eyes locked onto Felix. He maffled as he stared, then finally looked my way and bowed. "I'm sorry Milady. Had I known, I wouldn't have interfered. I wouldn't have spoken ill of..."

I cut him off. "Don't worry about it, good sir. I understand. There's not a soul here that doesn't understand your distaste for the king." I smiled to assure him I wasn't offended.

"Please, Milady, call me Gregor. This is my son Liam." Liam gave a questioning gesture to Gregor. He was still angry. "No, Liam. I believe we can trust them."

"You can," I agreed.

"Sorry, Liam means well. He's wary of anyone with ties to King Talbot. The nobles of Realta have never treated anyone who is different well. With his being mute, he is different."

"Understandable, mate," Felix addressed Liam. "And I'm sure my being a pirate weighs other uncertainties,. You can trust Merinley, she is not like others."

"That's nice to hear, I pray she can be the good influence my daughter..." Gregor stared off, not finishing his statement. The old farmer stepped timidly towards Felix and reached out to touch his face. Felix gave him a wary look, and Gregor pulled away before making contact. "I am sorry, Captain. I lost myself for a moment. It's just that for a minute there you reminded me of my Rosalie." The old man's eyes welled over.

"Don't worry about it," Felix responded. He reached down and picked up the sword Gregor had dropped. "You have a fine sword. It's from the palace if I'm not mistaken? How did you come by it?" He handed the blade back to the farmer.

"It was a gift from my son, my Rosalie's husband."

The old farmers odd behavior, speaking in vague unfinished sentences since we revealed ourselves, preoccupied my mind. Something important lurked there, waiting to pounce. He certainly held a fascination for Felix that only added to the mystery. The more I thought on it, the further away an answer for it seemed.

"Milady." Gregor broke my wandering thoughts. "Please, help yourself to what you need. Liam, son, would you run along and get these fine folks a loaf and some cheese for their journey?" Liam nodded and headed back to their home.

"Thank you." I appreciated of his offer, even though I couldn't be sure if it was our shared dislike of King Talbot or his fascination with Felix that garnered it. In the end, the reason didn't matter. What mattered was we had what we needed to get to Realta.

Felix offered his gratitude as well, and a friendly handshake to the old man. Gregor's hand trembled as he took Felix's and his eyes welled over again. Yes, something definitely lay there under the surface. Something big that I just couldn't work out.

As soon as Liam returned with a sack holding things his father requested, Felix's men hasted into the wagon. Felix and I offered our gratitude once more and followed suit.

"That was strange," Felix commented as the wagon pulled out of the wagon house and on to the divot laden dirt road. "Good, but strange."

"Indeed it was. Though, I'm thankful it did not come to a fight." I pulled my hood back over my head as I looked back at the old man who helped us. He still watched with a lost and dreamy face.

CHAPTER TWENTY-THREE

he signs of King Talbot's distressed mind grew evident as
we rolled into the market square. Once the busiest part of
the city was sparsely populated. Market-goers were few in number, and
there were even fewer vendors. Children tagging along with their
mothers or fathers solemnly clung to them instead of exploring playfully between stalls or poking grubby fingers into chicken coops.
Everyone walked with nervous steps, as though they walked on
eggshells. The stockades at the center of the market increased in
number. All were occupied.

Fear and depression hung heavily in the air.

These changes devastated me. This was not Realta. Realta, despite
the hardships its people suffered before, used to be full of life. Hope.
This place held nothing but heartache. I should've asked to come back
after Felix rescued me. It was selfish of me to follow my heart.

The wagon groaned to a stop outside the gates of Bua Tur and a
large stone took up residence in my belly. The temptation to tell Felix
that I changed my mind whispered to me. I wanted nothing more than
to tell him I wanted to go back to The Fura and never look back. But
the sadness that filled the surrounding city urged me on. It cried for

help. My knowledge wouldn't only ease this new suffering but would lead to a new era in Realta. At least I hoped it would.

Looking around, taking in the scene as I steeled myself, something strange about the gates jumped out at me. Only one guard on stood on duty. His crisp uniform a stark contrast to the weary look he wore, like he'd stood watch for an exhausting amount of time. It seemed Talbot had his men spread even thinner now; probably all over Realta in search of me. That was the only logical explanation as to why he left the gates so unprotected.

His lone position played in our favor.

We were all on high alert as we climbed off of our borrowed wagon to approach the palace gates. Domhnall took the lead, as planned. The guard rolled his eyes at our approach. "King Talbot is not granting audience to anyone. He's done with being charitable since he lost his fiancé. Take your bleeding hearts elsewhere."

"I believe King Talbot will be glad to see us," Domhnall retorted with a jolly air. "We come with great…"

The guard cut him off. "Are you deaf, monk? I said to take your business elsewhere." The guard, distracted by Domhnall's audacity, didn't notice the monk who slipped to his side.

"I would listen to my brother, were I you," Felix whispered a mild threat in the guard's ear. I saw a flash of his dagger poking the guard in the side. "King Talbot will be wanting to see us, without question."

The stunned guard looked over his shoulder. A flash of recognition crossed his face and he opened his mouth to sound the alarm. Felix's hand moved faster than the guard's mouth, covering it before he could utter a word. "I wouldn't do that," Felix ordered. "Alert anyone to our presence before I allow it, and they will be your last words."

Fear trembled over the lone guard's eyes as Felix removed his hand from around his mouth. "Why would you think King Talbot would want business with you, pirate?" Whether it was Felix's threat or the fear of the King's ire, the guard's voice quaked.

"We stumbled upon something of his in our travels; something I think he desperately wants back." Felix gave me a wink. The signal the time for me to reveal myself arrived. There was no turning back once I did.

I stepped forward from between Smith and Hawthorne, removing the hood of my cloak. "I believe you should be doing something now. My fiancé will be very displeased if he's left waiting to receive this news."

The guard took a few moments to compose himself before he sounded for the gates to be opened. "Open the gates and alert the King. Milady Merinley is returned."

Felix smiled, patting the guard on his cheek and removed his dagger from the side of the shaken sentry. "Good lad. I'm sure you will be rewarded justly for allowing the rescuer of His Majesty's beloved into the palace."

A troupe of guards poured out of the gates the moment they opened; their weapons drawn. "It would seem these men don't trust us, Cap." Hawthorne quipped as Felix and his men were surrounded.

"Did we expect anything less?" Felix remarked back. His men laughed in response. The guards shifted uneasily, unsure of what to make of the pirates' confidence. Normal men quaked at the power of Relata's finest. Or at least the power behind them.

The Captain of the Guard separated himself from the rest of the men. "You will surrender any weapons you have on you before you enter the palace, Captain Wade."

Felix signaled his men to obey the order, "Gladly." Their daggers and swords clattered on the stones.

"Is that all?"

Felix grinned and stepped forward. A few jumpy guards took nervous steps backwards as he approached their leader. He unhooked his firearm from his belt and boldly handed it over. "Keep her warm for me," he said with a wink.

"Milady Merinley," the Captain of the Guard addressed me. "I'm glad to see you. If you'd follow me, King Talbot awaits in the throne room."

The guards kept their weapons fixed on the four pirates as we were led to the throne room to meet with King Talbot. I could feel his irritation before we even entered. There was something about the simmering anger that bothered me, even though I was more than aware King Talbot didn't have the warmest disposition. If he truly worried about me after my abduction, shouldn't he feel even the slightest bit of happiness to see me back safe?

As the doors to the throne room were opened, King Talbot's face told a story completely different from the mood that hung in the air. His bored face lit with a false smile as he rose from his throne. Like a reunited lover, he ran to greet me, arms stretched wide. In another grand show of happiness, he lifted me into his arms.

I didn't believe his exuberant show for one moment; I knew him too well. From the looks on my friends' faces, they weren't buying it either.

His mask of happiness faltered when he spotted Captain Wade and his men. His hatred for Felix wafted over me. Felix returned that hate with interest. King Talbot's mouth formed into a sneering smile as he planted a kiss on my temple. When he finished his exaggerated greeting, he placed my feet back onto the stone floor and led me by the hand to the throne. Again, making a grand show of how much he missed me. Of the relief he felt at my return.

Instead of taking the throne, Talbot offered up the seat to me. I sat in the ornate chair, my hands admiring the lush purple fabric that covered the seat, back, and arms. A strange hollow sound met my ears as my feet tapped the floor right next to the throne. I peered down to find a new addition to the throne room. Or perhaps it had always been there and I hadn't noticed. There were small holes dotting the floor around the throne itself. I thought it strange. Talbot noticed my discovery and his eyes glimmered with a knowing smile, sending a chill through me. There was something very wrong with the minute exchange.

I felt a sudden and violent repulsion by the beautiful seat. King Talbot placed a heavy hand on my shoulder, as if to hold me in place, and positioned himself to my left, as if to trap me.

The guards advanced towards the throne, pushing Felix and the men along with them. They were on guard, unsure of what the pirates might do next. Felix's face remained calm, though I sensed he battled anxious and angry feelings. Our plan's success hinged on what would happen next.

"Captain Wade," King Talbot acknowledged, "What is it that I can do for you?"

I answered before Felix could, "Your Majesty, Fe… Captain Wade has saved me from a horrible fate and returned me to you." Talbot tightened his grip on my shoulder, his way of reminding me I should be silent.

The gesture didn't go unnoticed. A flicker of anger crossed Felix's face, but he corrected himself. His neutrality was key to our success, something we'd discussed at length while planning.

"Yes, that I can see. But surely he hasn't done this out of the goodness of his heart. Even you should know that pirates don't work that way. Or has his assistance made you forget this? I thought you were clever."

Even though the insult stung, I didn't let it show. Talbot needed all the ego stroking we could provide. I shook my head. I had no intention to speak up again unless he asked me to.

"Well, Captain Wade? What can I do for you?" Talbot sneered.

Felix stepped forward. "Ah, yes, that is something you are so right about Your Majesty. I'm a great pirate and a very bad man," Felix mocked. "I was quite tempted to keep your sweet young fiancé for myself. She is supremely enchanting and I could have loads of fun with her. But my love of coin far exceeds my attention span. Why keep a girl that I'd tire of quickly when I can be rewarded handsomely?" Felix kept his eyes on me as he spoke, lust dripped from his tongue. If I didn't know better, I'd have sworn his lust was for the coin he spoke of.

"Indeed." Talbot's attitude switched to annoyance. "Well, I believe a handsome reward can be arranged…"

"And a pardon." Felix interrupted. "I deserve a pardon. I went the extra mile for you, saving you the trouble of killing her kidnappers yourself, you see. Something I didn't have to do. I could have left them free to try again. You are most welcome."

King Talbot let out a quiet growl. "Bold words Captain Wade. Milady Merinley?"

The sound of my name coming from Talbot's lips chilled me. Only because he addressed me directly, I had to respond."Yes, Your Majesty?"

"What think you of Captain Wade's bold request?"

"I don't know what to think of his request, as I know you are better suited to make such weighted decisions," I answered strategically, playing into Talbot's ego. "Though, I'm certain that Captain Wade has given me much to be thankful for. Were the decision mine, I'd think he deserved anything he wanted as his reward." The double meaning of my words weren't been lost on Felix. He flashed a quick grin my way.

"The girl knows what she's talking about," Felix responded, receiving yet another scowl from Talbot. I didn't need to use my gift to see how entertaining raising the king's blood pressure was for him. He enjoyed this venture more than I thought he would. I had to admit, I enjoyed watching it.

"I'm inclined to agree with my bride to be. I do know better of these situations. And because I'm in a generous mood, I'll agree to a pardon, a little price for the return of something so valuable." Talbot descended the few steps from the throne and moved to meet Felix head on. "To further show my gratitude, I invite you to stay a few days here at the palace so that we may properly celebrate your heroic actions. A Hero's Ball if you will. You're more than welcome to take advantage of what the palace has to offer. I'm certain you'll find the Quaintrelle quite welcoming. I know they've been a comfort to me in my despaired state."

I wasn't surprised by King Talbot's unfaithful words, but Felix didn't hide how he felt about them. His eyes narrowed, his lips pursed. His expression only lasted a moment, though. Long enough for me to worry the whole deal would be blown in my defense. Luckily, Felix cooled and offered a hand to seal the accord. As an extra jab, his feet remained planted, making Talbot come to him. The King prickled and then conceded, taking a step down to take Felix's hand. The pirate chuffed, besting his adversary in this small manner.

Seeing Talbot and Felix side by side, their similarities were obvious, to me anyway. Maybe because I looked for them. Their heights and builds were the same. Their eyes held similar shape, though were different in color. Felix's eyes were intensified by high cheekbones that Talbot lacked. They also shared the same long straight nose and masculine jaw. The final similarity was in their ears, which again were same in shape, but Talbot's were much smaller.

I understood why Felix's features were grossly exaggerated in his wanted posters. Had they portrayed him realistically, any keen-eyed citizen might have noticed the similarity between King Talbot and Captain Wade. Talbot certainly didn't want anyone making that connection, even though he didn't know why his enemy looked like him.

I was surprised that no one else noticed. Then again, no one else thought to look for it.

Talbot broke me from my thoughts. "Now if you'll wait here and excuse Milady Merinley and myself, we have much to catch up on, as you can imagine. I'll send a valet to show you to a guest suite."

"If it's all the same, Your Majesty, my men and I will seek lodging in the city. Of course, we'll take you up on the offer of using palatial amenities. It would be a crime not to. How often does a pirate get to live like a king." Felix knew which words to use; which words would vex his foe the most.

"If that's your wish," Talbot replied with faked indifference. "Come along Milady, I'm sure you are weary from your ordeal. I'll escort you to your suite."

I stood, taking King Talbot's offered elbow to keep up appearances, to keep him in the dark. Keep him appeased. We exited the throne room leaving all behind. Sadness overtook me as I left Felix's sight and an overwhelming feeling of dread settled in me. I wondered if I'd just traded my freedom away permanently.

A TENSE SILENCE developed between Talbot and I as we made our way through the palace to my suite. It was torture. That awkwardness lessened now and then with elated greetings from palace staff we passed. Each one expressed their joy at my return. My returning smile was genuine, but it also masked my unease. Not one of them gave notion that they suspected I was anything but happy to be back.

Talbot broke his formality and shirked my hand from his elbow when we entered the empty corridor leading to my suite. After walking a few steps further, he grasped my arm in a vice-like grip and forced me to the side of the corridor, pressing me up against the rough stone wall. The sudden attack sprang tears to my eyes. While I expected some annoyance, I didn't expect my return to be met with violence.

"What do you think you were doing back there? I thought I made it clear that I was in charge," he hissed.

"I merely did as you asked. I gave my opinion on Captain Wade's request," I replied with a shaky voice.

"Yes, and you answered in his favor. You left me no choice but to give into the criminal's request for a pardon. I would've looked bad otherwise. You do not want me looking bad, do you?"

"I am sorry, Talbot."

Talbot jerked me forward only to push me right back into the wall. "Do not address me so informally. I'm your superior and always will be."

"I'm sorry, Your Highness," I corrected.

He rolled his eyes and scoffed, "Your being sorry doesn't change anything. At least we can rest easy knowing that the pardon will probably be voided rather quickly. Captain Wade and his men are likely to find someway to get into trouble." A foreboding shiver rolled through my veins.

I nodded just to appease Talbot and he released my arm.

"I believe you can make your way to your chambers from here." He glared into my eyes one last time, the coldness penetrated me deep. His boot squeaked on the floor as he turned on his heel and stormed back the way we came. I dared not move or even breathe until the sound of his footsteps died away.

I finished the short walk to my chambers on shaky legs. The deep cold feeling Talbot bore into my heart would not ebb. All I wanted was to be on The Fura, safe and warm Felix's bed. In Felix's arms. Since that was impossible, I set my mind on a hot bath. The moment I opened the door, my tension resided a little more. Anwen stood waiting for my return, one of my woolen robes cradled in her arms and a welcoming smile on her face. My heart leapt at the sight of her. I missed my dear friend and confidant immensely. Her smile faltered when she noticed the tears that laced my eyes.

"Everything alright, Milady?" Anwen asked.

"Yes, all is well. I'm merely relieved to be home and tired from my journey. Tears of joy," I said pointing to the stains upon my cheeks.

She gave me a questioning look and eyed the red finger marks that Talbot left on my arm. I should've known better than to lie to Anwen; she saw through almost everything. She moved on, though, knowing me well enough to that I would share when I felt ready to. "Well then, let me draw you a hot bath so you can wash away the weariness of travel, the pain of what you likely went through. You can regale me with your story while you bathe." Anwen wrapped me in a tight hug. "I'm so relieved to have you back home, my dear girl."

Seeing Anwen again was a bright spot in this. I missed the company of another woman fiercely while on the sea. Yet, I couldn't help but feel a darkness about being back. I reminded myself I would see Felix again, and he had his pardon. I just hoped that King Talbot's prediction proved false. Felix and his men wouldn't do anything to have the pardon revoked. Or worse, that Talbot would concoct some new law that would guarantee it.

CHAPTER TWENTY-FOUR

he turnout for the Hero's Ball reached numbers like no other. Everybody who was anybody desperately wanted to find out who the mystery hero was. My name, once again, slid across the tongues and lips of an entire room. My name and gossip of my mystery hero. I entered the Hero's Ball upon the arm of King Talbot. Applause and cheers filled the room upon our entrance. The happiness that hung in the air was overwhelming. The people were glad I had been returned. Perhaps they hoped, as I did, that King Talbot would mellow with my return. That the strict regulations he passed would be revoked.

If all went according to my plan, Realta was in for better changes than that.

I drank in their hope and joy, letting their feelings overtake mine. Each step into the ball shifted increments of my tension away and replacing it with borrowed happiness. Without it, the night would have been awful. Unbearable even, despite the promise of being near Felix for a few short hours. Though those promised to be absolute torture for completely different reasons.

Only a few days had passed since my return, since saying goodbye to Felix. I missed him already. So many times I decided to walk the halls of the palace in hopes of catching a passing glimpse of the man that stole my heart. I hadn't seen any trace of him or any of his men.

The walk to the dais seemed an eternity. Well wishers stopped our progress every few steps to display their pleasure at my return. Talbot's irritation bubbled each time, though he never let it show outwardly. He accepted their words with feigned gratitude, barely acknowledging they happened.

At last we took our places on two thrones that sat on the dais to watch over the ball as we waited for our guest of honor. My insides were made of humming bird wings as I waited for him. I watched over the celebration, my eyes flitting to the doors every minute or so. After what seemed a lifetime of anticipation, the herald blew his trumpet. The ballroom doors opened.

"Ladies and gentlemen, make way for our honored guest, Milady Merinley's savior, Captain Wade," the herald announced.

The crowd gasped collectively as Felix stepped past the herald and into the ballroom; Hawthorne, Domhnall, and Mister Bimble on his heels. These were the last men these people were expecting to see being honored by King Talbot. Their tittering became the music the pirates marched to.

My breath, however, caught when Felix entered the room. My heart stopped. It was if I were seeing him for the first time all over again. Here was the version of Felix only I knew existed, a whisper of who he didn't know he was. He wore a striking blue coat, adorned with gold piping and gold buttons, and dark trousers that fit just right. The coat made his eyes stand out from across the room. They sparkled a hint of mischief when his smile cut across his face as he took in the reactions to his appearance. That smile released the air caged in by my lungs, like the world had been righted once more by it.

I couldn't take my eyes off him as they made their way to greet us. He looked even more handsome than ever, he looked regal. He looked like he belonged. He acted like he belonged.

The men stopped at the foot of the dais and bowed. The murmurs exchanged between the ball attendees fell silent.

"We are deeply grateful for your actions, Captain Wade, for

returning my betrothed to us unharmed," King Talbot announced in a shocking and uncharacteristic move. Normally his steward did all the talking for him. Speaking to his people was beneath him. "For your actions, I'm offering you and your men a pardon. Your past crimes against Realta are forgiven from here on out. I look forward to watching you as you enter this new phase of your lives." His words were easily interpreted; he looked forward to seeing them fail.

Felix and his men bowed deeper, a wordless gesture to show their gratitude for the pardon. His eye caught mine as he stood full height, a knowing smile crossing both our mouths. The small exchange had my heart racing and my mind replaying every touch we shared. I heated at the memories, and from thoughts of future stolen ones.

King Talbot continued. "In addition, to honor your heroic effort, I concede the honor of my fiance's first dance this night, to you."

"Thank you, Your Majesty," Felix accepted the honor. "May you get everything you deserve, and more." Felix turned to me, extending his hand, "Milady?" Slipping my hand in his, a slow burn crept its way from my fingertips and coursed through me. I felt like I could breathe again. He escorted me on to the dance floor, stopping in the center and pulling me in a wide circle to dance position.

The music swelled into a melancholy waltz, a tune I recognized as a short one. The time in Felix's arms would be limited by its length. I intended to memorize the seconds spent there with him.

My body naturally wanted to snuggle closer to him, to absorb every ounce of his touch. Make the most of this short interlude. I had to fight against the urge. Distance needed to be kept to avoid suspicion. Even though Felix had the pardon we wanted, our actions still had to be careful. One little slip up had the potential to ruin it all.

"You look positively ravishing tonight, Sweet," Felix spoke low so that only I would hear him. "I'm having a very difficult time of keeping my hands in their proper places." He tightened his grip on my shoulder as if to emphasize his words.

I winced under the gentle squeeze; not a great deal, but enough for Felix to notice. His face flashed with concern. Using his thumb, he pushed aside the fabric covering my shoulder ever so slightly. His eyes became stormy at the discovery of the faded bruises Talbot left there just days prior. His chest rumbled. I couldn't allow him to explode.

"He was mad that I agreed with you about the pardon and grabbed me harder than he meant to." I knew the excuse was thin, but I needed to assuage Felix. I didn't need him to lose his temper and do something brash, something that would cause him to lose his pardon. This cage would be unbearable without knowing I could secret away to where I really wanted to be.

"If that buffoon has hurt you…" Felix started.

"I'm fine, Felix," I interrupted. "Be calm, please. Think of the plan."

The storm in his eyes weakened. Felix understood. He returned his focus to the dance. "This reminds me of the first time we danced."

That night flitted across my memories, the foreign feelings he stirred in me then. I never expected to see him after that night. Never expected anyone to mean so much to me. Little did I know then, Fate had other plans for us. "You mean when you tried to steal my mother's necklace."

"Pirate." He chuckled his one worded reminder. "I am so very glad I did. You turned out to be much more than a tasty strumpet that I could dazzle with my charm, and make off with a treasure."

"My mother's necklace is hardly the treasure you claim it to be in comparison to the other jewels I wore." I scoffed at his choice.

"Oh, I had my reasons on why I chose that over others."

"Really?"

"Well, Sweet, I asked you to dance with the intention of stealing a necklace on the sly. Stealing a treasure from you gave me an excuse to be close to you. But, I found that desire waning once we were on the floor. I felt enchanted from the minute you took my hand. I almost changed my mind about the planned theft. I only took your necklace because I felt a strong need to have it, I had been unsure of what made me feel that way. Now I am certain it was to lead you into my life. To bring to me the best treasure of my career."

I blushed at his confession. Id been immediately attracted to him from the moment I first looked into his blue eyes. The memory of our first meeting shifted into more recent memories of our time together. Heavy desire filled me.

"Careful, a look like that would cause me to forget our deal and take you here and now. I think the hanging would be worth it. I am missing sharing my bed with you."

A chill coursed through me at the thought of it. I bit my lip and straightened my frame. Remembering to keep up appearances proved much harder being in the arms I had grown so accustomed to. "Me too," I confessed as the last notes of the song played, shattering my heart. Those notes meant the time had come to return to Talbot's side.

Felix escorted me back to the dais, to Talbot. Anger and sadness emanated from him as he did. He was not looking forward to giving me back again. "Thank you, Your Majesty, for allowing me to dance with Milady. You are a lucky man indeed to have a partner like her on your arm." He turned to me and kissed my hand in a gentlemanly fashion. "Thank you, Milady, for the dance."

Felix's departing gesture became a warm thread binding my heart together. The only thing that kept me from falling apart then and there. A beacon of our promised reunion to come. That warmth dissipated the moment I looked to Talbot, replaced by the chill of my current loneliness. My fiancé appeared as indifferent as ever to my presence at his side. He stared with uninterested eyes and an arrogant heart over his subjects. The rest of the ball had to be spent at his side, being ignored and observing the festivities. I was to be tortured watching Felix and his men enjoy the ball as I couldn't.

The night wore on. The uncomfortable silence at my side was making the ball more like a chore than a celebration. The happiness of the crowd did nothing to help, I was truly miserable glued to the throne I sat on, forced to watch young wealthy maids in attendance make advances towards what was mine. His refusal of each one did little to lift my spirits.

It wasn't long before I couldn't bear being a bystander.

"Your Highness, might I be excused I asked. "I'm afraid these festivities are too much too soon." Talbot made an uninterested motion with his hand. He didn't care whether I stayed or went. I took my leave as fast as protocol allowed.

Cerisse caught me by the elbow as I exited the ballroom and insisted on accompanying me. Even though I wanted to be alone with my thoughts, I didn't refuse her company. In truth, having someone to actually speak to eased my angst.

"You are very lucky Milady," she commented, leaning into me as we strolled through the dimly lit palace halls.

"How so, Mistress Cerisse?"

"You are. Mistress Anwen saved you from servitude. You became a highly sought Quaintrelle. King Talbot wants to marry you. You're then kidnapped, then rescued by that dashing pirate, Captain Wade." She laughed at her last remark, 'Well maybe not lucky to be kidnapped."

"No, that wasn't lucky. But yes, very lucky I have been returned."

"But Captain Wade! He is devilishly charming. It couldn't have been all that bad spending time with him. I know I wouldn't mind spending time with him, or his man with the one arm." Her eyes took on a far away look as she twirled her golden locks. Her heart perked as she thought about him. I wondered if she felt what was forbidden to her when she did, as I had when I first met Felix.

"Domhnall," I named him. "He is kind and spirited, strong too. His missing appendage has no hindrance on him at all."

Cerisse repeated his name. I suspected she would be back at the ball to charm him later. He'd be lucky if she did. To garner her attention wasn't easy. Cerisse was dedicated to the job. With my change in station her schedule had doubled, many of my old suitors seeking her out in my absence.

"It must've been exciting to be with them," she implied.

I smiled. If she only knew the truth of her words. "I was lucky Captain Wade didn't decide to keep me for himself. I've missed my friends here."

"I don't think I would mind so much being kept by that pirate." She nudged me with her shoulder. "He certainly had his eye on you tonight."

Alarm rang in my head. If Cerisse noticed, others most certainly did. I prayed Talbot had been too distracted by his indifference to notice. I hadn't gotten anything from him that suggested he caught on to the way Felix watched me. I decided to dismiss her remark. "Probably wishing he had held out for a bigger purse. He is a pirate."

"I think not Merinley, you've always been able to hold the attention of all you meet. You have that charm that draws them in even if they know there is no hope."

"You're sweet, Mistress Cerisse. That was all just our training, which I always faked my way through. My heart was never in it. You were the one to watch."

"Thank you, Milady. But, I think you undersell yourself. You were always so modest." She took my hands when we stopped at the corridor to my suite. "It really is good to have you back. Realta just wasn't the same without you. Bua Tur was not the same." Mist clouded over her eyes. There were horrors there, in her eyes, once she let them take over her frivolous talk of scandal. Horrors she didn't want to speak of. What had happened to her while I was away? Whatever it was had scarred her.

"Would you want to join me for a tea?" My invitation to her stemmed from a hope she would open up and release her dark secret.

"No, I should be getting back." Her smile erased all traces of the sadness that had been in her moments before. "I have a one armed pirate to attend to." She winked as she turned to leave. Domhnall didn't stand a chance against her.

Anwen welcomed me with a pleasant greeting as I entered my suite. She waited in the sitting area with a pot of chamomile tea and biscuits, and had set out a nightgown and robe for me to change into. A fire blazed in the grand fireplace near the bed, making the room warm and inviting. She followed me, saying nothing, to the privacy screen to assist me out of my formal gown. Her nimble fingers made short work of the silken ties down the back of the dress. My body relaxed a tiny bit more with each one loosened. The cumbersome dress plopped to the floor with the final tug, pooling around my feet. Anwen left me to the rest after helping me step out of the puddle of fabric.

I listened to her fading steps and soft humming while she flitted about preparing my bed for the night. Lavender filled the air when she shifted the pillows, releasing the scent of the sachets hidden there. She worked so hard to ensure my comfort and happiness in this place. I suspected her extra effort was meant to distract me from reality. From being Talbot's betrothed. Her dedication drove my determination to finish my mission here. She deserved some happiness in return.

I quickly finished undressing and slipped on the thin night dress. Snatching the robe off of the chair, I wrapped it around myself as I exited the privacy screen to join her. There was a lot she and I needed to discuss.

Anwen was already seated and sipping on her own cup of tea.

"Anwen are you certain you don't have Apoidean blood? You always seem to know just what I need." I sat across the tiny table from her and brought my own cup up to my lips.

"How was the ball?" she deflected.

"Boring, if I'm to be honest. I obviously left early."

"Obviously," Anwen laughed. "I bet it wasn't as boring as you say. A little bird told me the guest of honor caused quite a stir," she teased. Anwen knew all about my abduction, and the affair I had with Captain Wade while in his company. What she didn't know was what I suspected of his true identity. I was bursting to fill her in.

"He was the belle of the ball," I joked. "Speaking of, there was something I needed to talk to you about. An urgent secret matter."

"Oh?" she leaned forward, interested in the intrigue I offered.

A crash from the small garden just off of my suite interrupted me. We jumped from our seats immediately, and I grabbed one of the dull knives used to spread jelly on the biscuits. It offered little as a weapon, but I still wielded it as though it were deadly. With the right pressure it had the potential for real injury. Anwen's steps matched mine as we rushed to see what had caused the chaos.

Taking caution, I opened the glass garden door and stepped outside. The grass felt damp from the nighttime air and all I could hear were the crickets chirping. I had to rely on my gift to help me out the intruder. I searched out with my mind for any feelings from them. I sensed someone almost immediately. A rustling in the flowering bushes to my right alerted me where this person hid.

A shadowy figure emerged from the bushes; emanating irritation. Anwen screeched behind me. Her outcry startled me and I tripped over something unseen. My robe fell open and my nightdress tangled about my hips from the fall. Anwen froze in place just inside the garden door, her mouth hanging agape in shock.

"Not the welcome I had expected, Sweet. But I do so love it," Felix crooned softly. He stepped through the brush and offered me a hand, pulling me intimately close to him. My head filled with his ocean air scent, sending flurries of heat through me.

"Felix! Why are you sneaking about my garden?" I shot a nervous glance at Anwen. Even though she already knew all about him, I wasn't sure how she'd react to the pirate being in my room uninvited.

My glance over at Anwen alerted Felix to her presence and he released the close embrace he held me in. "Pardon my intrusion, ladies. I got lost," he announced with an awkward flourish.

Anwen gave him an incredulous look, rolling her eyes. "Oh please, Captain Wade. Merinley shares everything with me, I know of your time together. Who could blame you for falling under her spell?" She smiled. "I'll excuse myself and leave notice you do not wish to be bothered Milady. Send word that you are resting."

"Thank you, Anwen. Would you mind preparing my bath before you go? I think I'll be needing one now."

"Of course Milady. It was a pleasure meeting you Captain Wade." Anwen bowed out and disappeared from our sight.

"You told your maid about us?" His eyebrow quirked upwards and a flirtatious smirk pulled the corner of his mouth. "How scandalous," he teased.

"She's much more than a maid, Felix. Anwen was my Quaintrelle mentor. She's been my guiding star ever since. She is like a sister to me. We can trust her."

Felix scooped me back into his arms and rested his head on mine."I had to see you once again before I leave in the morning. We make sail early, giving me no chance to return to the palace before we do."

They weren't truly sailing far. Felix intended to stay as close as he could for a few days more. Though he still had obligations that would take him miles away, he'd return as frequently as possible. "I'm glad you did. We haven't arranged our rendezvous yet."

"That we have not, Sweet." He squeezed me tighter and nipped at my ear. "Though, I do believe I heard something about a bath. I would be more than happy to assist you; a little rendezvous perhaps?" Felix wiggled his eyebrows suggestively.

My skin flushed. "Tempting, but no. It's too dangerous here. Despite my orders to be left alone to rest, I doubt King Talbot would follow them if he were so inclined. In his opinion, he doesn't need to abide by anyone's wishes. Better to not tempt fate. Not tonight anyway." I placed a small kiss on Felix's neck. "Where shall we meet?"

"Perhaps Fenian Cliffs, the men enjoyed the cove there. Domhnall has bonded with the old farmer who let us borrow his wagon. I'm certain the old man wouldn't mind if we intruded on him for a few days before we must tend to our responsibilities."

"Fenian Cliffs? I think I can arrange a trip out to thank the family that assisted my return. King Talbot couldn't argue against a diplomatic move like that. Two days from now?" I suggested.

"I'll be waiting, Sweet. Very, very anxiously waiting for your arrival." Felix's lips met mine. The short, meaningful kiss a perfect goodbye. He released his arms from around me and began to disappear in the shadows of the garden. He paused at the edge of the border, "Are you sure you don't require my assistance with your bath?"

"Go, Felix. I'll see you in two days time." I laughed at his persistence. When he made it over the garden wall, I turned back and headed inside my suite. The warm bath Anwen prepared was calling to me, promising enough comfort and warmth for the time being.

CHAPTER TWENTY-FIVE

I sat at the dressing table in my chambers, humming to myself as I brushed out my dampened hair. I redressed in only the robe Anwen provided. My bath had been luxurious and the perfect ending to the day. The night had been wonderfully bittersweet. Tortuous and breathtaking all in one, with a restful night in sight. Best of all, I had my first outing from the palace planned for in a few days. My lips still tingled from the stolen departing kiss from Felix. Goose-bumps appeared on my skin at the memory. My heart skipped a few beats.

As I reminisced, someone entered my chambers. I assumed it was Anwen with another cup of tea, I called to let her know I had yet to leave the bathing area. After a few moments, heavy footsteps echoed towards me, far too heavy. Not Anwen. I looked over my shoulder, waiting anxiously to find out who defied my request to be left alone. To my surprise, Talbot stood across the room from me. Even though I told Felix otherwise, I did't expected him to ever seek me out. In my experience, Talbot avoided me as much as possible. His mood was light, which probably accounted for the visit.

I rose once I noticed him and offered a small curtsy in greeting, holding the folds of my robe together. "Your Majesty, I apologize for my impropriety. I didn't expect you this evening."

Talbot offered a wry, drunken smile. "I wanted to ask if you would join me in my chambers. I can't help but feel very drawn to you since your return, you've been positively radiant these past few days and I'm finding myself desiring your company more than I expected to." Talbot's eyes lit with a cruel lust as he stared at me across the room, his words felt insincere. I sensed he was up to something. My intuition screamed at me that his intentions were not as he said.

"I'm flattered by your compliments, Your Majesty, but I must decline your invitation. I'm delighted to be back home, as you might imagine, after the ordeal I endured. That being said, I know how lucky I was that no harm came to me while captured and I desire now more than ever to be a pure bride for you."

His light mood shifted when I hesitated, fueled by something dark.

He stepped towards me, annoyance underlying the concerned façade we wore. Instinctually, I wanted to step back as he moved forward, but I fought it. I didn't want to make him angry. Talbot reached out for me as he neared. He grabbed my arm, squeezing with all his might. "Lying whore," he whispered, leaning in close. His wine scented breath washed over me. Trouble was brewing.

My eyes welled. "I don't know what you mean," I stammered.

He squeezed even tighter and pulled me a hair's breadth from him. "You know exactly what I am referring to." Anger flared in his eyes and he shook me. "Do you think me blind? Do you think me a beef-witted man? A merry-Andrew, perchance?"

Too nervous to speak, I shook my head in response. Tears streamed down my cheeks.

"Don't think I missed the way you interacted with Captain Wade whilst he held you on the dance floor? The motley-minded scoundrel certainly kept a close watch on you as well. Hell, when you first returned he certainly looked as though he wished to kill me when I, your fiancé, the only man allowed to touch you, welcomed you home."

I tried to diffuse the situation, "If my behavior towards him had been at all improper, I can only blame my former training. Old habits are difficult to lose. Captain Wade's certainly not the first to take fancy to a Quaintrelle." King Talbot considered my words. After a moment, I plead,"Please let me go, you are hurting me."

Shock filled me when the back of his free hand smacked into my cheek. "Quit your lying," he hissed as he shoved me into the dressing table. I crumbled to the floor sobbing. "I know who you are, whore. I wouldn't be so concerned had you been acting as a Quaintrelle does. It was your awkwardness; your acting contrary to your training that betrayed your feelings for the man."

"Talbot, I…"

He charged at me, growling, his face a deep shade of red. "Watch your informality! I didn't give you permission to speak!" He backhanded the other side of my face. "Had I even had the slightest inkling that your abduction would be handled by such incompetent fools, rather than the man I sought out, I wouldn't have ordered it in the first place."

His accidental confession sent my head reeling as if he struck me again.

Talbot's face looked surprised for a moment, telling me he did not mean to admit his part in my kidnapping. He recovered his composure, his surprise switching to a wicked, arrogant, sneer. "Yes, my dear intended, I orchestrated your kidnapping. A play I learned from my grandfather. He used the method to rid himself of pests. Though, I used it to garner more power. My grief gave me liberty make 'poor ruling decisions' for years to come. I should've known you could entice even the most hardened criminal to rescue you, enticing is what you do well." His hand brushed my cheek as a lover would, and his eyes wandered hungrily over me. My blood went cold. I feared he meant to take me, despite my previous refusal.

I shied away, maffling words that refused to come. As soon as my mouth opened he delivered the fiercest backhand to my face yet. My face tingled near numbness from the strike.

Talbot stood over me, leaning down so his face leveled with mine, he clicked his tongue in a chastising manner. He grabbed my face roughly, "You are mine, Merinley. If you want to pretend your wish is to purify yourself before we are wed, fine. But I'll ensure it is so. You're forbidden to leave Bua Tur until our wedding day. You'll be under constant guard, and you will answer my every beck and call. We will be wed in three months and then you will share my bed whether you wish to or not, as it is a husband's right to have his wife." Talbot paused for a moment before speaking again, "If Captain Wade is seen anywhere near the palace, I swear that his pardon will be hastily revoked. He'll be charged with treason. I think you know what that means."

He shoved me away and straightened himself before leaving me in a crumpled mess on the floor. I buried my face in my hands and cried. What had I done? I wished I'd listened to Felix and stayed with him, a life on the run would've been better than this. I doomed us both.

Shame took hold of me. I didn't even try to defend myself, something I was more than capable of doing. Somehow, Talbot's fury rendered me helpless.

Talbot's voice boomed moments later, making me jump from my skin. "Tend to your charge." The heavy door of my chambers slammed closed. Moments later nervous, soft steps padded across the floor. I looked up from my defeated position. My tears fell heavier when Anwen stepped into my line of sight.

Her face crumpled when she saw the pathetic state Talbot left me in, covered in tears and pink swelling where he had lain hands on me. There was nothing to be said. No explanation needed for her to know what transpired.

"Oh, Merinley," she gasped in horror and rushed to my side. "How can I... Should I send for Captain Wade?"

"No!" The word flew from me with such assurance I even surprised myself.

Everything in me screamed for Felix. I needed his arms around me and his strength. His fury. But, if he went after Talbot before I had the evidence I needed, no hope of saving anyone remained. "He must stay away. Talbot will kill him if he comes back."

"Surely, you do not mean that. If he knew what happened here." Anwen countered, confused by my adamant stance.

"He can't know. Not yet," my voice staggered desperately. "But, I need you to go to him. Let him know that I'm not able to leave the palace, but not to worry. My plan still stands."

"What plan?" Anwen asked.

"The plan to stop the wedding. To find a way to save Realta. It's vital he doesn't know what Talbot did to me tonight. I know him well enough to know that he will make a rescue attempt on his own otherwise." I paused, emotionally exhausted.

"Surely if we tell him of what Talbot's done he'd be more than willing to help with the rebel plot to dethrone him." Anwen was wrong. She didn't know Felix the way I did.

"No. If Felix found out Talbot harmed me, he wouldn't help the rebel plan. He'd knock the castle doors down in a rage and exact his own personal revenge."

Anwen looked confused at my request. "Surely that would be a good thing. Wouldn't it?"

I realized I hadn't yet shared what I suspected about Felix with her, what I knew to be true all the way to my bones. I'd been too busy preparing for the ball to tell her before. "We need Captain Wade to be cooperative and not come storming in with no plan. If he even comes near the palace, he will be arrested. That can't happen. His role in our mission is bigger than you know, than he knows. I think it's be better for you to figure that on your own, but I will give you a clue. All I ask is that when you meet with him look upon him closely. Say nothing to him of what you see, he doesn't know how connected he is to everything."

THE MORNING after my missed meeting with Felix at the Fenian Cliffs, nervous energy ruled me. I could barely stand still for the dressmaker as she fitted me for dresses Talbot approved of, including my wedding gown. She glared at me each time I made any sort of movement. I couldn't help myself though, waiting for Anwen to report back was killing me. News of Felix, and whether or not Anwen interpreted my clue, was all I wanted to know.

As planned, she went to Fenian Cliffs in my stead to relay to Felix the altered news of my captivity. I expected her back at any moment. Every time I heard someone move past the doors, I jumped. Every time I jumped, the dressmaker poked me with one of her sharp needles. A mild reminder that the more I moved, the longer the fitting would take.

Anwen came bursting into my chambers just as the dressmaker finished up. She buzzed with excitement; she had to have figured it out. Her contagious excitement took over the mood of the room, even swaying the dressmaker's sour demeanor. Though, she figured Anwen's mood came from seeing me in a mock up of my wedding gown and it was her pride that boosted her own mood. She had me spin to show off her work before ordering me to take it off so she could take it to make the final adjustments.

When the dressmaker finally left, Anwen's excitement burst into words. "Captain Wade's Declan's son, isn't he?" She spoke in fast and hushed tones. The constant guard King Talbot had me under made us take precaution with what we said.

"I believe so," I replied, matching her whispers with my own. "Tell me about your meeting with him, I'm anxious to hear anything from him. Then I'll reveal what I know." Anwen nodded once in response. "How is he?"

"Captain Wade sees through your excuses, and curses King Talbot. He is a beast caged, but mostly mad at himself for not standing his ground on your return. Although, we both know that it's impossible for anyone to deny you anything you set your heart on. He believes it's too risky to relay messages from his end, but he'll try to wait for word from me on any plans."

I mulled over his decision. While all I wanted were his words to hold me over until we were reunited, he was right. Trying to send messages held too much danger. We couldn't risk them being intercepted by the wrong person. After the night of the Hero's Ball, I was wary of what Talbot was capable of. If he found out, who knew what he would do.

Anwen prodded me out of my thought, "Now Milady, what do you know of Captain Wade's parentage?"

"Honestly, not enough to make the identification positive, but enough to stand on. I believe that if you can get to the convent and seek out Sister Maria's personal records we'll have the absolute proof needed to take action." I relayed to Anwen what Felix revealed to me on that drunken, ecstatic, night on his boat, how he was born and raised at St. Ludo in the Eira Mountains. The very place Prince Declan's bride had birthed their son. I spoke of the striking similarities I saw when Felix and Talbot stood side by side. "He is the right age to be Prince Declan's first born son, just a few years older than Talbot himself. The pieces all fit for him to be the man the rebels are searching for. We just need the documents for absolute proof."

Anwen gaped at my revelations, "I can't believe it. Captain Wade has to be the son of the old nun's Rosalie. It's almost unbelievable that the true heir has been living right under the king's nose all this time, and causing him much grief at that."

My subconscious opened up when Anwen mentioned Rosalie, bringing Gregor and Liam to the front of my mind. Suddenly I knew what had nagged at the back of my mind when I met the farmers. The reason why they hated King Talbot and his grandfather so much. Why Gregor had grown wistful looking at Felix. His daughter was Rosalie, Prince Declan's secret bride. Felix's mother.

"Merinley," Anwen alerted me out of my haze. "What is it, you grew distant a minute there."

"I was remembering something. An encounter with a farmer we had on our way back to Realta is all." I gave one last thought to my discovery before continuing, "We must get the nun's records."

"I promise, dear girl, that I'll get to that convent and find those records before the wedding. I couldn't live with myself if it were in my power to keep you from marrying that fiend and I didn't do so."

CHAPTER TWENTY-SIX

*O*ver the course of the next week, true vileness of my fiancé came to light. I thought I knew the extent of it, but I'd been blind at best. He'd done terrible things while I was gone. Things that I couldn't believe the people thought were the actions of a grieving man. Or perhaps it was their fear of him and his new found masochism that kept their tongues at bay.

I witnessed first hand the harsh new rules of trade and market. Both were now overseen by watchful soldiers. They patrolled the market to keep an eye out for illegal wares. Anyone caught with something from restricted places received punishment, either whipped or placed in the stockades. When the market closed for the day, the soldiers were ordered to collect half of each merchant's earnings as taxes. Anyone who resisted was punished.

I heard gossip of the awful new laws surrounding the military. King Talbot gave orders for any man witnessed to be able bodied enough to fight for him would be forced to join the ranks of his growing army. On top of that, King Talbot set up a special training camp, hidden in the forest between Bua Tur and the Eira Mountains. His current soldiers didn't train at this camp. This camp homed boys stolen from their mother's arms, boys as young as three years old. There they were to be conditioned to be obedient at all cost and trained to be nothing but soldiers. Soldiers that would never question orders.

Then there were the changes to the Quaintrelle. My sisters no longer held any autonomy over their roles in the palace. They had to accept invitations and requests, especially when coming from Talbot's closest allies. Over two thirds of their earnings went right into the royal coffers rather than their own. Talbot took away their chances at normal futures, at having families. Quaintrelle were forcibly sterilized so the threat of children no longer hindered their careers.

My heart broke for my former coterie. No wonder Cerise felt so filled with horror that night I spoke with her. She, and all the others, were more slaves than treasured jewels.

But all this wasn't the worst of what King Talbot had done. He enacted Prima Nocta. The so-called benefits he gained from this law, made him proud. He enjoyed the way his stories about his right as King made me cringe. He bragged about the wedding nights he took the groom's consummate roll in. He delighted particularly in regaling about a young couple that thought they could wed in secret, but their priest betrayed them, snitching to King Talbot of their planned union to save himself. King Talbot had his men hide near their secret wedding spot and arrested them the moment they thought they'd won.

He had the priest killed, even though he had made sure the law was upheld.

Talbot had the man imprisoned, beaten, and tortured for three days. Each night he would have the man brought to his chambers. There he was forced to see and hear what King Talbot did to his wife. On the third night, after the king had his way with the woman one last time, the man was decapitated right in front of her. He had the woman dragged, naked, to the stocks and left there for a week, even though she had died four days in. She became an example to those who thought they could defy King Talbot.

My stomach churned as he laughed about it.

What horrified me even more, the people didn't rise up. The rebels didn't seen fit to act when these monstrous rules were enacted or enforced. My confidence in the rebels waned when I learned of their inaction. I began to doubt their commitment to their cause. I hoped that would change when the time for action truly came.

To top it all off, everything I did seemed to ignite Talbot's anger. Anything I did that he considered out of line, became a punishable offense. I was hit and pushed more times than I could count since the Hero's Ball. I tread around him with careful steps, made myself as small as possible to avoid his wrath. But no matter how careful I thought I'd been, I found I could've done something better. Been smaller. Less heard. His temper cracked irreparably and he'd gone from angry and overbearing, to violent and controlling. A true monster. Worse than a monster. A demon.

I was wrong to return, I chastised myself daily for it. Nothing came close to being fixed with my return, and no glimmer of a better future anywhere to be seen. I only added myself to his warpath, and held no power to do anything except pray for the rebellion to start. For the people to revolt. For Felix to save me. For something to happen that would take me away from my waking nightmare.

Things took an even darker turn during a dinner with Duchess Emile, who came to visit her son with an envoy of ambassadors to discuss new deals between the two kingdoms. Her visit was more of a formality than a happy, long awaited reunion. A way for her to save face with her son and her people. A guise of a family united covering their political motives.

As expected, Talbot's disinterested mother excused herself early from the meal. She didn't have the stomach for political talk, or so she said. Part of me thought she just wanted to be as far away from her son as possible. There was no love lost between the two.

Duchess Emile surprised me when she invited me along with her, to "Leave the men folk to their discussion of things we had no business in". I immediately stood, seeing my opportunity to escape Talbot for a short time, and possibly get to know her a little more. When else would I get the chance to delve into her mind and learn more about the man who was set to be my husband? Maybe she had insights that could help me get out.

Talbot's hand shot out, grabbing onto my wrist and yanking me down to my seat, "You're not excused. Mother, take your leave alone." She didn't hesitate to leave, without so much a second glance at anyone. Her abandonment stung more than it should have.

The rest of the meal, I sat in uncomfortable silence, knowing something horrible was coming.

"I have something special for you," Talbot sneered when the last of the envoy had left the room. He held my wrist in a vice like grip, pulling me from my seat and leading me with hurried steps to the throne room. I barely kept up without stumbling. There he led me up to the smaller throne he brought in for me, throwing me in it with enough force to nearly topple it. Talbot towered over me, making me shrink into the rich velvet cushions. The crazed look on his face made his green eyes appear glow. It terrified me more than he ever had before.

He had something horrible planned.

Talbot grabbed my hands away from my face, squeezing my wrists and twisting as he did. I cried out which earned me a backhand to my right cheek. He pulled me from my throne and crushed me against his side. Burying his face in the side of my hair, he took a deep breath, "It really is a shame you are unwilling to share my bed. I do love the way you smell when you are afraid. It's so very alluring, your fear. I'm going to gain so much pleasure in breaking you."

My body quaked from revulsion, from fear. Nausea ebbed in my stomach.

"This just might bring me just as much pleasure as bedding you." Talbot kicked his throne over and reached down, sticking his fingers through the holes in the floor where it sat. He pulled and the floor tile lifted away. A coffin sized, dark chamber sat open in the floor.

Seeing the tiny prison he intended to leave me in, deepened my fear; my body broke out in goosebumps. Talbot shoved me into the chamber and replaced the floor tile, landing hard at the bottom and scraping my hands and knees. The grate clanged into place moments later. When I looked up, Talbot was grinning at me through the holes.

"You are a monster," I seethed.

"And you are mine to do with as I please," King Talbot mocked as he towered over the hole. "It pleases me to see you caged. Enjoy your stay, I have a marriage to bless."

I heard scraping as he lifted the throne back into place. The little room grew darker. What little I was able to see of Talbot, disappeared. He hummed a jaunty tune, which mingled with his heavy footsteps; both echoed through the throne room like a dirge. The heavy doors open and close. I was alone.

I curled up into a ball and cried myself to into a fitful sleep.

AN UNKNOWN TIME passed before being woken by the floor banging and rattling. I uncurled my head from under my arm and peered up. Talbot grinned down at me before someone entering the room made him to look up.

"Your Majesty," a somewhat familiar voice filled the room above me. "It's a pleasure to see you. But, I was under the impression your bride-to-be would be joining us for this meeting?" At these words, I realized the voice belonged to the priest set to officiate our wedding.

"Milady Merinley is indisposed at the moment." I shuddered at the underhanded half-truth Talbot used. "I assure you, though, that I have her blessing to make any decisions on her behalf."

"I'm glad to hear it. You know how women can be about their weddings." The priest and Talbot laughed together.

I didn't want to hear the conversation. Using my hands to cover my ears, their words muffled. I didn't care to know the details of this wedding that I hoped would not happen. To distract myself, I thought of Felix. But, my mind would drift every now and then to the reality of my situation. It wouldn't allow me to escape.

The sound of scraping broke me from my light daydreaming. Light filtered down into the dank hole in the floor. The tile lifted, but I still didn't look up. I had no desire to see Talbot. His hand wrapped around one of my arms. With a violent yank, he pulled from my tiny prison.

My body ached from being cramped in the small chamber for so long. I stood with my head down when his hand left my arm. I said nothing and made no move to get away.

"You know, my little whore, I have to say I didn't enjoy that as much as I thought. Don't get me wrong, I enjoyed it immensely, but I rather think our wedding night will be far sweeter. Until then, you can expect to spend time here when I'm displeased." He placed his hand under my chin and lifted my face level with his. "This is to be our little secret. Should you alert anyone to your presence, there will be other special treats in store. Have I made myself understood?"

I gave no response, which only infuriated him. My silence earned yet another hand mark on my face.

"Get out of my throne room, and be sure no one sees you."

My feet couldn't move fast enough.

CHAPTER TWENTY-SEVEN

he morning hung still. Not even the birds sang, their aubade solemnly marking the occasion. My wedding day, the day that I knew would be the worst day of my life. Unless someone stopped it.

I didn't want to wake, remaining silent and still with my eyes closed against reality. The core of my body ached from repeated abuse. At least King Talbot had used enough sense not to lay hands on me where bruising would be visible with this day approaching. It was for his own protection and not a favor to me. My comfort meant nothing. The appearance of his hands being clean meant everything.

A soft knock at my chamber door announced the arrival of Anwen. Despite what I wanted, I opened my eyes and sat up as she entered. Anwen carried a tray with tea and a small breakfast for me that I refused. My stomach churned. Eating anything at all was unappealing. All I wanted was escape, a task that would be impossible considering the constant watch Talbot had me under.

I sensed Anwen's sadness the instant she entered. Her eyes told me all I needed to know. No rescue had been planned. I would have to marry my monstrous fiancé. I lost complete faith in the rebels in that moment.

While this sad realization angered me, hope still lingered that Felix would make an appearance. Knowing him, it would be at the most dramatic moment possible. Right before "I do".

I listened to Anwen move about the suite as she prepared for the day. I rose to join her when I heard the distinct sound of the baths being heated. The time to pull myself from the warm security of my bed had come. I plodded, without motivation, to the bathing area.

I took a seat on the bench near the bath and watched her as she added the fragrant floral oils that made the water silky and inviting. Staring blankly at the rising water, I got lost in the hollow thoughts that filled my head. I felt nothing when Anwen knotted my wild curls on top of my head to keep my hair from getting wet, then gently prodded me out of my daze. I disrobed and slid into the warm water. The hot water released the pain from my aching body but did nothing to ease the ache in my soul.

My eyes closed for what seemed to be mere minutes, but when I opened them again the warmth of the water had gone. Anwen gave me a sad smile, "I didn't want to disturb you Milady. You looked so at peace for the first time in weeks."

I stepped out of the cool water and slipped into my woolen robe as Anwen un-knotted my hair. "He knows it's today?" I asked uncertainly while Anwen rubbed more fragrant oils onto my arms and legs.

"He does." Those words were enough for the calm I found in the bath to linger a few minutes more. Felix was my only hope. He had to come. I repeated those words in my head as Anwen led me from the bathing area to finish readying me for my wedding.

The calm obliterated once we re-entered the main area of my suite. The dressmakers had arrived while I bathed. My wedding dress hung near the dressing partition. A lump immediately formed in my throat and I forgot to breathe.

In truth the dress was beautiful, fitting of a royal wedding. Made with the finest golden eggshell colored silk with lace sleeves that belled from the elbows and a massive array of skirts blooming from the fitted bodice. The bodice itself sparkled with delicate crystal detailing. The train and veil were made of the same lace as the sleeves and were longer than need be. Despite the beauty of the dress, I didn't love it. To me, it was nothing more than a fancy stockade.

When Anwen and the dressmakers were done with me, I looked beautiful, despite the sadness in my heart. The gown hid the bruises on my legs and core so all that was seen was beautiful lily-white skin. My dark hair was pulled into a loose up-do and dotted with white flowers. I made a beautiful bride. A beautiful bride for the wrong groom.

For a fleeting moment I imagined I wouldn't be meeting Talbot at the end of the aisle, but Felix instead. That brief idea lit me from the inside. My wordless prayer played again. Felix had to come.

"There's the happy glow of our beautiful bride," one of the dressmakers quipped. "Now you are radiant. King Talbot will be breathless when he sees you."

The mention of Talbot was enough to pull the glow from me. I sank back into reality, becoming so empty and dead inside that I felt nothing from those around me. Even my gift was broken.

I RODE ALONE in the royal carriage to the cathedral. The wedding venue was set to be filled by all the nobility within the borders of Realta, as well as from our allied nearby kingdoms. Even Duchess Emile promised to attend. But, the bridal guests were next to none, even then few for whom I cared for. I'd see my Quaintrelle friends, but palace staff wasn't allowed to attend the wedding, and that meant Anwen wouldn't be there. I've even settled for Kizzy and Aunt Rowena to attend on my behalf.

I didn't allow myself to cry; no matter how much I wanted to, I had to be strong and endure. Talbot wouldn't defeat the tiny thread of hope I desperately clung to.

Felix had to come.

My fiancé had warned me days earlier that I must look every part the blushing bride, I pulled all my remaining strength and thought of Felix yet again. Perhaps if I pretended my marriage would be to him, I'd make it through and avoid Talbot's ire in the end. I couldn't bear to endure a beating on top of what I knew else I must do tonight, if I was not rescued.

Felix had to come.

The carriage pulled up to the front of the cathedral and my heart pounded like a caged beast against my ribs. Before getting out of the carriage, I pinched my cheeks to make them rosy. I had to don the appearance of a blushing bride. This was it; there would be no getting out of it now. Soon, I'd be Talbot's no matter what happened, unless…

Felix had to come.

The doors to the cathedral were flung open the moment I reached them. A grand flourishing trumpet called, followed by a dulcet wedding march. I entered the church, taking in the beauty inside that I could not fully enjoy. Every row of pews, and every alter were lavishly decorated with the finest arrangements of expensive flowers and yards of flowing white taffeta. If this were a happy day, it would have been a dream to look at.

My feet moved as though they were encased in frozen lead as I made the march from the cathedral doors up to the altar. All the faces watching me blurred together. I marched to what felt like my execution.

Felix had to come.

My mantra reminded me what I needed to look happy. I thought of the warm embrace of Felix's arms and the way my heart melted at each beaming smile.

Felix had to come.

My eyes fell on Talbot, who stood in his place next to the priest. I couldn't deny he looked handsome, despite wicked gleam in his eye. I focused on the parts of him reminded me of Felix. I had to convince myself that my fantasy was real. I needed to in order to finish my bridal march. Otherwise the day might end disastrously for me.

I closed my eyes for a few steps, really focusing on tricking my mind. When I opened them again, I smiled. My trick worked. Talbot was gone and Felix stood in his place. I took his hand and joined him at the altar.

CHAPTER TWENTY-EIGHT

elix did not come.

As soon as I uttered "I do", the fantasy I wove in my head dissipated, the need to pretend happiness faded. Felix disappeared, Talbot appeared in his place.

My newly appointed husband ushered me down the aisle and out of the cathedral. I let him drag me from the hallowed building and into the awaiting carriage. My fight diminished; no one stopped this from happening. Those I trusted to keep me from being wed to the tyrant had abandoned me. Worst of all, Felix had not stopped it.

I wondered if his feelings for me changed when he realized our plan failed. Decided I wasn't worth the trouble. My heart cracked, filling me with a pain more unbearable than I ever thought imaginable. My mind became so consumed with grief that I noticed little else.

The carriage ride bumped and blurred past. Time meant nothing. Tears flowed down my face with abandon. I didn't care about appearances any longer. I hoped my swollen red face would turn my husband's appetite against him, but I knew all too well that he wouldn't care. I belonged to him, I had become property, not a partner. Property for him use as he willed.

Talbot promptly left me in Anwen's care the second the carriage stopped at the palace. Her eyes appealed sorrowfully to me, the apology she couldn't say aloud dancing there. I couldn't look at her. In my heart, she had betrayed me, too. She promised the rebels would stop the wedding, that our plan to reveal Felix's right to the throne would come first. Now, she was preparing me for my wedding night. No apology she had could make up for that.

"Make her ready," King Talbot said, hastening away.

Anwen led me by my elbow into the royal chambers, which occupied nearly the whole upper floor of the wing facing the towering Eira Mountains to the north. My feet dragged each step.

As we passed the near wall sized window, I could imagine King Bern standing there, smiling a wicked smile to himself as he thought of how close he had hidden his son's bride. Of his victorious control over his son. I couldn't help but think I would much rather a prison like hers than the one I would occupy for the rest of my life. How ever long that may be. For all I knew, once Talbot had his heir, my life would be forfeit.

I hoped any child we had wouldn't be Fae blessed as I had been.

As Anwen closed the door behind us, she opened her mouth to say something.

"Don't, Anwen. Whatever words you have are too late." I stifled a new batch of sobs. "Just undo my ties and leave me. I can dress myself."

"But," she began.

"I said no. Do as I ask, it's the least you can afford me."

"Yes, your Majesty." She loosened my corset and dress in silence. "You'll find what you need behind the partition," she said woefully. Another apologetic look dressed her pretty face. Tears filled her eyes and she fluttered a hand over her mouth. Finally, she left with her head hanging low; her quiet sobs were cut off when the heavy wooden door clicked into place behind her.

I sat on the ornate bed I had to share with the man that made my life hell these past months. My body felt so heavy, like my sadness had become a physical thing pulling me down. It grew heavier and heavier by the second. I rubbed my hands over the decadent blue blanket that matched the swooping drapes above the bed. While I did, a horrible image of the night to come crossed my mind. I shuddered at the pictures in my head. Flashes of pain and shame. Based on the horrific ways King Talbot had placed his hands on me since my return, I dreaded what he might do to me now I belonged to him. Now that there was no need to hide the abuse.

He warned he would have me, willing or no. I imagined fighting it would only lead to things more dreadful than I dared to think about.

Heavy tears fell from my eyes once more, spattering onto my lap in a pluvial nature. I stared at my silk gown. The spots my tears made seemed to be screaming my lament to the world. They taunted me.

Felix did not come.

The sound of larks outside broke my trance, reminding me I needed to move. Talbot wouldn't be happy if I wasn't ready for him. I steeled my resolve and plodded slowly to the partition. Grabbing the side, I gave a tremulous sigh. I could do this. Being a former Quaintrelle; I had already been well trained in bedding men I did not want. I could do this, or so I thought.

I knew there was a chance my training would be pointless. Now that my heart had known real love, it was much harder to recall my training. I closed my eyes and rounded the edge of the partition.

"Hello, Sweet," a familiar and unexpected greeting knocked the wind from my lungs. I stumbled back in shock. As my eyes opened, I saw him sitting in the dressing chair, looking dashing in his charcoal gray jacket. A twinkle gleamed from his eye and a half smile adorned his face. I saw my lacy, white dressing gown hanging in his left hand. "Now, tell me again, for what reason was it pertinent that we return you here?"

I flew at him, unsure of what I would do when I got close enough to touch him. I was so angry and heartbroken that he didn't come sooner or stop the wedding. I wanted to slap his charming face. At the same time, I was overjoyed to see him my caged heart was tearing free of its bonds. I wanted him to hold me close and kiss me the way he did at the tavern on Apoidea.

He stood tall, ready to meet whatever I hit him with. The confident stare on his face solidified what I knew I would do. As I approached my arm flew back as if on its own volition, preparing to strike. Felix never flinched. My hand met his face, leaving an angry red mark as evidence. His nonexistent reaction somehow comforted me. Another round of tears broke free; tears that were angry, sad, and happy.

I fell into his broad chest and let the tears flow. "Why didn't come, why did you not stop it?"

"Because, Sweet," Felix lifted my chin, "imagine the scandal. The fearsome, and recently pardoned, Captain Wade spirits away with the Queen of Realta; on her wedding night no less." His words mimicked what he said months before. He loved the idea then. He was reveling in it now. A dramatic rescue if ever there was one.

A playful grin spread across his face. "But first, I think you should change. I'd be blinded trying to carry you off in that frock." Before leaving me to dress, he wiped away the lingering tears and kissed my head. A warm feeling rushed through me. A feeling that I feared I'd never feel again.

A fire rekindled in me. I could feel hope building outward from the darkness that filled me this last months. I dressed in the dressing gown in haste, only noticing how little it actually covered once I put it on. The plunging neckline left little of my breasts covered, and the delicate white lace emphasized my marked body. Each bruise was easily seen through the sheer lace pattern.

I thought of how silly it seemed that little girls would often dream of wearing the purple of royalty when playing childhood games; how terrible it was that I wore it on my skin rather than as a dress. No girl had ever dreamed of purple skin.

In my head, I wished that Anwen hadn't been in charge of readying my honeymoon attire. An escape in this dress would be bound to draw attention, even if I wasn't the queen. With a deep cleansing breath, I left the privacy the partition had given me, with excitement coursing through my veins. I eagerly wanted to see the man here to save me.

The ever-playful Captain had sprawled himself across my marriage bed, waiting with a gleeful glint in his blue eyes. He hopped up at my appearance and rushed to greet me. He smiled in approval at the revealing gown, but just as quickly his mood dampened. Storm clouds crossed his eyes when he noticed the bruises that were hidden beneath my wedding gown. I could tell a new hatred for King Talbot budded within him as he passed over each mark. "Oh, Sweet. What has that monster done?" As he studied me his obvious anger rose further.

After a moment, his face brightened as fast as it had darkened; though the hint of storm still lingered in his eyes. His firm hands pulled me close, "Better scream, Sweet, this is, after all, a kidnapping."

I smiled and loosed a beautifully constructed call for help.

"Perfection," Felix winked as he slung me over his shoulder. He ran for the balcony. Felix didn't slow his pace; he meant to hurl us over the side. I screamed again, this time with real fear.

"Don't fret," he whispered. "I have a plan."

My head jerked up at the sound of someone entering the suite. Two guards and Talbot rushed in just as Felix hurled us over the balcony edge. Their faces, in masks of horror and rage, peered over the balcony as we landed into a makeshift rescue cot that a couple of Felix's men were waiting with. Felix dragged me from the cot, making good show of abducting his prize. My limbs flailed, pretending to struggle against him. I screamed another cry for help as he hoisted me over his shoulder once more. Felix turned and saluted Talbot with his free hand before taking off towards my freedom.

The king's face became beet red as he spouted curses at Felix and his own guards. The guards scrambled to obey his orders, but it was no use. We were long over the garden wall before anyone had time to stop us.

Smith and Mister Bimble waited for us on the other side of the palace walls. Felix set me down only for me to be swept right back up in a bear hug from Mister Bimble. Joy filled the air. My heart filled even more seeing these two. In the short time I'd been on The Fura, these men had grown to be like family.

Smith hugged me in turn and handed me a long, heavy cloak to cover myself with. Running around in this very revealing dressing gown hadn't been ideal, but it had been necessary. I thanked Smith and threw it around my shoulders in a flash. We were off once again before I'd finished tying it closed. Smith took lead and Mister Bimble brought up the rear. If Talbot's men caught up with us, he was best suited to defend us.

The worry of being caught lessened the further into the wood we went, where the trees grew closer together to create a maze of sorts. The dense underbrush masked our footprints. Despite the added protection of the trees, our defenses never completely dropped. Not even when we reached a hidden clearing connecting with a seldom traveled dirt road where Domhnall waited with Gregor's wagon.

"Hey now. There she is!" he exclaimed rushing forward to greet us. Behind him, Liam popped up in the wagon and waved ecstatically before clamoring into the driver's seat. Mister Bimble climbed up next to him. Smith, the two men that held the cot, Felix, and I hurried into the back of the wagon. In moments, we were off into the darkening woods. Despite our head start, we still needed to get as far away as fast as possible.

I snuggled into Felix's side for comfort and warmth. A blissful relief began to creep into my bones, happy to be free yet again. I knew that this time would be very different from the last time. King Talbot would pursue finding me this time, with vigor and venom. Felix had embarrassed him and taken what belonged to him. His pride was at stake this time.

"How did you breach the palace? Talbot has his men alerted to apprehend you if you ever came to the palace."

"But his men are fools, Sweet. At least those he left behind at the palace today were. Getting in was easy with a simple disguise, finding the royal chambers, however, required assistance."

"Assistance?"

"Your Anwen. She is a gem."

I realized then that she'd tried to alert me to Felix's presence in the royal chambers. Her heartbreak hadn't come from my being doomed, but because I'd scorned her. Dismissed her with a coldness I'd never shown her before. If only I hadn't let my feelings get in the way and allowed her to speak. If only my sorrow hadn't made my gift fail. "She knew? She was trying to give me good news and I dismissed her out of being hurt. Blamed her for betraying me. If ever I see her again, I'll make it up to her."

"That will come in time. All that matters now is that you are safe," Felix commented.

"The danger is not over yet Felix. Talbot will be seeking revenge this time," I emphasized.

"I know. I'm looking forward to it."

WE SAW no sign of Talbot's soldiers following us when we returned the old wagon to its owner, who greeted us with fervent concern.

"You used my wagon to kidnap the queen? And took my son along for the ride?" Gregor laughed, though his fear wrapped around him like a heavy blanket. His eyes scanned over the group, and after a moment he shook his head. "Seems everyone is accounted for and safe, despite your foolish game. Better be off quickly, Your Majesty, before your soldiers find you."

"Please, just call me Merinley. I want to thank you for all of your assistance, sir."

"Gregor." The old man corrected me as well. "Don't think anything of it." Gregor's eyes drifted over to Felix, that same wistful mist crossing them. "You have a fine man here Merinley. Don't go getting yourself back in that wretched man's grasp."

"I don't plan on it, Gregor," I replied.

Gregor turned to Felix, "You and your men can count on my help anytime, Captain Wade. Any enemy of King Talbot is a friend of mine."

Felix laughed and shook Gregor's hand. "Thank you, Gregor."

With no time for idle chatter, we left Liam and Gregor as soon as the other men were out of the wagon. The rest of our escape would be on foot until we reached The Fura, still nestled deep inside Fenian Cliffs.

CHAPTER TWENTY-NINE

I laid in bed, my mind far too active to allow me to sleep. I thought back on the events that led me there, feeling waves of sadness when I remembered that I was married. Legally, I belonged to a man I didn't love. I was the wife of a monster. I tried not let my thoughts settle there, reminding myself that I'd been saved. Felix saved me and took me back to The Fura, where I belonged.

I shoul've been nothing but relieved.

But my mind couldn't stop circling back to dark thoughts, about the ramifications of our actions. Should we be caught, Felix would hang. It was likely I would swing next to him in the gallows. I shuddered with the morbid thoughts, disturbing the sleeping captain.

Still heavy with sleep, he propped himself up on his elbow, using his free arm to drag me into him. He soothed away my thoughts of death with the gentle tickle of his fingers on my arm. Wrapped up near him, it was easy to feel safe and let my worries abate. He'd use everything in his power to keep me so. Twice now, Felix had saved me from horrible men. Still, I couldn't stop the fear completely. King Talbot could do far worse than the inept abductors from so long ago. With a valid reason to use it, he had an entire army at his disposal to hunt us down.

"What bothers you?" Felix whispered in my ear, his voice husky with sleep.

"There's too much in my mind, I can't sleep. I'm worried. What happens if he catches us?" I didn't need to name who.

"Have I not demonstrated how good I am at saving you?"

"Of course." I pressed a light kiss to his cheek. His words reminded me whatTalbot let slip about my original abduction. It was news Felix needed to hear. "It was Talbot, you know."

Felix nuzzled into my neck, "No, Sweet. I do think I did the rescuing."

"Not what I meant," I gave him a playful shove with my shoulder, then turned to face him. "He ordered the kidnapping, all those months ago. He hired a man to take me, the man that hired those thugs from the inn. He never anticipated my return and thought his grieving state would allow for him to do as he wished without the people complaining."

Felix stared at me in disbelief,"Who told you this?"

"Talbot did, after the Hero's Ball, after you left my chambers. He came into my chambers asking me to join him in his bed. When I refused he came at me like a storm, furious and unrelenting. He said he saw how we looked at each other during the dance he allowed us to share.

"When I tried denying it, he beat me. He was out for blood." I paused with the fresh memory of that night; I had never been so terrified in my life. Tears clouded cloud my vision as I continued. "When Talbot is angry his lips are loose. He accidentally let it slip that he was responsible for my abduction. When he realized what he'd done, he let it all out, including that he ordered the abduction to gain sympathy from the people. Then he told me that I belonged to him and threatened to revoke your pardon if he saw you near the palace again."

Anger built up behind Felix's eyes, yet he remained outwardly calm. "Sweet, you are safe now. I will protect you with my own life, that wretch shall not lay hands on you again." He paused a moment in thought, "Did he let slip who it was he hired?"

I shook my head. Talbot was smart enough to keep some of the details to himself.

"That makes it harder to use against him. I do know a few scoundrels that specialize in hiring third parties to keep their employer's hands clean. I'll figure this out, it could prove useful against Talbot."

I sensed that the time had come to reveal what else I knew; to reveal to Felix his role. Still, I held my tongue, nervous about how he would take the news. My withdrawal of words didn't go unnoticed.

"What else, Merinley?"

"That may not be necessary." My hands nervously twisted the blanket. Revealing these things to Felix threatened to change everything. He could take the news in any unpredictable way. "There's another way to make him fall. A better way."

"And that would be?" Felix sat up a little more, inching closer to me as well.

I pulled away, putting space between us. My heart raced from the uncertainty in my head, of how to share the rest of what I came to realize all those months ago. Why I left. I decided to start at the beginning."There are rebels in Realta. They have information that will be detrimental to Talbot's position. I have little hope that they'll use it, though. The rebels have had this information for months and they have done nothing that shows conviction."

"What do you mean?" It was Felix's turn to pull back, but not from nerves. He was amazed, confused at the revelation.

"They mean replace him on the throne."

"How? Surely any qualifying noble to replace him would be just as bad, if not worse. The lot of that family tree are vile, reprehensible," Felix seethed. His distaste for noble families in Realta ran deep. I didn't blame him one bit for that. None of them had ever shown any trace of goodness. None, save Prince Declan. His mother was to thank for that.

"Not necessarily, there's at least one good one. The rebels have intelligence on this person that will rip Talbot from his lofty perch and keep any of his known kin from replacing him."

"Known kin?" I had Felix's curiosity piqued.

I bit my lip and searched Felix's eyes. This part proved the most difficult to divulge. "I need you to listen with an open mind on this. This part may be the hardest to believe. And it may not be something you wish to hear."

"Go on, Sweet. You have my word." His strong hands wrapped around mine, and his blue eyes became soft with compassion. But, I could feel the worry swirling in his heart. See the uncertainty on his furrowed brow.

"King Talbot should never have been crowned. He is not King Bern's rightful heir. Prince Declan had another son." Felix gave me a crooked, puzzled look. A look that said the idea had never occurred to him. I suspected it hadn't, why would it have if his identity had been kept from him his whole life. I delved into the story of how Anwen and I had pieced together, about the diary and about Prince Declan's first wife and child.

"If there's another heir it will be hard to prove on more than a few old documents and the words of a retired Quaintrelle. You say you found all this out from Prince Declan's journals?"

I nodded furiously. "There is more to it than that, something huge and even more seemingly far-fetched. I believe that we have found out the true heir, Declan's first born son." Felix leaned forward, his eyes wide and eager for the next revelation. The one I feared most. I swallowed hard, unready to reveal this part. Unsure of how he would react. "This is all tied to St. Ludo," I chickened out, heading the conversation in a wider circle. "Where you were born and raised." I suggested, hoping he would follow the crumb.

"Yes, I told you that. What does that have to do with this?"

I inhaled deeply. Felix didn't understand. "King Bern hid Prince Declan's wife there. Prince Declan's son was born at that convent."

"What? Are you saying that you think…?" Felix paused, unable to finish the question. He ran his hand over his face, which looked overwhelmed.

"I'm saying that I know you should be King of Realta."

"How can you be so certain?" Felix's heart warred with the idea.

"The evidence is there. You are the right age. And, no offense, you do resemble Talbot. Not identical, but close enough if one were looking closely they could easily see the relation."

Felix stood from the bed and paced, deep in thought. He was silent for several minutes.

"What are you thinking, Felix?"

"Firstly, asking to be returned was a terrible idea. Secondly, I have serious reservations, doubts. Fate really has dealt a strange hand here, if everything you say is true," he laughed wryly and paused for several long minutes with his back turned to me. For a moment, I thought the news broke him. I thought he might refuse to believe it.

I got up and crossed the cabin to him, resting a hand on his shoulder, "Are you alright?"

"Yes," he nodded, turning to face me. "I'm good. Now, whether or not what you say is true, whether or not there is some other true heir to the throne of Realta out there, or if I am, it'll be met with doubt. There will be accusations of lies and trials to go through. It will not be easy. But that's not our immediate worry. There is also one other problem, Sweet"

"What is that?"

Felix took my face in his hands and stared into my eyes. "Even if you can prove it and the throne is no longer Talbot's, you are. A change in position will not change that you are his wife. I hate to imagine what he'd do to you, should you be involved in him losing his power. The only way to be certain that that monster is no longer a threat to anyone, is if he's dead. I intend to be the man to slay the beast." Felix scanned me with his eyes, his gaze stopping on each visible bruise. "When next I meet Talbot, he shall suffer greatly for each and every time he placed his hands on you, and then he will know my sword."

CHAPTER THIRTY

Once again, I found myself setting toward the shores of my childhood home. We figured that word of my abduction wouldn't have reached the neglected Apoidea, yet. For all we knew, they weren't even aware of the wedding. Nothing could be done about it if they knew, but it didn't matter to us. Apoidea had been my home. Felix and the crew were loved by the whole island. These facts made it less likely the people would betray us. Still, we harbored on the far side of the island, away from any habited area, and the main port, just in case.

We weren't taking any unnecessary risks.

As Felix, the crew, and myself walked through the market it became apparent there would be no playing at being part of the crew this time. My secret, the lies I told, had been outed. From the looks of it, for some time. Tattered wedding announcements hung limply on the doors and windows of many of the buildings. Seeing my face plastered next to King Talbot's everywhere I turned was a sickening reminder of recent events. A reminder I belonged to him in the eyes of the law and God.

The people we passed didn't seem to care.

This time the men scattered throughout the market, going to where ever they pleased. There was only one place I wanted to visit, the tavern. I had a promise to keep.

The distinct sound of Esme's delighted squeal greeted me the moment Felix and I stepped into the tavern. My eyes followed the sound and spotted her coming at us from the main seating area. Seeing her again felt amazing. After the last time, I knew our friendship had no bounds.

She sprung at me, wrapping me in a tight hug, "Merinley! Oh, I probably shouldn't be hugging you like that. I mean, Queen and all." She backed off, but she looked like she wanted to explode out of her skin. "I can't help it, I have to hug you! It's so good to see you again. I never expected to after those fliers were hung. But that makes me wonder. Why am I seeing you again, and in the same company?" Her eyes darted in a playful manner between Felix and me.

"Good to see you too, Esme. I see you had your baby." I tried changing the subject by drawing attention to her now flat stomach. I had little desire to speak of anything to do with King Talbot, even though I knew I had to eventually.

"I did. He is so beautiful Mer. I wish he were here so you could meet him. My parents took him not long ago, giving me a much-needed break." Esme bubbled excitedly about her baby.

"I'm sure I will."

She nodded and jumped right back into what I could tell she was dying to talk about, what I dreaded discussing. "We were all shocked here when we learned you were marrying King Talbot. You should have seen the shade of green your Aunt Rowena turned when she found out. It was the best thing I have ever seen. Anyways, after how you were with Captain Wade here last time, we were all convinced you were with the pirate. Even Kizzy said you were. What is going on?"

"I kidnapped her, of course," Felix jumped in, still feeling prideful about his latest adventure. His long arms wrapped around me possessively.

"Oh my goodness. What?" Esme laughed.

I knew there was so much more explaining to do. "How about we sit down somewhere and I'll tell you everything."

"Looks like you'll be busy for some time," Felix whispered to me. "I will be close if you need me." With a quick kiss, he left me, going to sit at the bar so I could speak with Esme alone.

We moved our conversation to a seating area near the tavern's fireplace, which roared with an inviting blaze. I made no hesitation once we were seated. I told Esme my story; from my aunt and uncle selling me up to Felix rescuing me after my wedding. Every word had Esme rapt with emotion.Tears stained both our cheeks when I finished.

"Why didn't you say anything when you came back?" Esme sniffled.

"I didn't think anyone would believe me. I should've known better." I confessed through lowered lashes, ashamed I had so little faith in the people of my home, the people that loved me and my parents.

"That is ridiculous, Mer," she chided playfully. "Of course we would've believed you, and we would've made sure certain people knew we did."

"Thank you, Esme. That means a lot to me." The way she spoke made me think perhaps everyone on Apoidea already had an idea that my relatives were less than reliable. It did nothing to make my sheepishness wane. I should've thought better of my people and less of my own trials.

"Thank goodness for Captain Wade, making you safe. I'd hate to think of the life you would have had as King Talbot's bride."

"Yes, Felix has been my saving grace, but we are far from in the clear. There's a hazardous road ahead for us before we can really be safe."

"That you do," she agreed.

Our conversation drifted to more pleasant topics, leaving behind the darkness of Talbot. We talked for hours, only breaking when Esme was needed in the tavern. She grilled me about my time as a Quaintrelle, how I met Felix, and for every detail about my adventures with him. Talking with her was cathartic, healing deep wounds from being torn from my childhood home. When dusk settled over Apoidea, the time came to head back to The Fura. I hated to leave, even though I knew I'd see her the following day.

THE TIME APPROACHED to leave Apoidea, even though it was one of the safest places we could harbor. Felix, with advice from Cook, ordered we only stay a day or two in safe ports. There would be no visiting places with strong ties to Realta until our problem resolved. We were on guard for the time being.

The Fura bustled with activity. All hands were called upon to ready the ship to sail. Every rope in the sky high maze above the ship wiggled in anticipation of the open sea. Each man moved confidently around the rigging. A well oiled machine after years of experience. Their movements were like a dance, hypnotizing to watch and deftly executed.

I would've loved to stay on deck, watching them. Doing so would have put me in the way, a dangerous place to be on a bustling ship. Instead, I helped the only way I could. My place was in the galley, helping Cook take inventory. Clara sat on the edge of the table watching me, hopeful I'd toss her a scrap now and then; which I obliged when Cook wasn't looking.

"Merinley, Cap's lookin' for ya." Hawthorne came bursting in. He grabbed a pickled egg from the jar on the table, shoving it in his mouth with gusto. The move earned him disgruntled looks from Cook and Clara, the little ix because he didn't share. Hawthorne, not bothered by upsetting the older man, took another egg and laughed, his smile bright against his midnight skin.

"Where?"

"In the cabin," Hawthorne replied.

"Can you take over for me Hawthorne?" I asked, swiping a stray hair out of my face. No matter how tightly I pulled it back, some of it always escaped; as was the unwritten rule of curly hair.

"Sure thing," he smiled, dimpling his cheeks. "Anything to get out of helping Nigel in the crow's nest." Cook grumbled under his breath, not wanting Hawthorne and his bottomless stomach anywhere near the supplies. Clara, on the other hand, chirped excitedly and jumped to his shoulder. She was far more likely to get fed all her little heart desired with Hawthorne there.

I wiped my hands on my pants and headed out and up towards his cabin. Our cabin.

I found him pacing; when he saw me enter he beamed at me. My heart fluttered, as it always did when he looked at me with that smile on his face. The one that made him look dashing and goofy all at once. His unique smile that I couldn't help but return.

"Felix, Hawthorne says you asked for me."

"Indeed I did," he crossed the room, gathering me up in his arms and kissing my cheek. "We have an important task on shore before we make sail."

"What is it?"

"A surprise."

I groaned. Surprises hardly turned out well for me. Almost every surprise I experienced, changed my life, turned it upside down; mostly not for the better. Granted, there were few that turned out for the best, but the odds were not in my favor.

"Why the face? This is a good thing, Sweet. Trust me." Felix's eagerness perplexed me. I had no idea what he had in store for me that would have him so excited.

I gave in. Felix never steered me wrong, but apprehension sat in my stomach like a stone.

"Not that way," Felix pulled against my hand. We turned away from clear path that led to the market. My surprise was not there, like I assumed. Surely what he had in store was not in the tiny group of houses considered the village. Most Apoideans lived scattered about the island, nestled in clearings in dense woods that covered most of it. That left one place that made my heart thump nervously in my chest.

Felix turned onto a path thick with overgrown ferns and wild-flowers and my heart sped up double when the path confirmed what I worried over. We were headed to the secluded cabin where the Elders met.

"Felix?" I questioned his confident sense of where he headed. "We shouldn't be out here without invitation."

"Trust me." His blue eyes sparkled with excitement. Whatever he had up his sleeve had him positively gleeful. My curiosity inched higher, despite my better judgment. Why would he bring me out this way at all? He spent enough time on Apoidea to know that no one went to the Elders' cabin without permission. Doing so was disrespectful, not only to the Elders, but to the magic of the island. Our Fae lineage. It simply wasn't done.

The Elders' cabin looked exactly as I remembered. Rough hewn logs made up the body of the cabin. The roof, shingled with circular cuts of the same logs, adorned with a spider web of moss. The eaves dripped with honeysuckle vines and thick boughs of wisteria. Simple chimes and charms made from shells and bones hung from the eaves. There were no windows, keeping the secrecy of what happened inside from the outside, and only one door, sky-blue and carved with images of the natural world around it. Bees, ix, and other fauna and flora. Built within a large circle of overgrown, red and orange mushrooms, surrounded by verdant flora and large trees with beehives within them, the cabin was the center of the Apoidean Fae ancestry.

I felt transported back in time as I stared at the cabin. A knot formed in my throat, and my feet glued to the forest floor. "This is my surprise?" I stammered.

"Go on. Knock." Felix stood against a nearby oak, that foamed with fermenting honey from the hive inside, with his arms crossed over his chest and his signature smile on his face.

"I can't. We're not supposed to be here. It is sacred," I countered, fighting the urge to march back to The Fura.

"Just do it, it's fine." Felix gave a little wave of his hand, urging me forward.

Tentatively, I walked up to the cabin and reached up to the door and prepared to knock. I hadn't been to this sacred place since my parents died. Being there rushed all of those long past feelings back to me.

Feeling small, and alone despite being surrounded by the entire community of Apoidea as they mourned the loss of an Elder and his wife. I hesitated as the memories washed over me.

Before I could knock, the door swung open wide to reveal High Elder Tam, the oldest member of the Elders. Like the cabin, little had changed about Elder Tam over the years. I recalled when I first met her when I was small, jarred by her appearance; she really did appear to be a witch. She was old, bent, and wrinkled with knobby joints. Her eyes were the same shade of gray as the wild halo of hair on her head. A few wiry gray hairs grew from a mole on her chin. A large fang stuck through her left ear and another dangled from her right by a delicate chain. After all these years away, I found her witch-like appearance comforting.

She welcomed me with a big hug. "Merinley, daughter of Elder Nicholai, we have been waiting for you. It's time for your Ceremony of Gifts. "

Bleary eyed, I turned to Felix, who looked even more satisfied with himself than before. "They came to me Sweet, asked me to bring you here." I broke free of Elder Tam's hug and threw myself at Felix.

"Thank you!" I couldn't help but fall into kissing him, getting lost in his lips. This was the second best thing he'd done for me. Kidnapping me was the first.

Elder Tam cleared her throat, reminding us that we weren't alone. I turned with a sheepish smile and looked back at Elder Tam, my cheeks flushed from passion, and embarrassment. "Sorry, Elder Tam."

"Don't be sorry for your joy Merinley," Elder Tam's eyes nearly disappeared in her wrinkled face when she grinned her snaggle-toothed grin. "You've had too much sadness in your life to deny yourself to freely express your happiness." She motioned for me to join her inside.

Entering the cabin, there were no words that could describe how I felt. I thought I'd never take part in this sacred ritual. Yes, I knew I had a gift; but I'd always been curious how different it would be if I had been properly guided. If my parents weren't stolen from me.

I entered into the anteroom and expected Elder Tam to follow directly behind, but she didn't. She still stood at the door, watching Felix. "Elder Tam? Are you alright?"

"Yes, Merinley. I think your Captain Wade should join us." Her eyes had yet to leave Felix; she stared with a knowing smile. A smile that meant her gift shared something important with her about the rogue that stole my heart.

"But Elder Tam, it's forbidden for outsiders to see our sacred rituals." I remembered my father stressing the importance of our sacred rituals to the Apoidean people, the importance of keeping them from being seen by those who didn't understand. Those who judged.

"I invited him did I not? Captain Wade is as much one of us as if he were Apoidean born. He can be your anchor as we perform the ritual. If you like, that is."

Elder Tam's blunt and endearing explanation warmed me. Letting him join the ritual, as an anchor no less, meant a lot. The anchor was traditionally a family member meant to support the person undergoing a ritual. Felix acting as mine was a great honor. She wouldn't allow it if she were not sure of his loyalty. "I would like that very much, Elder Tam."

She nodded once and called Felix into the ritual cabin. I could tell the honor elated him as much as it did me. There was no other living soul that I'd rather be there with me. He bounded up to the door, scooping my hand into his and kissing the back of it.

We entered the cabin together, hand in hand, receiving greetings from each of the council members. The Elders were all seated on low chairs arranged in a circle. At the center of the circle sat an empty chair large enough for two that sat a few inches higher than the chairs the Elders sat in; it was surrounded by sixteen lit candles. Felix and I were to sit in the center chair.

Along the walls of the cabin hung portraits of all of the Elders of the past. The chair set out for me faced one special to me, my father, Nicholai. Too many years had passed since I'd seen his face, even in dreams. The gesture from the Elder's was touching. It was like having my father there. Misty tears sprung to my eyes, and I fiddled with my mother's locket. A sweet feeling of being whole filled my heart.

"Your father?" Felix asked, grabbing my hand. I could find no voice within me, so I nodded. "He had your spirit, that's easy to see." His arms wrapped around me, in comfort. The moment was sweet, bonding.

Elder Tam interrupted, asking me to take the seat in the center of the circle. "Merinley, daughter of Elder Nicholai, this Ceremony of Gifts is unusual. Your life path did not allow for you to follow this rite as those who came before you. Your life was meant for things bigger than what this island could offer." She hobbled close to me, inspecting me carefully. "I can see from your aura that you have magic. When did that manifest?"

"Early, Elder Tam. I can't remember a time without it." The Elders all knew of my gift already, there wasn't much they weren't aware of when it came to the Apoideans. Most of the island knew as well. When I was small, I had difficulty not blurting out what I sensed about how others felt without them telling me. My gift was no secret here. Asking about it was simply ceremony.

"What is your gift, Merinley?" Elder Tam asked.

"Empathy. I feel what others feel; I feel their desires and needs as if they are my own. I know if they intend on doing good or harm."

"Yes, that is part of what I have seen for you. And the other?"

"What do you mean?" I asked.

"What few outside this room know about me is that I do not just see the aura of others; I read them. I can divine things from their past and am privy to the path their life will take."

"You know what is to come?" I was amazed at Elder Tam's revelation.

"No, Merinley dear, what I do is much simpler. While I can catch glimpses of a person's past from the memory that surrounds them, I can't see the future. I only see the direction their life should take, what their purpose is in life.

Your aura tells me you are as rare as I, maybe even more. Not only did your gifts manifest early, you have three powers my dear child; one is yet to surface. That unknown gift is itself a rarity, for a gift to bloom so late. I can't tell you what your inactive gift will be, though I do know its readying itself to emerge. I can also tell you that your empathy ability is still growing, that it will grow for as long as you live. You may even be able to influence emotions someday."

Elder Tam's assessment astounded me. Astounded and confused. "Elder Tam, I don't have more than one gift. Empathy, that is all."

"Well, sometimes we surprise ourselves. Do we not?," her wrinkled face lit with secrets. "Now, let's get on with the ceremony and find out what we don't know."

"Captain Wade," Elder Durriken said. He was a stout bald man with caring brown eyes and wiry black hair, took control over the next part of the ceremony. "In this next stage of our Ceremony of Gifts we will be inducing Merinley into a sleep state that should encourage growth in her gifts. During this sleep, she should be able to get a sense of what her gifts are. A Fae journey of sorts.

The more we know about gifts often encourages them to grow. Your task is to hold her, your presence will be felt and will remind her that all she sees is just a dream. This is the purpose of an anchor. As Merinley is older than usual for this ceremony, we know the risk of her becoming lost in this dream state isn't as great as with one younger, but we still ask this of you as tradition calls for it."

Felix showed he understood with a quick nod. They removed the chair I sat in from the circle, and instructed Felix to sit on the floor first. Next, I was instructed to sit in front of him so that I may lay with my head in his lap when instructed.

Elder Durriken gave me a snifter of the honey produced by Apoidea's large bees laced with valerian root to help me sleep, as well as wild canary grass to produce visions. The drink had a sickly sweet flavor; I had to force myself to finish the small dose. The concoction took effect immediately. Warmth spread through me, making me feel as though I was made of the sweet honey potion. The room seemed to slow and my limbs felt heavy, encased in stickiness.

"Merinley, you need to lie back," Elder Durriken's instructions sounded muffled, and far away. I laid back, placing my head in Felix's lap. "Felix, place your hands on Merinley's arms and keep them there until she wakes."

I looked up at Felix; he wore a serious expression. The potion Elder Durriken gave me made him appear fuzzy and glowing. I wanted to touch his face, to feel the light surrounding him. But my hands were too heavy. "You shine," I giggled, slipping into darkness.

There were no visions. I existed in darkness barely aware of Felix's hands on my arms. I heard distorted tones of the Elders and Felix talking in the empty space. I wondered if this is how this ceremony happened for everyone, or if I could hear them because I was older than normal.

I woke slowly. My head pounded and all the warmth seeped from my bones, leaving ice in my veins. The dim room came into focus. Felix helped me sit up and hugged me close to him. His delicious heat and scent enveloped me. Someone handed me a cup of what I thought was more of the honey concoction; I tried to refuse it.

"Water," Felix whispered in my ear when I pushed the cup away. "It will help ."

With a shaky hand, I accepted the cup, and drank with greed, not caring that it dribbled down my chin. The water washed away the remaining traces of the honey mixture. Nothing ever tasted better.

Elder Tam's face appeared over the edge of the cup, slightly out of focus. Despite not seeing her clearly, I saw questions etched into her face. More accurately, felt them. She waited, patiently for me to finish, shifting. "Tell us, Merinley, what you saw in your sleep." She stepped forward the moment the last drop of water passed from the cup to my lips.

"Nothing. I saw nothing, but I could hear you, sort of. It was like hearing underwater."

"That's most strange." She scratched at the hairy mole on her chin. "Very strange. Are you sure you saw nothing?"

"Without question."

"Do you use your gift purposely, let it do as it wills?"

"In truth, Elder Tam, no. I've had to keep my true self hidden all these years, out of fear. Only a few I trust illicitly know I'm Apoidean, fewer still know I'm an empath. Did the ceremony not work because I didn't nurture my gift enough?"

"No, though suppression does explain some things; such as lack of growth in ability. It could also be why you're unaware of your second gift and why your third has yet to emerge. I think your second gift may be visions, but it is weak so the potion hardly had time to work before your body rejected it. If it were strong, the potion wouldn't have worked at all." Elder Tam walked across the room and points at a portrait of a past Elder, a woman with short golden hair that framed her long face. "Elder Ruelle had visions and the potion didn't work on her either."

Elder Durriken came and squatted next to where Felix and I sat. His golden brown eyes studied me with care, as if looking for evidence of something, "You have visions?"

"No, I…" I thought back to the dream that I had when I had been unsure whether or not to return to Realta. The dream that pieced together Felix's story with the one Anwen told me of Prince Declan. Then my memory flitted to the morning that changed everything. My sixteenth birthday. I recalled the dream I had just before waking and the warning my mother offered in it. "Maybe." I told him of the dreams I had, leaving out the details of Felix's identity.

Elder Durriken nodded and smiled. "Yes, your second gift very well might be visions. A very special gift to have."

"Begging your pardon, Elders," Felix interrupted. "I need to be taking my leave now if my part in the ceremony is done. There's much to do before we set sail."

"Of course, Captain Wade. Thank you, again, for agreeing to bring Merinley to us. She won't be long behind you." Elder Durriken replied.

"It was my pleasure," he replied. "I'll see you in a little while, Sweet." He kissed the top of my head."Will you be saying your good-byes at the tavern before you return to the ship?" I nodded, leaning into him again. "Good."

With one last kiss, Felix left the cabin and headed back to the ship. I had to keep my time with the Elders short if I was going to have enough time to visit Esme. There was so much I wanted to ask them about. But there wasn't enough time to cover it all. There was one thing I had to know before I left. "Elders, I know that my having multiple gifts is rare and would be beneficial to our people. Should I return to Apoidea where my gifts could be of most use?"

Elder Tam answered, "Merinley stop. I see you conflicting your head and your heart. You have a strong sense of duty, just as your father did before you. Do not let your sense of duty eliminate what your heart desires.

"Yes, we would benefit greatly with you among the Elders; but your path lies with Captain Wade. Your paths are intertwined and would be even if your life had been different. Stay on your current path. Follow your heart, listen to it, you will find that it leads to good things."

I considered her words for a few minutes, looking back on the road my life had been on; the road it was heading for. She was right, how often had I given up what I wanted for the sake of others? To do what was expected of me? More than once that sense of duty landed me on hot water. My current situation being the result of my insistence of doing my duty, was. More than enough evidence of that.

"Thank you, Elders, for all you've done for me today." I offered my hand to each of them. "This has been the most wonderful honor, and I'll never forget this kindness you have given me."

There was a lot to think about on my walk toward the tavern. I'd discovered so much during my time with the Elders. Those discoveries gave me a lot to think about on our journey.

CHAPTER THIRTY-ONE

My mind tumbled like a raging waterfall as I made my way from the Elders' towards the market. I wanted to stop in the tavern before I made my way back to The Fura. Seeing Esme one last time before we left held a significance in my heart. I didn't know if I would see her again once we left these shores. She'd been my best friend, and more than understanding of everything since my appearance back on Apoidea. No questions, just love. I had to see her, and perhaps catch a glimpse of her baby boy too. I owed her a goodbye, just in case.

The jingle of the door's bell could barely be heard over the delighted squeals of a baby as I entered the tavern. My heart squealed in delight too. I followed the noise to the back of the room, pushing past the crowded tables. There I found a scene that stopped me happily in my tracks. Esme sat in a chair, her head resting in her propped up hand. Her gaze falling in adoration across the little table at her sweet little one, snuggled in the large muscled arms of Mister Bimble. His face performed acrobatics, creating the silliest faces I'd ever seen. No wonder the babe laughed so rambunctiously. I probably would've too.

It was endearing to behold.

Esme spotted me, lifting her weary head from her hand and waving me over emphatically. "Mer! How was your ceremony?" she asked the moment I reached the table.

"You knew?" How was it that I was always the last to know about anything big happening to me?

"I just learned of it. Mister Bimble told me when he came in."

The giant of a man looked up from his game, "Cap asked me to wait on ya, escort ya back to the ship." He instantly returned to making faces at the baby, who squealed once more in delight.

"It was good, a lot to take in." I smiled at the scene before me. "He is really good with him."

"I know. I wish I could keep him around all the time. Maybe I'd get more rest." Esme was silent for a few more moments. "Do you want to hold him? Give our friend here a chance to rest his face?"

"I would love that." Mister Bimble transferred the boy to my arms, stretching his in relief once freed from his sweet little captor. The babe began to protest at first, letting out a little squawk of displeasure. "Hello, little man," I said to him sweetly. He immediately quieted and looked at me with his wide curious eyes, as if to study me. I looked back into his little face and fell in love. After a minute he decided I wasn't that bad and cooed, his little rosy cheeks bugling with the shape his little mouth made. He had Esme's wide, curious eyes and the sweetest baby chub. "He looks much like you, Esme. What's his name?"

"Merin, in honor of my best friend," she reached out and grabbed my elbow tenderly.

She named him for me. The tribute was moving and unexpected. I never expected that I still meant so much to Esme. It was almost as if we had never parted, had never lost touch. She treated me like I didn't suddenly disappeared from her life, then just as suddenly reappeared. She was a true friend. I wiped an errant tear from my cheek as I snuggled her little one, breathing in his baby scent. "He is absolutely beautiful, Esme." I lost myself in the simple moment, and for the first time, dreamed of having a moment like it again.

Once again, my mind fleeted away to revelations of my ceremony and thoughts of another life with Felix. One where I had never been sold, never been in Realta. A life where I met Felix on Apoidea. Would we be sharing something like Esme and her husband? Have a babe of our own? Or would we be sailing the waters of the world, a thorn in the side of Realta and a savior for those they oppressed? The idea seemed a long lost dream.

The reverie was broken when Hawthorne barged into the tavern. His chest heaved as if he had run the entire way from The Fura to the tavern. He gasped for air twice before finding his words. "Bimble, Merinley, time to move it. Realta soldiers have anchored in port and will be in the village shortly."

The news jarred me. I expected soldiers to make an appearance here sometime, but not so soon. Apoidea was low in priority to Talbot, nor did he know it was my birthplace. This was the last place I expected he would dispatch his men.

I kissed Merin's little head and handed him back to Esme with a one armed hug. We said a quick goodbye. There was no time to linger, time was of the essence. Hawthorne, Mister Bimble, and I flew fast out of the tavern. I prayed we'd get back to the other side of the island undetected. I knew the chance of that was slim, according to Hawthorne they were close already.

Minutes after we fled the tavern, we were stopped in our tracks. A small group of seven soldiers meandered into the market. Each carried a satchel filled with rolled parchment pieces. They hung the new posters, not even bothering to take down and discard the wedding announcements still plastered on every available surface. I couldn't be sure without looking, but I had an inking those new papers were reward posters. With the way the men were scattered, there was no way we wouldn't be spotted.

Sure as the sun sets, one of the men, a gangly fellow with an orange beard, spotted us. There was a moment of hesitation on his face, fear even. His call to his brothers in arms caught in his throat, coming out garbled. It didn't matter, they had already spotted us anyway. Their faces held the same fear as the first man's. Every one of them kept their eyes locked on Felix's intimidating First Mate. Mister Bimble did that to many.

Mister Bimble had a mighty reputation. Not only for his size. His fighting skills were whispered ghost stories amongst soldiers of many nations. Legendary. He was feared and worshiped. All of that was there on the faces of the Realta soldiers. Despite his legend, they meant to engage. They had to. Their orders likely left them no choice.

"Halt!" A short soldier with bad skin and a small gut called out with a slight tremor in his voice. "Surrr, surrender now or face the full power of King Talbot."

My companions chuckled, no intention to obey feeble orders. "Get behind me, Miss," Mister Bimble instructed. "I'll get you to the ship, I promise." The giant man lumbered forward at full speed with Hawthorne at his side. They plowed into the trembling soldiers, a torrent of fists and teeth.

The fight was unfair. Hawthorne and Mister Bimble knocked out the majority of the soldiers within minutes. Three remained. Hawthorne took on one in a match that seemed even. Mister Bimble wrestled the other two at the same time. In truth, I believed that the two pirates were taking their time with them; letting off a little steam and enjoying the combat. Their laughing banter as they fought certainly supported that theory.

Movement just behind the fray caught my attention. One of the fallen soldiers rose from the dirt and attempted a hobbling run toward the port. He meant to return to their ship and gain reinforcements. Mister Bimble and Hawthorne were too busy with their current matches to notice, it was up to me to stop him. I couldn't let him get to his ship. I took off in a run towards the melee and called out for Hawthorne to throw me one of his short blades. He seemed confused at my request but followed my order. He pulled his dagger from his boot and tossed it in my direction.

I caught the weapon by the handle, the cool metal stung my hand. The slight inconvenience didn't give me hesitation. Quickly measuring the weight, I spun the blade in my palm before dropping to my knee. I drew a breath and threw the sleek weapon, which flew fast and true. The brawling men's attentions were drawn to it when it soared past them; their gaze followed it. Their faces gaped as it hit the mark;

sinking into the back of the running soldier's leg, just above the knee. The soldier tumbled into the dirt with a cry.

Inspired by my display, Hawthorne and Mister Bimble made short work of their foes, knocking them out with brute punches.

"Well done," Hawthorne congratulated me.

"Oh, I'm not done with the fool yet." I wanted to see what they were plastering the Apoidean market with.

We approached the soldier, who lay bemoaning his injured leg. As we neared him he scrambled in the dirt. It wasn't until we were next to the soldier that I saw how young he was. He couldn't have been more than thirteen, though tall for his age which was why I mistook him for being older. His baby face dripped with sweat and his dark eyes filled with fear. My insides seethed with guilt and anger towards my estranged husband. This child knew nothing of being a soldier. He was merely an expendable body.

I crouched, pulling the knife from his leg. "Mister Bimble, would you restrain him please?" I asked while wrapping my scarf around the wound. "I apologize that I had to harm you, but I couldn't let you get away. My freedom is too important." I felt bad about resorting to injuring him, I'd never had a problem with any of Talbot's guards. Sure a few of them were loyal to him, as well as like-minded. But, for the most part, they were just boys and men doing their jobs. Keeping bread on their tables. Following orders. "We'll tie you up, when your comrades awaken you can return to your ship. We'll be long gone before then."

"No, please, Your Majesty. Do not leave me. King Talbot won't be pleased when he learns of our failure here. He will kill the lot of us for failing," he hiccuped between raking sobs. Genuine fear rolled off him. Tears streamed down the young soldier's face as he begged for his life. "Just take me with you, lock me up if you must. But don't leave me. Please. I don't want to die," he pleaded with waterlogged brown eyes. "Don't let him kill me."

"Mister Bimble, what do you think?" I asked.

The first mate hemmed over the proposal, scratching the chin hiding under his fiery beard. "Cap is not going to like it. Could be a liability."

"He's just a boy. I have already maimed him, I won't be responsible for condemning him to die. Trust me, he's not trying to deceive us." I paused for a moment and made a brash decision. "He's coming with us. Smith can properly patch his leg. If Felix has a problem with him, he can take it up with me." I stood, brushing the dirt from my hands while glaring at Felix's men. Nothing they said would get me to abandon the boy.

"Yes, Ma'am," Mister Bimble conceded warily. Without further discussion, they agreed to take the boy to The Fura. Hawthorne didn't take any chances and bound the boy's hands with no struggle.

While he placed the boy under arrest, I jogged over to the nearest new paper hanging in the Apoidean market. Even though I was certain they were notices for Felix's head, I wanted to read the page for myself. I needed it confirmed. To see what we were up against in terms of the temptation set out for bounty hunters.

I tore the paper down, along with one of the wedding announcements, which I allowed to flutter to the ground. Nothing could have prepared me for what I saw when I read it. It was not a call for bounty hunters, or a poster marking us as wanted. The flier was different announcement altogether. An execution had been planned for in three weeks time to punish the treasonous accomplice to my "abduction".

The treasonous accomplish in question; Anwen.

My vision narrowed, and a stone took up residence in my stomach. Cold shivers raked over my body. Talbot planned to execute Anwen. While she did facilitate Felix entering the honeymoon suite, she didn't deserve the king's wrath. Knowing how King Talbot's wicked mind worked, I feared that he may try to torture information from her first. That he would gain all her secrets before she hung. He might even do it publicly, just before the execution. Talbot's sick mind would get a lot of pleasure from that. Anwen knew so much about the rebellion and the conspiracy to dethrone Talbot. She knew a good percent of my secret. Should she spill her knowledge, any chance we had would be diminished to near nothing.

I folded the paper up and hid it within my belt. Running was no longer an option. It was time to do something. Anwen had to be saved.

"WHAT IS THIS?" Felix barked at Hawthorne. He glared at his returning crew with a skeptical eye, none too pleased to see the state we were in, or the young soldier with us.

"Ask her." Hawthorne nodded in my direction as he led the young soldier past.

"Merinley?" He turned to me, crossing his arms across his chest and a hint of surprise in his steady voice.

"He's a child. I couldn't just leave him to suffer. I injured him, now I'm going to fix him up and protect him." I met Felix, mimicking his stance.

"Protect him? He is a soldier. King Talbot's crony."

"Barely! He was a mess in the market. It's like Talbot slapped a uniform on him and put him on a boat. He's a child and no threat to us. I *know* he's no threat," I challenged. "You can trust me."

Felix, understanding my emphasis, ran his hand over his face and groaned. "You are certain?" he asked after a moment.

"You know I am."

Felix marched up to the young soldier, who quaked in Hawthorne's grasp. He stared him down, eyes squinted and lips pursed; intimidating by any standards. "Are you going to give me trouble, Boy? Because if you give me trouble, I give it right back and then some. You do not want that."

"No, no Sir. No trouble," he stammered, sweat rolling down his brow. "I swear."

"He stays in the brig, and needs to give up any information he knows." Felix commands.

"Of course," I agreed, "but, he needs to be treated well. Show him he can trust us; that we won't turn on him." He suffered enough abuse from his superiors as they answered to their king. I wasn't going to stack any more cruelty on top of that.

"Anything you want," the soldier adds, showing his compliance with eagerness.

Felix gave a curt nod, implying he was satisfied there'd be no problems with the boy. "Someone go get Smith, he'll take the boy to the brig and care for his injuries.

I accompanied the young soldier to the holding cell with Smith. I wanted to assure him that he could trust Smith with his care. Aside from being able to give him the medical treatment he needed, Smith was the man I trusted most to assuage the boy's fears. He was the least threatening member of the crew.

After that, I made my way back to the cabin. The whole way there my mind was preoccupied with the memory of my last encounter with Anwen. I was selfish and tuned her out; turned her away. This was my fault for sure. If I'd given her a chance to speak, she may have escaped Realta with us. She'd be on the ship with us, not being tortured and played with by that man. We would've had more time to plan out a way to bring Talbot down. Instead, we were being forced to act unprepared.

Felix wasn't alone in the cabin when I got there, not surprising considering our current situation. It made sense for him to be in counsel with his First Mate and a handful of other crew members. Instead of finding them in deep conversation about our next move, I was greeted by Mister Bimble regaling them with the scuffle in the market.

"I had no idea she'd actually hit the boy with the blade. Ya don' hear of court ladies being able to actually wield weapons. When the blade sank in his leg, well, that was impressive. Made me realize the Cap' was not speaking in metaphors when he bragged of her skill with a dagger." He laughed boisterously and slapped Felix on the back. The rest of the men all joined in.

Their laughter thinned when they noticed me, growing silent. They appraised me with new admiration, with the knowledge that I was more than what I had seemed in my time with them. Their acceptance of me shifted into something deeper. Well most of them anyways. Nigel still glared at me like a rat stowing away in a barrel of grain.

"Could I have a moment with Captain Wade, men?" I asked.

"Men." Felix's command only needed one word for them to follow my request.

I handed the notice of execution to Felix, "Talbot's set a trap."

"This doesn't feel like a trap," Felix said as he read it. "It's more of Talbot being, well, Talbot."

"It is a tap." I bit my lip, and tears began to well in my eyes.

"How can you be so sure, Sweet? He could honestly just feel like executing her just because he's angry. I wouldn't put it past him," he argued. In any other situation I'd have agreed. This was different.

"I know Talbot better than I'd like," I countered, keeping a sob at bay. "Tell me, what if someone took something of yours, some piece of property and you happened to have something of theirs that was important to them. What would you do?"

He thought a moment and then begrudgingly admitted, "I'd use it as bait to get what is mine."

"Exactly. To Talbot, I'm property, nothing more. Valuable property. He knows I left willingly, despite what we tried to make it look like. He knows, he just plays along to save face. If the people knew I ran off on our wedding night, it wouldn't look good on him. He's putting on a good show while baiting me with someone I care about."

Felix nodded in eventual agreement. A sly look spread over his face. "We take the bait. This is the perfect reason to go back to Realta. We try to save your Anwen. I end Talbot. But we're going to need some help."

"From where? The rebels have done nothing to prove they are anything other than lily-livered. They've done nothing with any of the information they've been given."

"From old friends of mine, the Lesh," Felix said with a nonchalant shrug.

"Lesh?"

"I believe you would know them as savages, Sweet."

CHAPTER THIRTY-TWO

There were so many pieces that needed to fall into place in order for this mission to succeed, but there was little time to do it. The only way we could even hope to succeed would be to send an away team ahead of us. The team would need to be small enough to not draw attention, but large enough to split up.

Domhnall and Hawthorne were the first to volunteer for the task. They both were eager to end Talbot's reign. To my surprise, Nigel also volunteered. I knew he felt neither here nor there about why we were doing this. He didn't like me and wanted me off of The Fura since Cook had threatened him. Possibly before. I suspected he only volunteered for selfish reasons, to either be away from me or because it was a means to get me off of the ship permanently. In the end, five men were selected to be dropped off at Fenian Cliffs.

The young soldier we acquired on Apoidea with was to go with them. The boy was little help with information about Talbot's plans. He had, as suspected, been given a uniform for a meager promise of two pence a week, and no training before being shipped out. He did, however, turn out to be a hard worker, once he proved to be trustworthy. Felix didn't mind the boy being on the ship, and found he liked the boy. Still Felix had no intention of taking him to Lesh with us. He didn't want the kid to cause problems there with the prejudice he was likely raised with.

The selected mens' orders were to make their way from the cliffs to Gregor's farm to acquire horses to take them on the rest of their journey to Realta, and to leave the injured young soldier in the old man's care. In Realta, they'd separate. Hawthorne, Nigel, and a third member of the crew would wait for us there. I hoped they'd flush out some rebels that were willing to take action as well. There wasn't much hope there, only a shred, so I wasn't holding my breath. As for Domhnall, he and his partner would continue on into the Eira Mountains to Saint Ludo. There they'd search for Sister Benedict's documents to prove Talbot should never have been crowned.

That wasn't Domhnall's only mission. I pulled him aside before he and the others were set to leave The Fura at Fenian Cliffs.

"What is this?" He asked when I handed him the letter. Instead of grabbing it from me, he let it fall at his feet. With a huff, I scooped it up and held it out in front of him.

"Something very important. An urgent message for Gregor and his family, only for them. Don't tell the others you're delivering this message. This is secret. Not even Felix knows." I made stern eye contact with him to make sure he understood. "Make sure they get this when you stop there."

"But why keep Captain in the dark?" Loyal to the core, Domhnall didn't like deceiving his captain.

"He will know, in time. I promise this is a good thing. You will not get in any sort of trouble for keeping this secret from him. In fact, I think you'll end up being very happy for your captain."

He took the letter hesitantly. Domhnall had ill feelings about keeping secrets from Felix. Yet, he also trusted me. Eventually the potential happiness this favor would bring won out. "Alright then. I will make sure this is delivered."

I watched the shore of our destination inch closer as we sailed in. My anxieties about Felix's decision to enlist the help of the Lesh erupted like wildfire with each minute that passed, despite everyone's insistence that they weren't what I had been taught in Realta.

I heard little of Lesh during my years on Apoidea. Or maybe I just paid no attention, too consumed with what had happened in my personal life. My first real recollection of hearing about them came from when I lived in Realta. Frightened whispers about the savages to the north swept through the servants quarters. Booming declarations of the evil that lived there were made by soldiers and nobles alike. Even the Quaintrelle were fed propaganda against them, especially after self defense had been added to our lessons. Lessons on the extreme horrors of the "Savage Lands" accompanied the exercises our trainer had us do. The most emphasis being on that there were no people there. There were monsters that disguised themselves in the skins of their victims.

Admittedly, on many nights, I had nightmares from the tales. Of creatures maiming my sisters and wearing their skins to get to me.

I should've realized I'd been taught falsehoods about most things that were looked down on by Realta. Just like the lies they spread about my homeland, the truth about Lesh was skewed to cause fear. Still, that fear they instilled in me played at the back of my mind.

We dropped anchor in the harbor with no need of hiding or sneaking in. The men hopped into action preparing the longboats to get to shore. Down below, the harbor mirrored the bustling activity of the ship. But it was not because of the ship's arrival. Men and women tended to tangled fishing nets strewn in the water and across the beach. Children played down the shore, splashing and squealing in the clear waters. No one seemed to pay any attention the large ship that had just pulled into their midst.

"Why do they seem to not care that we are here?" I inquired of Mister Bimble.

"They care, Miss. But the Lesh are patient and respectful when it comes to their friends. They give us time to settle before they swarm the shoreline to wait for us." Even as the long boats splashed down and the call for going to shore went out, the Lesh continued on with what they were doing.

"But how do they know you're ready?" Mister Bimble didn't

respond with anything more than a lift of the corner of his mouth. Instead, he raised a fat, white horn to his lips. The horn emitted a low melodic hum when he blew into it. "That's how," he replied when he finished blowing.

I looked back over the harbor to confirm his claim. The people stopped what they were doing and flocked towards the shore. Many of them were shouting and waving their arms in excitement. Felix and his crew were just as welcome in Lesh as they were in Apoidea. Living examples of the old adage about enemies and friends.

Despite their friendly appearance, I was still on edge. Something seemed off to me.

The first mate followed me to where the crew descended into the longboats. Felix waited there for me, wrapping me in his arms when I met him. "Are you ready?"

I was far from it, but there was no choice to be otherwise. If Felix said these were possible allies, this meeting had to happen. I nodded once, my underlying nerves tied my tongue.

"Come then," he took my hand and helped me over the side of the boat.

In the longboat, I could not help but let my inaccurate teachings infiltrate my mind. On top of that, I felt nervous about what these people were like, and how they would react to me. I was, after all, a stranger to them and still the queen of a land that hated them. Felix was their ally, not me.

The ride from The Fura to the shore of Lesh tormented my mind. The closer we got to shore the stranger I felt. The feeling intensified when it was time to exit the longboat and journey into the crowd waiting for our arrival. The moment my feet stepped onto the wet shoreline, I realized what was wrong. I couldn't feel them. For the first time in my life, my abilities were rendered useless for no reason. I stopped in my tracks.

"Felix, something is wrong," I pulled on the sleeve of his coat to get him to stop as well.

"What is it, Sweet?"

"I don't feel them," I whispered nervously, eying the approaching crowd of strangers.

"What?"

"I cannot get a read on their emotions. I've never been rendered blind by such an amount of people. One or two every once in a long time. Never a whole group. It feels wrong."

He put an arm around me, laughing lightly, and encouraging me to continue onto the beach. I resisted still. "Everything will be fine. These are good people. I'm sure there's a good reason why you're having trouble reading them." The way he spoke made it seem like he had an idea of what that reason was, but he wasn't sharing. His assessment didn't make me feel any better about the situation.

Before I felt ready to move forward, the Lesh had already reached us. "Ah, Cap-ee-tan Wade," the man breaking through the crowd called out. His height impressed me, he may have been taller than Mister Bimble even. He wore clothes made of furs and leather. His graying black hair had been knotted in strange snake-like ropes and his body marked with intricate inked designs. His approach indicated he was the man in charge. "I hear you have irked the King of Realta, yet again."

"Aye, that I have Sy. I even dare say that I've finally beaten his distaste for you." Felix stepped up to the man and they embraced as old friends.

Sy grinned with an air of mischief when he saw me hiding behind Felix, "I see that you have indeed, old friend." He slapped his friend on the back and laughed. "This must be why."

"Sy, may I introduce Merinley, Queen of Realta." Felix guided me around him with a firm grip and a reassuring expression.

I cautiously greeted Sy. I'd never been in this situation, not being able to read a person at all. I held my hand out in a timid gesture and curtsied.

"A pleasure, to meet you. You must be special indeed for Cap-ee-tan Wade to risk life and limb for you." He took my hand and kissed it.

A slight shock resonated through me when Sy made contact. I pulled my hand away in surprise, not because I had become more apprehensive. The opposite had in fact occurred. I felt a wave of relief with the shock. For a brief moment, I'd been able to feel his emotions, and they were just as surprised as mine.

Sy's eyes widened in accordance with what he felt. He unleashed a friendly but wicked grin with matching laugh. "Apoidean! Very intriguing. I wonder, does your husband know?"

I blushed, feeling naked that he knew my secrets without my sharing it. I shook my head in response. "I may be young, but I'm not a fool." I looked the large man over and questioned, "How did you know?"

Sy let loose a full-bellied laugh, "I like her, Cap-ee-tan! Come then, I tell you over a meal and we will discuss the purpose of your coming here."

We followed Sy and a handful of his people along trail lined with dried grass that led to a village made up of large tents and small lean-to stables. As we strolled through I began to see these people less and less as the savages that Realta painted them as. Everything I saw painted them to be no more barbaric than any other people. No evidence of them being monsters could be seen.

Sy's tent loomed high over the others, intricately decorated with beautiful glyphs of various animals and human figures. Though his tent had a distinction that set him apart as their leader, it didn't feel like a status symbol. His tent placed him as being of his people and sat in a place that they could access him with ease.

This man was a true leader. One of his own people. Equal. He was how the leader of a nation should be.

Outside of Sy's tent a large wolf-hound and a black cat nearly the same size as the dog lounged. As we approached, they stood and lowered their heads ,as if bowing. I astonished at their unique behavior, figuring his animals were well trained. Sy noticed my reaction to the large beasts and gave me an impish wink and toothsome grin before nodding to his furry guards.

Inside the tent, there were large, colorful rugs made of both fur and woven wool draped in heaps about the floor. Some smaller, woolen mats were arranged in a circle near the center of the tent. The mats surrounded a clay vessel of some sort that is releasing some steam from the top. A faint scent of something spicy swirled within the steam, filling the tent.

Sy sat on one of the mats and indicated for us to join him with a sweeping wave of his hand. "Now, my friends, I understand you seek my help to take care of a mutual, king sized, problem."

"How did you know that we came to ask for help and not a place to hide?" I asked.

"You told me, much like you told me who you are. You see," a man and a woman entered the tent, interrupting Sy. They were carrying rustic, stone trays of food and drink. He motioned for them to bring the trays over. The man was lanky, tall, and had a mop of scraggly gray hair on top of his head and adorning his chin. The woman, whom also had a great height, had striking golden eyes. She moved in a feline way.

They laid the trays on the ground between us and took up their places, flanking Sy. My eyes moved over the offering of foods. One tray held an array of vegetables and fruits, many that I didn't recognize. The other offered a large roasted gourd of some sort that had been sliced into large chunks.

Sy continued on, without missing a beat, drawing my attention back to him. "You see, I am like you. Like Apoidea, Lesh was once Fae lands. We descend from them, as Apoideans do. They've blessed me gifts beyond that of most humans. Many of my people been blessed. I, for example, can read all about a person with a touch. I know that you were sorely mistreated and sold by those you called family. You are extremely powerful and caring. And you will do anything for the people you love."

"Was that what that shock was? Your gift?" I inquired, fascinated.

"No, our Fae blood recognizing one another."

"I've never felt that before, I mean when I've touched others from Apoidea."

Sy looked amused, "Of course not. I take this the first time you met someone of Fae descent not from Apoidea?" I nodded. "I thought so."

"There are others? Not just Apoideans and Lesh?"

Sy smiled and gave a slight nod, "Yes there are, all over the world. That shock, as you call it, is Fae signature; a way for different clans to recognize they are meeting someone like them. An ally in blood. You cannot always tell one descended of Fae by looks."

"Aside from the Lesh that is, Sweet," Felix said. I looked at him with wonder and mild aggravation that he knew this but didn't share. He was enjoying watching me discover all of this, and I knew deep down why. He didn't inform me about Lesh's secrets because he wanted me to discover them on my own. He wanted to experience my learning about those like my people.

"Why do you say that? I see nothing different about them, other than that many of them are quite tall."

"And that is signature of shared blessing of Lesh that have been blessed," Sy informed me. "You see, our blessings vary; much like those of your people. Except with your people, most only receive one blessing. The rare few more. Here, those who are blessed, are blessed twice. One individual and one shared. I shared that mine is the ability to know a person by touch. Zuri here," he nodded towards the woman who came in before, "is incredibly fast. And Grove has a calming effect like no other." Sy motioned toward the scraggly man.

Every Lesh granted gifts from their Fae lineage had two gifts. The idea fascinated and amazed me as much as learning there were even more people out in the world with Fae ancestry. All these years I thought my people were alone in that. Never once did I question that thinking, but only because I didn't know better. Apoideans were so isolated by their contract with Realta, I wondered what else we were ignorant of.

"What of the shared blessing?" My curiosity peaked when Sy mentioned their shared gift.

"How about we show you?" Sy grinned.

"Oh, yes!" Felix crowed and rubbed his hands together in excitement. His reaction told me that something amazing could be expected.

The three Lesh stood in unison and each began to remove their fur and leather clothing. As they stripped down, I leaned to Felix and whispered, "What is going on?" I couldn't think of what kind of shared gift would require them to be naked.

Felix's face beamed with delight, "You are going to love this, Sweet. It is spectacular."

I turned my attention to the now naked trio, gasping in unexpected surprise. Their bodies contorted in painful angles. Hair sprouted from every surface of their bodies. A painful howl erupted from Grove, and his body lurched forward. He doubled over to place his hands on the floor before him.

I watched them, fascinated, realizing what their shared gift was. They were shape-shifters.

The horror tales spun by Realta of monsters that wore human skins clicked. Their fears of the unexplainable and unknown turned the Lesh's shared gift of shape-shifting into nightmare inducing tales to sow distrust.

Their painful looking transformations finished in minutes. Every trace of humanity erased fro them. Zuri transformed into the black cat that had been outside when we got to the tent. Grove, the larger than average wolfhound. He turned in a playful circle and panted happily. Sy transformed into a great white bear, bigger than any bear I'd ever seen.

Their transformations made me think I could be astonished no further. When I heard Sy's voice in my head, I was doubly so. *"You see now, Queen Merinley, what our shared blessing is. This the reason for our great height when we in human form, our bodies need be able to contain the animal within. You will see during your time here, we also have some of our people are quite diminutive as well, they transform into smaller animals."* Sy continued on to explain that the shape-shifting gift didn't manifest until a Lesh reached their full growth. He also explained how when they were in animal form they communicated telepathically.

Sy finished his explanation and he changed back into human form. The process looked even more painful than the transformation into an animal. I didn't envy them the process, and didn't think I could handle such a thing myself. He re-dressed and sat, selecting a slice of the roasted gourd. "So now, we discuss what we can do for each other," he said between bites.

"My guess is you already know exactly what we are here for, but to be clear, we need muscle. Fighters. King Talbot plans to kill someone that means a great deal to me, soon. He means to do this solely to punish me, to draw me in. We need to save her, and in the process save Realta too. In short, we want to get rid of Talbot. He should not be king." I explained.

"Yes, that would be a good thing. You will take the throne yourself, Queen Merinley?"

"I'll no longer be Queen when Talbot is removed. Women, as you may already know, aren't allowed to rule in Realta. Sure there are queens, but in name only. They have no power."

"So who would rule?" he smirked and flashed his eyes at Felix.

"A better man, who happens to be the rightful heir of Realta's throne. Talbot was wrongfully crowned." I said.

"Interesting," he smirked. With his gift, he likely already knew. Had known for years. He just wanted to hear it out loud. "You are certain of this heir? Certain they will not be as corrupt as others?" Sy asked, adding to his ruse.

"There's no doubt in my mind that they will be a far better leader than Realta has seen in ages." My words caused a wave of apprehension to emit from Felix. I squeezed his hand in mine, hoping the gesture would ease some of his nerves. He squeezed back, but I still sensed he had doubts about his role; about his ability to rule. I had no such fears.

Sy's eyes danced between the two of us. "Indeed, he will." He reached out and held Felix's shoulder, confirming that he already knew. "I would be honored to be part of bringing such a worthy man to the throne of our neighbors. Perhaps peace can build between our lands at last."

"And between many more," I added.

"If you knew, why didn't you say anything?" Felix asked.

"Would you have believed me?" Sy chuckled.

"I'm still struggling to wrap my head around it." Felix rubbed the back of his head, "So, what do you say, old friend?"

"I say, about time."

Relief washed over me. We had the help of Sy and his people. Certainly, with their help, we held a much higher chance of accomplishing our goal. We just needed to make a plan.

"Now, how do we enter Realta without detection?" I asked.

"Ah, Sweet, I have no intention of sneaking. I'm bringing the fight to that foul excuse of a man, and I wish him to quake in fear of my coming."

CHAPTER THIRTY-THREE

An eerie silence hung over Realta. The port and streets were void of people. Vendor stalls were closed. The only signs of life were sea birds and rats. Even those seemed to be scarce, and ill at ease. The scene filled me with a sense of dread and unease. The emptiness was a bad sign. The only reason I could think of that Realta would be so barren, chilled me. That reason; the main square was packed with people. Packed with people ready to witness an execution. Their attendance mandatory, though I was certain many would attend just out of morbid curiosity. It wasn't every day one saw a former Quaintrelle on the chopping block, proving in the reign of King Talbot, no one was safe. It was sure to be a spectacle the people would whisper uncomfortably about for ages. If we didn't stop it.

Ice ran through my veins. Was it possible that we were too late? Did Talbot move the execution up? Had seeking out help delay us too long? I urged the men to make haste. We had to reach the main square to see for myself if we were too late to save Anwen from King Talbot's misplaced wrath.

We ran with the devil on our heels. Our feet thundering on the cobblestone echoed the terrified drumming of my heart. The entire way, the empty city became more and more unsettling. Every sound we made reverberated back to us, only magnifying the strange abandoned feeling.

We found the same emptiness at the main square. No one lingered about, save for Domhnall, Gregor, Liam, and a few men I didn't recognize. They were ragged in appearance. Their clothes dirty and torn; their faces wore masks of relieved exhaustion.

My own mixed emotions battled in my head. I was elated that the square was not the grisly scene I'd imagined. Where ever King Talbot had Anwen, she still lived. She would be broken and terrified when I found her, though. Those scars would be healed in time. It was better than brutal death.

On the other hand, fear still wove vine like tendrils into my heart. Fear that wherever Anwen was, it was too late. Fear we would fail.

Fear of losing Felix.

"Captain!" Domhnall trotted across the square to greet us.

"Domhnall, it is good to see you have made it here safely. Where are Nigel and Hawthorne?"

"They've gone out into the city, scouting for those willing to join us, we've had little luck so far. The only two to join us are these men." He pointed to the ragged pair I noticed earlier. Both were emaciated, hardly looked able to lift a finger without pain, let alone a sword. But, it was their heart that mattered in the end."We freed them from the stocks when we got here. They agreed to help us for our assistance."

The lack of help from the very people we sought to liberate stung. Even though there was a chance of Talbot winning, and doling out punishment to anyone involved, the good outweighed the risk. One would think so anyway. It said much that a people were so terrified of their ruler that they ran away from hope.

Still, I was glad for what help we had. We had our reinforcements from Lesh, but that still left us outnumbered by unknown numbers. These two men who bravely volunteered despite their weakened state added to our numbers, barely. For that I was thankful. Every extra body counted.

"Good," Felix nodded his approval. "How did your mission fare? Felix greeted his crewman with a slap on the back. "Did it go well?"

"Aye."

"I see Gregor and Liam are with you." Felix looked at the farmers curiously, uncertain of why they'd follow Domhnall.

"Yes, they insisted on joining me to the convent and then here. Said they had to be here."

"I thought they would, after the letter you delivered for me." I assessed.

Felix raised a quizzical brow, "Letter?"

"Yes, I sent them a letter through Domhnall. I thought they'd want to be here for this."

"Why would you think that, Sweet?"

"Gregor has a big stake in what we do here today. He'll see justice for his daughter, Prince Declan's first wife."

The confused look on Felix's face washed away into one of enlightened awe. He got it. An overwhelming rush of happiness rolled off of him. "Oh, you mean?" He asked with a hopeful tone.

"Exactly."

A bona fide grin took over his expression. He just went from orphan to having family. Blood family that could teach him about his parents the way no one else could.

"What?" Domhnall stood scratching his head. He didn't know the whole situation and I sensed that he didn't like being out of the loop.

"Don't pain yourself too much over it, Dom," Felix patted him on the shoulder. "Everything will make sense when the fight is done."

While the two men dove into a light banter, I spied Gregor across the square. He played with what he saw as a large wolf-hound. I knew the wolf-hound to be Grove. Liam sat nearby watching them.

I crossed the square to join the old farmer and the shape-shifter. A buzzing anticipation grew with each step I took. Before I reached them, I sensed the change in Gregor and Liam. They had a renewed fire in them, Gregor most of all. I assumed my news, that his grandson still lived, had something to so with his new outlook.

"I see you've made friends with Grove," I said as I stopped near them. Gregor and Grove stopped their frolicking and Liam stood to join his father; giving an enthusiastic wave of greeting which I returned. Grove trotted over to me and sat; his tongue hanging and tail wagging. I patted him on the head.

"The beast just ran right up to us a minute or two before you all arrived in the square," Gregor laughed. "He is a remarkable dog. Why am I not surprised that you know him, my queen?"

"I told you, I'm just Merinley, my friend. But yes, Grove and I are new friends." I heard Grove grumble about being called a beast, but that h'd let it slide since the old man was nice. "He likes you."

"You speak to animals then?" Gregor chuckled.

"No, Gregor. I just know."

"Should I phase, Queen Merinley?" Grove's voice echoed in my head.

I shook my head "How about you go round up your kin, Grove. I'm sure they have scattered about the city waiting for us." He barked and ran off.

"Well that's something," Gregor gave an astonished laugh. "You sure about being able to talk to animals?"

"He's Lesh."

"What now?"

I realized Gregor wouldn't know this name, just as I didn't until I learned better. "From the savage lands. I'll explain later. First, I want to know how you are doing."

"Well, I…" He looked off into the distance in wistful thought. "I'm hopeful for the first time in ages. It's all because of you, Merinley. Why do you think that Rosalie's child lived? In all the time Declan visited us before his death, he never once brought it up as a possibility."

"He visited you after he married Emile?"

"Yes, for some time. Then he got sick and began to just send gold coin our way, to make sure we had nothing to worry about during lean times. When he passed, we were just as devastated as when our daughter had been taken. Not because his gifts stopped. He was our son, plain and simple."

"I'm glad to hear it, that he was a good man." I said.

"He was. Maybe a little rebellious and hard headed, but good. He never stopped loving Rosalie."

"Well, let me tell you this. I don't think that Rosalie's son is alive. I know he is. I know he is as good a man as his father. And so do you." I shifted my eyes and looked at Felix and his men gathered across the square.

"I do?" he asked wistful, following my gaze.

"Yes, you do. I think part of you knew the first time you met."

"Captain Wade?" Gregor's voice wavered and his eyes filled with tears. I lifted my finger to my lips to indicate it needed to be kept secret. "Thank you," he whispered. He continued to stare at his grandson. I hoped that we would succeed so that they could rejoice with each other when this whole ordeal ended.

As we all milled about the square waiting for our comrades an anxious tension grew. The longer we stayed, the more likely it would be that we would be noticed by the wrong person. Each minute that passed left me feeling more ill at ease that we had not been. Something about being unnoticed for this long didn't sit right with me.

Focusing, I picked up on something. An anger drifted in on the light breeze, bringing with it a fear inducing sound. Footsteps, like drumbeats, amplified against the stone walls and ground. "Felix! The approaching footsteps belong to someone extremely angry," I warned.

"Men, ready your weapons!" Felix ordered. We were certain these unseen angry men were soldiers sent by Talbot to deal with us, and bring me in. Not only had Nigel and Hawthorne not yet returned with recruits, but few of the Lesh had returned from their exploration of the surrounding area. It wasn't looking good. We were going to be outnumbered, more than we had hoped to be.

A few of Felix's men hid behind the few random empty crates and stone pillars in the square. The rest of us gathered in a tight circle facing outward, preventing anyone from sneaking up on us. I saw Felix and Gregor give each other passing, meaningful glances as they took their places in the circle. Felix ordered Mister Bimble to protect the old man at all costs.

The out-of-time marching grew louder and louder with each second that ticked by. We settled into ready positions.

Minutes later, the approaching men came funneling into the square, led by Hawthorne. Men, women, and shape-shifters in animal form all marched behind the dark pirate carrying anything they could find that could be used as a crude weapon. Their tired faces were lit with passion. Here was the fire I'd hoped for all along.

Upon seeing the group of men and beasts, led by our friend, relief swept over our huddled group. There would be no fight, not yet anyway. Our numbers had grown more than I had expected them to. Our chances of winning this grew. We would still be highly outnumbered, but not as much.

Felix and I passed through the now crowded square, greeting the newcomers, to get to Hawthorne. Many of the people we encountered were delighted to meet me, to be able to speak with me rather than just see me in passing or as a silent observer. There were even a few familiar faces from within Bua Tur, including Mrs. James, Ingrid, Suzette, and the gardener whose tongue had been removed. Even a few faces I recognized as belonging to palace guards.

"Well, this is certainly something," Mrs. James quipped, hugging me. She joined in our walk. "Who would have thought it'd be you leading this?"

"I wouldn't say I'm leading this, it was merely extreme coincidence that I became so involved."

"Can I just say how sorry I am, sorry my friends and I lacked enough conviction to end this earlier. The odds against us seemed impossible. Once Talbot force enlisted boys, our numbers would've been no match for his. And now, he has…" her little hands flew to her mouth as she stifled the sobs escaping from her. She felt as much guilt as I did about Anwen's situation.

"I know," I finished, my own guilt threatening to break my composure. "He has Anwen. We'll get her back."

"Cap," Hawthorne interrupted when we reached him. "The word around Realta is that he knows."

"I figured," Felix responded, half amused. "Seems to me he's not planning a fair fight, otherwise this place wouldn't be so quiet."

"Just as we suspected, a trap," I agreed.

"But a trap that we know is a trap, still gives us the advantage. We'll just need to be vigilant when we begin our assault."

"Of course, Cap. I'll spread the word. When do we go?" Hawthorne was itching for a fight.

"Not long. Are your people ready, Ma'am?" Felix moved his attention to the small Mrs. James.

"We've been ready for a long time, it just took a real leader to light a fire," Mrs. James replied. "I knew Merinley was special when I spotted her at auction, but I never dreamed she would be the queen Realta deserves."

"I'm not in charge," I interjected. "If it weren't for Captain Wade, this would not be possible."

"A joint effort," Felix appeased, "between all of us. Every one of us is key to a successful coup. Now, go tell everyone to prepare. I think it's time." Hawthorne and Mrs. James took off in opposite directions; headed out to spread the word. I tried turning to do the same.

"No, you stay here." Felix grabbed my hand before I could go anywhere.

"Is there something else you need to tell me before we go in?"

"I mean, I need you to stay here, Sweet. Stay with Gregor, out of the fray. I need you safe."

"No. No, way. I know parts of this palace better than anyone. I'm more likely to find Anwen than anyone." It was true. I knew all the servants passages by heart, even after all these years. I knew the royal quarters too. And there was one place only I and Talbot knew of. A place I'd rather not think about. The probability of Anwen being there was high.

"We have palace staff members that have joined us. Like you said, this is a trap. A trap for you. I'm keeping you out of said trap; safe. I will focus better knowing you are not in there." Felix argued.

I didn't want to acquiesce, but Felix was stubborn. More stubborn than me. If I didn't agree, he was likely to make Mister Bimble tie me up and take me back to the ship to wait he battle out. "Fine."

"Thank you." He gave me a quick kiss and wandered off into the crowd.

I promised to stay with Gregor, who I knew was also itching to help in the assault. But it was a promise I didn't intend to keep.

CHAPTER THIRTY-FOUR

s soon as Felix and the crew were out of sight, I took off towards where I believed Talbot would be holding Anwen. I felt bad, sneaking away from Gregor and the others, but I had a hunch I needed to follow. It was entirely possible Talbot had Anwen hidden away in a place no one else knew existed. The tiny prison under the thrones.

I had to hurry.

I made my way into the palace, ducking in every alcove possible to avoid running into any of Talbot's men. And Felix's. My caution, though, proved lacking when I slid into a darkened corner without looking, and directly into a waiting figure. Our surprised screeches mingled together as our senses collected. Lily. I'd seen little of her after the incident on the way to the convent; since the kidnapping Talbot concocted. So little, I thought she'd left the palace. I wouldn't have blamed her, after I nearly cost her her life.

"Your Majesty! You're returned again!" She hugged me, eyes full of excitement and fear. "Come quickly, before the pirates notice you have slipped their grasp. I'll hide you!" Sweet, innocent Lily. Even after what happened to her on the road to Saint Ludo, she remained the wide eyed and naïve girl. She had no idea the real danger was King Talbot.

I grabbed her small shoulders as she made to take my hand, "Lily, listen closely please." I looked into her eyes to convey the severity of the situation. "I didn't escape their grasp. I'm with them. They didn't abduct me on my wedding night; I left willingly."

As my words sunk in, a mask of recognition crept onto her face. "That's a relief to hear, I was distraught over hearing Anwen being accused of being a traitor. She could never do something like that."

"We're here to rescue Anwen from King Talbot. He holds her prisoner for no reason other than to draw me here; he knows I left with Captain Wade of my own volition. There are men from Lesh, the savage lands, and rebels with us as well. They look to replace the throne. We need your help if we are to do these things."

Lily nodded at me wide eyed, "Yes, Your Majesty. I would do anything to help you and Anwen. You both have always been so good to me. You saved my life."

"Thank you, Lily. Do you know the small trunk that Anwen kept in her quarters, the one with the Quaintrelle seal upon it?" She nodded again. "Good. Were her possessions moved upon her arrest?" Lily shook her head. "That's good news. Can you retrieve the box for me?

"I will. What do you want with it?" Lily inquired.

"Bring it back to the throne room by means of the servant's entrance." I stopped, taking a quick look around to ensure no one would overhear, "Should there be anyone in the throne room besides me and Anwen, remain hidden until I either call or come for you. Do this no matter what."

Lily nodded, gathered her skirts, and took off on her mission. Bumping into the innocent young servant had been a blessing. With her looking for Anwen's puzzle box I could focus on finding Anwen and getting her, along with Lily and the puzzle box, back to where Felix had left me.

I continued to sneak through the corridors. Any time I thought I heard someone approaching, I hid in an alcove until I felt certain I'd been hearing things, or until they passed; this time making sure no one lurked in shadows first. I found myself stopping every few minutes in my caution. My pace had been slowed much more than I liked, but my stealth was necessary.

After long minutes of creeping along the abandoned halls, I came to the doors of the throne room. I placed my hand on the handle and paused, mentally preparing myself. The possibilities behind the door were frightening. No matter what I found, whether I found Anwen alive or not, the price my heart would pay would be heavy. The regret of leaving her, treating her so harshly, tainted any reunion between us. I'd never forgive myself for putting my dearest friend in danger.

The sound of feet on the stone floor interrupted my preparation. I reached out with my power to get an idea of who might be coming my way. An idea of what their intentions. I felt feelings of panic more than I did anything else. Whoever came this way looked to lay low, not to fight.

Just in case, I cracked open the throne room door and squeezed inside, turning to peek through the doors to see who approached. A flutter of relief filled me when I saw Nigel, despite the ill feelings he had towards me. He must have rejoined Felix soon after the invasion on the palace began. I made a whispered call to get his attention.

That was a mistake. The second the words left my mouth a foul intention wafted through the air, amplified by way he reacted to seeing me. It set my stomach in knots. A greedy and pleased fire lit within him when he realized he'd found me alone. He tried masking his sinister feelings by wearing a friendly facade. He didn't know I could see, or rather feel, right through him.

"Miss," he said with a hint of glee in his voice. "Thank goodness I found you. You shouldn't be alone, it's dangerous here." He tried to push his way into the room with me. I couldn't allow him in. I pushed back going into the corridor with him instead.

"Did Felix send you to look for me?"

"No, Felix did not." Nigel's face darkened, a corner of his mouth lifting in a vile smirk "But King Talbot did say that if I found you, I could do whatever I wanted before handing you over."

My ill ease with him clicked. He'd turned on us. He tipped Talbot off to our plan. I gasped at this realization just as he reached out to grab me. With all my might I shoved him away, he stumbled back surprised.

Just as he landed, Domhnall came bursting around the end of the corridor with Liam. Nigel corrected himself and called out to his old shipmate with false urgency. "We need to stop her. She's been working for King Talbot this whole time." Nigel pointed at me. "It's all been a ruse so he could rid himself of his enemy."

The men stopped between us. Domhnall looked at me then back at Nigel. After doing this a few times he burst out laughing and swung his fist into Nigel's face. The traitor fell to the ground unconscious.

Relief swept through me, "I'm so glad you did not believe him."

"I never liked that guy, always spread lies to get his way. Made fun of my arm, a lot. Why was he saying that?"

"He betrayed us to work for Talbot."

"Oh, really?" Domhnall drew out his short muzzled pistol from his belt and aimed at Nigel. Liam half-lunged and grabbed Domhnall arm, stopping him. Domhnall, confused, yelled at him. "What the… this ass deserves to die, Liam." Liam nodded in agreement, then grabbed the pistol away and shook his head while placing it in his own belt. He then drew his short sword and plunged it into Nigel's chest.

Domhnall chuckled. "Good call, a gunshot would've drawn too much attention." He turned his attention to me, "Good thing Felix sent us to look for you once he realized you had taken off on your own. Why did you sneak off?"

"I had an idea where Talbot could have hidden Anwen. I didn't say anything because I worried that there would be a trap."

The one armed man chuckled, "You two are peas in a pod, you know that. Hard headed and always putting your own asses on the line for the people important to you." After a moment he asked, "Do you want us to join you?"

"No, I need to do this on my own. If I fall into Talbot's trap alone there's still hope that the rest of you can take him down."

"Are you sure?" Domhnall raised an eyebrow at me. His worry was plain, not only for me but for Felix as well. He knew all too well what Felix would become if something happened to me.

"I'm certain. But I'm glad you came along." Since Nigel's betrayal, I realized I was ignorant to take off on my own. I should have had someone with me, at least to accompany me to the throne room. Someone needed to know my whereabouts in case things went sideways. "If you would find Felix and bring him back here, I'd be in your debt."

"Of course, Miss."

I watched the pair dash back around the end of the corridor and once again braced myself for whatever I'd find behind the throne room doors. I took a deep breath and once again pushed the doors open, walking into what I knew to be a trap.

CHAPTER THIRTY-FIVE

The darkened throne room echoed with my footsteps, each one synchronizing with the panic within my heart. I stepped with trepidation. I felt out through the dark for any spark of feeling. Any sign of life. I had to make sure my hunch had been right, that Anwen was hidden in the small dank cellar beneath Talbot's throne.

I knew that little cellar intimately; knew every crack in the walls and every inch of grate above it. I had lost count how many times Talbot had stashed me in there. I would cower beneath his feet, battered and defeated, as he dealt with royal business. During it all, I was always in his sight, in his special little prison that gave him so much pleasure and power. No one knew I'd been there those times. He'd sneer down at me every time he turned away good people in need. He'd smirk with pleasure seeing me powerless when castle staff would inquire about me.

The memory sent chills down my spine.

I used my gift for another purpose as well. To make sure there would be no surprises. That no ambush waited for me in the dark.

Almost instantly, I found a spark of fear. True, deep fear, and exhaustion. As if to confirm what my senses already told me, a faint whimper echoed from near the thrones. Anwen was exactly where I suspected. Damn Talbot.

I rushed to the dais. "Anwen! Hang on Anwen!" I breathed as I shoved the King's seat in desperation. The heavy seat barely budged. I dug in deeper and shoved harder. Anwen's cries increased in desperate hope as I continued to push and pull on the throne. The task began to seem futile, the frustration of coming this far and not saving her brought tears to my eyes. With a scream, I pushed at the throne, the legs lifted off the floor only to thunk right back in place. Finally, after several attempts, the throne toppled with a resounding thud.

The noise would certainly gain the attention of anyone near the throne room. In that moment, I didn't care. All my focus had to be on Anwen. The grate had been exposed at last. I could do what I meant to. I dropped to my knees, not caring about hurting myself, and gripped at the grate. Anwen's fingers clung through from the opposite side.

"Merinley," she whimpered through the iron bars.

"Everything is going to be fine, Anwen. I'm here. You are going to be fine," I assured her as I pulled. The grate, like the throne, proved more difficult to budge than anticipated. My arms strained with each pull. "Anwen?" I asked. "Do you think you have the strength to help me free the grate?"

"I think so," she said meekly. Together, we worked to free her; she pushed as I pulled. In no time, we had accomplished what I had set to do. Anwen was free.

I helped her from the tiny prison and she collapsed into my arms. Even in the low light, I could tell she lived in that hole for some time. Her usually shiny hair was dull and dirty, as was the rest of her. Her voluptuous curves diminished, she was practically emaciated. She smelled of her own waste. I cared nothing for any of that. I cared that she was free.

"Merinley," Anwen's sobbed weakly. "I failed you. I am so sorry, my dear girl."

"No, Anwen. Don't think that way. You did more for me than you will ever realize. I failed you. I was selfish, for that I am sorry. Now, I can right that wrong." I wrapped my arms around her depleted frame and buried my face in her hair. "You'll never guess what else I've done. I brought Felix. He and many others, including the rebels, are in Bua Tur right now looking for Talbot."

Anwen's eyes shone with happiness and pride, "Really?"

"Yes."

The sounds of slow footsteps and clapping pulled us from victory. The slow rhythm filled me with dread. In my urgent rescue of my mentor and friend, I hadn't heard anyone enter the throne room. I hadn't felt anyone enter. My senses leapt from me; ice poured through my veins. I knew who lingered in the shadows before they could be seen.

Talbot.

"How sweet, the whore Queen and her mentor reunited." Talbot's voice carried across the room, full of malice and hate. "I'm surprised, my wife, that your pirate let you out of his sight. I had so hoped to kill him in your presence, before throwing you into your favorite hole so you can think of your actions. I guess we'll just have to substitute."

Talbot's face glowed with wickedness as he lifted a firearm from his belt. He fired within moments, giving us no time to think or act. His slug soared across the throne room and burrowed its way into Anwen's chest, directly into her heart. Her face twisted in agony before going ashen. Her breath faltered. Her body went limp in my arms. Minutes after I had saved her, I lost her.

No.

A raging sadness coursed through me. I laid Anwen down gently, placing a final kiss on her forehead. When I looked back up at Talbot, he was laughing silently. That broke the dam holding me back. I flew up and towards my villainous husband without thought or care for my safety, a feral scream ripping from my throat. An unfamiliar power surged through my body, hot and volatile. Talbot's face remained even as he prepared to fire his weapon again. He aimed low, not to kill me; he aimed to hurt me. The satisfaction he would gain from torturing me outweighed that of killing me. That realization had been enough to stop me in my tracks. I heaved with anger and pent up energy, yet I froze in fear. What could I do against a weapon like that?

My hand rose in a desperate attempt to stop him from across the room. I berated myself in my head at how silly it seemed that I thought I could stop him from firing. As the thought swirled through my head, I imagined the weapon flying from his hand.

Just as I saw it in my head, the firearm flew from Talbot's hand and skittered across the throne room. Time seemed to stop as the weapon traveled and came to rest out of sight, in some far dark corner.

This brief display of a physical Fae gift gorgonized me, mouth agape and eyes wide in disbelief. Elder Tam, and Sy, had mentioned a gift that would show itself soon. Never had I imagined it would appear in a moment like this, nor that it would be anything like this. Apoideans rarely had gifts that were so physical.

I shook off my shock and turned my attention the matter at hand. I couldn't let this distract me from Talbot, doing so would be detrimental. I looked again at the wretch before me. Talbot's emotionless face matched my surprise. He stared after his firearm, into the darkness. His eyes shifted from the darkness back to me. His shocked expression changed into a terrifying new blend of fear and hate.

"Witch!" he cried out, charging at me. His outcry sent a chill of fear down my spine and I raised my hands once again, hoping that whatever I did would happen again. Nothing happened. Panic swelled with each step that brought Talbot closer. I had to decide whether or not I'd try my hand at fighting him, or if I would try to escape the throne room.

Knowing my husband had more strength, and the crippling sensation he seemed to have over me, I chose to run. If I could get out of the throne room to Felix, or anyone on my side, I'd have the help I needed. I prayed someone was close.

My best option would be to try to get to the servants' entrance that has hidden behind the heavy curtains hanging on the right side of the room. Lily would possibly be there and together we could get out of the palace.

I sprung into a sprint towards where the curtains hung. I pushed myself hard, forcing myself to run faster than I thought I could, sending every ounce of energy into my legs. But my hesitation cost me. Talbot nipped at my heels, howling in anger. Just as I reached the curtain, his hand grabbed the back of my tunic. He yanked and flung me backward onto the cold marble floor, causing me to cry out. The impact left me winded and my head spun from the sudden change in direction.

When my vision cleared, I saw Talbot leaning close over me. He seethed with anger and disgust. His hand reached down towards my head, grabbing a handful of my hair. He pulled me up, keeping his hold on me. Pain shot over my scalp, it felt as though each tug threatened to tear a chunk from my head.

King Talbot's eyes flamed as he glared into my eyes. He fumed; rage poured from him in torrential waves. I knew I was in for a beating far worse than I had ever received. "You are about to have an endless amount of torments visited on you." Keeping his grip on my hair he unleashed his next attack. The back of his hand met my left cheek. The sharp slap sent tears down my face.

Without words, he dragged me back to the thrones. The stone floor scraping at my legs while I flailed uselessly. When Talbot released his grip on my hair, he threw me onto the floor next to Anwen's lifeless body. My hand slipped in her blood. The sticky, slick mess sickened me; angered me all over again. I glared up at the monster looming over me and spat.

Talbot's lip raised into a snarl and he came at me again, "How dare you? You foul, deceptive witch!"

"Apoidean, not a witch," I seethed at him. "You are a monster."

Talbot's eyes widened before narrowing into slits, making his green eyes snake-like. Growling, he kicked me in the side, sending searing pain through my body. The kick was followed by another and another. I curled up in an attempt to protect myself from major damage. The fervor with which he kicked me confirmed he was out of his head. Because of my deception, he was ready to kill rather than maim. I'd have to somehow escape or gain the upper hand, or I would die. When he stopped, he crouched down to look me in the eye, "I always wondered why you seemed to win the hearts of all who met you. Now it all makes sense. You bewitched everyone, Witch."

He stood again and paced back and forth next to me, raving on and on about my wickedness. His ranting gave me a small window to make a plan. I needed to catch him off guard if I were to have a chance at getting away. If only I could repeat the accidental display of power from before. But I had no idea how I had done that; I doubted I'd be able to do it again any time soon. Powers took time to master. I didn't have time.

There had to be some other way to defend myself. My mind raced to think of something before he ended his verbal tirade. In moments, I knew I had something all along, and I berated myself for forgetting about it. The small dagger hidden in my boot.

I slid my shaky hand down my leg, leaving a trail of blood along my buckskin pants, and touched the inner lip of my boot. I felt the handle there and rested my hand over it, readying myself for a quick attack. Minutes passed, or so it seemed, but Talbot continued on his rant of half-truths about me. I needed to provoke him in order to attack. God, help me.

Using one hand and my legs, I began to scoot towards the doors. I moved slowly, both out of pain and out of necessity. To really get his attention, I simpered; sobbing in terror and pleading for mercy.

Talbot's attention rushed back to me, the plan worked. He came at me, a monster unleashed, bellowing deep and low. He was on me quickly, towering over me. My hair, once again, ended up in his fist, his other hand squeezed my cheeks into a painful pucker. His fingers wove closer and closer to my scalp as he inched our faces closer together. The time had come to make my move.

In one swift motion, I drew my dagger and thrust it deep into Talbot's leg, twisting the blade. He squalled like an animal and let me loose. I swung my legs around and knocked him to the ground. His head impacted with the floor with a solid crack. I hoped that would keep him down for some time. The beating I'd taken made getting up a struggle, but I managed to get to my feet before he recovered. I limped as fast as I could towards the doors of the throne room.

Pain shot through me with each step, hindering my escape. It was near crippling. I fought against the burning ache that begged me to stop, to lie on the floor and give in. There was no way I could give in to that. Getting this far had taken too much. Soon, I heard Talbot grunting and stumbling behind me. The wound in his leg and the head injury didn't keep him down as long as I hoped. I pushed harder, with the hope his injuries slowed him down. With each second that hope thinned and I heard him gaining on me. It was as if he was fueled by hate and would only stop when dead.

Through some miracle, I reached the doors and heaved them open, groaning in pain from the effort. The sight that greeted me renewed my strength. Felix, followed by a slew of his men, Lesh, and guards, near the end of the corridor, a tangle of swords and fists. Their advance was slowed by their brawling. I managed to call out in a hoarse voice. But the words were stolen. Angry arms wrapped around my waist, dragging me backwards.

Talbot spun me around and forced me over onto my back. His legs straddled either side of me, he sat. Blood dripped from his wounded leg onto my waist, oozing into my tunic. The crazed look in his eye was enhanced by unequal pupils. The hit on his head had done some sort of damage, just not enough.

Talbot yowled at me again, his words slurred, "You, wife, are more trouble than you are worth." A heavy fist met my body. "A. Lying. Scheming. Good. For. Nothing. Witch!" His meaty hands hit with every word.

I tried my best to block his hits, I needed only last a little longer. I turned my head to see the large group of men being led by Felix drawing closer. I feared if they didn't arrive soon, I'd be dead. King Talbot's fist connected with the side of my face, twisting my head to look the other way. He continued his assault.

My vision blurred. I needed to hang on just a little longer.

CHAPTER THIRTY-SIX

ime slowed down as I counted what might have been my last breaths. Footsteps, like a waterfall's roar, mixed with a rancor of muffled shouts and a high ringing in my head. I turned my head, reaching my hand out towards the men in the corridor. They seemed miles away. My vision blurred with tears and my head vibrated from the pain. Another blow to the head forced my head the other way once again.

I didn't know how much longer I could hold out.

"Ignoble curr!" A roar that could have only come from Felix, cut through the fog building in my head. A large figure, a streak of dark gray, flew into the stunned king. His weight added to that of Talbot's in the seconds before the men tumbled over me. The fierce sound of the scuffle that followed could only be described as frightening. I tried to watch the men through bleary eyes, but all I could see were blobs of color. I cringed in pain with each hit I heard, as if teach of their strikes were on me rather than one another.

I tried raising my hand to my face to wipe away the tears. The pain that shot through my body with the barest of movement was excruciating. I pushed through the pain, but it made the progress slow. A hand on my arm caused me to gasp aloud; I hadn't realized someone sat beside me. After what I just went through, my first thought was that I was being attacked again. I turned flailing with what little energy I had left, but my weak attempts were diverted.

"Hush now, Miss. I got ya," Mister Bimble soothed, helping me realize I was in good hands. His rough hands gently touched my face and wiped away my blood and seemingly endless tears. He gave me a sad smile as I focused on him. He was hurting. Grieving. We had suffered losses, big ones.

The squelch of metal entering flesh pulled my attention back towards the fight. My heart thudded against my ribs in the moments it took me to turn my head. I was afraid that it had been Felix that had met the end of a blade. Talbot had so far proved a slippery demon that kept going when he should've stayed down.

My fear abated. Before me, Felix loomed over King Talbot, loose strands of his hair falling over his shoulders and face. The tyrant lay on the cold stone floor; wordless guttural moans spilling from his mouth. His skin losing its color. For the first time ever, I felt real fear coming from the monster. With every gasp and groan his fear doubled, increasing exponentially until the moment his life left him.

Felix's shoulders heaved from the fight as he stood over his foe, watching him die. When he felt satisfied that Talbot lived no more, he turned away from him. His eyes met mine in an instant and his enraged expression melted into worry. My heart filled with relief. Felix kept his promise. King Talbot's hands would never hurt me again.

Or anyone else.

Felix rushed to meet me. Mere steps separated us before he could wrap me in his arms; tell me that our battle was over. He never reached me. Instead the throne room erupted into chaos as Talbot's personal guards made their late entrance. With one look at their leader lying dead on the stone floor, they sprung into action apprehending any man that wasn't one of their own. Except for Mister Bimble, who still sat with me on the floor. I didn't know if it was his position or their fear of him that kept him from their irons.

"You are under arrest for the murder of King Talbot." The Captain of the Guard barked as a pair of guards seized Felix.

Felix fought against the men, "He was a monster! Have you not seen what he has done to the people here? Your people. Look there, he murdered that woman!" His head tipped towards the bloody scene near the throne. "See what he's done to your Queen." his eyes and voice softened as he drew their attention to me. "That thing did not deserve to be called King."

Several of Felix's men struggled to get loose, to aid their leader, but were met with resistance from the guards. I nudged Mister Bimble. I needed him to get them all to stop; which he did with a loud and deep shout, "Quiet!"

I indicated to Mister Bimble to help me to stand. I had to interfere and set things straight. The time had come to use my role as Queen, as well as reveal all that I discovered in the time since I had become engaged to Talbot. I opened my mouth, but all that came out was a scratchy gasp. I slowed myself, and after a moment I found my voice, though still raspy and weak. "Unhand him," I commanded the guards as best I could. "The King has not been murdered."

The guards all stared at me in confusion, their grasp on Felix remained. I could see they were torn between their duty to obey their leader and the seemingly odd order I just gave. The Captain of the Guard stepped in after a minute, "My Queen, you are confused. Injured. King Talbot, your husband, lies dead by this man's hand."

"I am glad for it, for Captain Wade saved me." I retorted.

"Your words will condemn you, Your Majesty," he warned, even though I sensed that he knew Talbot had been a monster; that he felt relief seeing him dead. "No one wants to see you hang."

I wouldn't let the threat of treason deter me. "I stand by my words, Captain. Yes, I am beaten and weary, but I'm far from confused. I am as clear as ever, if not more." I moved to approach the Captain of the Guard, but the injuries I'd sustained caused my footing to falter. Mister Bimble, having stayed close for support, caught me. "That man there," I seethed and pointed to Talbot's lifeless form, "never had a rightful claim to the throne. By law, the oldest living heir is to be crowned upon the King's death. King Bern passed the throne not to his oldest living heir, but to his youngest."

The Captain of the Guard looked at me like I'd grown a second head. "King Talbot was the only living heir to King Bern."

"No, my good man, there's another. " I smiled at Felix, still in custody of the King's men. "An heir that had been kept hidden from even King Bern himself."

I looked towards the servant's entrance and called for Lily to emerge from her hiding place. My eyes were swollen to the point where I had to strain to see her. As she became clear, I saw that Lily awkwardly clutched a large box to her breast. Anwen's puzzle box. Her head turned about wildly, taking in the ghastly scene in the throne room. A sob escaped her as she spied Anwen's body and yet another when she saw the result of Talbot's rage on my face.

My heart twisted. I realized all the terrible things that she must have overheard while hiding where I'd instructed her to stay there. Had I sent her out of the castle instead, she wouldn't have been subjected to these horrors. Again, I'd been the root cause of her distress. She was one more in the growing line of people I needed to make things right for.

Lily stepped wide around Felix and the guards, as if fearful she'd be ensnared herself if she came too close. When she reached me she, held the box out towards me with trembling arms. She tried her best to put on a brave face as she did. Her swollen eyes, tear streaked face, and trembling lips wouldn't let her.

"Mister Bimble, would you please help me sit down?" The brawny first mate braced me as I lowered to the floor once again. "Captain," I said to Talbot's man, "would you take the box from Lily and place it here next to me?"

Still confused as to what I was doing, the Captain of the Guard took the box from Lily and placed it next to where I sat. I smiled, feeling a sad nostalgia sweeping over me, as I traced the Quaintrelle crest with my fingers. I drew in a cleansing breath, praying that Prince Declan's secret journal would still be hidden within the box. My hand instinctively turned the crest counterclockwise, just as Anwen had shown me a long time ago. A tiny clicking noise filled the air until the crest resisted. I moved on to the next step of the puzzle box.

With gentle fingers, I searched for the hidden button on the side of the lid. It only took seconds to find and press the button. A soft pop told me I had been successful in unlocking the box's hidden chamber. I lifted the lid and opened the box. Anwen's most precious items stared me in the face. Jewels, papers, little trinkets that seemed to hold nothing more than sentimental value. I pushed those aside and found the hole pressing the button had created.

Sticking a finger in that hole, I said a silent prayer once again, and pulled up to reveal the secret compartment beneath. There hiding under Anwen's things was the journal. A thankful sigh escaped my lips. The worn leather book was a welcome sight. The most welcome sight in the entire world at that moment. The secrets inside, written by Declan himself, were vital to proving Felix the rightful heir of Realta's throne. As was the letter from Sister Maria.

I turned to Domhnall, " I believe you have something for me?"

"Aye, Miss." Domhnall fumbled in the satchel he wore and produced a stack of parchment and a leather bound book. He shoved them towards me. I scanned the small pile of papers. My smile widened at what I found; a marriage document for Rosalie and Declan, Rosalie's death record, and the birth document of their child.

I set the documents aside and moved on to the journal hidden among the documents. Once opened, the journal revealed what I had hoped it would; the name of the nun to whom it belonged written in a dainty script in the front cover. *Sister Maria Benedict.* I placed my hand reverently on her name, thanking her for what she had done all those years ago.

"What is she doing?" I heard someone in the back of the small crowd whisper.

"Quiet, please," I shushed. "I need my concentration."

My fingers flipped through the pages, scanning the pages within the journal, trying to find anything that would support Declan's diary and the letter from Sister Benedict hidden in its pages. After a few moments, I found the passage I needed.

I read aloud:

· · ·

The Lord works in mysterious ways, and today His will has tested me. I, along with the novice Harriet, had been tasked with the care of our two pregnant charges this day. As He would have it, both went into labor within a short time of one another. It saddens me that we lost three lives in the process.

Rosalie, Prince Declan's bride, delivered her babe, a son, first. She suffered childbirth fever and lost too much blood. She passed on into His grace shortly after. Our unwed mother delivered shortly afterward. Her babe, a boy as well, was far too underdeveloped to survive this world. I believe the heartbreak of losing her child caused her passing.

My soul tells me what I did next was the right thing to do, though that is yet to be seen. Harriet and I may be exiled from the convent should this be found out. Out of fear for the baby prince's life, I took extreme steps to conceal his survival. I have switched the babies' identities, and forged false documents along with real ones in order to protect the boy.

My only regret is that I had to lie to Prince Declan. I sent Harriet to Prince Declan with a message telling him that his wife and son had both died, along with the documents recording the birth and deaths. It will mar my spirit forever that I kept him from knowing that his son really lived. I hope he can forgive me if he ever learns the truth.

Now it is up to me to ensure the boy is raised to be a good man. When the time comes I will reveal his true identity to him. Until then, he is merely Felix Wade, ward of the church. Only time will tell what God's will for the boy will be.

The room fell silent when I finished reading. All within hearing range were stunned with the revelations in the journal. They could've been knocked over by a feather.

A low whistle escaped Mister Bimble's lips, breaking the silence. "Damn, Cap's the bloody King."

CHAPTER THIRTY-SEVEN

"This is absurd. The evidence we've provided should be more than enough to prove Captain Wade has a valid claim to the throne." Anger coursed through me as I argued with Talbot's advising council. "We have provided every ounce of evidence needed in these documents, including a journal written by Prince Declan himself."

"Regardless, Milady, we need eye witness accounts from people who can personally say they know him and about his parentage. It is protocol. Surely you understand protocol?" The head council jabbed at me.

"Of course I understand protocol, my whole life in Bua Tur has been protocol. What I think you fail to understand is that I know protocol almost better than you. Quaintrelle know protocol, it's part of our job. That being said, I know that if this were about anyone other than Captain Wade, you'd have accepted the evidence at face value."

"Sweet," Felix stopped my tirade with a whisper in my ear, "the head council is turning purple. I think it would be best we just concede and agree to the trial."

"But I'm right, you know I am."

"That might be, but what is our alternative? We agree to the trial or we hang. I much prefer the first."

"We could still hang, even with the trial. These are Talbot's guys," I reminded him.

"And we should beat them at their own game."

"Milady," the head council called my attention. "Are we going to come to terms or are you going to continue to show us you do not deserve that chance?"

"What does that even mean?" I screeched in reply and charged towards the council. "You…"

"We accept your trial, council." Felix interrupted, wrapping his arms around me to prevent me from doing anything I'd regret.

"Do you?" The head council raised a cynical eyebrow at me.

"Fine. Yes, we accept your trial." I bit my words down, they tasted sour in my mouth. I knew Felix was right; it was best we play their game, even if it still killed us.

"Glad to hear it," the head council smirked. His beady eyes twinkled with the insignificant victory. "You have one week to gather your witnesses for trial. No less than four. At that time we'll hear their testimonies and weigh them against the documents provided. Should we decide in your favor, Captain Wade will win the throne." He paused, sucking his teeth distastefully. "When, I mean should we decide against you, the throne will go to someone else with a rightful claim on it. I do not think I need to tell you what will become of the pair of you."

"We know," I seethed somberly. No reminder was needed as to our fate should this trial fail. We'd join the ranks of Anwen, Smith, Hawthorne, and the dozen others we lost during the fight for the palace. Losses that affected all of us deeply.

If Felix and I were to hang, it would be a devastating blow to our remaining allies. A step backward for Realta.

"Good. Now for the unpleasant part," the head council mocked. "As you know, you are no longer Queen. You do, however, maintain your title of Milady. But, you have no political pull or power until the end of the trial. You are also confined to the borders of the city.

Captain Wade, on the other hand, being who he is, will spend the remaining days until the trial imprisoned, with no visitors. I am sure you understand."

"Completely," Felix appeased. "Were I in your position, I would do the same thing." His insult was subtle but effective.

"Effective immediately." A pair of guards immediately seized Felix at the head council's command.

THE WEEK LEADING up to the trial was stressful, to say the least. Not being able to see Felix, to work together at finding the witnesses we needed, only made it more so. I threw myself into preparing for the trial, racking my brain as to whom I could call on to witness for us. Sister Benedict was dead. Lily visited the convent to seek out Harriet. That was a fruitless errand as Harriet had left Saint Ludo decades ago. The only people I knew for certain that knew of Rosalie and Declan's relationship were Gregor and his family.

I thought he would be the only witness I could find.

When Cook stepped up as witness, I was shocked. He gave no explanation as to why, being as mysterious as he always was. Not knowing what he had up his sleeve, put me on edge. It isn't that I didn't trust the old man; I just wasn't sure if the council would accept his witness. His days as Captain Redmayne were certain to play a part in that. Despite the uncertainty, I was thankful for his help.

The week passed quickly and I still only had two witnesses, with one being a long shot. I was beginning to think all we had accomplished was freeing me from an abusive husband before condemning ourselves to death.

Things looked bleak. I was a mess.

A sliver of hope appeared at the eleventh hour. We had a third witness. Our friends from Lesh returned to Realta, with their leader this time. Sy wanted to witness for us.

"Sy! Thank you, so much."

"My pleasure, Queen Merinley," he insisted on using the title despite it no longer being true.

"How did you even know we needed you, though?"

"Cook sent this keirie."

"What is a keirie?" I asked, fascinated.

"Tis a Fae bird, able to travel far in the blink of an eye."

I shook my head in disbelief, "Cook never said anything about asking you to come witness for us."

"He did not, he only said you faced a trial to prove Cap-ee-tan Wade's lineage. It was my decision to come offer my support."

Sy's offer thrilled me, even though it was likely the council would reject his witness, too. His leader status meant nothing here, and in Realta's eyes he was a savage; soul-less. Still having three witnesses was far better than two. Perhaps there was a chance that the council would accept this.

"PLEASE STATE your name for the council," the head council began the questioning of witnesses abruptly.

"They call me Cook."

"We didn't ask for what they call you. We asked for your name."

"Sigmund Redmayne." The attending crowd gasped when Cook stated his true name. Many had believed him dead. Cook enjoyed their obvious shock. His face stretched into a mischievous grin as he gave the crowd a flourished bow, his gray curls bouncing with the motion.

The council head called for the excited crowd to hush so that the witness hearing could continue. "Now, relate to us why you believe that this man, this wanted pirate, is worthy of the crown of Realta."

"Gentlemen, I don't believe he is King of Realta. I know he is. I've known since the day he wandered onto my ship. A scrawny, big eared boy that was eager to join up. A fire in his belly against the cruelty he'd witnessed during his life on the streets of Realta."

"What makes you say that you knew even then?"

"Looks much like his parents, and unfortunately a bit of his grandfather. The ears were a dead giveaway of his parentage. Only ever saw ears like those on one man before then." Cook chuckled.

"Who would that be?"

"My friend, Prince Declan. He had some ears. He and his farm girl were the boy's parents. My greatest enemy, that beef-witted oaf King Bern, was his grandfather."

The council shifted in their seats, uncomfortable with Cook's ill words towards King Bern. Even though he had been long dead his legacy of fear still lived on. It was as if they thought he would rise from the dead and strike them down. "You were friendly with Prince Declan?"

"Well… we had an arrangement," Cook acquiesced.

"What sort?"

"That, council, is a secret I will not release. Not even by threat of death."

"Alright then," the head council chided and made a note in front of him. "Where did you meet them?"

"Fenian Cliffs."

"How can you be so sure the friend you speak of was not a liar pretending to be the Prince?" the head council's eyes narrowed onto Cook.

Cook met the council's glare with one of his own, irked by his insinuations. He hated being called a fool. "Because I had known the boy for much longer than that."

"How so?"

"It's safe to say I had seen the young Prince Declan during my time at the palace," Cook sighed as though he thought his answer should be obvious.

"What do you mean, your time at the palace?"

"Precisely that. Do I have to spell out everything for ya fools? Have ya all been blinded or made to forget the history of yer kingdom?" Cook sighed and rubbed his hands over his haggard face as he rolled his eyes. He was getting annoyed. I for one anxiously waited to hear his next words. He was full of surprises. "If ya take yer happy asses down to yer hall of records, ya will learn that quite some time ago, before I got wise, my face had been at every council King Bern called. One could even say I had even been his friend at one point."

"You were?"Genuine shock rolled off of the council and attending crowd. Yes, Cook was full of surprises.

"Yes, until I could no longer handle his moronic ideals. Until he became evil. When he betrayed people he should care about. When he broke my Vi… When he killed an innocent. Take yer pick. Simply, we had a falling out. I moved on to pirating and making my old pal's life harder. Cannot say I've ever regretted the decision."

"Do…"

Cook cut off the council's question, "No more insipid questions. I gave ya my testimony. Captain Wade is a good man, just like his father. He will make a fine ruler, and so on and so forth. Go ahead and call yer next victim. I'm finished with this thinly veiled torture." Cook walked away from the council, rejoining Felix and me.

The council themselves looked as if someone had just violated them. The crowd buzzed about Cook's testimony. I knew they would be for quite some time. My curiosity had certainly been captured by his whole story. I hoped he'd share it with me someday.

Felix raised an eyebrow at his old friend.

"What?" Cook snapped.

"You sly old man. You knew all these years and said not a word to me. Why?"

"Ya gonna question me now too, Boy?" he narrowed his eye at Felix. "Yes, I knew. I said nothing because ya didn't ask. Besides, if I had told ya, ya would have done something stupid. I was protecting ya from yerself. Now shut up."

Felix slapped Cook on the shoulder and laughed, which only garnered him a warning glare from the old man. The trial had certainly riled him up in ways I hadn't expected. His anger tinged with grief and loss. Someday, I wanted to hear his story.

Our attention was brought back to the council as they called up the next witness, Sy. The council began as they had with Cook, asking his name to establish his reliability.

"I am Sy, ruler of the Lesh."

"Lesh?" the council asked when the name did not sound familiar to them.

Sy looked at the council in confusion. He didn't understand that the people of Realta had been lied to about them; that they didn't even know their true name. Some time passed so I spoke up to clear the matter. "Our past rulers would have called the honorable Lesh savages."

A murmur moved through the room.

"That what is thought of my people here?" His question, with good reason, came laced with a hint of sadness. I understood all too well the hurt of being labeled something you aren't out of fear and ignorance.

"Sadly, my friend, yes. Something I intend to change," I condoled.

Sy nodded in understanding, but I still saw the sadness that had passed through his eyes. "My people are not savages, your people have been misled. We, like the honorable Apoideans, seem to have been wronged for our differences; our ancestral gifts."

"Ancestral gifts?" the council asked.

"I could show ya, but I don't think you like that. Magic, I hear, is feared by your people."

"Very well," the council brushed off his comments to continue the trial. "Please inform us why you believe that Captain Wade is heir to the throne? In what capacity are you a witness to his birthright?"

"He told me," Sy stated, matter-of-factly.

"Are you saying that Captain Wade has known his parentage all along and denied it?"

"No. I think I should say it differently. Cap-ee-tan Wade's soul told me. He had no idea until recently."

"What do you mean, his soul told you?"

"My own gift. I see all there to know about a man with a single touch. When I first shook Cap-ee-tan Wade's hand I saw glimpses of his far too brief time with his mother. A time he will never remember. True, I saw little of his father, except a kingly glow. But I can say his mother died surrounded by women of your God."

"Impossible."

"Not a believer then? Come now, Council Man, let me show you." He extended a hand out toward the council leader eagerly. I felt the fear build in the man he goaded out; the head council didn't want to accept. Sy saw his hesitation as well, "I promise Council Man, I do not bite. At least not in this form." A mischievous smile spread over Sy's face as he chomped his teeth together.

The council leader approached Sy with caution and took his hand. The Lesh ruler's face remained still and calm but suddenly contorted a little. I wished he were in bear form so I knew what he felt at the moment. He released the hand he held and leaned in to whisper in the council leader's ear.

Whatever Sy told him had his attention. His eyes widened, rimmed with shame. He turned and nodded to the rest of the council. "He speaks the truth." The council dismissed Sy after that. His power frightened them, especially the leader.

Sy didn't look pleased either. He obviously learned something disturbing about the head council when he took his hand. His eyes flashed a warning at the council leader before he stepped out of the spotlight, "You play nice now Council Man. I am watching."

After his turn to witness, Sy left the room without saying another word. I didn't have to be able to read his emotions to tell his anger boiled, that he needed to step away before doing something he'd regret.

"Do we have a third witness to hear?" The council leader called, his voice still a little shaky from his encounter with Sy.

Gregor stepped out and toward the council, Liam by his side. Gregor was visibly shaken; he looked to be a bundle of anger and fear. All the years of his pent up emotions were trying to escape. He anticipated having some sort of closure once the trial was finished. Once Gregor stood in front of the council, Liam gave his father's arm a squeeze. The silent gesture received a nod in response; letting the young man know he could return to the crowd.

The council, again, wasted no time getting started. "Name?"

"Gregor Varick, I am a farmer."

The council leader sneered. I felt his arrogant confidence return. He felt no threat from the old farmer. "What does a commoner like you know of royal affairs?"

He squared his shoulders, "I admit, as a farmer, I know little of royal affairs. But, I do know when a man is worth his salt. If I can make a difference I will stand up and try."

"Very well then. Tell us what makes you a good witness in this matter?"

"Captain Wade is my grandson. Born of my oldest, Rosalie; wife of Prince Declan, rest their souls."

"Funny, I thought the Prince had been married to Duchess Emile."

"True, he was. That happened after his real love was taken from him; first by his father, then by death. They met at market and courted for months. Married, in secret, despite King Bern's objections. She had just revealed that she was with child when King Bern stole her away, hiding her from us all. We only learned where she'd been hidden after she died in childbirth."

"So you raised him, knowing full well who he was without telling a soul?" The council accused.

"No. I did not. I don't know where or who he was raised by. We were told he had died, a lie. I can only assume he was raised by the nuns at Saint Ludo."

"So what makes you so sure that he's who he says he is?"

"I see her in him, my Rosalie. There is also resemblance to Prince Declan for certain. You may even see the resemblance between him and my son, Liam." Gregor motioned over to where Liam stood.

The council nodded as they studied Felix and Liam. The council leader then interjected, "Yes the resemblance is there. Which begs me to ask, what is there for us to believe that what you say is true? How do we know you aren't putting on an elaborate ruse here? That Captain Wade is not truly Liam's son?"

The council leader's question enraged me and I had to use my limited power to step in. I wouldn't let him abuse Gregor this way, or to put doubt into the minds of the people here. "Council, you are out of order. Gregor is not being tried for anything, nor is he being asked to prove anything. He is here to give his testimony that you are meant to weigh against the documents you were given."

Gregor, despite my objection, still replied to the allegation. "Aside from the fact that Liam is only twelve years older than Captain Wade;

he is mute, council. While he's capable and more than worthy of love he has chosen a solitary life, he has dedicated his life to helping me on our farm. Though, I do pray that he someday does find love. I don't wish him loneliness when his mother and I are gone." A few tears slipped down Gregor's face. His heart full of pride when he spoke of Liam; yet there had also been a tinge of guilt. He felt responsible for his son not having his own life.

I had no doubt that Gregor's wish for his son would be granted someday. He was handsome and strapping, not showing his forty odd years at all. Between my Quaintrelle friends and his new bond with his nephew, I didn't foresee him being lonely for long. I knew with complete certainty that Anwen would have adored him.

As for being alone, that already changed for Liam. In the short time since meeting, he formed fast friendships with Felix and his men. No doubt, he would be in good company for the rest of his life.

The council excused Gregor, allowing him to rejoin Liam on the sidelines. His son welcomed him with a heartwarming embrace. There was so much love there. Felix had lucked out with the family he should've been with all along. In that moment, I hoped with all my might that the trial ended in our favor. Not only to save Felix, but so he could have his family as well.

After Gregor, we had no more witnesses lined up. I knew the council had asked for four, but I hoped I could appeal to them to consider allowing the ones we had instead. From what I could read off of their feelings it would be a tough feat to accomplish. I bolstered my confidence and stepped up to the council.

"Milady," the head council said, "Surely you are not attempting to bear witness yourself? I am certain that we made it clear to you that you could not."

"No, that's not what I'm attempting here. I am hoping to appeal to you to consider the case with just the three witnesses."

"So, there will be no more witnesses? Just the three?"

"Yes, just the three that have already spoken," I admitted, feeling defeated.

"You may have once been Queen of Realta, but you're not above the rules of trial. If there are no more witnesses then we are finished here. Without the fourth witness, we simply don't have enough information to verify the information the council has been provided with." He paused and twisted his face in distaste, "Especially when most of what we have heard today hasn't come from entirely reliable sources."

The council's words stung and bile rose in my throat. My worst fear was happening. They were going to deny the claim. Still, I had to try to fight. "You can't deem to think that just because these men who have witnessed for Captain Wade are not what you consider your equal, that they are not reliable! Cook was once a valued member of court. Sy is the leader of good people. Gregor is a hard working citizen of Realta. Just because they don't meet your standards of snobbery does not make them unreliable. That fact alone should show their witness is more reliable than anyone you could procure."

The head of the council fumed at my speech. His face reddened and sweat accumulated on his brow. "And you are just a pretty toy that happened to garner the attention of a king," he shouted. "Rules say four witnesses are needed. You had three. Three that did not represent any shred of anything but the opinions of morally corrupted, biased outsiders." He took a breath to compose himself as he swept his hand over his face. "Without a fourth witness, the council has no choice but to…"

"Wait." A strong female voice rose from the back of the room. The voice sounded familiar to me. "I will witness for Captain Wade." The crowd parted to reveal Matron Hattie walking forward, head held high. "I think my standing in Realta is well enough to be considered reliable, by anyone's standards." She stopped when she neared Felix. "Hello, my little scamp."

"Sister Harriet?" He questioned.

"Yes, my dear boy. It's wonderful to see you, but this little reunion must wait." She smiled like I had never seen her do before; a smile that said she had found some peace. She walked the distance to where I stood before the council, "Merinley, dear, I am so sorry for your loss. Anwen was a good woman and friend, she will be missed greatly." In a move that surprised me, Matron Hattie embraced me in a warm hug.

She whispered in my ear, "Had I known what you were up to, I would've come to you sooner."

A curt, annoyed clearing of a throat pulled us out of the embrace. The head council stared at us, annoyance etched deeply on his face. Matron Hattie returned the glare with an eye roll added on.

"Another time, Merinley. I have our King to save." She gave me a wink as she sent me back to observe the proceedings.

The council wasted no time in getting started once Matron Hattie's attention turned back to them, "State your name."

"Harriet Turnbow, I am Matron to the Quaintrelle program." She stood tall and proud, ever the intimidating woman.

"You are known to be a moral and stern force for those girls. So, if you'll explain your reasoning behind standing witness for a man known for being neither moral or reputable."

"Forgive me council, but you are wrong there. The Felix Wade I remember was moral and strong. True, he held a rebellious and mischievous streak, as all boys do, but he was always kind, honest, and helpful. Respectful. Qualities befitting of any crown."

"How do you know Captain Wade?"

"That is quite the tale to regale. May I request a chair so that I may be more comfortable while doing so? My old ones aren't what they used to be." The head council nodded and had a chair brought in. Matron Hattie dusted it before sitting. "Before I was known as Matron Hattie here at Bua Tur, I had been well on my way to taking my final vows as a nun at Saint Ludo convent. Thirty-odd years ago, when I was just beginning my days as a novice, a young pregnant woman had been brought to us by none other than King Bern himself. He told us the young woman was dangerous and delusional; she claimed her child was Prince Declan's. Of course, we had no reason to doubt King Bern, we had no reason to believe he would lie to us. So we believed him, most of us anyways. Sister Maria Benedict sided with the young woman, whose name was Rosalie. Her faith in the girl never swayed."

"You did not believe then?"

"No, not for a long time anyway. When Rosalie went into labor, I assisted Sister Maria in delivering the child. Rosalie didn't survive. As fate would have it, another young mother that was with us also delivered a child that day, very close to the same time. Sadly neither of that pair lived either. Sister Maria insisted we switch the babies' identities to protect Rosalie's boy. She sent me here, to the palace with a letter for Prince Declan to give him the false news. I still thought her mad, but did as I was told. It wasn't until I watched him read the letter that I realized my mistake in believing King Bern. Rosalie had not been lying."

"What changed your mind in that moment?" the head council leaned forward in his seat, truly interested in what Matron Hattie had to say.

"Prince Declan's reaction. He broke down. He cried the tears of a defeated man, a man who had lost everything that he held dear. He wouldn't have done so if there was no truth to Rosalie's tale. After that, I swore to help Sister Maria protect the baby, to raise him to be a good man. We hoped to someday reveal the truth."

"And this baby would be?"

"Captain Wade, of course. I thought it was clear of whom I was witnessing for," Matron Hattie gave a soft chuckle. The crowd joined in, amused by her putting the head council in his place.

The council leader sneered at Matron Hattie's response. "I have a hard time believing that. You say Captain Wade is the babe born and raised in a convent. If that were true, why would he ever turn to being a lawless pirate? Aren't children born in convents raised to be servants of the church?"

"If you would stop interrupting me, council, I would already have told you." The crowd tittered again at Matron Hattie's boldness. The council had no idea who they were dealing with. No one got the better of Matron Hattie, who always got the better of those she went against. "When Felix was around ten years of age he ran away. I don't know why, nor do I care to know. The past cannot be changed. But I will say this; his abrupt departure caused me great guilt on top of what I already carried about keeping his true identity secret. The guilt led me to leave my life as a nun, in hopes that I'd find him and be able to guide him still. I had no such luck. Eventually, I took a job in the palace as

Matron for the Quaintrelle program. All the while, the boy's fate weighed on my soul. I feared him dead. Years later, I was overjoyed to see his face plastered on posters declaring him enemy number one, though often those posters skewed his appearance. I easily identified him and found it ironic he had become a thorn in his own family's side."

"That is a very great tale indeed. Which leads me to ask why you never revealed any of this?"

"I was afraid, council. King Bern's wrath would have been a terrible thing to suffer. I knew what he was capable of if I did try to reveal the truth. King Talbot was no better. I may have spent a long time cloistered away in a convent, but I am not dull. Self-preservation is a strong motivator," the Matron's admission was laced with regret.

"That will be all, Matron. Thank you. We will now deliberate on these testimonies and compare them to what evidence we have."

The mood coming from the council had shifted since Matron Hattie's witness. They all seemed as if they would now vote in our favor; all except the head council. He'd been appointed to the seat by Talbot himself for their like-minded opinions. I didn't worry about his vote, though. I knew he would be outvoted by the others; even with his extra vote for being the head of the council.

CHAPTER THIRTY-EIGHT

The atmosphere in the throne room buzzed with excitement, and everyone was in good spirits, despite the overcrowding. Never before had there been so many people in the throne room. Everyone had been invited to the coronation; nobles, merchants, peasants, everyone. There were even representatives from Lesh and Apoidea. Nobody had even the slightest wave of being uncomfortable coming off of them. There was no doubt that all in attendance were happy, no one minded being shoulder to shoulder with someone of a different class.

Just as I had assumed, Matron Hattie's testimony had turned the tides in the trial. The counsel almost unanimously determined that the evidence had been sufficient enough to prove Felix to be the rightful heir to the throne. The only one who had voted against it had been the head of the counsel. He resigned when he was outvoted, angry that he no longer held power.

The coronation had been a long time coming. The council pressed to have the celebration as soon as possible, once Felix had been named official the heir to the throne of Realta. But Felix insisted that it wait, that we weren't ready. I thought it sweet of him to consider my feelings in the matter. The throne room became a room I was unable to enter ever since the night we defeated Talbot. There were too many bad memories associated with it. Finally, we agreed that the room would have to go under a complete remodel before the coronation could take place.

We passed the time before the coronation in a state of transition. Everyone adjusting to the new ways of life. A big part of that was me figuring out my gifts, nurturing them for the first time in years. Felix was astounded when I shared with him the details of my fight with Talbot, and he was keen on helping me to develop my gifts further.

After months of renovations, the throne room was ready. The throne room no longer felt cold and dark, as it has always felt during the rules of the former Kings. The new throne room was light and warm. Heavy tapestries were replaced with brighter fabrics and more torches were added to lighten the space. The thrones were no longer large or draped in darkness. Felix had them replaced with more comfortable seats, very much like the ones in his cabin on The Fura.

Most importantly, to me at least, had been that the small dungeon at the base of the thrones no longer existed. Masons had filled it with stones until they were level with the floor, and the heavy iron grate had been removed. The flooring of the throne room also changed, in order to completely remove the evidence of the horrible prison. The dark stone flooring was covered with light wooden planking, which while seemed odd to the workers who had done the job, the new throne room seemed a perfect reflection of Felix.

Overall the throne room was simplified, nothing overtly ornate about it. It reflected what Felix aimed to be; a king who represented his people. Not one who lorded himself over them. The room was perfect, a welcoming room to all who entered it.

We walked together through the crowded room, interacting with everyone, with Cook, Domhnall, and two other guards in tow. The guards had been uncomfortable with the idea of their king being so relaxed about being among so many people. The first time Felix had insisted on taking a walk through the streets of Realta had them scrambling. They were unused to a king that wanted to be with his people rather than ruling over them from the towering castle.

"I've been thinking about something," I said in Felix's ear as we passed through the crowd.

"About what, Sweet."

"You."

"What about me?"

"You are taking all of this in great stride, Felix."

Felix has held his own, being thrown into his new position. His charm, matched with his leading abilities, won over many already. Relations between Realta and Apoidea and Lesh had already begun to heal. Nations that once avoided Realta sent ambassadors to meet the new king and establish relationships. Old allies had as well. There were those who were wary of a pirate ruling a country, but those were mostly those allies of Talbot's that had benefited from his family's rule. We knew that there would be an adjustment period for everyone. Especially for Felix, who had a lot to learn about running a country.

"You've jumped right in this new life without much hesitation at all. Are you not the least bit unsure." I asked.

"Of course I am. It took months of cajoling and bribery from Cook for me to even entertain the idea of being his predecessor. Now, I'm on the brink of ruling a kingdom. While King Felix does have a certain ring to it, this isn't something I ever expected. This was thrust upon me. I'm more unsure of this than I have been of anything. I simply know that putting on a good show is half the battle. The rest comes from trial and error."

We stopped and I placed my hands on the sides of his face and gazed into his eyes, "I know this is a lot to ask of you, and I am sorry for that. I'm confident in your abilities to lead, Felix. You are going to be a great leader. With the help of trusted counselors, and Cook, I am certain you will get the hang of it in no time."

It wasn't just my faith in him that told me he would be a great ruler. It was the people. Felix and I had already spent many afternoons amongst the people, wandering the busy market of Realta. He was never meant to be cooped up by four walls day in and day out. He enjoyed the freedom of being outside. At first, the people he approached didn't know what to think about their King interacting with them in such a casual manner. They were used to be ignored and abused. These were the interactions that won them over quickly.

"Thank you, Sweet. Your belief in me is all I need," he said with a quick kiss on my cheek.

His words filled me with warmth. Knowing that my belief in him made him confident, gave me the best feeling I'd experienced in a long time. I looked back at all we had been through in the short time we had known one another and realized things could be much different if we hadn't met. He'd come to mean more to me than anyone had before.

We continued our stroll through the crowded throne room and start back towards the dais, stopping on occasion to return kind words from those we passed. Yes, it was clear that Felix had already won the hearts of many here. Realta was witnessing the beginning of a new and better era.

As Felix sat on his throne, he pulled me onto his lap to sit with him. "I guess this day has made it official then. I am King Felix."

"Yes, you are. A king with a full plate, at that. Even though you have already done so much since the trial, there is a lot more to do."

"Aye, that is true," Felix agreed.

"I know I didn't have much experience on the throne before, but I'll help you along the way as much as I can.My Quaintrelle training has to mean something."

"Thank you, Sweet." He placed his forehead on mine in a tender gesture. "And I know precisely what to ask of you, as my first official task as King of Realta."

"What would that be?"

"For you to rule by my side, officially."

My heart fluttered and my cheeks flushed. I hadn't even expected this request to happen any time soon. In truth, I knew it would, but had assumed that it would wait until he had fully settled in Bua Tur. When our lives calmed down. "Are you asking me to be your Queen?"

"Would you?"

"If you think your people would accept me?"

His lips parted in his signature smile, "Without question."

Playlist

All for Love; Sting, Rod Stewart, Bryan Adams
Amazed; Lonestar
Roses and Violets; Alexander Jean
Let Me Be Your King; Katherine Langford
Bleeding Love; Leona Lewis
Far Away; Nickelback
This Love; Sarah Brightman
Fragile; Laufey
Human; Christina Perri
What Would Happen; Meredith Brooks
Master of Tides; Lindsey Sterling
Dandelions; Ruth B.
War of Hearts; Ruelle
Ship of Fools; Sarah Brightman
I'm Kissing You; Des'ree
Lovesong; Adele

ACKNOWLEDGMENTS

First, a few personal thanks.

To my family for all their love and support of my dream, and for and their forgiveness for all the nights of leftover meals.

To Liz, who first planted the crazy idea in my head that I could do this during our many geek filled evenings of chaos.

To Heather, who inspired me to chase this crazy dream for real by living her own. I know wherever you are, you are making it an adventure.

As someone not especially good at talking about themselves, I'm not sure where to start or what to say. Other than thank you. Thank you for giving a new self-published author a chance and picking up this book. Of Secrets and Crowns has been a long labor of love and imposter syndrome that I am overjoyed to be sharing with the world. I hope you find something to love within its pages.

ABOUT THE AUTHOR

Dawn J. Braithwaite is an emerging author from the glorious Pacific Northwest, relishing in the rain and weirdness found there in abundance. A mild mannered geek with a dark sense of humor, Dawn thrives on nerd and pop culture, and the written word. She lives with her three children, husband, and small menagerie of furry and scaled animals. For years she dreamt of sharing the worlds in her mind, saying "I am too small to contain the worlds within me".

Of Secrets and Crowns is Dawn's first book.

www.ingramcontent.com/pod-product-compliance
Lightning Source LLC
Chambersburg PA
CBHW061225310726
48971CB00007B/1950